FAILURE
TO
ZIGZAG

A Novel by

Jane Vandenburgh

1989   NORTH POINT PRESS   *San Francisco*

This book is a work of fiction: all characters are fictional;
all incidents in it, events of the imagination. The descrip-
tion of the sinking of the U.S.S. *Indianapolis* is, however,
based on the actual happening as recounted in Samuel
Eliot Morison's *Victory in the Pacific, 1945*, the fourteenth
volume in his complete naval history of the war. I am also
indebted to Richard P. Newcomb's *Abandon Ship!* in which
the stories of the survivors are compiled, and especially to
Nestor Mestas for his willingness to talk to me about his
ordeal.

The poem fragment on page 257 is by Mitsune and was
translated from the Japanese by Mamoru Osawa in his
article "Hardy in Japan," *Kanazawa English Studies* 11
(The Society of English Literature, Kanazawa University,
1968). It is used with permission.

The map on page 163 is from Morison, volume 14, page
323, and is used with permission.

I want to express my sincere thanks to those colleagues
and friends who have offered me their invaluable editorial
insight, particularly Diane Goldsmith, Emily Heckman,
Ross Feld, Kate Moses, Barbara Ras, Lisa Ross, Jack
Shoemaker, and Victoria Shoemaker.

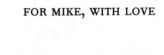
FOR MIKE, WITH LOVE

FAILURE
TO
ZIGZAG

Nothing is funnier than unhappiness.
Samuel Beckett, ENDGAME

I

VISTA DEL MAR

1960–1962

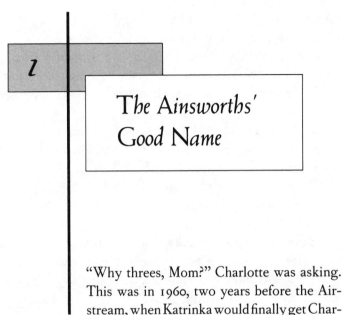

The Ainsworths' Good Name

"Why threes, Mom?" Charlotte was asking. This was in 1960, two years before the Airstream, when Katrinka would finally get Charlotte back for good. The two of them were sitting in a booth in the soda fountain of the pharmacy on Honolulu Avenue in Montrose, California. Charlotte was fourteen.

"Why not sets of twos?" Charlotte asked. "If they went out in sets of twos, it'd be a whole lot cheaper, did you think of that?" She was watching the bottom of her soda glass where a hard blob of ice cream blocked the end of her straw. Katrinka snorted and Charlotte looked up to see her mother smirking, arching one eyebrow ironically.

"Price is no object with some people," Katrinka said, "and these bastards are so damned rich they get no sympathy from me on the subject of mun-mun." She sharpened the ash of her cigarette on the rim of the little plate where her rainbow sherbet sat in a steel goblet, untouched, melting.

"But if they went out in sets of twos, it wouldn't be so noticeable, if you think about it. Why would they *want* to be so noticeable,

Mom? If they went out in sets of one, you probably wouldn't notice them at all."

Katrinka put the cigarette out with a hiss in the puddle that had formed beneath the sweating goblet. "That, sweetie, is just my point," she said, taking another cigarette out of the pack. "They want me to notice them, obviously. They want me to notice them and to fall in love with them." She lit the cigarette, then squinted at Charlotte through the smoke. "But," she exhaled, "I prefer not to get involved."

Charlotte was frowning hard, moving the straw through the root beer scum. Why was it, she wondered, that good things to eat always turned so quickly to garbage?

"Why are you acting so tragic?" Katrinka asked.

"It just doesn't make sense."

"All right then, Charlotte. Forget it. Forget I mentioned it." She snapped open her pocketbook and began digging out coins, holding each one to the window as if trying to see through it to the light. "And please remind me never to discuss anything with you ever again."

"Mom!"

"Well, really!" Katrinka was still poised with one eye squeezed shut. "What is it that you *want* me to tell you? That the psychiatrists of the state of California are following me in cars in sets of threes because they're trying to drive me crazy? Do you realize, Charlotte, that every other mental patient on Ward G-1 in the state hospital at Camarillo thinks the doctors are conspiring to drive her crazy?"

"But not you, right?" Charlotte asked.

Katrinka tipped her chin up. "I am," she announced, "much more original than *that*." She sucked her cheeks in and pressed her lips together elegantly.

Charlotte was frowning hard. "You say the one in the silver T-bird is Dr. Maudlin?" "Maudlin" was what Katrinka called one of the several psychiatrists she'd been *made* to go see; it wasn't his real name. Dr. Maudlin was the one with the office on Wilshire Boulevard: if he really was following Katrinka around in his silver T-bird, which Charlotte did not for one instant believe, then there might conceivably be some sort of sound psychiatric reason for it.

"One half, sweetie, thinks the doctors are trying to drive her crazy," Katrinka was going on, humorously. "Awwwwnnnd the other half thinks *she's* the Virgin Mary."

"But not you?" Charlotte asked again. In spite of herself, in spite of what she knew about her mother, she was holding her breath.

Katrinka smirked. "No one in our family goes in for any of that Jesus-and-Mary sort of crap, really really. All that is for Avenue B sorts of types. Remember the Crustanzos, Charlotte? Big she, little he? Talk about the body and *blood*."

Charlotte squinted. She did remember Tony and Sylvia, next door down the hill on Avenue B in Redondo Beach, but she didn't get the joke.

"Your grandfather may have once attended the Church of the Lighted Window, but it was only to place the muscles of his brain under the bi-homosexual spell of the Congregationalist minister with the finest speaking voice, and not because Lionel believes in G.A.W.D. If your grandfather believed in God, Charlotte, he would go around acting a lot less shitty, believe me. Is he being shitty to *you* these days?" she asked pointedly.

Charlotte dropped her eyes and automatically stopped listening. Conversations in her family had a way of always being the same. Her grandparents, and her mother too, all spent their days talking out into the same thick time, a time in which an act, particularly that of speaking, was never really done, never completed, but always seemed to hang suspended in the time that was yet to be. Charlotte experienced time differently, still believing in its ability to go forward, to progress. Time was different for her, she felt, because she'd been born after Einstein, who had changed time around. It was after Einstein, after Hiroshima and Nagasaki, that time had started to expand, to speed up, and the particles of matter had begun to fly from the center out and ever out.

She was going to shake her head when she realized that Katrinka had gone right on, as if she had herself already forgotten the question. "Awwwwnnnd all Winnie believes in is California land values, the Auto Club, and the man in the lousy attic." "The man in the attic" is what Charlotte's grandmother called whatever made a house creak and groan as it settled on its foundation. Which is really *gravity*, Charlotte reminded herself. She loved the reasonable way science had of sculpting cool words, ones that were exact, remote and shapely. It was the vocabulary of science, she found, that had the ability to cup itself around whole great chunks of chaos.

"Now *I* believe in truth," Katrinka said, pronouncing it "Awe-I." She looked up at Charlotte from the piles of coins she had assembled along the edge of the table. Each pile held pennies, nickels, dimes, or quarters, stacked in combinations to make twenty-seven cents. "Or aren't you interested in the truth these days?"

"Sure," Charlotte said, "but I have to go."

"You don't believe in Space Radio?" Katrinka asked her. Her whole face was lit up, humorous.

"It's just that I have a French test to study for, and a bunch of other junk that I have to do." Space Radio was what Katrinka, since Sputnik, was calling her voices. Katrinka liked to call the voices "Space Radio" because she thought it was funnier than the phrase for what they really were: "auditory hallucinations." And it probably *was* funnier, Charlotte realized, though she still preferred the latter.

"Go ahead then—be shitty about it." Katrinka snapped her pocketbook shut and peered down over her piles. "*Be* just like your grandparents."

"It isn't that, Mom! It's that I really have to go."

"Go, then, if you really *have* to." Katrinka looked out the window, her gray-green eyes no longer interested.

"I guess I can stay ten minutes."

"Lucky me," Katrinka said, but she did look back and her smile was small, real, triumphant.

They watched each other appraisingly. Katrinka wouldn't bring up Space Radio again, Charlotte guessed. Instead, she would pick something else that was equally sickening. "Awwwwnnd it's a good thing, too, that I'm *not* the Virgin Mary, when you think of what

happened to *her* poor bastard." Charlotte looked at her perfectly
levelly, saying nothing. Katrinka didn't need to talk about Space Radio—she was back on religion, which, to Katrinka, was the same
damned thing.

Katrinka smirked, then announced: "They tacked *her* poor bastard up!" She sucked her cheeks in and arched one regal eyebrow.

"Mom?" Charlotte asked. "Mom? Could you do me one small favor and keep your voice down?"

"Why should I?" Katrinka asked. "Have you ever known me to
keep my voice down in the past? Then why should I start now?
Awwwnnd just why is it that you want me to keep my voice down?
Because I'm claiming *not* to be the Holy Mother of Gawd in the soda
fountain of a pharmacy on Honolulu Avenue? Do you *want* me to
think I'm the Virgin Mary, Charlotte? Would that seem more *normal*
to you? That would make us Jewish, you realize? Don't you think we
have quite enough problems with persecution all on our very own
without adding all *that* to it?"

"It's that people's feelings get hurt when you make fun of their religion," Charlotte reminded her.

"Oh, I don't go by that. All my best friends are either Jewish or
Catholic and they're always the first to agree they're much too sen-
sitive to criticism. Anyway, sweetieheart, there isn't a damned soul
in this dump aside from you and me, so exactly whose feelings is it
that I'm supposed to be hurting? Unless you think we are so *very* interesting these days that we're being tape recorded by Jack and
Jackie? Or by the Ainsworths so they can play the tapes for Maudlin,
Moody, and DePalma?"

Charlotte had stopped listening. Instead, she was thinking about
the nature of paranoia, that it, like the color of one's eyes and the
shape of one's eyebrows and upper lip, might be a gene-linked trait.
The Sunday before, she had been standing in the dining room, taking some small pleasure in ironing her gym clothes, in the clean
smell of steam and in the physical act of pressing the required
creases into the damp and heavy cotton of the white blouse, the blue
shorts. The repetitiveness of the motion and its soft sound were

making her dreamy. Her face was tipped down, frowning. She was thinking of the Theory of Relativity, having just seen something on the subject on "The Twilight Zone" over at her friend Patsy's house.

She could hear her grandmother in the bathroom off the service porch beyond the kitchen, clinking things. Winnie was pretending to be using the toilet, but what she was really doing was working on a painting.

"Winnie!" Charlotte had called out. "Did you ever think about something like this? That maybe the Russian people are really *nice*, know what I mean? I mean, the people themselves, and it's really only the two governments that are enemies?"

Winnie came shusssshing, screeching but altogether silently, the muscles of her face drawn upward and out, made catlike by her fear and anger. She came on her quiet shoes, cowering through the three long rooms, all the while looking out the windows into the tops of the oaks, as if the dry and rustling leaves could themselves see and hear her. She carried a brush in one hand. In the other she held a sloshing glass jar filled with azure water. "Hush!" Winnie hissed, right into Charlotte's steamy face. "You are *never* to say a thing like that again, never even to *think* it! This is 1960! You never know *what* they may have invented! *Who* it is who may be listening!" Charlotte believed her grandmother was about to slap her. Instead, Winnie sloshed the jar of blue water all over the ironed gym clothes. The color bloomed, the smell rose up. The water wasn't water at all, but turpentine. Winnie had been working in oils.

"Your father's mother was Jewish, did I ever tell you that?" Katrinka was saying. "She was the diminutive red-haired type, the kind who likes to compare shoe sizes at a dinner party, in order to make a point about how large *boned* other women are. Her husband, on the other hand, was six three, which is where your father got his height. Eleanor Ann was so mentally ill on the subject of being Jewish that she always insisted on belonging to all the country clubs that kept Jews out—Chevy Chase, Oak Knoll, like that. Speaking of acting mental patienty! Jack and Jackie and the rest of the Roman Catholics? I mean really, Charlotte! *Fucked by God*, really *really!* Believe me, sweetie, 'fucked by *God*' is one sure way to get yourself locked right up."

Charlotte was perfectly silent, looking down at the palms of the upturned hands resting in her lap.

"I would like to discuss this," Katrinka said.

"Discuss what?" Charlotte was suddenly too full to stay awake. Eating made her tired, made her full and sick. She was so exhausted she felt ill. Winnie would make her eat dinner anyway.

"The issue of *paternity*," Katrinka said.

Charlotte lifted her face. Despite herself, she now was listening. Just the sound of the word caused an ache of longing at the back of her throat, as if someone were squeezing lemons.

"Well, it wasn't Joseph, obviously," Katrinka announced.

"You mean Joseph *Black?*" Charlotte asked. This was her father's name, the name of the man who'd died in the last days of the war when the *Indianapolis* was sunk by moonlight after having delivered the uranium for the bombs.

"Honey, we aren't talking about ourselves, *right this very second!* We are attempting to discuss the literary history of all this crap. The fact that even in the Bible you don't get a halo for marrying the mother of your own child. *If* you see what I mean. Even *if* she is so completely off her rocker that she walks around with a crucifix pinned to her pregnant belly button, calling herself such mentally ill names as the *Virgin* Mary and telling people she's been fucked by God. I mean really. I mean where would I be if Awe-I went around insisting to Maudlin, Moody, and DePalma that I'd been fucked by God?"

Charlotte's gaze was sliding away, off toward the gleam that was the pay phone on the back wall of the pharmacy. She was thinking of calling Patsy up. Winnie hated for Charlotte to say she was going to call someone *up*, but Charlotte could never remember to say "telephone."

"All right, then. So who was it really? If we assume she had not actually been fucked by God?" Katrinka asked. She pronounced it awwwctually.

Charlotte heaved a great sigh. "Oh, Awe-I don't know, *awe*-ctu-ally," she drawled. Since this was not a rational conversation, and Katrinka, as always, was talking largely to herself, Charlotte didn't see why it was so important that she keep trying to make sense. She was also falling asleep. "A. P. Giannini?" Charlotte yawned. Lionel worshipped A. P. Giannini and had once met him *personally*. That was in 1932 when the Ainsworths' First State Bank failed and was bought out by the Bank of America.

Thinking Charlotte was trying to be witty, Katrinka smiled. "Our *father?*" she asked. "Which *aren't* in heaven?"

Charlotte suddenly needed to take a short nap. She put her head down and rested the skin of her cheek right on the sticky tabletop. Sleep swam up. It was a yawning cavern, black and noisy as a sea cave, where the waves crashed, sucked at her, pulled her outward toward an ocean filled with bodies. By the third day, the sharks could no longer differentiate between the smell of the flesh of the dead and those who were still living. It was then, on the third day, that the sharkbites stopped, though the sharks did still swim among them, bumping up below the life net, gliding in and around benignly among the pale forest of dangling bodies. Flesh changed: puffed, whitened, became soft, then ulcerated. There beneath the surface of the tabletop the ship still lay, her pipes gushing forth fresh water, the shape of the superstructure, both fore and aft, now strung with bright lights, as if rigged out for Christmas.

"Charlotte!" Katrinka was suddenly screaming. "Are you swacked? Pie-eyed? Then why in *hell's* name are you acting as if you are falling-down drunk?"

Charlotte opened her eyes to the vision of Katrinka's face, her auburn hair sticking out from the way she'd been yanking at it. *This is my mother*, Charlotte thought, slightly shocked, as always.

"I just hate all this holy stuff, Mom," Charlotte said. "It just isn't *interesting* to me." She hated even the feel of the thin pages of the Bible, hated the way the paper stuck to the damp of her fingertips, how the reek of ink and gilt and piety seemed to come off on the skin of her hands. She had to close her eyes again against the thought of it:

the naked man tortured, dangling, his tongue swollen, his dying mouth given vinegar to drink.

"Well, Missy Miss, I'll have you know that half of the gals on Ward G-1 who *think* they're the Virgin Mary have actually been fucked by their own fathers. I have this on good authority."

"Space Radio?" It just slipped out.

"Actually, it was *Doctor* DePalma," Katrinka sniffed. "He was trying to get me to tell on Lionel and Winnie. He always likes me to tell how I am *truly* feeling, when it is none of his fucky business."

"Mom!" Charlotte shouted suddenly. "Mom! Don't you really think we could just please talk about something else? Don't you want to know how I'm doing in school, for instance?"

"How are you doing in school, dear?" Katrinka asked in her own voice, but by ventriloquy. "Just *fine*, Mom!" she answered herself, in Charlotte's own high and slightly breathy voice. "I'm getting all A's, as usual!"

"Mother!"

"Well, really, Charlotte. Why is it that you are so self-conscious? *Are* Lionel and Winnie being mean to you?"

"Let's talk about the cars, okay? All right? If cars are following you around in sets of threes, then maybe they're just trying to *help*." Her last word was thin and shimmery with air.

Katrinka sucked her cheeks in and announced: "When I need their help, I'll ask for it."

Out the window, moving away out into the blaze of sunlight, Charlotte saw a boy with broad shoulders wearing a woolen Pendleton. Hoods wore these shirts over white T-shirts even on hot days. The only hood in honors English was a boy named Bob Davidson, who spent long minutes staring at the side of Charlotte's face or brazenly right at her chest. He was smart but he didn't volunteer in class. He stared but never spoke to her. Even when asking her to dance, he just came up to her, took her hand, led her out onto the dance floor. He didn't dance like other boys. He held her against him, so she was wrapped in the length of his body. His clothes smelled like smoke. Once when a monitor tapped them for dancing like that, Bob Davidson dropped his arms, turned and abruptly left, abandoning her in the middle of the dance floor. He was very handsome, though he had narrowed, suspicious eyes and his skin was slightly wrecked. Charlotte always liked people better after she figured out what was wrong with them.

"Talk about psychotic!" Katrinka was saying. "Have you ever *listened* to a psychiatrist for any length of time? Most of them are Zero Sub Minus, I mean really. They all tend to name their children things like Sasha, have you noticed that? Sasha, Sasha, Sasha, or Sasha. Aside from which DePalma has admitted it."

"Admitted what?"

"That I am his most interesting case. Which is why the ones in cars are wasting all their fifty-minute hours watching me, no doubt."

"No doubt," Charlotte repeated automatically, though she was thinking about something else.

It was impossible to argue that Katrinka was not being watched since she was, as they both knew full well. Winnie sat in the Nash parked in front of the bank across the street, watching them as they did their visiting, and thinking about her money. She was watching Katrinka to make certain she didn't spend any of her twenty-seven centses on alcoholic beverages, and she was watching Charlotte to be sure she didn't squander her allowance on anything "wasteful" or "teenaged." These categories, in Winnie's view, tended to include such items as chewing gum, tweezers, U-No bars, makeup, safety razors, and 45-rpm records by Bobby Vee.

Having been raised by grandparents, Charlotte knew better than to waste her money on foolishness. She was saving her money for her college education, as she would have piped up to tell Art Linkletter had she ever been a guest on "Kids Say the Darndest Things." That was one of Lionel's favorite shows. Having been raised by grandparents, Charlotte knew all about thrift. She put every single cent that ever came her way into her account at the bank across the street, all of her allowance, also her lunch money, and the extra dime Lionel gave her every morning and ordered her to spend at Nutrition. She saved her money because she never needed it. In spite of being raised by the Ainsworths, she was still her mother's daughter. If she needed an item, teenaged or otherwise, Charlotte stole it, really really.

Charlotte was very good at shoplifting, was never caught, never even suspected. She imagined this had to do with the Ainsworths' good name in Montrose, where Lionel had been the banker, where he still did the marketing and got his hair cut. Charlotte also dressed like a child who was well brought up. She dressed like the sort of girl Nancy Drew's example encouraged girls to be, the type who did not chew gum or have pierced ears, who didn't go to the phone and call people *up*. The Nancy Drew-type girl first called out: "Oh, fawther! I shawn't be late!" then hopped into her little red roadster and went off to solve a tidy crime. Charlotte, on the other hand, knew she was the type who was liable to have committed it.

Charlotte shoplifted on Honolulu Avenue, where the Ainsworths were known, where they had their good name. This was also one of Katrinka's favorite places to do what Lionel and Winnie called her "acting up": talking to herself out loud, discussing whether or not the Virgin Mary had awe-ctually been fucked by Gawd, singing Johnny Mercer songs, dancing the hula in the Aloha Room with nameless drunken strangers.

Charlotte knew most of the merchants she stole from. Even if she didn't actually know them, they knew her, she imagined. She was recognizable as the Ainsworths' granddaughter because of the kinds of things they made her wear. Though Glendale High was a public school, they made her dress in what looked like a uniform: black and white saddle oxfords, the same kind Katrinka had worn when she went away to Cal; little white socks with tops that folded down; boxy plaid wool skirts that made a person look big as a house so no boy would ever like her; white blouses with the Peter Pan collars. These blouses were made out of a fabric Winnie revered: polyester blend.

It was Winnie who insisted on the braids. Hair in the eyes was one of the principal causes of nearsightedness and hair in the food was another of the things liable to make Lionel sick to death. The hair was braided wet, braided ferociously, to last the entire week.

Winnie parted it in the center with the jab of her knifelike comb, then plaited it so tightly Charlotte felt her scalp might rip. Her hair was so long and thick, the washing was itself a major chore; it fell to Lionel to accomplish these shampoos. Charlotte's braids were so long they trundled all the way down her back.

Other kids in Charlotte's school who had dead parents or other similar tragedies all wore the same sorts of crappy things. Even if they did dress in a more normal, teenaged way, Charlotte could pick them out by their dour, shadowed, defiant faces, or by the scared look that made their eyes jump, as if they expected to be criticized momentarily. Having no parents, she had decided, was like coming to school every day as an immigrant from a foreign country. It seemed to her that Lionel and Winnie lived in a place called Before the War, a country where the language was English, but words were used in a different way. Even the word "war" meant something different to them: the war they spoke of was the first one, the war of their own youth. In the house on Vista del Mar, where they never had visitors, conversations seemed to be performed as if by rote, the words chiseled in the air as if written in a play that was never done, one that had to be practiced over and over. "Can't you ever think of anything *new* to say?" Charlotte frequently wanted to scream at them. Screaming at Lionel and Winnie, however, wasn't part of Charlotte's "role," as Katrinka called it. Katrinka got words like "role" from the group therapy she was "made" to attend when she was at Camarillo.

Katrinka too repeated herself, always talking about the same damned things. Still, while her concerns remained the same, her version of how various events of their lives had transpired did evolve over time. She liked to tell what she called "my side of the story." Her side of the story was elaborated with each telling, Charlotte noticed, while Lionel and Winnie's version simply became more calcified. Katrinka was insane, Charlotte did understand and tried hard to remember. Katrinka had been diagnosed as such and the diagnosis had been frequently confirmed. Still, insane or not, she was easier for Charlotte to talk to than were her grandparents. Crazy as she was, she would never do a thing as mean as dump turpentine all over ironed gym clothes just because a person had said some dumb thing about the Russians after seeing some dumb show on the TV.

"So how's you-know-who?" Katrinka asked, referring to Winnie. Katrinka knew Charlotte had been thinking about the Ainsworths because being crazy had made her witchy. Charlotte knew what Katrinka meant because having a mother like that, having spent so much time trying to decipher what she was saying, had made Charlotte slightly witchy too.

"She bought a pair of pants."

"Christ Jesus! *Are* we going to have to have her committed? What'd he do, burn them?" Lionel had always hated the look of women wearing pants. Once, when Katrinka was at Cal and had been going through a phase of writing for *Pelican* under the penname "Sidney," she'd come down on the train wearing a jacket shaped like a man's and a pair of stylish trousers. Lionel had sneaked into her bedroom at night, taken them from her closet, and burned them in the incinerator. Charlotte was herself forbidden from owning any pants aside from the gym shorts, which were required.

"*He* was the one who helped her pick them out. They got them at Bullock's Pasadena."

"What is this all about?" Katrinka demanded. "Have they both finally cracked up completely? I promise you that when they do, sweetie, we're going to have to send them someplace very Oak Knollish, very Chevy Chase Country Club Without Negroes and/or Jews. Your grandparents are much too Glendale to tolerate the California-State-Mental-Hospital-at-Camarillo-type institutionalization, awwwwnnnd I do mean *really*." Her voice was now low down, confidential.

Charlotte went on. "She thinks the postman tried to see up her skirt when she went down the steps after the mail."

Katrinka tipped her chin back and nearly laughed. "Now why in the lousy hell would he want to do that?"

Charlotte smiled. "To get a peek at Herbert Hoover?"

Katrinka did then laugh, a short, throaty snort that exploded from behind the press of lips.

Winnie believed the flesh of her knees, when scrunched together with the ring made of a gathering of fingers, held the likeness of Herbert Hoover. She sometimes made Charlotte come look at this sight, just as she'd made Katrinka herself come to witness it when it had been she who was growing up in the house on Vista del Mar. "See?" Winnie had demanded of first one and now the other. Charlotte never saw anything aside from the scrunches of white flesh, but then Charlotte didn't really know what Herbert Hoover was supposed to look like. Even years later, when she had escaped from that thick time, she still searched any roster of the presidents for the one whose face most resembled Winnie's pale and dimpled knees.

"How's Mr. Tweedy?" Katrinka asked. Mr. Tweedy was Lionel's pet name for himself.

"Fine," Charlotte said. "The same."

They both smiled, knowing it was Lionel's dream to be the same, that every day since the bank failed he had tried to follow the same exemplary routine. He would rise at the same time, shower and shave, eat the same foods for the same meals, chewing with great exactitude, walk the same six miles. He read the same books over and over again, the complete works of Charles Dickens. He read aloud while lying on his back on the davenport. He preferred for Charlotte to listen, but he read out loud whether there was anyone to hear or not. It occurred to Charlotte that her grandfather tried to live the day in the same unvarying way in order to perfect it before he died. Just as he was getting it just the way he liked it, Katrinka would show up—down from the hospital or back from Sugarman's carnival—and the whole thing would go straight to hell.

"I really do have to go," Charlotte told her. "She gave me her last silver dollars, though, so let me pay."

"Oh, *gawd!* Not her last silver dollars!" Katrinka cried out. Winnie had a huge stash of them, taken in bags from the bank on the day it closed, but she always claimed she had no more left except these last two or three. She had been giving these last two or three to one or the other of them since 1932, saying, "Now, these are my very last silver dollars! Now, I want you to have them on one condition—you are *not* to tell Lionel! Do you understand me?" She handed them over knotted up in a fancy handkerchief, the bundle tied to look like something that would be carried by a baby hobo.

"These are her *very* last ones," Charlotte said. "Really, really." She smiled at her mother, then bent over her task, that of untying the hard grip of Winnie's many knots.

"Put that away," Katrinka said, waving one imperious hand. "I'm the mother around here and this is my treat." She said this grimly, out of the side of her mouth like a gun moll. She was busy now stacking the coins in a new way: quarters with quarters, dimes with dimes.

"Mom, really!" Charlotte said.

"Really really," Katrinka retorted, going on then in ventriloquy: "Now, I will be the judge of all this and all that, of who is and is not the mother around here, and of all things Nellie-ish and Tweedyish and all things monetary!" This voice was deep, male, authoritarian. It was Ogamer, Katrinka's old man character. She hadn't brought the dummies into the soda fountain that day, but the voices were with her always, except for when she could be persuaded to take her medication.

"All right!" Charlotte said. She did want the dollars, which still looked new. She liked the heft of them and the soft, deep shine that made them seem more valuable than paper dollars. Still, taking money from her mother, who was so poor she sometimes got public assistance, made Charlotte's skin crawl. Her whole epidermis, including her scalp, seemed to lift, to move. The skin was itself an organ, she knew, the one designed for the specific purpose of differentiation, to keep the self of a person in from the outside world. Was it scientifically possible, she wondered, for a human being to molt like a crab or snake?

"Anyway that Jew bastard Sugarman has given me my job back at his lousy crappy flea circus, so you don't have to worry about me on the subject of mun-mun."

"All right!" Charlotte said again, her flesh still crawling. She looked at the underside of either arm, where her skin felt like it was about to break out in hives.

Looking up from this self-appraisal, she noticed her mother's thin fingers gathering the coins. Katrinka's money was terrible to look at. It was clotted with some dark gunk into which were stuck the shreds of tobacco that always collected in the recesses of her pocketbook. Charlotte inclined her head, observing her own hands, which lay poised in her lap with the fingers curled and the palms turned upward. At times like this her hands tended to ache, pulsing in the center. She was always surprised that the act of leave-taking could cause such a physical and specifically martyrish pain.

"Oh, Lord God! *Now* what have I done?" Katrinka cried out, but Charlotte's mouth, gasping, gaping open, watering, couldn't speak to reassure her. She couldn't speak nor raise her aching hands, nor do anything at all aside from moving her heavy head slowly from side to side. As she cried, Charlotte kept her eyes tightly shut. She did this to try to keep her tears in, to keep her soul in, and to save herself from the sight of these, her gifts: her mother and her mother's dirty money.

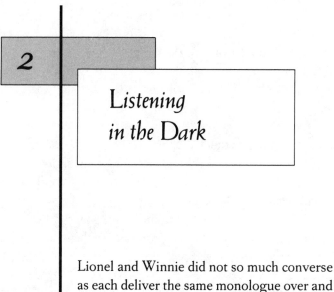

2

Listening in the Dark

Lionel and Winnie did not so much converse as each deliver the same monologue over and over. The major difference between them and Katrinka, Charlotte had decided, was that when they talked to themselves someone else was usually in the room. One of their favorite topics for ranting was what had gone wrong with Katrinka.

According to Winnie it was when Joe, Jr., died that Katrinka had turned, overnight, from a bright and hopeful girl into a paranoid schizophrenic. This was, Winnie claimed, the form of mental illness that had been clinically proven to be caused by the chemical properties of grief. Then too there was the issue of gumption. Katrinka hadn't one speck of gumption. If she had any gumption whatsoever she would stop all that ventriloquist business *this instant!* and go out and find herself a decent job. She should have stayed at the phone company. "Charlotte!" Winnie would cry out at this point, always as if she had just thought of it, "I want you to at least consider the phone company. Now, the phone company employs more women than any other company and it is a stable company, having survived the last depression. And when the next depression hits, people will still undoubtedly be so ill-mannered that they will rely upon the telephone, rather than sitting down to write a civilized note or letter." Winnie despised the phone for the way it would ring out in her house without her giving it permission. She would *not* answer it. Instead she would scurry to the bathroom off the service porch and hide until the ringing ceased. If, for some reason, she felt she had to answer it, she approached it furiously, as if she was back in the schoolhouse in Power, Montana, confronting the worst of her impudent boys.

Lionel, on the other hand, was of the opinion that the telephone was another of America's most magnificent inventions, like the cotton gin, the aeroplane, and Luther Burbank's hybrids. He went to the phone with a Republican optimism, believing it might be some powerful banker—A. P. Giannini? Lionel's own father?—who was calling him home. He would always pause then with his hand outstretched, realizing it was probably just Katrinka calling to ruin another of his perfect days.

Since the way Katrinka was *was not Winnie's fault!* Winnie would thank Charlotte very much to kindly stop looking at her so balefully. Didn't Charlotte realize that self-pity of just that sniveling sort was the first step on the road to insanity, that with parents like *hers* she had better be on the sharp lookout for her own abnormal tendencies? Winnie would frankly tolerate no more of *this*, which she disdainfully referred to as "the psychological," no more of the folderol about how insanity was engendered in the deprivation of maternal love. This was exactly the kind of nonsense that was manufactured to fill the pages of women's magazines. Winnie had no respect whatsoever for women's magazines—they made her quite cross! The articles were written for slothful girls, those who had nothing better to do than lie around all day staring into mirrors and plucking at their eyebrows! That was the type who had always made Winnie tired at Saint Helen's Academy; some too were Kappas, living with her in the Kappa house in Missoula. This type of girl was so lazy about taking a tuck in her buttocks that she was likely to end up relying upon a corset or a girdle!

Lionel had his own theory about what had happened to Katrinka: her brain had been pickled by alcohol. This was from drinking beer, beer, beer with the crowd from *Pelican* in the cellars of Eshleman Hall. That was up at Cal where Katrinka had been a fine student, a leader, an athlete, but had failed to graduate. "Now, Charlotte," Lionel would always intone at this point, "I am of the opinion that graduation is a very fine thing to achieve—do you understand me?" For emphasis he wrapped the long fingers of one mighty hand around the muscle of her upper arm and squeezed the bicep to the point of pain. He held onto the arm and rocked her slowly, hypnotically. Then he uttered the single word "*Drink*," saying it hotly against the skin of the side of her face so his breath made the little hairs move. "Now *Pelican* may call itself a humor magazine but your grandmother and I have never found anything funny in inebriation." He rocked her slowly, to let all this sink in.

When the phone rang, it was Lionel who went to answer it. "Hello, Dad," Katrinka said. "How's everything? How's mother?"

"What do you mean, *How's mother? Mother's* asleep is how *mother* is!" He was shouting, though trying to hold it down to a dull roar. He was standing at the built-in desk in the central hall of the house on Vista del Mar, right next to the bedrooms. He wore his cotton pajamas, worn so thin by laundering that they were nearly transparent. The top was unbuttoned down the front to allow his skin to breathe.

Lionel was staring down at the old, uneven floorboards, one arm held rigidly at his side. From the clenched fist of that hand two fingers extended, pointing straight down, as if holding an imaginary cigarette. The other hand gripped the heavy black receiver so tightly that the muscle of his upper arm had begun to ache and the bones of his knuckles gleamed a yellowish white through the skin. "Wellll," she was drawling now, "you allllways say Awe-I call only when I need something, so I thought I'd telephone to chawwwwt."

"CHAT!" he bellowed. "It's three o'clock in the morning!" He might as well yell—Winnie and Charlotte were both out of their rooms now. Though the night was warm, Charlotte's teeth were chattering. She wore no robe and stood clutching at her naked arms. Her nightgown, he saw, had suddenly grown too short. Her cheeks were sunken, sucked in, he was irritated to see. She liked to affect this look, he'd noticed recently, that of the starving Armenian.

The two of them were watching him beseechingly. He nodded his head once, then shook it: Yes, it was Katrinka. No, she wasn't dead yet. Winnie's own mouth was clamped so tightly shut that the dark of her lips had disappeared. Without her glasses, her eyes blinked huge, black, unfocused, and she seemed suddenly youthful, helpless. He thought of her heavy hair, the weight of it falling onto his hands when he'd unpinned it, when he'd let it down. Her gray hair now was permed into a short and nervous frizz.

"Wellll," Katrinka was saying, "if you're going to be la-di-da about it, I'll be the one to pick the topic of conversation. Let's be confidential, shall we, Lionel? Let's talk behind mother's back. Let's talk about when *you'd* quit smoking if *I'd* quit smoking? Let's talk about *tapering off.* You were the one who'd be the boss of the cigarettes, one Lucky each per hour. Remember your strolls after suppertime, uphill under the oaks on El Tovar and how you said the stars did press down so and explode right against your heart? There were thousands of men like you, Lionel, bespectacled, your socks clocked in hunter's green, still out of work, but still cheerful, still being supported by your wife's family's money, still getting a kick out of the Kingfish and Andy Gump. You were the one who was *not* suicidal, not one of the ones who went off the rooftop feet first after the Crash, one of the ones whose socks didn't match. The calls drove me boi-ing cuckoo! You and mother too and the way the two of you were together during your last great depression, with the beat-beat-beat of your tom-toms!"

"I don't know what you're talking about."

"You know exactly what I'm talking about, you lousy fucking hypocrite. I'm talking about *your* rules for *our* behavior!"

"I forbid you from speaking to me in that manner!" Lionel told her. "Have you been drinking?" The circulation now having retreated from all extremities, his bare feet and the tip of his nose were suddenly freezing. His blood pressure was building, going up and up. His temples throbbed but the blood could not get through. He would die, he knew, of having this person as his daughter.

"How do you like that?" Katrinka was saying to somebody else, someone behind her in the room. "Awe-I call to be sociable and he gives me that have-you-been-drinking sort of crap." Her voice rose. It was now so loud, so shrill, that Winnie and Charlotte could hear it, though they were several feet from where Lionel held the receiver out away from his ear. "HAVE YOU BEEN DRINKING?" she screamed. "Remember, Lionel? It was Prohibition. Your black shoes with their new black heels? When you and Uncle Mac chuckled to yourselves, brewing your beer in the bathtub? I could have you arrested for the things you've done."

"You are insane," he told her coldly.

But now her voice was softening, growing intimate, humorous. "You know, Dad, you used to be sort of sweet when you were all tanked up. That was when you used to like me. Know what? I liked you too. But never mind awwlll that. They're telling me I have to get off the phone. Give me Harold's number, will you. Phone numbers are just exactly the sort of information I cannot retain—the seven series of shock treatments, Dad. Dad? You know, when the brain lights up all at once?"

"You may not," he said, fighting to steady his voice. "I warn you. My brother has been dead for nearly five years, as *you know full well.* I forbid you from calling Jessie at this hour and upsetting her. Do you hear? Do you understand me?"

"Sure," Katrinka retorted. "Give me Uncle Lawrence's number then. I always was his favorite niece. He's leaving me all his mummun, did you know that? Banks too. I'm going to change their name to the First State La-di-da Bank of Katrinka Elmo Ainsworth. *If* you are very, very nice to me, I might consider giving you a job. I'm going to start you off as a teller, just like your lousy shitty father did. That man was an absolute bastard to you—can't you realize that, Lionel?—giving you a single bank in a one-horse town like Montrose, California, when Lawrence and Harold got the entire state of Iowa to divide among themselves. So you drive your crappy Naaaassh while Uncle Harold has his Lincoln Continental."

"Had!" Lionel choked, his face now purplish red, adding: "I drive a Nash because the seats fold down!"

"Give me Lawrence's number!" she screamed at him. "And be quick about it! I have to get somebody to bail me out of this stinkhole jail!"

"The squalor we have found her in," Winnie was saying. She stood at the window of the dining room, looking down through the trees into the street, wringing her hands in a dish towel. "Whatever did I do to deserve it?"

"Nothing," Charlotte said, automatically. She too was watching the Nash back out of the garage. The dust on the leaded glass windows and the thick clutch in which the oaks held the house made it hard to see the car, but she could feel the vibrations of the motor coming up through the floor from the stone garage. Now she saw the glint of chrome and heard the sound of the engine change as it backed up, then turned around and started forward. The Nash crossed the culvert and went on up the little slope leading out of the gully, before it disappeared under the canopy of trees standing at the back of the lot across the street, the grounds of a large estate. There, nearly a block away, lived the Ainsworths' closest neighbor. The little road crossing the stream washed out every year during the rainy season. Still, the city of Glendale hadn't gotten around to paving it. Winnie blamed this on the wealthy old woman who owned that land, imagining she had a profound influence with city hall Winnie had been unable herself to amass. The rich neighbor had no need to have the roadbed paved because her house fronted on Montecito, and she probably considered the Ainsworths' street just a dusty country road.

"What kind of God would give a person a child like that?" Winnie was asking. Charlotte didn't answer. The question was imponderable, and she was thinking of something else, of how the oak leaves looked like black lace against the silvering of the early morning sky.

"She does this on purpose, you know? She does it just to shame me. She could stop it *this instant!* if she chose to." Charlotte weighed this thought: she too liked to believe that Katrinka really could turn it off, that Space Radio was something she'd invented to pay Lionel and Winnie back for what Katrinka called being so lousy crappy shitty. "It is me she blames," Winnie was saying. "She doesn't blame him."

"No one blames you," Charlotte told her, automatically.

Winnie hissed. She hated to be contradicted. "Of course they do," she snapped. "Her doctors all blame me and so do you!"

Charlotte turned to look at her grandmother, staring from beneath the shadow of her brow. The two of them had the same bluish eyes, but Charlotte's right eye was also marked by a colored patch shaped like a pie piece, radiating out from the iris, the color of which was golden in some lights, or turned greenish, changing as Katrinka's own eye color did. It was this mark, this patch, Charlotte was inclined to believe, that had always allowed her, while not yet thoroughly crazy, to participate in her mother's point of view. It was as if she was able to witness things at once through her mother's as well as her very own eyes.

Winnie was right: Charlotte did blame her. She blamed her blackly, thickly, so heatedly that her heart was sometimes hurt by the pain of it, as if her hatred had inflamed the very sac in which the heart muscle needed to beat. Still, as their eyes now caught, locked, and Winnie's widened, and then as her face began to grow shiny under her granddaughter's hot look, Charlotte was herself surprised to understand that the fact was so purely obvious that even Winnie could distinguish it.

"I am the one she hates," Winnie sniffed, as she looked away. She was lifting the sharp angle of her nose somewhat pridefully, her voice beginning now to twist and yank. Charlotte hoped she wouldn't start crying. Whenever Winnie cried, she ran to the bathroom and began packing up her painting supplies; then she took the car and went off to the Mojave Desert for a few days, leaving Lionel and Charlotte alone to cope without a car. The Ainsworths always bought their cars from American Motors—the Nashes, then Nash Ramblers, then their Rambler American—because of the one feature they did so prize, that the front seats folded all the way down for Winnie's sleeping bag on her flights from home out into the desert.

"No, she doesn't," Charlotte said. "She loves us," she said. She listened to the distant sound of her own voice saying this: it was breathy, wistful, lifted. "She just has a different way of showing it," Charlotte went on. "You know? Because of the way she is?"

Winnie snorted contemptuously and turned to finish clearing the breakfast dishes. In spite of his daughter's being in jail, Lionel had gone for his regular walk, starting out when it was still pitch dark. When he came in, he had to give up the pleasure of sitting awhile in his red leather banker's chair where he allowed his skin to breathe. Instead he went right on to showering, shaving, then sat down to his regular bowl of mush. As always, he spent nearly an hour over it, stirring milk into the cereal until it was again entirely liquified and it dribbled extravagantly from the flattened silver soupspoon. He could somehow manage to chew mush though it was completely lumpless, completely wet with milk. He made the mush himself every morning: it was part Roman Meal, part Malt O'Meal, part wheat germ. On this morning, as on all others, he stirred, dribbled, and chewed, intent on his pleasure, his mouth and tongue whitening, utterly mindless of the calls from the Montrose police station encouraging him to take Katrinka back up to Camarillo.

As on any other morning, the Ainsworths were discussing that same thick past. This morning, it was another schoolteacher back in Power, how she'd suddenly burst into tears and had clattered from the room when Winnie showed up at school wearing Lionel's diamond. "Oh, that was Bessie," Lionel said. "She had such a crush on me!" He smacked and dribbled.

"It wasn't you!" Winnie cried. "I was the one Bessie loved!" Then Winnie whirled with her cat's face poised to catch Charlotte gawking and screeched triumphantly: "But there was nothing filthy in it, as there is nowadays, so don't get your hopes up!"

The second time the police called, it was Charlotte, with heart frozen, who'd gone to answer it. She could hear Ogamer in the background, singing the "Marseillaise." Katrinka was assaultive, the beleaguered sergeant mentioned. She was verbally abusive. Her voices were keeping all the other drunks up.

"May I help?" Charlotte now asked Winnie at the table, knowing she wouldn't be allowed to. Lionel could tolerate no one aside from

Winnie touching the dishes that touched his food. Charlotte hated helping, hated the utter futility of all housework, the way dusting was never finished and dishes and laundry were done and done only to be done again. This attitude toward housework was pure Katrinka, Charlotte knew, like the patch of greenish eye and the tint of her reddish hair. Attitudes descended. They came down just as actual insanity did. Charlotte thought of insanity as a thing in motion, like the abstract nude in one of Winnie's artbooks. Winnie was at the top of the steps, Katrinka at the bottom, with the merging ghosts strung between. It was called *Madness Descending a Staircase.*

"You should stick to the practical side of things," Winnie was now advising her. "I'd like you to go to work for the phone company or to become a nurse. Or you might do well to major in domestic science. There are so many new and wonderful things to learn about in that field, what with the new drip-dry fabrics that pack so well! You will want to marry someone willing to help you care for your mother. She will be your burden when Lionel and I are gone. Now, you'll want to marry someone quite different from yourself: not someone artistic, no one high-IQ-and-no-common-sense. If you first get a degree in Home Ec, you can always teach in the high school when your husband dies. I always did despise teaching, the way the children called me 'mama' and their eyes clung to my face and their soiled hands smudged the articles of my clothing. I would like you to learn to be more modest in your person, Charlotte, than you show signs of becoming. I want you not to dress in a way that encourages boys to look at you, or to drive past our house. I want you to keep a clean house and to learn to behave normally, do you hear me? Your mother has always surrounded herself with abnormality and she therefore gets no encouragement at all to live in a decent way. Oh, it was terrible, terrible! to live in a small town like Power where everyone knew our business! When I was pregnant with your mother, I could see the curtains in the parlor windows moving as I walked down the street. They were observing the shape of my person, telling one another just what it was that the town banker and the schoolmarm had *done!*"

Charlotte wasn't listening. She was staring out the window at the gully where the dirt road crossed the culvert. The dust the Nash kicked up was only now settling back down onto the roadbed. In the first low shaft of direct morning light, it looked, to her, like gold.

Lionel worried about germs in his food and hair in his food. Winnie worried about her own as-yet-undetected cancer of the colon. What Charlotte worried about was ending up crazy. She knew that being crazy was caused either by heredity or environment, though the experts couldn't say which. Either way seemed to make no difference. It was in her genes, obviously, like the color of the mark on her iris, and there she was in the same dusty house, being raised by the same people who raised her mother and in the same lousy way.

Winnie worried about cancer because her sister Trudy had died of it. Winnie believed cancer was caused by worry, and given the sort of daughter she'd been allotted, she knew there was no one in the world who worried more. The family doctor, Dr. Greenley, a devout Seventh Day Adventist and vegetarian, had advised Winnie to try to calm down the slightest bit. He favored the nutritional approach.

"Just try not to worry so much," Charlotte reminded her. "He said to eat a little less meat, remember? And a few more Loma Linda Vegeburgers, and to try not to take it all to heart." What Dr. Greenley, a man of science, had actually said was that Katrinka's fate was in the hands of God. Charlotte didn't mention this. She couldn't say the words or even think about them for any length of time without being silenced by her own great heaving sobs.

"How dare you be impertinent to me?" Winnie cried out. "Speaking to me of *vege*burgers! Are you trying to be funny at my expense? That's one of your mother's tricks, you realize? Lionel, will you speak to her? Will you remind Charlotte that she is to attempt to act normally? Will you also remind her that I am not a well woman?"

"Your grandmother is not a well woman," Lionel said.

Charlotte lowered her face, biting hard at her lips and cheeks, trying to hide what probably showed anyway, that she did think there was something deeply funny in it, not only in the very sound

of the word "vegeburgers" but in the way Lionel did so sternly intone on cue: "Your grandmother is not a well woman!"

"Look at her!" Winnie cried out. "She's beginning to look more
like her mother with every passing day!" Winnie hated to be reminded not to worry. She *needed* to worry. She imbued the act of
worrying with the power of prayer. It was only her worrying about
a thing ahead of time that kept it from happening. The trouble with
Katrinka was that she was always working herself up into some new
and unforeseeable calamity. Now, *how*, when Winnie was a girl at
Saint Helen's Academy, was she ever supposed to have imagined
herself old and unwell? And with the burden of a child to raise, and
the daughter, too, still to care for, a daughter who would not take her
medication, would *not* get better, who was not only alcoholic but
schizophrenic and who was *bound and determined* to act up in the
most public way imaginable, in roadshows and on network television, before Ed Sullivan's home audience of millions!

But it was Charlotte Winnie was really worried about these days,
because she was showing the same signs: the poor posture, the
smirking and other facial antics, and the boys! Why, boys were calling on the phone, then falling silent when Winnie answered. It was
at just this age, when Katrinka had grown her bosoms, that she had
begun to show the interest in boys. They should have sent her away
right then to boarding school as Winnie's own mother and stepfather had done. If Lionel and Winnie had, she might not have ever
started smoking and become so very involved in stage crew!

Boys were driving by the house now with their windows rolled
down, their radios blaring, all in their souped-up cars! Why, they
were going by to race up the fire trails, to park, to neck, to drink beer
and to throw down their trash! This was all for Charlotte's benefit.
Teenagers, Winnie had observed, were like animals when it came to
sex: they were drawn to it wheresoever they could smell it.

When Winnie had said "bosoms," Charlotte had mentally gone
off somewhere else, so by the time the words "smell it" came along,
she was nowhere at all around. She was, by then, in the laboratory,
observing very clinically within the pink and neatly boxed shape of
her grandmother's large intestine the whitish mass of an inoperable

malignancy. Charlotte saw it vividly, as if in a kind of technicolored X-ray, with the parts all lit up, moving and pulsing in just the way the bones of her own living feet had been demonstrated to her to be, once when she'd wiggled her toes to check the fit under the shoe-store's fluoroscope.

With Winnie now dying, and now finally dead, Charlotte could lift her face at last, imagining how it would be to ride with boys in cars. Her long hair was loose and flying. The air was perfumed with vinyl from the brand-new tuck 'n' roll, fragrant too with sage and the stink of distant skunk, and of boys' sweat and hair goop and of lint and the other things they kept buried deep in their woolen pockets. Their breath was hot and sweet, heavy with the taste of beer. She had a book now, a paperback, called *The Amboy Dukes*. It was about boys in gangs. It had rape in it.

"Well, you don't have to worry about that kind of junk with me, Winnie," she told her grandmother, automatically. She said this out loud, to make a joke of all of it. "Nobody ever calls me up anyway, you know. And even if somebody did call me up it wouldn't be anybody to ask me out to ride on fire trails, but would just be some dumb crud a year or two younger than me with arms about this big around calling me up to tell me I'm flat as a board." She was holding up a zero, the circle made of one forefinger, one thumb, intended to demonstrate the circumference of this crud-type boy's upper arm, when Winnie let out a banshee shriek.

"Younger than *me!*" Winnie screamed. "*Crud!*" she asked, turning toward Lionel, with her face contorted. "*Flat* as a *board!*" Wasn't this *just* the type of talk Katrinka had so frequently resorted to after stage crew, the type of talk Winnie had no intention of tolerating? Why just last week Charlotte had allowed another child in the high school to write on her blue canvas binder: "Flunk now—avoid the June rush!" "*Flunk!*" Winnie was screaming blindly, out toward the treetops, "as everyone knows full well is just one more way of saying that other word, the one her mother has always been so fond of, the one which is *the* most vile word in the entire English language!"

"You mean fuck," Charlotte enunciated mentally.

Why boarding school was the only place for girls like this, girls with *bosoms!* who spoke in such a slovenly way! who by their scent alone could draw boys up and onto the fire trails!

"Driving by in sets of threes?" Charlotte asked her mother, talking to Katrinka who was not there, via Space Radio, via E.S.P. Charlotte closed her eyes, concentrated, saw Katrinka there in the mists. Katrinka smiled and tipped her chin up, whispering back: "Threes," she agreed. She inhaled deeply on her cigarette.

It was to the Marlborough School in Los Angeles that the daughters of many important people went, Winnie was saying. Why, Walt Disney had himself sent his daughter Diane there! Charlotte, opening her eyes, saw that her grandfather was intrigued. He was not eating just then, still he smacked his lips and moved his mouth around, as if practicing for the next day's mush. Yes, indeedy! he was saying. Why, Walt and Diane Disney—Oh, to shake such a fine man's hand! Why, Walt and Lionel might take long walks together up Big Tujunga Canyon, remarking on the depth of the water table, on the state of the Auto Club, on Annette Funicello. He chuckled to himself, congratulating Walt on Disneyland. Why, Lionel and Walt might sit together on the Marlborough School Board of Trustees!

He was of the opinion that Charlotte might attend the Marlborough School but he saw no need for her to go there as a boarder. The school was just downtown, a short ride on the freeway, just the way he and Charlotte always drove when they went off to take Winnie's paintings to the framemaker. He would drive her, then pick her up. He moved his lips around the deliciousness of it: he was busy adding bumping into Walt to the sum of his perfect day.

Charlotte and Winnie watched him, each from under the shadow of her brow. Each was silenced by the sight of her own doomed future flying toward her through the Nash's windshield. Winnie wanted this teenagedness gone from her house, not brought back home every night by freeway—she wanted it stuck off and away in boarding school where it rightfully belonged! Charlotte, on the other hand, knew that Lionel, with his rapidly dimming vision, could no longer safely drive the car.

By acting up so publicly, Katrinka had always made certain there was never anything hidden about her mental illness. It was Charlotte's father, the war hero, who was not to be discussed, though he seemed to have died in such a normal, though drastic, way. Lionel wouldn't speak his name, nor suffer himself to hear it.

Lionel liked to sit like the sphinx in his red leather banker's chair at certain prescribed times throughout the day, with an arm on either armrest and his mouth shaped into a hard circle, breathing slowly in, then slowly out. If, as he sat cooling down after his six-mile walk, the name was casually mentioned, he would rise angrily and stride stiff-legged down the hall to the back of the house, with the sweaty shapes of upper legs, twin buttocks, and lower back all left there, clinging, shining and indignant, to mark the wreckage of the day.

It was Winnie who told Charlotte privately what there was to tell, that the *Indianapolis* was Joe, Jr.'s, first assignment, that the ship went down in the deepest waters in the world, that because of secrecy of the cargo the ship had been sailing under radio silence and was never missed. The *Indianapolis* was sunk just two weeks before the Japanese surrender. The families were not immediately notified that the ship was missing. It sank in twelve minutes. No SOS went out. There was no escort. The survivors were in the waters of the mid-Pacific for four days before the oil slick was sighted, quite by accident, by a single American flier who happened to be off course. It took another day and a half to mount the rescue, by which time three-quarters of the 1153 men on board had perished. Men died in war, Winnie said. It was normal, natural. Children lost their fathers. Charlotte wasn't to feel sorry for herself, nor to count herself so special.

Charlotte wasn't all that special. Why, Winnie had herself lost her own beloved father when she was only three. Louis Rutherford had been a great man, a banker, like Lionel, but good at it. Like Robert Louis Stevenson, Louis Rutherford had had a wide and poetic brow. (Winnie invariably thumped this brow in the sepia-tinted photograph she always pulled out to illustrate this point in the story.) Winnie's father had died alone in Hawaii where he'd gone to cure his TB. He died because of an old man at the bank, a clerk who'd coughed all over the books as they were being reconciled, which was the reason Winnie had always detested sick old men. Louis died at twenty-eight; Charlotte's father at twenty-six. Louis had had a lovely singing voice and had played a three-quarter-sized Washburn guitar, the one shipped back to Winnie and her mother on the mainland on the same sailing vessel that brought back Louis' body for the burial.

It was Winnie who had suffered, with losing her father like that, then ending up with a daughter so abnormally bizarre she had insisted upon changing her given name when she went away to college. She'd *said* it was because the registrar had told her there was another girl named Katherine Ainsworth at Cal, but Winnie had never believed that tale for one single second since Charlotte's mother had always been the type to make up peculiar stories, and was so odd, always, that she'd been the one and only girl on stage crew. Winnie didn't see why she hadn't picked "Kitty" for short, rather than going so far as to change it to "Katrinka *Lionel* Ainsworth!" And why the name *Katrinka*, a name that clinked and rattled like junk clanking in the wagon of a gypsy tinker?

"I haven't had a REAL vacation in forty years!" These words would erupt from Winnie suddenly, and always as if the enormity of the injustice had only then dawned on her. Since she hadn't had a job to go to since leaving the classroom in Power, Montana, to marry Lionel all those years before, Charlotte was always tempted to yell right back at her: "Vacation from *what*, Winnie?" though she never did. She didn't ask it as it was just that type of question that was liable to provoke the great sloshes, either the blue-tinted turp or the turkey gravy Winnie'd also been known to throw.

Winnie had as little use for Joe, Jr., as she had for her own daughter. Why had he been so hell-bent on marrying Katrinka when she was only one or two courses short of graduation? If she'd only graduated, Katrinka might have gotten by teaching art in the public school rather than having to resort to ventriloquism. Winnie also bitterly resented a comment Charlotte's father once made about the shape of Louis Rutherford's eyebrows. Winnie never mentioned just what this insult was. Still, Joseph Black, Jr., all these long years dead, had never been forgiven for it.

Charlotte imagined that what had happened was this: that her father, who'd married into the Ainsworth family rather than been raised in it, hadn't properly understood what it was he was supposed to have shouted when Winnie got out the sepia-tinted photo and began then to thump it in front of his nose. "Oh, *my God!*" he should have said. "Look at that wide and poetic brow! Why, Winnie, your father looks *exactly* like Robert Louis Stevenson!" He may have mentioned something instead about how Winnie inherited Louis' eyebrows, which were slightly bushy and were perfectly level, running above either eye without the pronounced arch that Katrinka's had, the arch she used to give her ironic words an even more exaggerated inflection. Charlotte, like her great-grandfather Louis, like Winnie herself, had ended up with the straight ones, the ones from under which Charlotte would peer out, trying usually to keep her face as plain, as deadpan, as Buster Keaton's.

What Winnie always said, finally, about Charlotte's parents was that they were too much alike. They were *just alike!* and they both made Winnie tired, and so did their artistic Berkeley friends. These friends had had funny names, which had served to encourage Katrinka in her own abnormality. Some had had three names—there was an Alec Something Something—and one of them had gone by his initials only. They had been artistic and they were funny-looking. They'd had drunken soirées and had talked their filthy language. What was wrong with Charlotte's parents was that they'd both had high IQs and no common sense! This was the type that had always given Winnie the absolute pip. She'd known some like that at the university at Missoula, but had never imagined her own child would turn out that way. She had never thought to worry, and, by not worrying, this very thing had come to be.

Although Lionel and Winnie pleaded with her doctors to keep her, Katrinka was always released from the hospital. One morning she'd been put onto a Greyhound bus at Ventura with a ticket for Glendale. Lionel had spent all the afternoon and on into the evening at the bus station waiting but she had not arrived. The last bus had come without her being on it, so now he was home again, and they were waiting for the phone to ring. Each lay awake in bed in the hot, dark, and ticking house, each listening for disaster.

Though willed to so do, the phone would not now ring. If it did now ring it might be the police, or it might be Sugarman saying Katrinka had found her way to the carnival and so was there safe with him. Or it might be Katrinka herself saying she was near Pershing Square, staying with a *very* close dear and personal friend of hers, a Negro, a Negro mental patient, a *male* Negro mental patient, someone she'd met in board and care. "Oh, he may be a little cuckoo," she'd tell Lionel, "but he's not as cuckoo as you," adding: "In the words, Dad, of Johnny Mercer." If the phone hadn't rung by morning, Lionel would go for his walk, shower, shave, slop his interminable mush, then begin to notify the authorities. He was very good at notifying the authorities, his voice becoming deeper, more authoritative with each of the calls he made.

Now as the three of them lay in bed, each was listening to the Dodger game to pass the time. Lionel had recently given Charlotte his own Sony portable radio. She'd washed the flesh-colored earplug with soap and water, then had rinsed it with alcohol, but within the plastic she still could detect the smell of his earwax. She now heard the game in three places: from within the scented plug guarded from touching the inside of her ear by the sheath she'd made of Kleenex; from the front bedroom where Winnie was listening on her big radio that had many bands, some that picked up police calls, some calls from ship to shore; and from Lionel's old Philco console, which stood in the study next to the daybed upon which he always slept. The Philco was imprecisely tuned. At Winnie's insistence, all the doors within the house were standing open. Since the house had come to contain someone who was so determinedly teenaged these days, Winnie was increasingly suspicious of the kinds of things that might occur behind closed doors.

Charlotte listened but could not concentrate on the events of the game. She listened only to hear the soothing voices of Vin Scully and Jerry Doggett announcing the plays. She loved the modulation of their intertwining voices, the way they did not yell except in joy, how they did not interrupt. She loved the way they were so kindly, so forgiving, even to the opposing players. She loved their intelligence, their godlike apprehension of baseball statistics. She had once loved baseball, too, but had now stopped. She had stopped at the same time she'd stopped loving her grandfather. She had once loved Lionel ardently, to the soles of his feet, loved him as she'd never loved her grandmother. This love had been based, it now seemed, on his good humor and his reason, on the rules of building trashfires and the game of chess, on the sound of his voice reading aloud from the complete works of Charles Dickens. She had loved him but did no longer and she could not really remember why. She thought it might be for the way he smelled after lunch, like coffee and peanut butter, or because of the look of food ever whitening on his working tongue.

Suddenly the crowd roared. On this night, Frank Howard had suddenly hit a homer so far up into the stands of center field that it may well be the longest home run ever. The crowd in L.A. Memorial Coliseum was wild. "Lionel!" Winnie called out excitedly from the front toward the back of the darkened house, "will you listen to that?"

What Charlotte could never stand about the Ainsworths was that they ranted and raved about Katrinka and what she'd done to them but were unable to concentrate on the simplest facts of grief. Their daughter was lost out in the night someplace. She was not safe, was never safe. They called to one another back and forth about the Dodger game, exclaiming over how fine and *tall* Frank Howard was. Charlotte moved the dial away from the voices of Vin Scully and Jerry Doggett, stopping at any bump of noise that might be the rock and roll on KFWB.

Outside, within the wired glass dome of the porch light next to Lionel's study door, a fat moth was dying, as the men in the water had died, slowly, over time. Each of the awful sounds the moth made was amplified by the hollow shape of the dome. She heard the thud of the body as it flung itself against the heat—the bumping made the moth sound huge, at least fist-sized. She heard, too, the airy flutter of the dusty wings being ripped apart on the wires. To escape, it needed to fly up past the white and mesmerizing glow of the bulb and out into the cool soft dark, but it never would. This was one of the things she, born to a dead father, had always known: that death, like life, did also exert its own sure pull. She heard the moth fall heavily against the hot glass, heard too the nothing of its waiting.

Charlotte waited too, hoping it was dead at last, but then the thumping started. She wanted it to quit, to die, DIE! to burn up, sizzle, expire! Death she could live with: she had seen the face of it on the brick mason lying on his back on a lawn on Montecito one morning on her way to school. Death she could stand, but not this other— the moth, the man on the cross, the ones in the water, her mother out there in the dark being drawn ever back toward the shock that lit up every cell of her brain. In electroshock all the synapses were caused to shoot off at once. Then there was the rest to fall back into, the velvety darkness, the clean slate.

The mason had lain on a bright green lawn within a swirl of leaves. The sky was low, gray, darkening. The press of clouds enlivened the hues of earth: the fallen leaves were peach-colored, golden, scarlet, russet. She'd stood on the sidewalk and had looked at him: he looked as if he'd been pitched from sleep into a more terrible dream. He had died, they'd thought, of a heart attack but he looked rammed, bashed, his arms flung up and out, his mouth agape. Someone came forward and used the mason's own dropcloth to cover him. The canvas was smudged with marks of dirty red. Still, the body showed from under it, the feet splayed wide apart, the hollow of each boot, between toe and heel, clotted with whitening clay. It was to hide his shame, Charlotte felt, at being caught dead like that, that they'd covered up his face.

It was torture to think that Katrinka was not safe. She was never safe, not on Ward G-1, where her brain was showered with the waves of sudden light, not here on Vista del Mar sleeping in the other twin in this very same room with Charlotte. Try as they might Charlotte and her mother couldn't keep one another safe from the other two, those two, the ones calling from room to room.

She pulled the pillow over her head and tried to imagine something her heart might bear. She thought of Bob Davidson, of the smoky smell of his Pendleton, of the way he held her to him on the dance floor. They rocked in one place, as if dazed, stupefied. She was wrapped in the heat of him, in the smell of cigarettes, her face pressed to the scratchiness of the wool. She thought of his thin and cynical lips, of his narrowed eyes, of the way he watched in class but would not volunteer. He was not like Charlotte, who said, always *said*, who was forever speaking out, just as her mother did, each one talking as if to save her very life. Lionel had already warned her about boys like Bob Davidson, hoods, having pointed out a low rider once from the Nash. "That, Charlotte, is a bean-oh. Now under no circumstances are you ever to associate with a boy of that type."

"You mean 'beaner,'" Charlotte corrected him. His right ear though was currently his deafer ear, so Lionel no longer heard anything over the motor's roar.

She thought of sneaking out her open window, of riding up the fire trail in Bob Davidson's car, of throwing beer cans from the switchbacks down onto the wooden shakes of her grandparents' house in a wide and sparkling arc. The colors of the cans—red, silver, golden—would explode out of the night like embers popping out of a brushfire. Whenever there were fires in the hills, whether along their own crest or way over in Bel Air, Lionel sat on the peak of the roof wetting the shakes with the garden hose, just to be sure. She was thinking of Bob Davidson, of his hard thin lips, of what it would take to get inside a mouth like that, of the way his weight might feel lying atop her on the new tuck 'n' roll, when she heard the real weight of her grandfather moving along the creaking floorboards past the telephone desk in the central hall. That was the house at dead center. That was where, during the next hundred years or so, the house would finally implode, if she or her mother had not yet set it on fire.

Though his only daughter was lost in the dark, Lionel came along now on his stiff legs, laughing to himself over the feat of Frank Howard. He was chuckling, literally going: "Ho, ho, ho." Charlotte could see him striding up to Frank Howard, one large fine man approaching another, extending the fingers of his fine, long-boned hand.

Charlotte heard him go into the bathroom, heard the water hitting water through the door, which had not been definitively closed. She thought of the shape of Lionel's fingers, of those long fingers holding the shape of his large man's penis, of the weight of his balls dangling in their sacks. She thought of each of her grandparents quite diagnostically, as under the fluoroscope, seeing the pale masses of their various malignancies and the large and throbbing shadows of each of their still quite vital glands.

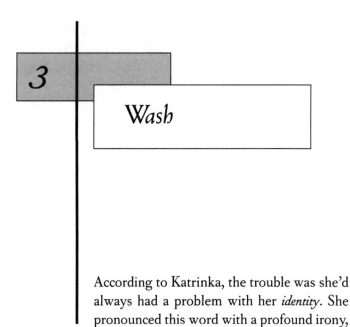

3

Wash

According to Katrinka, the trouble was she'd always had a problem with her *identity*. She pronounced this word with a profound irony, as if everybody knew there was no such thing. Katrinka seemed to think her mental illness was funny, which was why she'd filled in "mental patient" in the space for Mother's Occupation on Charlotte's birth certificate before she'd ever even been committed to Camarillo.

Unlike Lionel and Winnie, Katrinka was perfectly happy to talk about what had gone on. Her version, though, was different from theirs; it also evolved over time. It was her humor, the blank wall of it, that made it hard for Charlotte to know what Katrinka meant, really *really*. She liked to tell Charlotte how *bad* Lionel and Winnie were, though never really saying exactly what she meant. She liked, too, to talk about Cal, and about living with Joey in their crappy little house in Silverlake, the one that was falling down the hill. Katrinka's memories were at once vivid, lucid, but also so fragmentary that she could never give evidence in a court of law, Charlotte saw. Katrinka could remember a particular morning from the past as if it were yesterday, but couldn't remember the month or year in which the morning had occurred, could remember the phone ringing but not what the person on the other end had said.

Katrinka's memory was shot, she said, because of all the electroshock therapy which had drilled holes in her already half-cracked brainbox. "Awwnnd it's a good thing too, sweetiebaby, when you realize the things I can't remember are probably at least as godawful lousy as the rest of the shitty crap I have retained." Who needed, Katrinka wondered, to remember every single day spent lying on one's twin bed in the back bedroom of Vista del Mar, staring at the ceiling, smoking Lionel's Luckies that were being parceled out ONE TO THE HOUR and listening to the dual Wraths of Gawd broadcasting bad news from the living room? The voices of the Ainsworths, as Katrinka told her and as Charlotte already knew, did not call sweetly, each to each, but yelled, directed, ordered, boomed, instructed, warned with all the subtlety of a Ouija board: OH I WOULDN'T EVEN THINK THAT IF I WERE YOU! NOW I AM OF THE OPINION OH YOU MAKE ME SO NERVOUS LIONEL THAT CHARLES DICKENS WORKED AT THE AGE OF TWELVE IN A BLACKING FACTORY THE PIP! THE PIP! OH I'M GOING TO RUN OFF AND JOIN THE NAVY! THE NAVY! THE CHURCH OF THE LIGHTED FIRST STATE BANK OF JESUS H. CHRIST! HIS FEET SO CLEAN YOU COULD EAT OFF OF THEM, IMMACULATE! RESURRECTED!

It was the PIP! the PIP! and having the very voice of Winnie echoing in her brainbox—a voice like a headache—and having the cigarettes doled out to her ONE TO THE FUCKING HOUR! that always drove Katrinka a little boi-ing cuckoo! and right smack back to the mental hospital. At Camarillo, at least, she could buy her own lousy smokes at the canteen with her own lousy chits.

Katrinka's version of their disasters, that which she called "my side of the story," varied from the Ainsworths' in that it concerned the minute event, the way a person always tended to say a particular thing, or the color of the landlady's wash that was hung out on a particular Wednesday morning. Her version changed according to the vagaries of her memory, but certain points remained immutable. Katrinka had not, for instance, "cracked up" over the boys on stage crew, so Charlotte wasn't to go by that. Nor had she been driven insane by singing beer-drinking songs with the *Pelican* staff when she was away at Cal. Instead, she said, she'd always been the way she was, which was this: *non compos mentis.*

Or more precisely: Katrinka had, she said, always come unglued periodically, ever since she was small, and usually when Lionel and Winnie were themselves having a breakdown over something, or because of the pressure of public scrutiny, as when she'd gone on Ed Sullivan, or when she was a little short of funds. Being broke, Katrinka said, was the single greatest cause of mental illness, that awwwnnd having decided that you'd been *you*-know-whated-by-your-own-you-know-*who*, the specific details of which she and Charlotte most certainly would not go into since it was perfectly obvious to Katrinka that this was not something Charlotte could discuss without Charlotte's cracking up for good.

One part of the story Charlotte was absolutely not to go by was Winnie's tale of how Katrinka had suddenly "gone crazy" when Joey died. It had had nothing to do with Joey, with her meeting him, their drinking tee minny martoonies, their having artistic, funny-looking friends, their marrying, or their being *just alike!* as Winnie loved to exclaim. "Or his dying, if that's, really really, what you think we *ought* to accept as what his disappearance is intended to signify by awwwlll the powers that be," Katrinka would say. The powers that be seemed to include nearly everyone, Charlotte noticed, aside from her mother and herself. Joey's death was one thing about which Katrinka did not remain convinced. She seemed to believe it for awhile, then the conviction would simply erode away. She always spoke of him with such immediacy it did seem that he had just left the room.

"Well," Charlotte told her one of the times they were discussing this, "it is always hard to adjust to the loss of someone when there isn't a body to bury." She listened to the hushed, adult voice of her own self saying this. Whenever she found herself saying a thing like this it was as if another person, someone resting competent hands on Charlotte's shoulders, was speaking out from above her head.

Her mother sucked her cheeks in, inhaled deeply, sniffed. "Now, where in the *hell* did you get that tidy little bit of information?" She squinted at Charlotte suspiciously. "Did your father tell you that?"

"Mother!" Charlotte yelled. "I got it out of a book!"

"Well, he was Freudy-Freudy, and *that* sounds very psychological to me."

"It *is* psychological." She glared at her mother. "But he happens to be *dead*, remember?" She was always shocked that Katrinka, who wasn't stupid, had to act so dumb at times. She did it, Charlotte guessed, in order to be more deeply amusing.

"Well, we don't go by that."

"What do you mean, *we don't go by that?*"

"In our family, we do not go by 'the psychological,' as the headache must have mentioned. Just as we do not go by this business of the Virgin Mary's being flunked by God in the June rush." Since the episode of the blue canvas notebook, which Charlotte had told her mother (as she did end up telling her nearly everything), this was what Katrinka was calling the doctrine of the Immaculate Conception. Immaculate Conception had always been one rich source of her jokes, since it tended to offend so many people. Her Immaculate Conception jokes had not gone over well on Ed Sullivan. "Freud, *schmoid*," Katrinka then suddenly announced. She tipped her chin up and looked away. She was, Charlotte noticed, talking to somebody else.

"Well, what *do* we go by then?" Charlotte asked her. She was squinting, meanwhile, examining this thought: that from these four people—Lionel, Winnie, Katrinka, and Charlotte herself—Katrinka imagined that something called a "family" was to be construed. Charlotte didn't go by that—her mother was the only one to whom she any longer felt spiritually related and then only vaguely, intermittently, resentfully. Her one true parent, she often imagined, was the father she'd never met, the long-dead and vanished hero.

Katrinka smirked, listened, hiked up one eyebrow, for emphasis. "Oh, Awe-I don't know," she drawled. "Once a wish? Twice a kiss? Three times comes a letter?"

Katrinka's memory was so wretched that she seemed to hardly remember the Great Depression, in which Lionel had lost his money, or the Second World War, in which Joey had lost his life. This was the sort of large event that didn't really concern her. She never read the newspapers, preferring to get her news in other ways.

She couldn't remember Joey going off to fight the war, couldn't even remember his enlisting in the navy, yet she was able to recall even the order in which the laundry had been hung out to dry on the line outside her window on that particular Wednesday morning, the morning of the day on which his face was to vanish forever from her sight.

"Charlotte!" Charlotte opened her eyes to the pitch dark. They were there in the back bedroom on Vista del Mar, a place where Katrinka could never sleep.

"I want to discuss this!" Katrinka was saying, her face suddenly rosily illuminated as she puffed on her cigarette. She was sitting on the edge of Charlotte's bed and was bending over her. "This," she said, "is what I would like to discuss. It isn't the facts of our tragic lives which are important, don't you understand that? But the shape of things you can still see when you close your eyes?"

"Huh?" Charlotte asked. She could still see the shapes in her dreams, police cars and streets all weirdly illuminated, since she was still asleep.

"When you were born and Lionel put you in the shoe drawer? You didn't suck your thumb or a finger, but you tried to suck your whole damned hand. I can see it. I could always see it, even on the ceiling of Ward G-1! I can *hear* it, Charlotte, right this very minute, you going oink, oink, oink."

"You mean when I sleep I sound like a pig?"

"Oh, for christsake, sweetie! Can't you for once adopt the kinder, cuter interpretation of anything? Exactly why is it that you are so easily criticized? Because of the goddamned Ainsworths? Don't you really understand just how *sick* they are?" Charlotte, wide awake now, reflected. It was very difficult for her to remember that people in her family were mentally ill. It was a thing she seemed to need to learn over and over again, their eccentricities being such an intrinsic part of what was normal in their natures.

Another time when Katrinka was staying overnight at Vista del Mar, she woke Charlotte up to ask her: "Why is it so important to you that I *remember* things? Just why is it that I *must* remember? When everything that ever happened to us is just too damned crappy lousy! All right! Tell me what it is that I'm supposed to re-member and I'll *try* to remember it. I'll try to remember it, if that will make you feel better."

Charlotte, still asleep, told her groggily, "Mom," she said, "I don't even know what you're talking about."

"THEM!" she said. "The *lies.*" She made a slight gasping sound, as if she were struggling for breath. From out of the dark her face sud-denly showed in the glowing, then again dimmed. "Can't you really understand it? How unreasonable memory is, how it cloys, blinds my eyes, makes the ink of old letters swim and dance and all that crap, each with its own ghastly shadow? It is never possible to re-member the one single thing, sweetie. Memories adhere, come along together. You *do* know what I'm talking about. And why should we remember these things, the things too terrible to be borne? Who needs to remember lying on the bed in Ward G-1, lis-tening to thirty other mental patients all talking to themselves? Be-lieve me, sweetie, listening in the dark to mental patients talking out loud is one sure way to drive yourself crazy." Really? Charlotte thought, smirking.

Katrinka couldn't remember Joey's going off to war. She did re-member that it was a Wednesday morning when the phone had rung. She had been baking a chocolate cake, one out of Irma Rom-bauer. Through the front room window Katrinka could see the landlady hanging out her white wash. Katrinka reported this, then suddenly went lurching off in another direction.

If, Katrinka said, Charlotte was in such a need of memories, she ought to stick to the concrete. She should concentrate on nouns—on persons, places, and the look of things. Her father, Katrinka went on, had been very big on the *look* of things, on everything Frank Lloyd Wrightish, all that was Japanesy. There was the look, the feel of Joey's hair to think about—it was so dark it was nearly black, and was coarse, curly, wiry to the touch. There was the wide expanse of his tanned and freckled back, and the space between his two front teeth. Joey had been as gat-tothed as the Wyf of Bathe, Katrinka wanted Charlotte to remember. She instructed Charlotte to *remem-ber* this as if it were something Charlotte knew for herself, rather than something she was being informed of by her mother. And it did sometimes seem that the two of them had exactly the same life to lead, with Katrinka going blithely on ahead, and Charlotte coming along the same path, head down, picking up the shards and pieces.

Charlotte should concentrate on the look of things, Katrinka was repeating, thinking her daughter hadn't really been paying attention, on the gap between the two front teeth! Awwwnnd she should tend to the way things were always funny. Hadn't she ever noticed that when Winnie hopped into the Nash to run off and join the navy that she always drove into the desert, in exactly the wrong direction?

As she watched the orange tip of the cigarette swoop down to her mother's lips, glow brightly, then darken as it was lifted away, Charlotte suddenly thought: *My mother's life is like a poem in which all small things are bejeweled by meaning.* She would never have mentioned this aloud, however, because she knew Katrinka would have been insulted by it. Katrinka hated poetry. She hated it, she said, for the way it bleated of things better left to quietude.

The landlady had hung out the wash. She pronounced it *warsh*, because—like Maxine Bill on Avenue B—this landlady was an Okie or an Arkie. She had hung it out that day to make a whole great big hell of a goddamned point of how *white* her whites were when Katrinka's weren't. The washline was strung between the two houses. Katrinka and Joey had the Willys then. It was parked over the slope down at the curb. Their house was on the downhill side facing west toward Hollywood. The lights of Sunset Boulevard lit up the underside of the clouds at night. The landlady, who did her *warsh* with a regularity that could only be described as mentally ill, had the big house in front. Theirs behind was a real dump, falling down off its crumbling foundation. Joey'd been so low, he was painting the kitchen in three shades of blue to make a deep point about his depressive nature. Katrinka sniffed. She had never understood what people hoped to get out of what they called "depression." She had herself never spent a depressed day in her life and therefore she didn't go by it.

Joey was cracking up over having to work for his father, over having to hear the beat-beat-beat of the tom-toms at the office, too, over

Joe, Sr.'s, paying their Charg-O-Matics at the Jolly Boys Bottle Shop and at the tobacconist's when why *shouldn't* he, when it was he who drove them both to drink? Joey was blue, too, over Eleanor Ann, over her talking about them in the third person at the Blacks' dinner parties, parties Joey and Katrinka were *made* to go to since they were good for his architectural career. Eleanor Ann liked to quote herself, telling what she'd said that day at her bridge club: "Why, my dears, this is too exquisite! Their Bohemian phase! The poor, dear, dumb things! Their house, if I may say so, is a perfect hovel! With our Joey being AIA!"

The wash was white and that had meaning. There was wind that day and that had meaning. On the morning he left, he'd had no socks that matched. He'd gone off to die in a white dress shirt worn under his suit coat, with only the collar and cuffs and button placard pressed. Why was Charlotte looking at her like that, glaringly, accusingly? Charlotte should have married him herself, obviously, if she was so goddamned great at ironing that she was about to win the Nobel Prize in it, or *he* should have married Gervaise, Katrinka supposed, since he'd decided their lives were straight out of Zola. Better he should have been rich enough to have hired his own damned laundress!

When the phone rang, she'd gone to answer it—she did remember that. The washline was strung downhill between the two houses. She'd mixed the cake by hand, one hundred strokes, then she'd poured the batter into a greased and floured pan. She took the dirty mixing bowl out and put it into the landlady's Okie-and-Arkie trash. This was one of the last recipes Katrinka would ever attempt to follow—she hated to be bossed around by anyone, and that included Irma.

The phone rang. She went to answer it. There were rules to follow, Winnie told her, rules concerning tissue paper and the proper packing of shoes. Katrinka watched as the pieces of white laundry all lifted on the line together. The sky was white and the white clothes were lifting into it. Was Charlotte listening? It was this she was to remember: they were all being tugged, Katrinka knew, all drifting up, all being wrenched upward toward all that was not black but was whitey-white instead. The wind had lifted the line, then it subsided. That had had meaning. Every whack and whack of the wooden spoon too had meaning, and each snap and lick and ripple of the laundry, all the pieces hooked and fighting the line like fish.

Did Charlotte realize that her father had been an excellent sailor? That he'd spent every summer of his life sailing from the Blacks' house at the beach in his own ritzy-fitz little skiff?

Charlotte shook her head—no, she hadn't known that. About herself, her parents, there was still everything to learn. The very nature of their lives was mysterious, the events dramatic, the names of places and objects—Cal, Silverlake, *Pelican*, skiff with centerboard, Tinian, Leyte—of almost luminous interest to her. The words were thinglike, became objects to be picked up, weighed, turned over, as an artifact might be. The secrets in her family, she felt, lay just beneath the surface of these words, as huge and well-lit as the shape of the ship the men of the *Indianapolis* had all been prompted to hallucinate together. That was on the third day, after the shark attacks had stopped, when the men began to commit suicide, encouraging others to do it too, to slip their life jackets off, to dive back down to it. Madness, Charlotte understood, was something that could be held separate or it might be offered up to be shared. She knew this because Katrinka had always seemed perfectly willing to share hers with her.

Charlotte just wanted to get the facts straight. She felt like Jack Webb on "Dragnet," going "Just the facts, Mom." She imagined herself to be an interviewer, like Brenda Starr, Reporter. Their past seemed at times like something the two of them were conspiring to invent together, Katrinka with the small snippets of precise memory, Charlotte with the larger picture. Charlotte's job, she felt, was to stand at her mother's side as Katrinka put down the phone and stood staring out at the landlady's wash, and to take her by the elbow. *Who was on the phone, Mom?* Charlotte was to whisper, though at that point she had not yet been born. *Was it the War Department? Just tell me the simple words, all right? Just say what they said. Did they say he got a medal?* She wanted that, a weighty tangible thing that would stand for him. She wanted it to be worth a great deal of money.

Katrinka did not remember anything at all about all that. She re-membered wash, shoes, tissue paper, shoe drawer. She had held the phone out and away. She did not weep, never again would weep, even when the child she'd borne was taken from her arms. Not crying was a point of pride with her. She tipped her chin up so when she swallowed the movement down either side of her long neck was visible. She stared out at the laundry hanging on the line and Char-lotte, looking into the pitch dark, could see it too. "Frankly, sweetie," her mother was saying from the next bed, "I don't know what it is that you want me to tell you. Can't you see that? Can't you really see that nothing that I can say is going to do you any good?"

Charlotte was growing, was now nearly her mother's height. She would, one day, pass her. The thought of it, of standing next to her at the window, of taking her mother's elbow and looking directly into her gray-green eyes, made her heart hurt, grow huge with awe and pity.

Her mother's life was a poem, an aggregate, in which all the small jeweled things had to be chipped out and examined for worth, for meaning. There had been no body to bury, so Katrinka couldn't re-member it, could never get it right. Still, all these years later she could recite the order of the wash, see its white snap and ripple. The wash did mean, she'd tell you, and what it meant was this:

undies   undies   diaper   BRA!

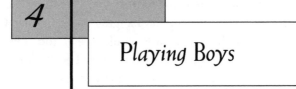

4

Playing Boys

Back in the days before stage crew and Cal, when Katrinka was more normal than she turned out later to be, she'd had one good friend that Lionel and Winnie very much approved of. It was this friend who grew up to be *the* Mildred Younger who placed the name of Richard Nixon in nomination for the Presidency of the United States at the 1960 Republican Convention! Whenever Lionel and Winnie started to get going about Mildred Younger! about Pat and Richard Nixon of Whittier, California! Katrinka would wink at Charlotte, arch an eyebrow, and tell her: "*Very* high up! Oh, Very! How very, *very* la-di-da fitz!"

Now Charlotte had a friend like that, a nice friend from a normal, happy family. Winnie said the words "normal" and "happy" in a way that was utterly grief-stricken—upon saying "happy," her voice broke the word into two desolate pieces. Patsy Johnson's parents were good Republicans, members of the Oak Knoll Country Club, recent converts to the Episcopal religion, exactly the sort of people Lionel and Winnie very much admired. Mr. Johnson drove Patsy and Charlotte to the dances at the YWCA where they often spent their time in the bathroom waiting for somebody good to show up.

"Well, at least someone asked you to dance," Charlotte told Patsy, one afternoon in the bathroom at the Y.

"Sorry, Char, but Williman Grottman is not a someone," Patsy said. "Williman Grottman is a mollusk who slimed in here from the sewer."

Charlotte thought this over. Williman Grottman, who was in their honors science class, was the worst boy in their grade, the worst, probably, in all of Glendale High. He had once told Charlotte that the spelling of his name came from a typographical error at the county recorder's office that no one in his family ever felt he had the right to fix. Charlotte knew she ought to be kind to him, to be kind, distant, aloof, slightly patronizing, but she couldn't be. When she saw him coming toward her she raced to the bathroom, terrified of having to tell him no, that she wouldn't be able to dance with him. She might have even wanted to dance with him, since he was so smart in science, but she couldn't allow herself that. She couldn't dance with Williman, or even say the word no to him, without being pulled down by her pity into the welter of their mutual and ghastly woe. Patsy, on the other hand, felt nothing at brushing him off. Shining a person on didn't faze Patsy in the slightest, while the act of rejecting someone else made Charlotte feel as if she herself were almost physically maimed.

"Face it," Patsy was saying. "No one good's coming. We might as well call up my dad and go home and kill ourselves." Charlotte was sleeping over at Patsy's house so they were going home together. Charlotte lifted her eyes to Patsy's in the mirror—each was slicking on more Icy Peach lipstick by Maybelline. What did Patsy have to kill herself over, Charlotte wondered. She had so much normalcy it made Charlotte sick—the two nice parents, the freckled little brother with taxicab door ears, the big house with symmetrical landscaping, the big black dog standing on his porch, drooling into his pools of spit. Patsy's abnormality was completely normal, Charlotte knew. It was a matter of common and minor wretchedness: menstrual cramps, braces, the few insignificant pimples. "It's just a face you're going through," Charlotte had mentioned more than once.

Patsy played competitive complaining in part, Charlotte knew, to guard herself against an envy of her good fortune. Katrinka called competitive complaining the game of "Compete-O." Vying for who was the most Poor and Pitiful Pearl Among Women was a favorite pastime on Ward G-1, one in which Katrinka refused to participate. She would not participate—still, whenever Charlotte complained about Lionel and Winnie, Katrinka would smile and say, "Oh, I know, sweetie! We *win!* You and I have it worse than all of the Christians, most of the Jews, and even some of the Negroes! *Gervaise, c'est moi!* and all that. Our lives, as your father used to say, were written by Zola, which is more interesting anyway than the lives of Mr. and Mrs. Tweedy, don't you think? who were written by Charles Dickens."

Katrinka, when bragging about all of their misfortunes, was generally humorous, but sometimes, inexplicably, she became angry. This was usually when she imagined that Charlotte was accusing her of being a lousy mother, though her being a lousy mother was a point beyond contention, having been proved for all time when Charlotte and Katrinka were living with Sweeney on Avenue B. "All right, then!" she'd cry. "What do you *want* me to do about them? Shall I call the police and have them arrested? Do you want me to take them to court and have them declared legally dangerous, incompetent and cracked-up-nuts, as they've done over and over again to me? Who would there be to raise you then? Unless you think you're so high up in the smartypants aspect of things, these days, that you can raise your own self, Missy Miss! Is that what you think?" Charlotte stared at her levelly, thinking, *If I had the money, if I had the car keys*, never mind that she didn't know how to drive.

"Can you see the two of them locked up in Camarillo?" Katrinka would go on. "Which *is* what would happen to them if people found out how bad they are. The two of them bent over, toiling in the mental patient lettuce fields? Being given electroshock therapy, Charlotte? Your grandfather without his feet up? Having to earn his own fucky chits for cigarettes? The *Ainsworths!* Being driven steadily more and more crazy by being forced to listen to the conga-bonga rhythms of jigaboos? Is that what you want?" *Yes,* Charlotte would think grimly, *Camarillo would serve them both damned right.*

Charlotte watched Patsy in the mirror—she was brushing on mascara from the small black slab that had been moistened with spit. Patsy might try out for the most pitiful prize, but she could never win it: she was smart, cute, nice. No one could ever win it if Charlotte was in the competition, so great was the luck of her cards. She had aces nobody even knew about. She had a royal flush: drunk, mad, dead, queer. She had this:

"Know what my grandmother told me?" Charlotte said.

"What?" Patsy's face was elongated, her cheeks stretched hollow by the opening of her mouth, as she brushed the blackness onto her lashes, her eyes rigidly held wide open. She had tiny golden freckles dusted over her cheeks and forehead.

"I shouldn't even tell you this," Charlotte said. "It's too sick." She waited, closing her eyes, imagining the best card she held, the lights of the sunken ship. She studied it for a moment, and then used it to cover over the next one, the whitening mouth of her grandfather as it moved around the chewed-up peanut butter sandwich. "She said they still sometimes have relations because it's good for one of his glands."

"Oh, my God," Patsy said. Charlotte opened her eyes and saw herself in the mirror, her brows lifted up, asking what she should find in this. Patsy had stopped brushing. Her eyes were blue, clear. "I think," she said, "that I am about to throw up."

They were back then at Patsy's that night, working on their personal appearance. Charlotte was reading a diet in a magazine and Patsy was painting her toenails. Each had already washed her face with Phisohex, then with Noxzema. They had plucked one another's eyebrows though Patsy's were so pale they were nearly vanished from her face, and the loss of even one or two hairs from Charlotte's own was probably going to cause Winnie to fly off into a giant hell of a tizzy, a real doozy, a fit which would be magnificent to see if watching from some safe place, high in the oaks, say, or from the other side of a plate glass window.

It was the look, the thought, of her own hair that always filled Charlotte with hopelessness. The braids went trundling down her back like her grandparents' twin sentinels. They made her feel like a refugee, as if she were another Annelli Verdonner. Annelli, like Williman, was another Charlotte felt she ought to be particularly kind to but could never quite bring herself to be. Like Charlotte's, Annelli's braids were obviously constructed by someone else—hers were white blonde, skinny, pinned up with ribbons in bun-shaped twists at the sides of her head above her translucent ears. They made her look years younger than anyone in their grade. The fact of braids, Charlotte had decided, had the effect of making a girl look old-fashioned, too well tended, too often handled. The country from which Annelli Verdonner had come had been taken over by the Russians at the end of the Second World War and had disappeared from the map of the world.

The more regular girls at Glendale High wore flips or pixies, bubbles or a single, bouncing ponytail. The point was not to be knockdown beautiful, which tended to stir things up, but rather to be cute. Moms of girls looked like Doris Day, their grandmothers like Mamie Eisenhower. A very stylish woman from the country club might try to look like a grayer, more Republican Jackie Kennedy, as long as she didn't look "Eastern." Looking "Eastern," sounding "Eastern," or sending your children east to go to school, they felt, all showed you thought you were better than everybody else. In Glendale, in 1962, it was better to be the same.

There were no Negroes living in Glendale then, by unwritten covenant. If anyone was Jewish in Charlotte's school, the fact was never mentioned. Even the hoods, like Bob Davidson, weren't real greasers since they weren't Mexican. Mexicans lived in their own neighborhoods and went to their own schools, and for the kids at Glendale High, were the stuff of lore. Mexican girls had deadly beehives, hairdos that were ratted up, hairsprayed, never taken down to be washed, used to hide razor blades for girl fights and for the breeding of black widow spiders. Spit curls were stuck to the cheeks of Mexican girls with little X's of Scotch tape, X's inexplicably left there after the curls were already good and stuck.

The cute, sweet, nice girls of Glendale High didn't swear. They didn't swear, scream, fight, or have pierced ears. They learned to dance at cotillion and learned their pleasant manners at charm school, where they also learned that manners, once learned, might also occasionally be ignored. They didn't get pregnant or have girl fights, which were fought by different rules than the fights of boys. The fingernails of Mexican girls illustrated this: they were long, sharp, and as red as if they'd already been dipped in blood. Charlotte knew all about girl fights, this being the way she fought the enemies in her dreams.

Boys' fights were different, were fought more simply, as men fought wars: to crush, to annihilate. In girl fights the impulse was less singular. Girls fought a fight to humiliate, to make the other ugly, to rip the blouse away, to tear off a bra and expose the other publicly. They fought with boys surrounding them and watching, fought so these boys would laugh and cheer.

"We could iron it," Patsy was saying. "Or we could use that stuff Negroes use, that junk like a perm that reverses the process?" They were trying to figure out how to make Charlotte's hair fall straight. Because it was braided wet it fell down her back in a curtain of waves when they let it down. When brushed out Charlotte's hair, like Katrinka's, turned wild, electric. Patsy's parents were out and they were babysitting Brian. He was in the den down the hall watching TV. They were in the bedroom with the door locked, drinking rum and coke.

"But it would stink up the house," Patsy went on. "It always stunk up the house when Mom used to give me a Toni. We're not supposed to stink up the house when my parents are out." She had cotton balls stuffed between her toes, a trick, like the use of orange sticks for cuticles, they'd gotten out of charm school. "Why don't we just cut it?" Patsy asked. "I mean, what could they really do to you if you came home with it trimmed?"

"Throw me out of the house."

"Oh, come on."

"I mean really." It seemed to Charlotte they'd thrown out Katrinka for less, for winking across the Thanksgiving dinner table, for humming Johnny Mercer tunes meaningfully and in Lionel and Winnie's direction, for commenting that the rectal way both Pat Nixon and Winnie each held her lips illustrated a trait of personality called being "anal retentive." It was from Charlotte's father that Katrinka had learned these Freudian sorts of insults. *Penis envy*, she might have the elegant voice of her dummy Nellie Platter pronounce, diagnosing down from on high as Winnie, standing in a bloody apron with fists tightly clenched and the tuck firmly taken in both of her buttocks, was going on and on about how the still-raw Thanksgiving turkey proved she *ought to have been born a man!* "Or," Charlotte added, "they might send me straight to Camarillo."

"We coulda least bleach some streaks in it," Patsy was going on, "so you'd look kinda like a surfer, except the peroxide would probably stink up the house. We could wet it and put it up on orange juice cans?" She looked over, lifting her scanty eyebrows, "except then you'd have to sleep like that."

"Sure bet," Charlotte said. Patsy dropped syllables out of words and further contracted most contractions. It sounded cute, her saying *pro'bly, prac'ly, 'zackly, din't, woun't, coun't*, and *shoun't*. Charlotte would have liked to talk like this, dumb for boys, but if she had Winnie would have pro'bly smacked her.

"Wann'nother rum'n'Co'Cola?" Patsy asked. She was drunk too, so in addition to the teenage accent she'd started to sound like Mrs. Johnson, who came from Butler, Georgia. People often turned into their parents when they were drunk, Charlotte had observed. Katrinka, drunk or sober, did Lionel and Winnie perfectly, but when drunk she seemed sometimes to be possessed by them.

Katrinka too had other ancestors rattling around in her dummies' trunk, where one of the psychiatrists had once suggested she try to keep the voices confined. The voice of one was like a monster's —this was Big Mother, Charlotte believed, Winnie's mother, who called out gutterally, going *KATH-er-ine! KATH-er-rine!* as if from the grave. Or it may have been Big Dad, Winnie's stepfather, or Winnie drunk herself, doing her own parents. It might have been Winnie drunk, except that Winnie didn't drink. She didn't drink even though her teetotalling Seventh Day Adventist doctor had ordered her to sip a small glass of sherry medicinally one-half hour before bedtime. She was to sip it, Dr. Greenley said, and she was to try to calm down. Charlotte had heard Winnie in the front bedroom at bedtime, trying to calm down. She was sipping, weeping. She was singing one of her favorite George Gobel tunes. "Life is just a bowl of sherries!" she sang. It was from Winnie, obviously, that Katrinka had inherited the feeling that she had the right to change the words to songs without regard to copyright.

"Know what?" Patsy was saying. "I think we should call him up. It might make a whole lot of difference if he knew how much you love him."

"Oh, Awe-I don't know about that," Charlotte drawled. She was drunk herself, so she was taking on aspects of Katrinka.

"We coulda least try," Patsy said. "Coun't hurt." She licked her lips and rubbed the tip of her nose with the back of her hand. What would it be like, Charlotte wondered, to be someone else, to be a person like Patsy who was just a person, just a simple, sweet, smart girl who didn't feel the need, as Charlotte did, to be herself and everybody else besides, who didn't have to be the judge of everything sitting high up in the oaks watching all the day's proceedings and with no small measure of disdain?

"It *couldn't?*" Charlotte corrected. She was veering off now schoolmarmishly, off now toward the Winnieisms to correct for the Katrinkas. She enunciated this next carefully, as if crossing a trout stream in Montana on slippery rocks. "Oh, I sin-cere-ly doubt *that.*"

"Well, waddaya wanna do then?" Patsy asked, looking up from her toes, which were shining, dazzling. "Wanna play boys?"

"No," Charlotte immediately snapped. But they always said that—it was the way it was played.

"You mean really, Char?" Patsy asked. "You think we shoun't anymore?"

"No," Charlotte said, and she was humiliated to hear her voice coming apart, becoming husky, ragged, as voices did when they became overladen with desire. It was the desire of others Charlotte preferred to think about—she hated to be reminded of her own. She preferred her perch high in trees, looking in through the dusty diamond-paned windows at all the pitiful souls, all twisting, dangling, made limp, weak, by the tightening of themselves all along the core of their oblique and archaic desires. Charlotte was made so sad by the needs of people that she sometimes felt she might weep.

"No," she said again. "Just as long as we, you know, stop the way we said we would when you do the confession."

Patsy had to go to confession before she was confirmed at Saint Nicholas Parish at the end of the school year. Patsy and her younger brother had both undertaken the instruction. It was from their catechism class that Patsy had learned there were no drool-mouths in heaven—no cute angel puppies, Father Bob had informed them, no dogs of any kind—and this had caused a crisis in Patsy's faith. She wasn't certain she had much interest after all in going to a heaven run by people who'd decided dogs do not have souls.

Patsy had already decided she was not going to confess to having played boys with Charlotte. She would not utter the words, shape them out into the musty air of the dark confessional, then have Father Bob, who sometimes came to dinner, sit there with his eyes *interested, knowing,* as he looked up after pouring pan drippings over his Yorkshire pudding.

She would have confessed, Patsy supposed, if Charlotte had been a real boy. Doing real things with real boys also was not allowed, but it was at least expected. There was something deeply wrong with this, they both felt, that Patsy could not confess it and be cleansed of the guilt. It was so wrong that they'd made up their own rules about when to stop.

It was that they were girls together, Charlotte knew, though the shape a person's body took seemed to make so little difference really in what a person thought he or she was capable of. Bodies were bodies. They seemed to want the same sorts of things—to eat, to be allowed to sleep without having their life jackets stolen, to be rescued finally from the middle of the ocean, to see things and hear things once again that made them happy, even if they had to be hallucinated, and when dying, to get it over quickly.

Charlotte was lying under the covers now beneath the white eyelet canopy. Her toes curled in, the joints cracking audibly. Patsy flounced over to the door, opened it, yelled down the hall to Brian to *turn the TV off and brush!* Then, going back to her vanity table to flick the little light off there, she swayed her bottom from side to side, doing this just as the two of them did when moving down the sidewalk to the bus stop, counting to get their feet in step, making sure the pleats of their skirts swished from side to side in unison. If the hems of their skirts weren't even, if one wasn't yet short enough, they'd roll it up higher at the waist. Their little white socks were stuffed in gym bags and their legs gleamed in cinnamon-hued nylons attached to the garter belts they'd taken from Mrs. Johnson's dresser drawer without asking.

Patsy marched away to the door as they went together to the bus stop, but when she flicked the switch on the vanity lamp and came back toward the bed, Charlotte could see in the light falling through the curtained window that her head was inclined and her expression had become somber. She was, Charlotte saw, practicing being penitent.

The light through the window was cast by the street lamp on the corner of El Tovar. It stood above the gully that had been carved out by the flooding creek, above the little dirt road that Winnie couldn't get the city of Glendale to pave. On a night like this when there was mist in the air, Charlotte could look out the dining room of Lionel and Winnie's house and see the haloed glow of this same street lamp through the dark mass of oaks.

Charlotte was lying on her back with her eyes nearly closed. The night was moonless. Out in the center of the lawn, the Johnsons' dog lifted his head and mooed. Bingo, who was a standard poodle, had never in his life either woofed or barked. His habit of mooing was the reason Patsy sang this song to him: "I can tell by your mooing that you are a cow-dog. You can tell by my mooing that I'm a cow-dog too. We can tell by our mooing, that we are both cow-dogs. I won't go to heaven 'nless my dog goes there tooooooo."

Bingo now stood on the lawn and lifted his baying head at something wild—deer or pheasant or coyote—off in the hills in the chaparral. "Shaddup!" Patsy told him softly, at the window. "Shaddup, Bingo, 'cause somebody's trying to sleep."

One of the rules of playing boys was the pretense of sleeping. Charlotte, with her eyes tightly shut, could hear Patsy coming to the bed, feel her weight on the edge of the mattress. She was now folding back the coverlet, the blankets, the sheet. She lifted the top of Charlotte's cotton pajamas, moving gently, so as not to awaken her. The sudden air on Charlotte's skin was chilly; her toes curled again. She was naked now from the waist up, smelling Patsy's shampoo, feeling the soft brush of her hair as it fell forward. She was exposed to the light, to the air, to the soft touch of Patsy's breath.

"Think of him," Patsy commanded. Her breath was hot on first one nipple then the other. This was part of it, pretending it was boys. If it was boys doing it, they wouldn't really turn out to be queer. "You're thinking?" Patsy whispered and Charlotte nodded yes, her eyes still closed.

They breathed together now, each in a shallow way, each waiting to see which side she would choose. The counting didn't start until the first touch, the first sharp heat of lips, of tongue. Then Charlotte had to stand this great feeling all the long way up to one hundred.

They were good at this, better than boys could ever be, as good as boys would be if they would ever bother to learn. Patsy's mouth was there then on Charlotte's nipple. She went slowly at first, then bit harder, taking the tip in her teeth and fluttering the end of it. She took the hard part of the nipple and pulled back. That was so Charlotte would be forced to cry out.

Charlotte needed to cry out—it was part of it, the way it was played. Still she could not. She needed to cry out, to protest being brought out of numbness and into feeling, to protest the ridges of Patsy's two front teeth, which were still scalloped from when they grew in, to complain about the feel of the wires of her braces. She needed to cry out, yet she couldn't. She was drugged, inert, as heavy as fog and as splayed out, as splayed as the stupid girl in the book, the one being held down by the gang of boys in the storeroom of the theater. They put her on the tabletop and did it while the movie played so her cries could not be heard. This, Charlotte knew, was the girl's own dumb fault, for failing to zigzag.

She could not cry out, could not be heard—still, she needed to, as saying the name was part of playing it. "Bob," she said, and she heard the way it was ragged in her throat, the way it told Patsy how deeply she was feeling it: the need, the desiring. "Bob," she said again, and heard the sound floating up like moaning. It was she who was moaning it, but she wasn't there. She was high above the canopy of oaks, staring in through the windows at them from under the shadow of Winnie's bushy eyebrows. "Two girls in bed!" she was shrieking, out of the treetops. "The spectacle!" And Charlotte was just tricking Patsy. "Oh, Awe-I never cared for it," she would tell Patsy disdainfully. "*You* were the one who always started it." She would announce to her grandchildren: "Oh, yes, as girls we did love one another, but there was nothing *filthy* as there is nowadays!"

If Patsy were a real boy Charlotte would cry out. She would let a real boy hear her wanting it, and she would hear him too. She would do things to him, whatever it was he wanted, and she would listen as his voice broke up, wrecked by the swells of feeling.

She was still counting, the sharp feeling dulling. She'd get to a hundred, then do Patsy's first side, then Patsy would do Charlotte's other. Patsy would go last. Going last always went to the one who had the guts to start it.

Patsy's nipples were different, softer, pinker, smaller. They got silky when they were wet. They smelled like spittish toothpaste. After the last turn they had to stop to keep from really being queer. They'd stop for the night then; soon, they would discontinue. That was so Patsy might receive absolution and remain with the pure of heart.

This, Charlotte decided, was exactly what she hated about Patsy: she still believed there were rules that people went by. She was such an idiot, such a dumb *girl*, that she believed there was a God who beamed down on them, like the moonlight through the tree limbs, who gave a good goddamn about what people on this earth had decided to do. Patsy still really did believe in the fact of sin, that one might be absolved of it. Like the rest of her family, Charlotte had never gone by that.

Charlotte saw Patsy going off across the wide green lawn in her white communion dress, dressed like she was on her way to a little marriage of her own. She stopped to pat the head of the dumb black dog, who, like Charlotte, wasn't getting into heaven. He lifted his head toward the hills and mooed at nothing. God, Katrinka always said, had been invented on Avenue B by Maxine Bill and the rest of the Okies and Arkies from Pork Hollow, West Virginie. They needed God to keep track of the sins on their souls because their education was so poor they'd never learned to count past ten.

Charlotte was drunk so faces swam on by like fish in cloudy water. The dead were here now, here now—Laddie Bill and the brick mason—now here, now here, then not. Lionel's face came forth through the water, the interior of his mouth whitening around the chewed-up peanut butter sandwich. Charlotte and her mother had the winning hands: dead, mad, drunk, the mouth of him, and now this: queer. She knew this trick, covering the thought of one worse thing with the image of another, the thing that could be better understood. She saw the shadowy shape of the sunken cruiser that went down in the deepest waters in the world yet lay waiting, waiting, just beneath the water's surface, the hundreds of pale bodies dangling up above. It was the worst disaster in U.S. naval history and it belonged to her.

She thought of Bob Davidson's face, the shape of his sullen mouth, the squinted bright blue eyes, the line of his lips that would not open to volunteer. If she got into Marlborough she would, after the end of the term, never see him again. She thought of getting his hard mouth open, not as a kiss but rather as a form of invasion.

Her eyes were wide open staring up. She no longer felt anything at all and was not counting. Patsy's hair was silver in the light from the street lamp, her skin spotted by the dots of purer illumination falling through the holes in the eyelet. Patsy raised her face to Charlotte, alarmed. She was asking, with her vanished eyebrows up, if it wasn't yet her turn. Her chin and lips were shining.

Charlotte nodded and they traded places. She wiped the wetness off herself with the edge of the sheet, then let the top of her pajamas fall back down. Patsy had arranged herself back on the pillow with her arms flung up, this way, that way. It was just as the mason had fallen dead among the leaves. Patsy didn't know these things, couldn't know these things, as Charlotte saw them, all swimming by in the dark, transparently, as if she too lived with the ghostly men in the ship at the bottom of the ocean, she alone with the eyes to see. It was now and now and now with the dead men lying there and them leaping too, their clothes on fire, going into the burning sea. The fuel oil burned for hours but there was no one there to spot it. No SOS had gone out. This was Katrinka's whole point, exactly: if God had decided to come back as a little baby, why would he choose to be born in such a lousy Dogpatch shitpile, and why to such a mental patient who hallucinated holy ghosts and was married to a man so old he only did it for his glands?

There were no rules that Charlotte went by. Patsy would get to one hundred but Charlotte would not stop. Her nipples were soft, rosy, lazy, and needed to be chewed in order to stay up. She pressed with one hand on Patsy's belly right behind the pelvic bone where Patsy liked it. Pressed there, like that, she felt the need to pee.

She would press there, make Patsy cry out and call them, a whole gang of hoods. Charlotte would invite them over. I have a girl here, she'd say, here on the tabletop. She would help them hold her down. Then Patsy would have a real reason to cry out, real boys to confess about. She would cry out but it would not be heard over the sound of the ship's exploding, the torpedoes hitting one, then two, the engines still going at full ahead, powering down and into the darkened sea. It was their own fault, for failing to zigzag, for being caught in the light of that single moonbeam, seen by the sub five and a half miles away. With luck like that, Charlotte knew, no boy was ever going to marry her.

She would press there to make Patsy say the words she needed to say, speaking them out to be heard in the air. "Do it," Patsy cried, her

face looking tortured, her voice ripping up. "Please, do it to me."
The boys would come and she would be as naked as the men were
when they went into the sea. She'd be spread out, exposed, as low
down as gravity, lying on the table, waiting, waiting, as the ship
waited still, for each and all like Father Bob and the holy ghosts, for
the rest of them who felt they had such goodness to dispense, the
rest of the pure of heart.

5

Great Expectations

It was her grandmother Ina Boggs Ainsworth of South English, Iowa—according to Katrinka—the prominent wife of the prominent town banker and very high up, therefore, in all the la-di-da crap, who taught her sons, Harold, Lawrence, and Lionel to be bankers. Ina did it in this manner: she cut three slices of hot apple pie of wildly unequal size and set them out in the center of the kitchen table for her three boys to fight over. This, Katrinka claimed, was the way Lionel got the white dot-dot-dot of fork marks all over the backs of his hands awwwnnd, since he was the youngest, smallest, weakest, his profound feelings of bi-homosexual inferiority. Pie, Charlotte knew, was responsible for other things as well, for the sugar diabetes she wasn't supposed to know about but did. She actually knew all about it, how it was robbing him of his eyesight, as it had already stolen away the function of his islets of Langerhans.

As a boy he was coddled, dressed on the stove in cold weather, kept in short pants and curls until a very late age. Still, Lionel grew into the man all the schoolteachers were intent on marrying. They loved him for his auburn curls, for his freckles the size of a turkey's egg all over his handsome face. Lionel and Winnie had gone away to marry so Bess and the rest of Power wouldn't be able to *scrutinize*, as Winnie liked to put it. They were married in Missoula in the parlor of the Kappa house where Winnie lived when she was in school. The wedding took place so early in the morning that most of the slothful girls were still upstairs asleep in bed—when they found out they hadn't been invited to the wedding of a sorority sister that was just downstairs, *well!* Winnie always sniffed a loud sniff of great satisfaction at this point in the story. The twenty-four silver teaspoons with the Greek letters on the back were a gift of the Kappas; they matched the silver soupspoons, now all uniformly flattened by the forty years of the pressure of Lionel's mush-filling mouth. Charlotte, having heard this story a hundred times, had stopped listening to it, had stopped worrying over the size and color of the freckles on a turkey's egg, or what exactly was entailed in being a "Kappa." The freckles, the curls, the auburn hair all were gone, though Lionel still did wear short pants. He went out each day in his khaki walking shorts with his thin shirt flapping open, the better to expose his shiny white and mole-strewn chest to the air that it liked to breathe.

Lionel now had no-color hair buzzed off so short by Rico the barber that the transparent hairs shone all over his oiled scalp like filaments of glass. Rico's was on Ocean View, right around the corner from the bank and the pharmacy in Montrose, just at the spot where, according to Katrinka, Lionel had once stood in his undershorts and gartered socks and had thrown silver dollars over the heads of the depositors as they ran on the Ainsworth First State Bank. Like Vista del Mar, Ocean View Avenue had no view of the sea.

When Rico cut Lionel's hair with clippers, he left a short fringe in front that stood straight up with pomade. This "hairdo," as Winnie called it, was the same one as little boys like Patsy's brother often got. When he came in from the barber's, Lionel liked to pose in profile for Charlotte and to ask her if he resembled an aircraft carrier. Charlotte never smiled at this joke anymore, never did more than squint at him and scowl. "A real Beau Brummell," Winnie would snort, looking up from the dining room table where she was pounding together stretcher bars.

Winnie's saying that was her part in the conversation, her line, to be delivered always in the selfsame way. Charlotte had her own lines too, lines she now refused to offer up to the old man who was too deaf to hear. She wanted to be dead, too, to be deaf, dumb, blind, or simply vanished, gone. She would die young, she imagined, as her father had, die and get it over with without having to go through all the arduous living.

Her grandfather, having finished his walk for this day, his shower, his shave, and the dribbling of his mush from the flattened spoon, now was up on his stiffening legs heading for the couch. This day, he hoped, would end up as etched in perpetuity as the shape of the Greek letters on the backs of the silver teaspoons. He was an old, old man, Charlotte saw, a man once handsome or even beautiful, one who did or did not resemble a person of one or the other sex, someone named Beau Brummell. He was a man who, despite his faltering eyes and glands, still held out hope that his life would turn out well. He was, this day, reading his favorite book in all of Dickens, out loud and for the umpteenth time, a book whose reading was bound to give Winnie the pip in more ways than one, Charlotte suddenly understood. She watched him, getting up, walking, sighing, humming to himself contentedly, and still faintly chewing. This is what she had once loved her grandfather for, she realized, the greatness of even his slightest expectations.

He read aloud while lying on his back on the couch, with his cigarette dangling from the stiff fingers of his hand. Right next to this hand stood the wooden and brass smoking stand he'd had imported from England when he was a bank president. All Lionel needed to do was raise his hand slightly, to touch the rim of the ashtray with the side of his long ash and it would burst into a dusty gray shower of nothingness.

He read aloud until Winnie came and stood, with tuck taken and fists tightly clenched, over him, yelling down that he simply *must* hush up, that she could not bear another moment of it, hearing that same damn story over and over again for forty years! that it was making her so nervous she was running off to join the navy! She banged out to pack up her things, to go out to the desert, or off to look at real estate. Lionel had by then begun to read silently, but with his lips moving over the words so he could feel the rhythms of the passages working in the muscles of his throat and mouth.

One of the greatest moments of his life was recalled by his reading aloud: it was when he was seventeen that he had delivered the valedictory address to his high school on the botanical genius of Luther Burbank. Lionel still knew this speech by heart and went out occasionally to the back of the lot near the incinerator to pronounce it out into the smoky air. Before Charlotte had become a teenager and had begun her job of leaving him, a task she now worked on bit by bit every day, she used to go out there with him. She helped him lug the well-packed brown shopping bags that were full of burnable trash to the clearing where the switchbacks started up from the dirt road's dead end. The clearing was a widening there to give the fire trucks a place to turn around. They stood next to the untrimmed boxed hedge of the long-abandoned Victory Garden, where green shoots slanted ten feet into the air like sloping botanical exclamation marks, while he said such words as *hybrids* and *cultivar*. Since Charlotte's desertion, Lionel now gave the Burbank address for the pleasure of the squirrels alone.

When Charlotte was very young she had loved the sound of Lionel's voice. She loved the way he pitched it low and intimately over the words of a book. She listened to it as she played with her paper dolls, moving them along the piped edges of the cushions at the other end of the long davenport. The dolls were caricatures, painted by her mother and sent in manila envelopes from the hospital or from Sugarman's carnival. Like the four dummies, whose comic, pushed-in faces were still profoundly familiar, there were strong likenesses here too—Winnie had looked at the wide and poetic brow of one doll and had burst into tears. There were also Big Mother and Big Dad, who came along in a cutout covered wagon. Great Aunt Bertha Hopkins and her daughter Little Winnie came with a grand piano that folded down out of a wall of a foldout Victorian house. There was one who was unmistakably Katrinka, standing hands on hips, in a pair of stylish trousers. There was one of Joey, too, with his dark hair and the space between his two front teeth. The way he was grimacing made it seem like he was looking into the sun.

Her mother knew many things, Charlotte felt, but nothing really about the point of paper dolls: to make them pretty, to make them with lots of clothes. The ones Katrinka made came with nothing to change into and the clothes painted on were done with such vehement detail that there was no way really to react to them at all. All she could do was hop them up and down in their costumes on the end of the davenport and hope they didn't start making sounds. Possessed at times by others, Katrinka had never questioned her right to possess the parts of other people—their faces, words, accents, inflections, costumes. That sort of entitlement, Charlotte knew, was a function of her mother's schizophrenia, so she was ever wary of finding it in herself.

The dolls were painted on the thick and bumpy watercolor paper that, because of its high rag content, was very expensive. Winnie bought this paper for Katrinka, along with the paints in tubes and the sable-haired brushes that came to a perfect point when tested wet. This was Winnie's part in the effort on behalf of Katrinka's rehabilitation. The art supplies were not intended to be used for such frivolity as paper dolls, the nonsense for which Charlotte was—in Winnie's opinion—much, much too old. The expensive paints and paper were meant to help Katrinka make her own way in life by learning to concentrate her artistic talents on good, common sense sorts of subjects, the commissioned portraits of very important people, say, or the cute, sweet, nice sorts of things that might help her get a job at the Disney Studios in Burbank, or to work by mail for Hallmark Cards.

Charlotte no longer listened to the words of Lionel's stories but to his tone in reading them, which seemed to tell her more. He liked the Pip-type story best, the type with orphans in it, those who got the good, rich parents in the end. She was an orphan, the throb in his tone confided, and he, who'd once had good rich parents, was now an orphan too. It was the orphans who came forth always from his reading so finely dressed in the raiment of his love. Lionel's tone told it: he wasn't the father of this huddled group or the mother either, but one of them himself. The waifs issued forth, then huddled with Charlotte at the end of the davenport along with the feet she too had once loved. These were feet so lovely that it must have been a shock for them to find themselves still attached to such a failing man.

Lionel believed his long and shapely feet were a sign of his good breeding. He even seemed proud to have bequeathed these aristocratic feet to the daughter he so despised. It was possible, he said, to tell much about a person from his feet and the state of his shoe-leather. That was the reason he so often took Katrinka shopping at Red Cross or at Florsheim. This, along with the replacement of her broken, lost, mangled, or thrown-away eyeglasses, was his part in the rehabilitation.

Lionel did not himself ever wear shoes in the house since he felt it was the right of his feet to be allowed to breathe. He had always taken such good care of them that even in advancing age the skin was still uncallused, the toenails clean, clear, and neatly trimmed. His toes were long and expressive of emotions, wriggling in satisfaction at the good parts of a story, or curling in on themselves in an attitude of supplication as the time drew near to lunch.

The pads of the toes of the feet were rosy, and rosy, too, were the balls and heel. This pinkness shaded away into a creamy white that rounded onto the top of the foot. This was a pale color into which it was possible to look deeply and to see. The feet were skinny and well muscled from all the long miles of walking accomplished during all those perfect days. The tendons and long bones and joints showed through the skin to demonstrate their articulation. The hollow of each high and well-formed arch was shell-like in its curve and color—a pinkish, yellowish white, as smoothly waxen as a candle. Back when Charlotte had still loved her grandfather, she'd enjoyed her detailed examination of these well-tended feet, which did seem like twin characters to her, other members of their family.

She'd grown up there at the end of Lionel's couch, as her mother had before her. Of the Ainsworths, he had been the one who was kindest to her. She played with the dolls Katrinka sent and she knew

things she could not know. She knew the sound of the voices of
people who'd died before she was even born—Big Mother, going
KATH-er-rine! Joey saying inscrutable and jokish things: *flea circus,
notions counter, hole-in-the-wall.* She listened, as her mother had, to
the throb of Lionel's orphan voice, to his promise that they would all
get the good rich parents in the end. Charlotte no longer believed
him, if she ever had. She grew up in a house where she now knew
there was no view of the sea.

She knew the lie of him intrinsically, had learned it, it seemed,
from studying the bones of her own sad feet. Katrinka had, in her
own oblique way, done what she could to confirm it. Their own two
lives, Katrinka told Charlotte, had been written by Emile Zola,
Joey's by Siggy Freud. And from the stark pitch Charlotte's own
thoughts had begun to lately take, she *knew* she knew the truth of it:
they all had failed to zigzag. Katrinka, growing up herself on that
long couch, had been rendered by it rudderless, powerless, lines
knocked out, helpless too at the job of rescue.

"It's just been too godawful lousy, hasn't it, sweetie?" Katrinka
would joke, to ask the thing that could not be said. She would raise
Charlotte's face to her own with the three cold dots of her fingertips
placed beneath the chin. "I mean, really *really?*" Her green gaze
would swim over Charlotte's features—eye, eye, lips, cheeks—and
her own eyes might widen in awe of whatever it was she saw there:
herself? Joey? the two again together? or for that moment, maybe,
Charlotte alone and singular, Charlotte as she really was?

"I mean really? Just too crappy shitty? Hasn't it, sweetie?" she
would then plead, though pleading humorously. "Hasn't this life of
ours just been hell on fucky wheels?"

Lionel taught Charlotte to balance a ledger checkbook, the opening
gambits in chess, and how it is that a pawn might become a queen,
the stratagem that most interested her. He also instructed her in the
proper burning of trash. The trash they took together out from under the big oak where he'd once built Katrinka a treehouse. The
walls and roof of it now were gone, or had never existed, but the
floorboards still rested in the fork of three large branches, the planks

crawling with black ants. The limbs of this oak were entwined with the yellowish green witch hazel, a parasitic plant, she learned from *Compton's Pictured Encyclopedia*, incapable of producing its own chlorophyll. The clumps of it were so dry, so pale, so weightless, they hardly seemed alive. She sat in the treehouse and looked at it. She went there to stare or read. She read the dictionary or the volumes of *Compton's* or her books on the naval history of the war. She didn't normally *play*, as she'd never been entirely certain what this really entailed. For this reason her mother called her "my sober little pig," then laughed at Charlotte's look of bewilderment and hurt, saying, "Oh, for christsake, sweetie, can't you ever for once be teased? Don't you really get it? That coming from *me* that's a compliment?"

Lionel liked a good clean fire, one started with the rinsed-out milk cartons that burned so well because of the wax impregnated into their sides. The wax grew watery as it was melting, the letters of the cardboard blistering, then swimming in black oil. There was an audible poof when the fire took hold and the pure white smoke carried back away from the chimney and off toward the brush of the drying hills. The chaparral was the same greenish purplish gray as shadows, as the sweaters Winnie once knit for Charlotte and for Lionel in a tone she called "heather," as the chests of the mourning doves that filled the air of the canyon with their low cooing.

Winnie wore Lionel's flannel shirts and stood at the rail of the back porch with small fingers in the sides of her mouth to call the quail down out of the hills. "*Whirrrrt!* Whoooo are yoooouuu?" she whistled. She'd learned birdcalls from Big Dad on the summer ranch in Montana. She could call pigs too. She wore a flannel shirt over her dress, the dress put on to prove she wasn't what they always called "mannish." And in a bluff voice that was suddenly lower—a man's? a rancher's?—she'd announce: " 'Speck they'll be along here now, pret'darn quick." And the mother quail did then come, out from the shadows of the underbrush, with her chest puffed and her black plume bobbing to one side of her paler head. The babies followed her in a ragged line, like a drunken, scrambling army.

The Ainsworths' house wasn't part of Verdugo Woodlands, the development of newer "homes," as they were always called, where the people were richer. Their house was mock-Tudor and stood alone on its street in its own solitary jog in the canyon. Deer came down from the hills to pull at the asparagus that still shot up behind the garden hedge and to eat the milky green grapes from the arbor that ran along the back of the house. This was a variety of grape that remained ever small, hard, sour, and cloudy inside, the result, Charlotte guessed, of the shading by the overgrown oaks that robbed the house of sunlight.

When Charlotte was growing up, Winnie was always so worried about money that she had the habit of slipping a quarter from one pocket of Lionel's shirt into the other every time he opened a packet of cigarettes. These quarters went into the pot of money she referred to as "my own private funds." Her own money was always invested in real estate. Smoking was, in her opinion, a vile and filthy habit and she had absolutely no intention of going broke over it.

This was before the freeways, when Charlotte and Lionel drove out country roads to see Katrinka at the hospital or to find the carnival, playing this or that stinking hellhole dump of a hole-in-the-wall. "Hole-in-the-wall," Katrinka said, was what Joey called anyplace that wasn't London, Paris, or the city of New York. Even the names of the towns amused Katrinka. "A-*zu*-sa?" she'd ask the air. "*Es*-con-*deeee*-do?"

Winnie refused to go on these expeditions because she didn't want to risk her life on the roads with the Sunday drivers. Lionel and Charlotte drove out alone in the Nash through flower fields, where the light was colored by the pink, yellow, and purple blurring upward into the mist. These fields were worked by the Japanese, who could be seen bent over in the rows in their wide sloped hats, men and women indistinguishable. "Now, Charlotte," Lionel pronounced as knowingly as if he were really talking to Luther Burbank, "the Jap garden is an interesting botanical phenomenon and is found to be a great deal more fertile than that of the white. These are the reasons. The Japanese, by all accounts, is a remarkably industrious worker, and he employs the very valuable resource known as 'night soil.' " Lionel smiled smugly to himself as he drove on, he and Luther Burbank having chuckled and shaken hands over that one. She had long since learned from the dictionary what the term really meant; still, by concentrating, she could even now dredge up the darkness, the loamy mystery that had come with the words when they were first heard.

It may have been that the sunlight dissolved the colors of the flowers in the middle distance or broke it apart on the mist from the sprinklers or that the heat from the soil radiated upward and made the color shimmer in the air above the fields. For whatever reason, color did spill out and up from the blooms in the fields when Charlotte was young and Los Angeles was still a garden. The sky was tinted by the pastel hues of the stock and the snapdragons, and by the wide fields of bright red and yellow glads. The smell of the flowers spilled upward, too, and even the fertilizer had a rich stink to it, drying lighter on the blacker earth.

The roads ran east along the base of the foothills of the San Gabriels through little towns called La Crescenta, Arcadia, San Dimas. The farther east the Nash went, the larger were the ranches and the greater the distances between towns. The orchards were of orange and plum, lemon, walnut, lime, grapefruit, the trees all planted in rows that lay straight to the road in both diagonal and vertical directions. Almond trees there bloomed, the flowers on the black earth, falling white as snow. All this was simple, might have been simple to describe, except that Charlotte had been raised in a way that had entirely skipped simplicities, such notions as *mother, father, snowfall, childhood,* or what *notions* even were.

This was before Katrinka married Sweeney and they went to live in the butt-built development on Avenue B. It was when the Nash still smelled of the sharp stink of onions, when there were hay wagons. The highway west to Camarillo was laddered by blue-green shadows cast by the eucalyptus standing as windbreaks along the edges of the fields. The sun was low because they went so early on a Sunday morning, the day when there were visiting hours. Katrinka would be neatly dressed in the knit suit from Bullock's that Winnie had sent along the time before, worn with the well-constructed Florsheims. Her face would be calm, clear-eyed, pale. As she bent to kiss Charlotte's cheek, her lips were cool and fragrant with tobacco.

To Lionel she lifted her face and directed perfect, nonironic questions: "How are you feeling, Dad? How is Mother? Is she getting any rest? Do her knees still bother her going down the steps? She wrote that she has been in contact with a company that makes a home funicular."

Hands poised on hips, Lionel would answer shortly. Katrinka did not go near him—he would not tolerate being touched by her. He waited in the family waiting room while Katrinka and Charlotte went out into the sunlight and across the lawn. Lionel never sat down while waiting, never even smoked, though it was allowed. He stood with hands on hips and waited, purely waited, his lips pursed the whole while into a hard dry O.

The food was good, Katrinka told her. The mental patients worked to raise it themselves in the hospital fields. Her work was teaching art on the children's ward. "I am very good at it," she said, without irony, but also apathetically, without humor, interest, or much conviction.

"Do they?" Charlotte asked, having to halt herself to keep from crying. "The children? Do they ever make you think of me?"

Katrinka searched Charlotte's face, with eyes and eyebrows pained. "Oh, sweetie," she pleaded. "How can I make you understand? The children—all the people—are here because they're *sick*."

Her labor earned for Katrinka the right to art supplies and also the chits that she could spend on cigarettes and jars of instant coffee at the canteen, which had a snack stand. They went there when they left Lionel so Katrinka could buy Charlotte a U-No bar. Rather than spend the chits, Katrinka used real money, part of the fifteen dollars Lionel and Winnie gave her each month as an allowance. This buying, as always, made Charlotte feel she might faint, cringe, keen, so physical was the assault of her love and guilt and sorrow. As they walked on up to the ward, Charlotte and her mother held hands. She had wanted the candy bar, and Katrinka had wanted very much to give it to her, but now Charlotte was too choked to eat it and it melted from the heat of her hand within the bright silver of its wrapper.

They held hands, though Charlotte could hardly bear to do so, so aware was she of the delicacy of the bones of her mother's fingers. She had understood this fragility since birth, it seemed. She understood it: she had not forgiven her. She held her mother's fingers lightly in her own, in order not to harm them, but the knowledge that they would be so simply crushed made her want to squeeze them harder. She could kill her mother, she'd always known, using nothing more than the strength of her love.

Charlotte's own hands were nothing like Katrinka's. They were stronger, mightier, more like those of the fatherless girl who'd grown up riding horses on the summer ranch in Montana, the girl who went trout fishing and raised pigs for college money. Winnie hooked her fingers in the sides of her mouth to call the quail and those birds did come, damn it! Like her, Charlotte was not helpless, was capable of anything, even maybe another soul's destruction. She watched Winnie at the dining table, banging together stretcher bars, pulling the canvas over them, whacking the staples in, slapping the aromatic fabric with gesso. The paintings she brought back from the desert were good, full of sky, sand, and light, the kind of bending emptiness that Charlotte would learn later was modernness. It was the painting of a landscape that now was rid of the people it once held. Winnie's hands, even in old age, were tan and hard and muscled. They were the hands of someone good at horsewhips and tools.

Katrinka brought Charlotte up to the ward to meet the nurses and technicians she spent her days playing Scrabble with. Patients lay smoking on their backs on their beds, or read the Bible, or sat smoking on the cracked Naugahyde couches in the dayroom, where the TV played "I Love Lucy" and no one ever laughed. Lucy tried to act like a mental patient, Charlotte saw. She was funny, Charlotte supposed.

Above the beds in the ward, lined up fifteen to a side, were the watercolor portraits Katrinka had done in exchange for cigarettes and jars of Nescafé. These portraits, she'd once explained to Charlotte, were intended to make each mental patient look more noble than she really was, more intelligent, funnier, more beautiful or holy. "I'm very popular around here," she often said.

The drives on Sundays were less predictable if Katrinka was working at Sugarman's; then the Nash might head south along the beach cities or north up the coast as far as Oxnard. The carnival played out in the San Fernando Valley when no one lived there, yet, aside from walnut ranchers and movie stars. The carnival could be seen in a grassy schoolyard or in a newly mown cornfield next to the pale and glittering pastel stucco of a recently poured Pentecostal church. This stucco rotted easily, exfoliating a halo of sparkling paint into the already corn-dusted air. These churches were always done in the pale colors of dyed Easter eggs, colors that vibrated against the bent blue sky. The carnival went up in the open fields being cleared out to make way for subdivisions. The portable Ferris wheel glittered in the emptiness like a giant mechanical dandelion. Seeing it, Charlotte's heart would careen between hope and dread.

She hoped her mother would be there, would act all right, that they would be able to "get through" the visit. "Getting through" things—as in *endure*—was Katrinka's best hope for them, that the two of them could just hang on until things did get better. Charlotte needed to *get through* living on Vista del Mar, as Katrinka did working for Sugarman, as they both did this particular visit with Lionel, whose voice tended to go da-*dum*, da-*dum* in rhythm with the high blood pressure throb of his temples, as if he intended to die right then and there, just to punish them. They had both had to *get through* living on Avenue B. *Get through* was pronounced through gritted teeth.

Charlotte hoped she would act normal; still, when Katrinka did act normal—as in the hospital when she was given shock and had to take her medication—she didn't seem like herself. She seemed instead like the paper doll Winnie would have done of her: flat, sober, dressed in the steel-blue Butte Knit suit and the sturdy good-common-sense sort of shoes. Katrinka was more peaceful, surely, but she also seemed lost from herself. When the voices were gone she even seemed physically smaller.

Coming upon the carnival, Charlotte especially hoped her mother would not be drunk, that Lionel's voice would not go da-*dum*, da-*dum* on the evils of drink all the way home in the Nash, that Winnie, with her wide brow furrowed, wouldn't join in from the top of the thirty-seven steps, not even waiting until they were inside the house to begin the inquisition. "No," Charlotte would tell her, when Winnie asked, first thing, if Katrinka had been drinking. "At least I don't think so."

But usually Katrinka had been drinking. First, she'd drink down a Rhinegold as fast as she could—that was to help her *get through* having to go out to lunch at the goddamned Miramar Hotel with Lionel. Then, she'd take a big swig from the indigo bottle of Evening in Paris that she kept on the vanity table. "That," she said, winking at Charlotte in the dim light of her trailer after first gargling, then swallowing, "is so *he* won't know I'm stinko."

Apart from its terrible manners, Winnie loved the twentieth century—the advances in soil management and the invention of the jet plane and Walt Disney's domed cities where there would be weather control. She loved medical science for the way it had eradicated TB and smallpox and was working on a cure for cancer, one that might be developed in Winnie's own lifetime. She was waiting, too, for science to come up with the nutritionally perfect pill.

Winnie loved the freeways, particularly the straight and modern Harbor Freeway that took her off to the land developments in which she had invested. The freeway, she maintained, was a much safer way to travel than poking along on the country roads with the bumpkins and old men in hats. She drove the Nash in the fast lane, to get away from them. Charlotte, crouched on the front seat and hanging out the rolled-down window, was the spotter: "There's one, Winnie! He's got on a fedora! And he's in his shirtsleeves and suspenders! Look! He's chewing on a piece of straw!"

Winnie stomped the accelerator hard, her head hunched forward, elbows held aloft, the tip of her hawkish nose sharp against the blur of speed. She went seventy or seventy-five, saying it was common knowledge that you might go as fast as you wanted in the fast lane, as long as you were a member of Triple A. The speed limit of sixty-five had been posted only to remind the men in hats that this was not a country road.

Winnie loved the Triple A, which kept Republicans in Sacramento, which brought in the flood control that had paved the Los Angeles River. This river, Charlotte noticed, was not a normal one since it had no water in it. It had been paved to look exactly like a freeway, though it carried no cars and had no lane lines. There was a chicken wire fence along the edge at the top of either slope. Below there were tumbleweeds and boulders. It carried runoff only when the entire alluvial plain was flooded, when all of the other roadways carried their share of water, too, away to the sea.

Triple A, Winnie felt, could be called upon at any time, for Emergency Roadside Service. For this she carried her emergency dime. Triple A might save her if the Nash stopped on the freeway anywhere near Watts, where the sky was darkening with the haze of TV antennas. The children of Negroes ran barefoot, Winnie had observed, while their fathers bought white Cadillacs on their checks from public assistance. They all laughed at the Kingfish on their TV sets. They had natural relaxation but not much in the way of gumption.

While on the Harbor Freeway passing Watts, Winnie pressed her lips in intently and stomped the accelerator until the speedometer read ninety. She pushed with the silent rubber of her ripple-soled shoes. She and Lionel wore identical sandals, ordered by mail through an orthopedic catalogue. Unlike Lionel, however, Winnie wasn't the slightest bit vain about her feet. What she liked was the sure grip the soles gave her going down the steps to the car or to get the mail.

Sometimes bumpkins strayed into the fast lane, forcing Winnie to brake. Old men in hats always brought out in Winnie the profound need to cough and sneeze. If she coughed too hard, she might wet her pants, so she gripped herself there, going "Oh! Oh!" keeping one grim hand on the steering wheel. If she had to sneeze while driving, why, she might lose control of the car. She worried about this obsessively: what if, while in the fast lane, she were to sneeze and be forced to squeeze her eyes shut for an instant and in that blink of time something terrible should happen—a Cadillac appear, say, there in the lane before her, a Cadillac driven by a shiftless Negro singing "Ah Gots Plenny o' Nuffin" (when it was his *own damn fault!*) and going only two or three miles an hour? Why, she would crash the car!

If Winnie felt a sneeze coming, she would widen her eyes and set her face with all the force of her will, then put the Nash into neutral. That there might, too, be cars behind her held no interest for her. As the urge to sneeze approached, she might coast; then, if she did truly sneeze, she would brake as hard as if she had suddenly come upon the piece of the sky where the world dropped away. Flinging her right arm rigidly out like a signal corpsman's to keep Charlotte from flying through the windshield, she sneezed, braking hard. Once she'd sneezed, she then sat up again, one brown arm resting on the rim of the open window. That was how she was—regal, bolt upright—when a hoodish boy, a bean-oh really, on a motorcycle pulled up next to her, riding on the meridian to get close enough to her to flip the bird right in her face. She did not respond to this, or him, but sniffed as she always sniffed after sneezing or while in the presence of something slovenly or teenaged. She sniffed and informed Charlotte, as she always did when the fit was past and the sneezes might be tallied: "Once a wish, twice a kiss, three times comes a letter."

When the Ainsworths were together in the car, Lionel always drove, though his driving was even worse than hers since his eyes were so bad. He drove her because Winnie's driving him would have made her seem mannish. Though she said often enough that she wished she had been born a man, this was something they evidently thought they were keeping hidden from the world.

Before the freeways, each little town like Montrose had its own downtown and downtown Los Angeles was just the largest of these. That was where Charlotte and Lionel went to take Winnie's pictures to the framers. "Going to the framers" was another of the expeditions Winnie would not go on. She didn't want the framers to see her because they had looked at her paintings. The name of the city was pronounced by the Ainsworths with the gulped-down "g," as in *angles*, while Charlotte and Katrinka said it out more into the air, more with the sound of the *angels* in it. Before the freeways, it had only a few tall buildings, and these were built short, for earthquakes. The Atlantic-Richfield building was the grandest one. It was black, with white and gold filigree on each of its tiers, so it looked like a witch's wedding cake. There were also the city hall and the library and the phone company at Ninth and Hope. It was there that the Ainsworths had made Katrinka work for a while after Joey died. "Ninth and Hope," Katrinka would sometimes laugh, when she was talking out loud to her smoke. "Ninth and *Hope?*"

Though Lionel drove, Winnie helped. She sat up rigidly on the bench by the window, gripping her door handle and ordering him: "Now, Lionel! You can change lanes now!" He would veer then, without looking, through all lanes of traffic, with his turn signal flashing. He drove a direct diagonal path. Once in the leftmost lane, he would settle in, doing seventy-five or eighty.

"Oh, you make me so nervous!" Winnie might mention to him, as the horns sounded and the brakes squealed. She would then add, "Your clicker's still on."

One day he could no longer hear her, though she had raised her voice. "Lionel, I *said* your clicker's on. Turn your clicker off, I said." Charlotte, lying low on the back seat in order to slowly and secretly chew her Wild Grape gum, was reading the colored funnies. She looked up, wondering if Lionel might be being defiant. She sat up and saw his face in the rearview mirror, the eyes stony behind his glasses. He was gone, there but not there, the body just a sack of what still was left of him. The hands still gripped the wheel but did so in *rigor mortis*.

"Lionel!" Winnie was screaming. "Oh! you make me so tired! Turn your clicker off this instant!" But he made no sign that he saw or heard anything, just sped ahead mile after dizzying mile. Charlotte went back to the funnies, chewing the gum surreptitiously against the cup of her cradling hand. *The wild ride of Ainsworth McGoo*, she told herself, inventing the comic strip she would write just to be able to stick the two of them into it. She could hear her grandmother clutching at the door handle, muttering and whimpering.

"All right, now!" Winnie said, finally. "There's the sign for Glendale—you can start to move over now, and for heaven's sake, click the clicker the other way." The turn indicator kept clicking the same way it had been, though: *that*-way, *that*-way. "Lionel!" Winnie screamed. "There's the second sign. You *must* start to move over this instant!" but the Nash sped on and on, breezing along at eighty. "Oh! you make me cross! Oh! you make me tired. Stop this *this instant!*" Winnie cried. Then, in a voice that was perfectly heartbroken: "Lionel, you have just passed Glendale by!"

Charlotte was sitting up by now with her arms folded along the back of the seat. She saw his face in the mirror. His pupils were the size of tiny pinpricks. They might all die now, in a fiery freeway car crash. She was vaguely excited by this idea—the thrill of it pounded in the pit of her stomach.

When the Harbor Freeway gave way to the Pasadena, the curves tightened so the Nash barely clung to the road. There were brushy cliffs here, Charlotte saw as they flew by them, from when this had once been a wooded canyon. Her head was aching now, pounding with a nausea that came tinted by the colored ink of the funny pages, perfumed by grape-stinking gum. She was going to die, she realized, and it wasn't even going to be very interesting. Why, she was wondering, if more and more people were coming in all of the time, as Winnie claimed, did the streets all seem to be becoming more and more empty? There was a coldness in the world now that never before had existed, the damp of the shadows of concrete overpasses which the sunlight never touched.

The freeway finally ended in Pasadena, spilling the Nash out onto Colorado Boulevard. Lionel suddenly knew just where he was going. He sat up straight and turned right, with the clicker still clicking left, into the empty parking lot of Bullock's, where he braked, turned off the key in the ignition, and slumped forward against the steering wheel.

"YOU!" Winnie screamed. "You might have killed us with your shenanigans!" She took her big fists away from the hollows where she'd had them pressed against her eyes. She slammed his shoulders with her handbag. "YOU!" she screamed again. "Your own father warned me of the trouble I would have with you! Thrown out of Grinnell for public drunkenness!" She was trying to push him out of the car with her straightened arms, but he was resting heavily, as if he'd fallen soundly asleep. "You never graduated!" she screamed at him, placing the ripple soles of sandals against him and shoving. "Get out! I'll be the one who does the driving from now on!" Her Herbert Hoover knees were showing below her pushed-up hem.

Now, she was out of her side of the car and walking around. He still slumped against the wheel. She yanked his door open and tried to move him by shoving and pushing him over. He slumped away from her blows and she got in, first adjusting her prim lips, then the side mirror. She bent forward to fiddle with the lever that would allow her to rock the seat forward. She yanked and rocked, but the lever on the passenger side had not been released and Lionel had not obeyed her instructions to help her. She again ordered him, but he was still slumped over, saying nothing. Winnie happened to glance up then into the rearview mirror and see Charlotte watching her. Charlotte's face lit up instantly with a bright hot flush. Winnie, who seemed only then to remember that Charlotte was with them in the car, turned around and slapped her.

Charlotte's mouth was hanging open. She could not manage to close it even to hide the big purple wad of gum. She'd been slapped only once before in her entire life, and that was by Sweeney on Avenue B, and Sweeney had slapped her, not in cruelty, really, but in a kind of pitiable desperation. Avenue B was the sort of place where children were slapped. Children there were slapped, whacked, spanked, paddled, whipped. Maxine Bill, hanging her body from her kitchen *winda* out into the foggy morning, would yell, "You get in here before I take down your pants and beat your filthy butt with your daddy's belt!" The words were held by the fog and stayed.

I have not had a real vacation in forty years! Winnie was screaming. Charlotte was going to Marlborough! she was going as a *boarder!* she was going there to learn to act like less of a slut and whore! Winnie knew all about Charlotte's little secrets, Winnie was going on, all about the sorts of things she wrapped up in brown paper lunch sacks and carried out to the fire to burn! She knew about Charlotte's filthy things and secret things and the wrapped-up halves of liverwurst sandwiches and the other pieces of perfectly decent food! Everything that had ever happened to her was Charlotte's *own damned fault!* Lionel had his weaknesses, Winnie admitted, but it was Charlotte who played on them, just as her mother had! With their see-through nighties and their Nightie-night, Lionels! and all of those Breck shampoos!

Charlotte stared into the face before her, saw how canted it was, how deformed by fury, and understood then that it wasn't human, but rather a thing deranged. Her heart was expanding, growing suddenly large with the swelling thought of it: *the Ainsworths are insane.* They were insane, demented, *crazy*, and were, therefore, not invincible, as she'd always imagined them to be. *They are insane,* she thought, and understood that this meant they might be tricked, that she and her mother still might get away.

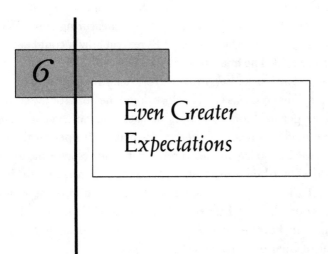

6

Even Greater Expectations

Lionel had always been the one to wash Charlotte's hair. When she was too small to reach
the sink, she'd lain on towels that he'd set out
over the cold tiles of the counter. Her hair could spill down behind
her into the bathroom sink and her clothes would not get wet. She
had gazed up at him then, at the beauties of his face. When she had
still loved him, it was possible to see in him the freckled boy, the
charming rosy-cheeked young man, the dapper personage Winnie
called Beau Brummell.

Now when she looked at his skin, Charlotte noticed that it was
emptying. The colors had faded and his flesh now hung loosely
away from bones that were still in him but were somehow diminish-
ing. He smelled strongly of his lunch, of the peanut butter on whole
wheat, of coffee and cigarettes. She was bathed in the same thick
smells that had once been just as strong but then hadn't bothered
her. When she was small she had lain before him and had peacefully
picked at the gold foil label of the shampoo bottle which she held,
her head resting on the one bunched towel. That had happened, she
knew; still, she did not really remember it.

While she could not remember, she now knew things. She knew that he washed her hair too deliberately, too thoroughly, taking much too long. He sudsed it once, then again, rinsing in between with water mixed in Winnie's big Pyrex measuring cup—Winnie grew rhapsodic on the virtues of Pyrex, on how it could take both heat and cold. The final rinse was a cold as pure as that of window glass on Christmas Eve in New York City high atop Rockefeller Center. This cold was used to close down the pores of the scalp and seal out germs. Lionel and Winnie each knew of several children who'd died as a result of their pores being left open or their hair being washed so late in the evening that it didn't have time to dry— a child went to bed with a wet head and was found dead in the morning. Charlotte imagined these wet-headed children as a line of ghosts out following Lionel in his slate-gray slicker, doing the same six miles in the rain—her mother was one of the pale, slight orphans ahead of Charlotte in the line.

After the shampoo, which was conducted religiously every Sunday afternoon, Charlotte sat on the floor in front of the davenport so Winnie, behind her, could do the braiding. Next to Saturday, which had Perry Mason, Sunday was the best night for TV, with Disney first, then Ed Sullivan. When Katrinka had gone on Ed Sullivan, she'd had an agent, and a TV station had been talking about her having her own program. Ed Sullivan flew her back to New York City. A photographer rode along in the limousine that was sent out to Idylwild to meet her. Each of the dummies was put into a separate seat for the publicity shots. She had all four dummies by then—Miss Priss and Buttercup, in addition to Ogamer and Nellie Platter, who were the originals. Shelley Winters happened to be on that same plane and had had her picture taken kissing Ogamer. She was a starlet then and hadn't wanted Katrinka to end up standing alone in all that ritzy limelight.

Katrinka had told Charlotte all this when she called long distance from the bar high atop Rockefeller Center. She had other big news too: she'd been out to Jones Beach that day to see the Atlantic Ocean, and guess what? It was *green!* This was on Christmas Eve.

While Charlotte's hair was being braided, she held the rubber bands for Winnie. These came off the L.A. *Times*—for some reason Winnie referred to them as *bandeaux*. Charlotte also held Louis' shaving mirror, which she could tip up to see alternating patches of her own and her grandmother's wide and poetic brows, Winnie's now quite rumpled with concern over the straightness of the part. Winnie's comb caught a snarl and pulled. Hair braided by Winnie was yanked and intimidated—it *would* stay braided the whole damned week. The silver of the mirror was mottled, the ivory it sat in as yellow as an old man's teeth.

The Sunday after Lionel's wild ride, he'd gone into the bathroom, as usual, to set things out as if everything was still the same. Charlotte was astonished: they were crazy, but *this* crazy? She stared at her grandmother, who stood by the dining room window examining the small pale watercolor she'd just finished framing. Winnie's lips and furrows were set in displeasure. She'd used Bon Ami to clean the glass—the can had a little chick on it and the slogan reading, "Hasn't scratched yet." Charlotte didn't really get it. Winnie, tipping the glass to the light, had found something, a speck of lint or dirt trapped on the inside. Though the back was already sealed with the brown paper she had first wetted, then glued and stretched to dry, Winnie was now beginning to take the whole framing job apart to do over.

From the bathroom, Lionel called her and Charlotte went, as she'd always done. She stood in the doorway, knowing she knew something, that knowing it made her different. She stood with her hands on her hips and watched him, the way he'd set all the various items out, the things with which he hoped she might be cleansed. He had put out the folded washcloth, the face and bath towel—all in matching colors—the bottle of Breck, the mirror with its disintegrated silvering, the four fresh ink-stained *bandeaux*, Winnie's own wide-toothed tortoise-shelled comb. Because she knew things, Charlotte could see things now with her mother's eyes, see how it must have been with the two of them together and alone, when he was all tanked up during his Great Depression.

His hand was reaching out to her. He turned the palm of it upward, seeing her seeing him. He did that in order to seem humorous, pathetic. *I am just an old and disappointed man,* his smile was telling her. *Humor me.* The crinkles at the corners of his eyes were deepening. He turned his hand upward, to show he was harmless, pitiable, but he didn't believe it really. He wanted her to come to the sink, put her face in the cradle of her arms, and bend over.

"No," Charlotte said. Her voice was rising into the wet air, air fragrant with Dial soap and with the sweet-smelling pink mold that grew in the plaster surrounding the tub. The word rose and she with it. Together they wobbled, thinned out—with every day now she was better perfecting her vision, her weightlessness, her invisibility. She knew things, had said something. Now, though, her teeth were chattering and she had to talk like a ventriloquist, with lips and teeth together.

But Lionel hadn't heard her and still reached out. "No," she said again, shaking her head so he would see. "I'm not," she told him, waving all of it and him away with one hand. "I have to go somewhere, there's something else that I have to do." She had no idea of what she meant, only that it was true. She knew something else: she was going to get away with it. To know this was a shock, a thrill, like getting away with murder.

His eyes were widening behind his bifocals. He staggered slightly, then again reached out. He'd heard her but he didn't understand. She tipped her chin up, defiantly. She felt her eyes squint and her face turn humorous. He looked at her and saw that she was her mother's own true daughter, and he then buried his face in the largest of his clean and hopeful towels.

No longer was there an urgency, so she chewed her gum openly, folded her arms and rested one hip against the doorjamb. When he took the towel away, she saw that the anger or fear or weeping had reddened the whites of his eyes, making the irises appear a bright and vivid green. "It was only that her hair," he said, haltingly. "Her hair was so like yours. When I unpinned it, when I let it down."

Charlotte wasn't exactly certain which of them he was talking about—he probably wasn't either. He'd dropped the towel to the floor and stood now with both hands outstretched to measure the heft of hair. He stood with palms turned upward, as if weighing two bags of gold.

Charlotte knew it now with absolute certainty: she was going to get away with it. Knowing this she walked through his study and out the back door to go to sit in the treehouse. She waited there until dusk, past the time when a shampoo might safely be performed, all the while anticipating Winnie's coming to the screened door, screaming for Charlotte to come in. In fact, Winnie never screamed anything at her ever again.

It was as if Charlotte had, in that one afternoon, finally become absolutely invisible to them. She stared at the chimney smoke being carried off toward the back of the canyon—her grandparents had started to burn their trash in the fireplace when the use of incinerators was banned—and understood that she had no more weight with them than that.

She held no weight with them; still, she had eyes and she now knew things. She could now see, suddenly, through her grandfather's eyes, as well. On all those afternoons when Winnie was out looking for real estate or had slammed out to go join the navy, it was Lionel's habit to lie on his back on the davenport with the lights off. He lay in the gathering darkness resting his eyes from the reading of the day, and listened for Katrinka to come up the steps. She opened the door and he saw her there, framed in the blaze of sunlight that jabbed through the canopy of oaks. When he saw her, his long fingers lifted. He reached out to her past the smoking stand, his palm turning slowly upward. His smile was slight, lips tremulous. Did she remember that he was an orphan too?

Through his eyes Charlotte saw the shape of the girl silhouetted in the doorway. The light behind was blinding, though, so, try as she might, Charlotte could never see her face.

Charlotte hadn't gone on that trip east. Still she remembered it more vividly than she did the events of her own life, than sitting, say, at the age of twelve in her undershirt and underpants on the examination table in Dr. Greenley's office while he blushed and stammered, responding to Winnie's demand that he tell Charlotte the facts of life. Charlotte couldn't really remember this at all, only thinking *blah, blah, blah*—the facts of life being exactly the kind of thing she did not want to hear from some old man while she sat before him in her underwear.

She remembered the trip east instead, how in the weeks before it Lionel had actually acted as if he were proud of Katrinka and had bragged about her at the barbershop. He told how she had an agent and the people in Hollywood were interested—oh, this was sure to be a really, *really* big shoe! Charlotte remembered it: how the snow was falling on Jones Beach, twirling down in fat, loose flakes that melted when they hit the sand, how they were as big and wet and sloppy as goosefeathers.

Charlotte didn't know how big a goosefeather was, any more than she knew the look of a turkey's egg or what was meant by the chick who hadn't scratched yet. She didn't know these things because she had no firsthand experience with poultry. Still, like the chick who hadn't yet scratched but looked as if it soon intended to, she was starting to figure things out.

Every afternoon when she came home from school, she sat in the treehouse and thought of things. She no longer went to Patsy's because Patsy now spent her time with her boyfriend. Charlotte sat in the oak to stay out of her grandparents' way. She had to avoid them until school was out, when she would be relinquished to Katrinka and the Airstream.

She hadn't known before what goosefeather-like snow was, but now, as she concentrated, she was starting to be able to see it. She sat with the ants in the dusty heat and stared at the drifting smoke of her grandparents' fires. Their house had been built in a canyon above a creek that dammed up nearly every year during the rainy season, when the gully became clogged by boulders, by silt, by ripped-up vegetation. As the once-dry creek became a river, and the river choked itself and no longer had anywhere to go, the road washed out. The mountains, the hills were all being worn away, would all, one day, be washed out to sea. In spite of Triple A, in spite of Flood Control, the Ainsworths were not safe: either fire or water was one day going to get them.

She imagined her father's wide tanned shoulders, the gap between his teeth, his expert hand on the centerboard of the skiff sailing along right at the surf line. Even when he was young, Katrinka said, he had always been in danger. Charlotte saw the fat white flakes of snow falling into that green sea, saw the waves swelling and the naked men with their bodies dangling.

She saw Lionel young, saw him lying on his back as he rested all the various parts of him. His pale hand was reaching out of the gloom, reaching out and turning. She saw the shape of the girl who stood in the doorway and slowly came to him. Katrinka had never had a soul to protect her, Charlotte knew. She hadn't had even the raging drunken crazy mother Charlotte herself had had, the one who called long distance at three in the morning, long distance, collect, and person-to-fucking-person for Lionel Elmo *"Pédé"* Ainsworth, LI-O-*NEL!* with socks *clocked* in hunter's green! to tell him he'd better mind his own fucky business, *apropos* of Charlotte, because if he laid one hand on her, Katrinka would have Rufus, her Negro mental patient boyfriend, come straight over from Watts with all of his Negro mental patient friends and beat the crappy shit out of him.

Charlotte sat watching the dead dry clumps of the parasitic plant. She picked up a clump and weighed it, remembering what she could not know. She remembered her own father dragging the sleeping bag from the trunk of the Willys and out onto the dunes near Benicia. Across the dark water the ships lay in drydock at Mare Island. They were hung, she knew, with netting for camouflage. She knew about camouflage, the covering of one dark thing with the draping of another. She took the darkest thing she had and obscured the shape of it, hanging its rigging with lights. She lit up the ship as the shop windows had been in Manhattan the week Katrinka was there for Ed Sullivan. Charlotte pressed her eyelids with her fingertips, pressed until her eyes ached and the lights began. These lights were red at first, then traversed the spectrum, running red through orange to orangish yellow, from yellowish white to white. At white, they changed, bursting bluely out of pinpricks. From pinpricks they grew to the size of stars, stars flying out and out. This was as in shock treatment, she felt, when the waves of light were worked to obliterate all sight.

Lights were strung by her in memory all along the ship's super-structure. These lights, brought on by the numbing pressure of her fingertips, were what she used to construct a screen. Dr. Greenley had once told her that he could use the pinprick of his lighted instrument to see into her brain. He could see, he'd said, that she had a good strong brain, just as she had good strong eyes.

She had good eyes, good vision, a good mind. Still, she could use the lights to stop the sight of this: a memory, something she both could and could not see. The memory was of the moment that she'd sat on the examination table in Dr. Greenley's office and had begun to know something. He was trying to tell her something. He was saying that it was only through the grace of God that some would find salvation. She had good health, good eyes, a strong brain. She had His grace. She would need to use it.

She closed her eyes again, pressed with her fingertips, and brought forth from the darkness the lights of the places she'd never been. She sat on the beach on that snowy day and saw how the storm had slushed up clouds of sand that showed through the greenish swelling of the translucent waves. The swirls of stirred sand took on the shapes of bodies. The bodies of the naked men were made to travel the course of each wave's crashing, so as it crested, then broke, the body turned inside out.

Charlotte too was inside out. She lay on her back on the davenport, raised her hand by the smoking stand and saw the shape of the girl coming forth to her. She saw her own hand reach out. She was in the water now, the saltwater which made her buoyant even as it caused the flesh to change. Charlotte herself was weightless—it was the twin stones of her two dark parents who'd always made her sink.

Weightless and without a past, she remembered her mother's life instead. She sat in the bar high atop Rockefeller Center drinking highballs, looking out the cold black window at the same snow she'd seen falling on the beach earlier in the day. The storm had filled the streets of Manhattan with an absolute darkness. She was with Watson, her friend from the *Pelican*, who'd moved east, and with some other people from the TV show. The men were all growing increasingly fascinated, she noticed, and their wives increasingly less so. This was on Christmas Eve.

The streets had been lit up when they'd come downtown from the hotel but the sights were now erased by the darkness of the storm's low clouds. Katrinka sat with her back to the cold black glass, one freezing elbow resting on the chromium ledge, which was as highly polished as a mirror. There, on the surface of the chrome, she noticed that the snowflakes were, that night, falling upward instead of down. She announced to the others that Ed Sullivan had undoubtedly arranged this in honor of her—he had much greater pull, those days, with the Jews of that town than Jesus ever did. Several people smiled but only Watson laughed. Watson wanted to go to bed with her.

This, Charlotte knew, was what death was: the falling out and away into nothingness, that pitch, that arc, those arms akimbo. She knew something else about this—the stepping off, the flying out—but couldn't, just then, remember what it was. Memory was tricky: she tried to remember it—that which she knew—but she couldn't see past the probe of Dr. Greenley's lighted pinprick, the red, then orange, then gold. She pressed her eyes and brought on the numbing lights of the sunken ship. It had been sunk in July but it was all decked out for Christmas.

Bodies existed for a while in three dimensions, then were transmuted into smoke. They were smoke, sand, the words of those she'd never heard, the touch she'd never felt. The dead had no weight, no heft. She had no self left aside from the various parts of them, so she wasn't to be governed by the same rules. She had no gravity, unlike the rest of them, unlike her two dark stones. Nothing real had ever happened to her; still, she could remember all of it, the way the water warmed by day but the warmth never penetrated, never moved down to touch their numbing, puffing feet. White sharks bumped up among them in the moonlight. She pressed harder to stop the sight of that. The ship came forth. Men, certain men, did kill themselves. Certain men were those who let loose their grip on the net.

Charlotte had come forth from the two of them with a dark shape clutched in either hand. She pressed her eyes until her brain hurt, then she understood it: she was their poem, the only future her parents had ever had.

She might, she knew, fly out one day, off from a silver ledge and into a dark night where fire danced on water or bodies were shaped by the weightlessness of sand. She might fly out to be true to them. She knew this: she was their own true daughter, not by accident, but through the sheer force of her own will.

She might go out, fly from the silver ledge, but she would not fall. She'd been given shape by the words of them, but she was orphaned now and had no weight. Her palms ached with sorrow, but because her hands were empty there was nothing now to pull her down. She was sand only, or smoke, or the words the two of them had said, had said. She had no substance and so might fly. She was her mother's vision of the silent flurry of those defiant snowflakes, those twirling up out of the dark streets below.

II

AVENUE B

Winter 1955

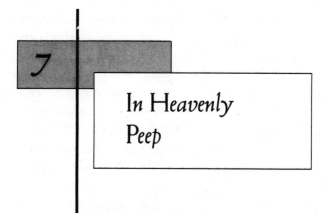

7

In Heavenly Peep

One day near the end of 1955, when Charlotte was nine, Katrinka showed up married. She announced it as soon as she got out of the blue sedan, telling Lionel she was *married*, that she'd come to get Charlotte, who was *her* daughter, and that there was nothing the Ainsworths could do about it.

"Your mother and I," Lionel called down the steps to her, "have asked you repeatedly to telephone before arriving here."

"I wanted you to meet him," she went on, lifting her face to Lionel, who was halfway down the steps. She had emerged from the car and had started up without bothering to close the door. Now a man was getting out of the driver's side.

"Dad, this is Sweeney. Sweeney, this is my *father*. But don't call him that—he prefers 'Lionel,' don't you, Pops? And you can call me *Mrs.* Sweeney from now on when you discuss me at the barbershop—I think we could do with a little more formality around here. Familiarity, as you always say, does breed contempt."

"Believe me," Lionel told her, coldly, "I do not discuss you at the barbershop." He stood in the center of the steps, blocking the way, with Charlotte peeking out from behind him. The big-faced man in a blue suit was at the bottom of the steps behind Katrinka. His hair was kinky, golden, plastered down with shiny hair goop.

Lionel had finished his walk and was now allowing his skin to breathe. Although it was a chilly day, he had on shorts and a thin shirt that was open down the front. His feet, on the cold bricks, were bare. "Is he aware of your psychiatric history?" he boomed down.

"He doesn't give a shit about my psychiatric history, do you, Sweeney?" She was pulling off one yellow glove, clicking open her pocketbook, digging in the bottom for cigarettes. She stuck one in the side of her mouth, struck a match, lit it, then tossed the match, which was still smoking, off into the brush growing down the slope next to the steps.

"Besides," Katrinka said, inhaling deeply, then exhaling, "all Sweeney wants is somebody to be nice to him. He just lost his mother so you goddamned well better be nice to him, or he'll crack up right here on your steps."

"Have you informed him that you cannot cook?" Lionel asked. "That you have no skills in home economics?"

"Why is she cowering like that?" Katrinka asked. "Charlotte, get out here this instant! What are you afraid of? Are Lionel and Winnie being mean to you again?" She reached past Lionel and grabbed Charlotte's wrist. "Isn't she beautiful?" she asked Sweeney. "I told him all about you," she said, "the night I picked him up in a bar in Hermosa Beach."

"Very pleased to make your acquaintance," Sweeney was saying, generally. He wiped his hand on his pants before he reached it up toward Lionel, who ignored him.

"Charlotte!" Katrinka said. "Where are your manners? Say hello to your new daddy."

"I thought you said the other one might still be alive," Charlotte whispered.

"Oh, hush," Katrinka told her. "Will you please make an effort not to be babyish on my wedding day?"

Winnie was out by then, at the top of the steps, wringing her hands in a dish towel, so Katrinka called up triumphantly, "Mother! This is Sweeney, *your* new son-in-law!"

Lionel's voice was revving up. "And who, may I ask, performed this alleged ceremony? Were there blood tests performed? Are there false documents involved? Now, I am of the opinion, young man, that you might feel you may gain access to our holdings by this maneuver, but I assure you, she has no legal standing whatsoever, as *I* am the conservator of both her person and her property."

"What he's interested in," Katrinka turned around to inform Sweeney, " is whether or not we have con-sum-mated our marriage; isn't that so, Lionel?" She pronounced *marriage* in French.

Charlotte's stomach twisted; she wished her mother wouldn't make jokes like that. Sweeney, too, seemed shocked. His whole face moved in a shudder that passed across his forehead, then he blinked both eyes hard. He was chewing his lower lip, a lip as red as a woman's wearing lipstick.

Winnie, crablike, was descending, right foot, right foot, right foot, her brow corrugated with worry. "Get your things," Katrinka told Charlotte. "We have a house now, on Avenue B in Redondo Beach. I'm going to be a happy homemaker, Mother. Aren't you delighted? I've already enrolled Charlotte in Tulita Avenue Elementary."

"You may not enroll her," Winnie said. "Mental patients have no right to enroll anyone in anything."

"He says he's a machinist," Lionel turned and called up. "Says he works for McDonnell Douglas. He owns the house—he bought it on the GI Bill."

"What branch of the service?" Winnie snapped.

"Navy," Sweeney said, answering for himself.

By the way her eyebrows moved, Charlotte could tell Winnie was interested. "We can have that checked," Winnie told herself. "But did he actually marry her?" she called back to Lionel. "Why would a normal person want to do a thing like that?"

"Because I'm *nice*," Katrinka said, extending one long white arm to gather Charlotte to her. As always, Charlotte tried to resist her. As always, her mother's cheek was the softest thing she'd ever felt.

Sweeney's house was green stucco, paneled up to the bottom of the windows with knotty pine, as if flooding were expected. All the houses in the tract were identical, aside from the colors, which went pink, green, yellow all down the hill.

The houses on either side of the street were built to mirror one another, so when Charlotte went to play at Cheryl Bickford's, the kitchen seemed to have hopped over to the other side. In this oppo-site kitchen, Cheryl's mother Audrey made batches of Toll House cookies by the voluptuous process of "creaming" the butter and sugar together. Charlotte and Cheryl were allowed to help, if they remembered to wash their hands.

Cheryl was an only child—not only that, but, as Katrinka said, she was the *perfect* child, a child from outer space. She had every color of Crayola, all still pristine in the largest crayon box, all still with points and wrappers intact. Those crayons and the smell of the cookies baking and the warm waxy smell of the skin of Cheryl's fin-gers made Charlotte love this girl as she had never loved another. She loved Audrey, too—the way she smoked, the way her bright red lipstick was painted way wide of her mouth, the look of her neat hair and her shirtwaist dresses.

The crest of the hill was four houses up, the ocean eight blocks down from there on the other side. Sweeney's house faced north-east, looking off toward downtown L.A. in the distance. Beyond that was Glendale, Charlotte knew, at the base of the distant moun-tains. These were the mountains that were being rubbed out, erased.

At the foot of the hill was the big field the kids said had been a Jap garden before it had been bought up by the developer, who then went bankrupt on Avenue D. This was the "butt" who, according to Gail Bill, still owed her mother Maxine plenty of things: trees and lawns, sidewalks, a garage. In this field there were swampy places where Charlotte found tiny frogs after the rains—they were no big-ger than her thumbnail. It was in that field that John Hamberger once fired his bow down a gopher hole and brought a dead gopher up, hanging limply on the point of the arrow. There was no victory in John's face at all, just surprise that a gopher hole really was *that*, that a real gopher had been lurking there below, as if waiting to die.

At the top of the hill there was a flat block where Charlotte rode the two-wheeler Sweeney had given her. She rode it with her skirt and slip hiked up so her legs showed. He hadn't known there was such a thing as a girl's bike, with the crossbar on the diagonal. Gail Bill mocked the bike, mocked Charlotte for her high thin voice that enunciated, that said, *thank you very much* and *actually* and *yes, please, I would* if she was asked if she'd like something to eat. The only one on Avenue B who appreciated those sorts of manners was Audrey Bickford.

It was the heart of winter. The wind pressed constantly in off the ocean. It was so strong that it had already blasted the color from the uphill side of each of the houses, so the black and white grit of the stucco stood out away from the pastel colors still left in the depressions, making the houses look gray. The wind ripped clothes off the circular clotheslines, sending them creaking and singing. The shirts torn from the lines billowed open and started tumbling down the alley in a cloud of pale sand.

The wind carried kites so far east from the crest that they vanished against the color of the roofs in the next subdivision, so far away they finally went down from the sheer weight of the four or five balls of string attached to them. The wind was a rough ocean that the flock from the pigeon club sailed out upon, soaring, eddying, forming a dark cloud of swirling bodies and gliding wings, until one of the tumblers fell out of the cluster, descending almost to the ground in circles, before saving itself by flapping back up. John Hamberger said it was the trick pigeons used to get away from hawks.

Charlotte was the first girl in the pigeon club; she got to join because John Hamberger had given her one of his own pigeons, a red. He was the boss of who was in the pigeon club because the coop had been built by his father in their backyard.

The wind slammed doors in Sweeney's house, doors that sounded hollow because they were. Charlotte found that out when she saw the hole he kicked in one of them when he was mad at Katrinka over something. The door was a thin empty box built of plywood.

The rooms of the house sounded hollow, too, because they held

so little furniture. The one room that was very full was where Sweeney and Katrinka slept; it had been his mother's room and had a
complete bedroom set, bought by Sweeney when he had come
home from the war. It had a huge mahogany bed with a solid headboard that went almost to the ceiling, curling back at the top like a
scroll. The headboard sat diagonally against both of the corner windows, blocking out all the yellow light from the sandy backyard. It
sat diagonally, Charlotte supposed, to indicate that although Katrinka was living in a tract house in disguise as a homemaker, she
had absolutely no intention of becoming the slightest bit conventional.

The surface of the matching dressing table was shoved up next to
the bed; it held Katrinka's overflowing ashtrays and the bottle of
Evening in Paris. The surface was seared by many long purple
dents, as if it had been pressed repeatedly by a slender burning finger. The wood of the tabletop also bloomed with white clouds made
by hundreds of circles, the marks of the sweating beer cans.

Charlotte's room used to be Sweeney's. There were no curtains
on the windows. The furniture was obviously a boy's. On the
dresser and the nightstand were the things he'd once made in wood-
working shop. There was a lamp base but no lamp, and a stand for
something to balance on. These items had been decorated with a
woodburning kit in designs that looked cowboy-and-Indian.

Charlotte's top sheet had gone to the Brownies to be made into
placemats, so she slept with her arms touching the scratchy blanket.
Charlotte thought of Winnie, of the way she ironed the still-damp
sheets as they came off the line. The smell of these sheets, even
hours later, was full of the heat of the iron, of wind, and of daylight.
Winnie loved Bobby Burns and in utter secrecy wrote poetry, which
she then read out to Lionel, who said he liked it. Then she would cry
out, "You do not!" and crumple it up. Winnie had once changed the
words to the "Now I Lay Me" prayer so Charlotte wouldn't have to
say the words "If I should die before I wake." Winnie had changed
the prayer's words to "Happy and well may I awake, and this I ask
for Jesus' sake." This was to teach Charlotte the lesson of being op-
timistic. Life was, as Winnie liked to say, just a bowl of cherries.

Katrinka cut up a library book and taped the pictures around the room. Charlotte went to sleep looking at them, awed by her mother's lawlessness: Katrinka wasn't afraid of Maxine Bill, who was the boss of the housewives; she didn't care if she was invited to Maxine's lousy bingo parties or not. There was Madeleine running around the room, along the wall of the quay, getting away from the nuns; Katrinka was like that—brave and clever. Charlotte was the other, more conventional type, she thought—one of the little girls who followed along in two straight rows, keeping an eye on her mother.

Maxine Bill was at war with the developer, the "butt" who'd promised the lawns, the sidewalks, the streetlights, the sewers. What she was really mad about, though, was the garages, which should have been built along a *paved* alleyway. She had called the developer a "butt" to his face. This was Maxine's favorite word. It was Maxine who boomed the awful words out of her kitchen window: "Now you get your filthy little butt in here right now before I whip it with your daddy's belt and give you something to *really* cry about!" Charlotte played with Maxine's oldest daughter, Gail. Gail was fat and already had breasts. She had a loud and terrible voice, just like her mother's.

The women on Avenue B all stayed home except for Ann next door up the hill—she had a job. She and Bud had no children because she had something wrong with her parts. The husbands worked in the aircraft factories or as electricians or plumbers. The best job was Dick Bickford's; he was a cop with the city of El Segundo. The one with the worst job was Tony Crustanzo, who sharpened knives. Maxine's husband Willy was an automobile mechanic, and often had parts of an engine lying around on the living room floor. *That*, Katrinka said, was because he had only gone far enough up in the School of Hard Knocks to learn how to take a car apart awwwnnd had never learned how to put it back together.

Because his father was a wop, greaser, dago, because his brother Tony, Jr., was a crippled gimp, the pack of kids led by Gail picked on Nino Crustanzo. Gail called out to him, "Hey, dago greaseball, come on over here so's I kin kick your butt!" Charlotte would have gone to Nino, taken sides with him, helped him push the wheelchair up the hill to fly kites, except she didn't have the guts. Charlotte's own standing on Avenue B was too precarious.

She gained status by having a father who had died in the war, then lost it by having a mother like Katrinka. Was Charlotte *sure* Katrinka had been on Ed Sullivan? Was she *really* a ventriloquist? Could Charlotte *prove* she wasn't nothin' but a crazy drunk?

Gail, at thirteen, had one goal in life and that was this: to have Elvis Presley sign his name in ballpoint on the flesh of her boobs, "Elvis" on the righty, "Presley" on the lefty. Gail had it figured out, as Charlotte told Katrinka: she was going to put Band-Aids over the words to keep them from washing off when she took a bath. "Well, thank Gawd she'll only have to go through all *that* every three or four months," Katrinka commented.

Charlotte didn't really like Gail, either, but now she played with the Bills because she wasn't allowed over at Cheryl's. It was partly Katrinka, the way she'd driven the rainy day carpool after drinking her breakfast beers, dressed in her bathing suit and black high heels and the green silk kimono Sweeney had brought back for his mother from Occupied Japan.

But it was Charlotte and Cheryl, too, who'd gotten in trouble with Audrey. What they'd been doing was boosting one another up the clothesline pole, then sliding down with their legs wrapped around it, their dresses hiked up and their slips out of the way. They slid down the pole slowly—it was chilly and pitted from the salty wind. They were doing this over and over again, taking turns, hugging the pole so the cold metal caught and tugged the fabric of their underpants and pressed right at the place where you pee. Audrey, looking out the window, noticed them doing it, screamed at them, and sent Charlotte home. Cheryl wasn't to play with Charlotte ever again, even though it was Cheryl, the neat and perfect girl, who'd been the one who discovered how to do it.

When Nino pushed his brother up the hill, the wind lifted their long dark bangs, reddened their thin faces. The wheelchair was old, wooden, heavy; Charlotte could see by the grim strain in Nino's face how hard it was to push. She wished she had the guts to go and help him. The other kids watched silently as the boys struggled up against the push of the wind. Tony, Jr., held the kites on a lap so flat his pants seemed empty of legs. The kids watched in awe; the polio had come from a place they had all been: the swampy frog ponds at the bottom of the hills. Any one of them might have gotten it, except the rest of them had gone to Kaiser-Permanente and taken their shots.

When the boys had passed, Gail began the chant: "Can't *stand* those Crus-*stan*-zos! Can't *stand* those Crus-*stan*-zos!" Katrinka once told Gail, with immeasurable scorn, that her Crustanzo chant was the cleverest thing that had ever come out of her dim brain. Gail rolled back her upper lip, believing she'd been paid a compliment.

Tony was going broke in the knife shop. Sylvia was so pregnant it was probably twins. The boys had holes in the soles of their thin shoes and holes in their crooked teeth. The Crustanzos were behind on their rent. "Tell them," Katrinka ordered Sylvia, handing her a breakfast beer, "that you cannot get blood from a turnip." She had Sylvia over for breakfast beers. She had Sylvia over all the time now, since they both were shunned by the other housewives. Maxine no longer asked Katrinka to Wednesday bingo, and she had never invited Sylvia. Katrinka didn't care. "Public opinion," she liked to say, "no longer worries me."

The snapper was a bobby pin bent back on itself and spring-loaded against the unbent prong. Gail used it to make the other kids mind. She would let it fly across the room, though it could put out an eye, or she would come up from behind and snap it right against the skin of someone's neck, leaving a purple mark. She snapped Charlotte once on the thumbnail and the pain was so terrible Charlotte thought she would die before it was over, that it would freeze her jaw and brain. It was pain that traveled out, pain that went on and on and on.

"Well, snap her the fuck back," Katrinka said, when Charlotte told her.

"I don't have one."

"Oh, honestly, Charlotte, I'm sure you can come up with something. Sic your grandmother on her. Or tell her she's going straight to hell for being so nasty. The Bills all love that going-to-hell type crap."

"She says I'm going to hell for not being baptized by total immersion. She says I'm a Jew for not being baptized at all."

"Tell her she's going to hell for Elvis on the righty and Presley on the lefty." Charlotte sighed; she wished she could think of these things at the time. "Why," Katrinka asked, "are you worried about hell, my sweetie? Anyway, you shouldn't be—this is it. Hell is right here on earth. See?" She pointed out the window to the rutted street, which was being dug up for the sewers that the county was putting in. The topsoil of the yards had either already blown away or had never been delivered, so the sand of each lot spread far out onto the chunks of asphalt. There Nino was pushing the wheelchair in his ruined shoes, slipping backwards as though he were walking up dunes.

When Gail Bill laughed, her upper lip rolled back and showed the thin strip of pinkish skin that attached the lip to her bright red gums. Her teeth were very little. She threw her head back and laughed like that when she used the snapper. She snapped the kids to get them to turn their stuff over to her when she took them shoplifting at the five-and-ten down on the Pacific Coast Highway.

She popped the snapper at Charlotte from behind fences on the way to school. She peed in a milk bottle and told Charlotte she'd have to drink it. She threatened to rub Charlotte's face with the peanut butter scar on her upper arm, a scar that came *off* on you, Gail said. The skin was dark brown from elbow to shoulder, and shiny from the way it had hardened after it had melted. That, Katrinka said, was where Maxine, who was criminally insane, had burned her daughter with hot grease when she was frying hog jowls. Hog jowls, didn't she know, hon' chil', was *the* most favoritest thing in Pork Hollow, West Virginie, where Maxine and Willy Bill and all the little Bills and the rest of the Okies and Arkies all hailed from? All except Laddie Bill, who was cute and had come, therefore, from heaven.

Charlotte smiled weakly. It wasn't God or hell she was afraid of: it was Gail Bill.

Sweeney sometimes put Charlotte up in the attic through a trapdoor in the hallway, so she would be able to play. There was nothing to do up there, so she sat on the trunk that held her mother's dummies, staring at the boxes of Sweeney's dead mother's things. Everything up there had the same reek of dust and rotting cloth.

The dummies' clothes smelled like old women because they were made for Katrinka by her Great-Aunt Bertha Hopkins, who lived with her daughter, Little Winnie, in the town of Orange. Aunt Hoppy had always made doll clothes for Katrinka, so when she became a ventriloquist it had seemed natural that she should continue. Aunt Hoppy was the only person Charlotte had ever met who didn't seem to think Katrinka's being a ventriloquist was odd in any way. That was because she and Little Winnie were so very odd themselves.

The attic was stuffy; the air full of pitch. There was no floor, so Charlotte had to be careful not to step off the rafters or she'd fall right through the plasterboard of the ceiling. She never knew exactly what might qualify as playing.

Below her, in the kitchen, Sweeney and Katrinka were having an argument. He was probably complaining about the food Katrinka served him, Charlotte decided. The night before, Katrinka had served a long loaf of unsliced French bread stuffed with an ear of corn and surrounded by canned peaches. The peach juice sopped into the bread. Sweeney, blinking, his face twitching, had told Katrinka it was the worst thing he'd ever tried to eat.

And he was right, Charlotte thought. Even Katrinka hadn't disagreed. She had smiled her indulgent, what-a-dumb-shit-you-are smile at him and told him that if he was such a big shot, he should take them out for a lobster dinner on the Rainbow Pier.

In the kitchen now, Sweeney was slamming cupboard doors. Charlotte heard the whomp and the jingle of the refrigerator shuddering closed. The front door opened, then slammed with its empty, rattling slam. Then the car started up and moved down the hill, slowly, around the heaps of dirt from the excavation. She walked down two parallel rafters to peek out the vent: Sweeney had driven away.

Charlotte went back, sat down, and began to weigh her feelings. Sweeney did try to be nice with the bike and the attic and giving her the dimes for bags of pigeon feed. Still, he wasn't her real father and he had forgotten her. Besides, *nice*, according to Katrinka, was one of the lousiest things a person could turn out to be. She heard the toot of the Helm's Bakery truck at the foot of the hill on Tulita and thought of the roll-out trays of jelly doughnuts. She was very hungry. There was no sense getting attached to Sweeney anyway since he was going to divorce Katrinka if she cooked him any more of her creative economy dinners.

The best thing about Katrinka, Charlotte thought, was that she thought food was so funny. That was why she did things like shove a corn on the cob up a loaf of bread and serve it sopping with peach juice. Sweeney didn't get it: the dinner was a joke. It was a joke on Winnie, who, like Dr. Greenley, deeply believed there was something profound about eating—that spiritual health could be found in it, that food held scientific truth. That was why Winnie insisted that Charlotte resist sugar and what she called "the synthetics." That category, though, included almost all good things: jelly doughnuts, ice cream, tuna sandwiches served on white bread with a sliced pickle, and potato chips. Lionel got the sandwich for Charlotte sometimes at the soda fountain in the pharmacy on Honolulu. He would have coffee and a nice slice of coconut cream pie. This was secret eating, done behind Winnie's back. The pie, in particular, was something she was never to find out about.

Once, because Charlotte had asked him, Lionel had bought a loaf of white bread when the two of them were doing the marketing. Winnie was livid. She had stood in the kitchen with her brows shoved together, systematically running each slice under the faucet. The pulp she had gotten from this went into the Pyrex measuring cup to see how much food it really amounted to. It just wasn't anything, Winnie had said, opening her fingers to show them the white and tan glop that remained after she'd wrung the water out. It wasn't anything, and she did so hope Lionel would resist the temptation to waste good money on such foolishness again. Cheerios, too, were reduced in this manner, the one time he'd brought them home for

Charlotte. Cheerios came down to little more than a tablespoon of glop per bowlful.

"Mom?" Charlotte called down through the trapdoor. "Mom? Mommy? Can't you hear me?" She thought Sweeney might have hurt her mother, but then she heard the slushy sound of Katrinka talking to herself and laughing.

"Baba?" Charlotte called, though she hated this word. It was a joke, made from the name a sick child says when calling for her mother. It was horrible; still, Katrinka sometimes went by it. "Mother!" Charlotte demanded, but from the kitchen she heard the rasp and the cough and the cackle.

Charlotte assessed the drop. The house was modern and the ceilings were low, so it wasn't that far, not like going out the window of a bar high atop Rockefeller Center. She cradled her elbows in the corner of the opening and lowered her legs and body. She dangled, really needing to pee, then she swung down so her hands broke the fall for an instant before her weight pulled her fingers free.

Katrinka was sitting at the kitchen table in the spotted kimono, staring out the window. The table was cluttered with beer cans. The tops of some of them overflowed with cigarette butts. Sauerkraut had been dashed about and lay on the floor like clumps of white seaweed. Ketchup and mustard were spilled as well. Katrinka turned to Charlotte with her face lit up with amusement, her eyes bright as the green silk she wore.

"Why didn't you come?" Charlotte whispered, her chest so tight with anger that she was having trouble getting the words out. She rubbed elaborately at one knee, which had not been hurt when she landed on her own two feet. "Why didn't you *help* me?" she asked her.

"Oh, honey baby," Katrinka said, waving a match back and forth to put it out. She shrugged hopelessly.

"Mothers are supposed to help their children," Charlotte told her.

Katrinka narrowed her eyes and glared hard for a moment before she said, "Zat so!" and looked back out the window. "Why don't you tell it to Winnie, then? Churchill 2–3226. Or go live with Aunt

|||||||||||||||||||||||||||||||||||

Hoppy and Little Winnie in Orange—I'm sure they'd *love* to have you. Or go move in with Audrey, if she's so wonderful. Or Bud and Ann. Bud and Ann I'm sure would love to have a little orphaned bundle of you darkening their doorstep."

Charlotte dropped her eyes. The thought had occurred to her.

"If you *must* know, Missy Miss," Katrinka said, stretching her long white arms way over her head and keeping them there while she went on talking, "the reason I did not come to get you is that I had every confidence you could get down by yourself."

"But I could have *killed* myself!" Charlotte shouted at her, the words jumbled by her choking and tripping over themselves to get at Katrinka, to make her feel bad.

"Oh, I sincerely doubt that. For one thing you're too much like your grandmother. I never saw anyone whimper as much as that woman does and be so goddamned good at taking care of herself all the while." She still held her arms up, as if she were being robbed.

After a moment she stretched and whispered and then sucked her cheeks in to announce, "At any rate, this is pure Zola, Charlotte. *Je suis Gervaise*, and all that. Awwwnnd, my own sweet baby, it's all I can do to help myself these days, in case you haven't noticed. In case you haven't noticed—I am in way over my head."

L'Assommoir was Katrinka's favorite book, though Charlotte wasn't altogether certain her mother had really read it. Joey told its story to Katrinka; Katrinka then told it to Charlotte. It was the story of the washerwoman in Paris who'd had one simple wish: to die between clean sheets in her own bed. But her life was bedeviled by hardships and degraded by a drunken husband and a drunken lover. Finally, after succumbing to drink herself, Gervaise had ended her days in squalor. She had died lying on filthy rags beneath the stairs of the boardinghouse that had turned her out. She had crawled there like a dog to rest.

The title had no equivalent word in English, Charlotte's father had informed Katrinka, and Katrinka informed Charlotte. *L'Assommoir* was the blow delivered to the animal in the slaughterhouse, the blow from which an animal did not recover. The instrument that delivered the bludgeoning was similar to a sledgehammer. The same, her father had felt, could be said for life its very self.

Charlotte had listened attentively to this, as she did to anything that concerned her father. He had been able to speak French and German and to read Latin. Katrinka hadn't seemed to learn another language—still she was apparently able to speak them all. She was the opposite of dogs, Charlotte felt, who know all languages, yet can speak none.

The tale of Gervaise was the saddest story Charlotte had ever heard; still, Katrinka didn't seem at all depressed by it. The works of Emile Zola even seemed to amuse her. She said the tale of the Crustanzos was written by Zola, as was the rest of Avenue B, with the exception of the Bills, who were just too subnormal to be tragic in any way. The Bills, Katrinka said, were lower down than either jazz or gravity.

Katrinka painted Avenue B in tinted Glass Wax on the front windows to decorate the house for Christmas. There were Santa and his reindeer, and the flatbed truck filled with Girl Scouts, their voices lifted, the words etched into the Glass Wax clouds over their heads, singing "Hark! the Herald Angels Sing!" as the truck bumped along trying not to fall into the sewer. There was Bud and Ann's crushed peppertree sapling, buried beneath rubble from the street. And there were Nino and Tony, Jr., and fat Gail and fatter Maxine, and Gail's little brother Laddie, who had on a Davy Crockett cap and had his clothes on inside out and backward. Laddie was singing: "Thum one's baking gingerbread. Nith and brown, betht in town. Thum for me thee thaid."

And there in the corner on the cobbled streets of Paris were Gervaise and her daughter Nana and Emile Zola, all etched into the Glass Wax, all sitting in an outdoor café. Emile Zola, Charlotte understood, was her own father, who, as author of their lives, was never really with them while he still had always somehow been.

Lionel and Winnie came early on Christmas morning, bringing it with them. They would not come in the house. They stood in the cold fog on the concrete slab that was the porch and grimly handed out presents. Sweeney, in his terrycloth robe, waited with his forehead twitching a little in expectation. Even though he was an adult, Charlotte noticed, a *grown man*, he still *hoped* for something, she saw. Winnie gave him a pair of socks and a package of Black Jack gum.

Charlotte got some dresses from Bullock's, the game of Clue, *Bleak House* by Charles Dickens, a chessboard and pieces, and a perfumed doll in a plastic dome that was for collecting, the smell of which made her sick.

Katrinka got an apron, dish towels, a file box full of helpful household hints that Winnie had cut from the newspaper and glued on three-by-five cards or had written out on the cards with a Rapidograph pen. There was also a bar of Fels Naphtha soap and a box of Bon Ami cleanser. There was a box full of art supplies and a copy of *The Joy of Cooking* by Irma Rombauer.

Then Charlotte gave her gifts: pencils and pens stolen from the five-and-ten, a bookmark she'd made out of a piece of sheet for Lionel, and the placemats from pieces of sheets she'd made for Winnie. Each of these items was decorated with ironed-in crayons; the edges were frayed to a depth of two inches. The fraying had taken six weeks of Tuesday Brownie meetings. Charlotte had thought she would die before she finished the placemats; the tediousness of pulling one thread out, then the next made her vision wobble and her head ache.

She walked them to the car, vaguely worried that someone was forgetting something. She wanted to ask Winnie for another sheet. She wanted to tell her about the laundry never getting done, but couldn't do that since it would be disloyal to her mother.

Each of her grandparents took turns grabbing her upper arms in a firm grip, then moving her forward to be able to kiss the air at the side of her face. Winnie, frowning meaningfully, whispered, "Churchill 2–3226," and slipped her something tiny and white, wrapped in paper and taped. In tiny letters with the Rapidograph, she'd written: *This is your dime for an emergency.* Charlotte was to keep it in her pocket at all times.

The pigeon John had given her was called a "red," but it was actually russet, with a white hood and leggings. The tail feathers were reddish brown that graduated to a pinkish beige, and the tips of them were creamy. She was so beautiful that Charlotte named her Juliet.

The beachies tried to join the flock to get the good feed. They were fat from the popcorn and trash they lived on at the pier and, being wild, were hoggish. John tried to keep them away by firing his bow and arrow. He had a target set up at the back of the Hambergers' lot. He was going to teach Charlotte to hit it. He stood with his arms around her, showing her how to place the cleft of the arrow against the string, how to sight down the shaft toward the bull's-eye. She could feel his breath on the side of her face as he spoke, telling her these things. She heard him, but she wasn't listening. Then, just as she let the arrow fly, Laddie Bill ran in front of the target to get to the other row of kids. It was an accident, as with John and the gopher— she hadn't aimed at him, hadn't shot him on purpose.

"You put my brother's eye out!" Gail Bill bellowed, running to him. "God DAMN you to everlasting hell!" Charlotte saw the mouth with the ridge of skin, the little teeth. Her own mouth, too, was gaping. She had never been in so much trouble in her life. She was going to jail, like her mother always did.

The kids were all around Laddie, who lay on the ground. Charlotte pushed by them, remembering something: the arrow had hit and glanced off, not staying in as it would have had it gone deep into an eye. His face was smeared with dirt and snotty tears and blood. "Look at me!" she ordered him, and she held his hands away from his bloody eyes. He opened both of them, bright blue eyes surrounded by the smudging of brown and red. The arrow had hit his cheekbone and bounced off, leaving a little slice, a tiny cut, white where the fattish tissue showed.

He was never mad at Charlotte over it; he was never mad at anyone. He was old enough for kindergarten but he didn't go. He collected animals: stray dogs, a parakeet with a withered claw, hermit crabs that he kept in a milky mayonnaise jar. He was one of the children in the middle of the Bill family, but he was off by himself, away from the pack, raising himself. Katrinka loved him for his cuteness. Charlotte, on the other hand, loved him for being a walking miracle: the single human Bill.

Maxine decided the only way she was going to get her garage was to go on "Queen for a Day." Since the award was made on the basis of the official applause meter, she made all the ladies of the neighborhood go with her to clap.

All the women of Avenue B talked of the rooms of the house as *my* kitchen, *my* front bedroom, *my* hall, but Katrinka seemed to own only the bathroom of Sweeney's house, these days, where she sat on the toilet drinking beer and letting the wash soak in the bathtub.

On the day the women all went to Hollywood to clap for Maxine, the kids stayed home from school to watch on the Bills' television set. One of the reasons the Bill family was the boss of the neighborhood was this TV—they were the first family to own one. Charlotte stayed home, too, though she didn't care about the program. She stayed home because it was Friday, when she had her violin lesson after school. Katrinka had pawned Charlotte's rented violin.

Gail was making sandwiches in the Bills' kitchen, using a whole loaf of white bread, spreading peanut butter on slice after slice, licking the knife in between. She made Charlotte one, moving the knife back and forth over her scar, pretending to use that, too. "And here's a glass of milk to flush it down," she told Charlotte.

Charlotte took the sandwich and the glass of milk, saying nothing. She wasn't hungry, and she would have gone home, except John was supposed to be coming over to see the program. She waited until Gail turned her back, then she threw the sandwich out into the ice plant through the door at the side of the kitchen—Laddie had gone out and left it open behind him. His scar was white, small, like a moon slung low, the shape of a tiny cutting from a thumbnail. His cheekbones were scattered with chunk-shaped freckles, the same color as the peanut butter. The point of the arrow had missed his eye by a quarter-inch.

This wasn't Maxine's day. The other contestants were a girl who had only a few months to live who wanted to go home to Minnesota to attend her high school reunion, a blind lady married to a blind man who needed veterinary help for their Seeing Eye dogs, and a lady whose son had had polio and needed special shoes so he would be able to play Little League baseball. Charlotte saw right away that Maxine didn't have a chance. She thought about luckiness, what it was, how you got it. The luckiest one on this show was the one with the worst luck, since that was the kind of luck that won. This time it was the dying girl who got to go back to Minnesota, who got to ride in the golden Cadillac and get her makeup done. Lucky her.

It was early in February, a foggy yellow morning that had ebbed into a foggy noonday. The sun was flat, a cold disk from which no heat eked. There were no shadows of houses or of Bud and Ann's single broken peppertree, which was the only tree left on Avenue B. Charlotte could see it as she looked out the window by the kitchen table.

When the phone rang, Gail was on the floor sitting astride Kent Hamberger, who was a year older than John but in the same grade because he'd flunked. She was tickling him so hard and had been at it for so long that his face was inflamed and he looked like he couldn't breathe. John had not come up the hill, and Charlotte wasn't supposed to go to John's house when his mother wasn't home. Katrinka was made furious once when Charlotte went there and was with him alone, although all they'd been doing was making a package of chocolate pudding.

Gail's lip was still rolled back from laughing as she got up and went to the phone. She was laughing so hard with all the muscles of her face that even as she took the news she couldn't change them: the man at the five-and-ten they all stole from was calling to tell them Laddie had just been hit by a car while trying to cross the Pacific Coast Highway, in the company of a pack of dogs. As she repeated it, she was still grinning.

It was all Charlotte's fault. She kept crying, thinking of the scar on his cheek, the way his face had looked when it was smeared with snot and blood, how one eye then the other had peeked up at her, out from his squinted weeping. She sobbed as she knew she would for the rest of her life. Her own ill will had brought this on, her bad wishes had made it happen, so profound and thorough had been her contempt for his entire family, and so strong was her wish that evil might befall them.

Katrinka was sitting on the edge of Charlotte's bed, drinking beer and talking softly to herself. She got up and clomped off down the hall in her black high heels, still whispering, to get another beer. It was as much Gail's fault, she said as she came back in, for not tending to him, or it was Maxine's fault for having six kids in the first place when she obviously cared much more about getting the crappy garage, but it certainly was *not* Charlotte's fault because of the lousy dogs and their coming to get a peanut butter sandwich!

Charlotte cried and cried. Katrinka stroked her hair and face and drank her beer and sang a lullaby. She sang two songs year-round without regard to season. One was a Christmas carol, the other was "Summertime" from *Porgy and Bess*. When Katrinka sang "Silent Night," as she did that night, she sang their own version, from the way Charlotte had heard the words when she was small, when she had thought it said, "Ground round version, mother and child," believing it was about her own mother and herself and what they were having for dinner.

Katrinka sang it that way now, in Laddie's memory, with Charlotte lying below, watching the light from the hall illuminate the planes of her mother's face, studying them for sadness. She had never seen Katrinka cry, and it was her own crying that her mother seemed to like least about her. Like everything else, Katrinka seemed to take it personally.

Katrinka was thinking of someone else, Charlotte imagined. She lifted her chin and sang in her low voice that became reedy and thin at the top of the climb, going up: *Sleep in heavenly peeeee-eeeep!* and then thickening, getting throatier again as she came back down: *Sleep in heavenly peep!*

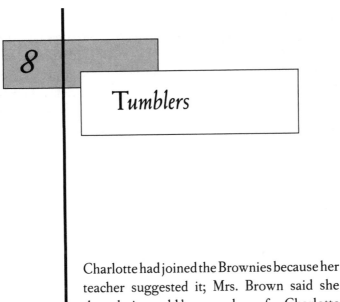

8

Tumblers

Charlotte had joined the Brownies because her teacher suggested it; Mrs. Brown said she thought it would be a good way for Charlotte to make friends. Almost immediately, though, Charlotte realized it would be impossible to be friends with girls like these, most of whom were as neat as Cheryl. Cheryl, too, was in this troop, but wouldn't speak to her. It was easier to be friends with boys. John and Kent were nice, and the other boys in the pigeon club weren't as big on cleanliness as the Brownies were. The red pigeon John had given her turned out to be a male, the leader of the flock, so Charlotte changed his name to Romeo.

The Brownies were getting ready to "fly up," which was what these people called becoming full-fledged Girl Scouts. In order to fly up, you had to complete some projects, such as making hot chocolate for your whole family, or setting the breakfast table for your mother, or packing your father's lunch box—*helping*, in other words. Charlotte, though, could not help. Even the thought of having to help made her feel insane, as if she might go crazy with rage and boredom, as had nearly happened while pulling the threads from the placemats, week after week after week, all the while smelling the air of the school cafeteria.

But the worst thing about the Brownies was the twenty-four boxes of Girl Scout cookies Charlotte was required to sell. She had no hope of ever doing it. Every girl on Avenue B was a Brownie or a Girl Scout; they had all lived there longer than Charlotte and knew people to sell them to. Even Bud and Ann, even Sylvia, had all bought theirs.

She was sitting in the bathtub, telling this to her mother, who sat on the toilet with the lid down, drinking a beer, keeping Charlotte company. Charlotte heaved a great groaning sigh; it was the same sound Katrinka made in the aisles of the Frontier Market as she pushed the shopping cart. It meant all the wifey business was really getting her down. People stared at her when she made that noise, believing she was having a heart attack.

"Never mind, sweetie," Katrinka said. "I'll buy one carton and make the Ainsworths buy the other." Charlotte looked down at her chest and stomach, shining with Zest. She lathered herself even more carefully, then stuck a washcloth onto her skin as if it was the top of a strapless ball gown. The ends of her braids were wet.

"Winnie won't let him buy them," Charlotte reminded her. "Sugar's poison to his system."

"I don't give a shit about his system," Katrinka said. "He can buy them and burn them in the incinerator, for all I care. He can throw them to the dogs." Charlotte stopped breathing, thinking. She raised her fingers to her eyelids but still could see the little moon-shaped scar, thin as the edge of a dime. "I'm not talking about *cookies*, Charlotte! I'm talking about family loyalty."

"You'll have to ask him privately," Charlotte told her, looking up. Their eyes caught. They studied one another for a moment, before Katrinka's face suddenly emptied. She then drank down the rest of her beer in one great gulp and stood up. "What complete shitasses they are, really really!" she said, stomping down the hall in her high heels. She had on the kimono and a full black slip, but no hose and no bra. Sweeney hated for her to dress like that, but now he was working the swing shift at the plant. He liked that shift because he didn't have to be home for dinner.

Katrinka wasn't cooking the creative economy dinners anymore. She was subsisting, these days, on the hops, grains, and barley used in the brewing of Miller High Life, which was, she said, one of nature's most perfect foods. Charlotte was getting by on chocolate sandwich Girl Scout cookies and U-No bars.

Katrinka clomped back in, flipped the lid up, yanked her underpants down, and peed. "How much are they?" she asked, over the sound of the urine rushing into water.

"Fifty cents a box."

"Times twelve." Katrinka was trying to figure out a way to get the money. Drinking beer while sitting on the toilet and trying to figure out how to get money was what she did most of the time, most days, now that she didn't drive the carpool or go to bingo at Maxine's. Like Gervaise, though, she still did the laundry. She did it in the tub and saved the quarters Sweeney gave her for the laundromat for shopping at Blackie's Liquors. When Charlotte wanted to take a bath, Katrinka moved the wash to the sink in the bathroom or the sink in the kitchen, pulling it along the hallway, in wet cardboard boxes, which she got from Blackie for this purpose. If both sinks were full, she pulled it out the kitchen door. The linoleum in the bathroom had begun to buckle and puff; the sweet pinkish mold was flowering from the cracks.

"I'll tell Sweeney he has to give it to me," she announced. Charlotte looked down at her stomach, which she heaved in and out, trying to figure out if she was fat. She couldn't decide, so she ate another cookie. Sweeney, she knew, would never give Katrinka money for anything—he even paid the charge himself down at Frontier. He wouldn't give Katrinka money since he had found out she'd pawned the diamond wedding set he had given her, then lied, saying the rings were lost. These had belonged to Sweeney's mother.

"Well, we have to do something to make money. Maybe I'll open a beer-and-lobster joint down on the pier. Your father and I always thought we'd be good at something like that. We thought we'd have a dump but name it something college-educated: *Sans Souci* or *L'Assommoir*. Like that. The best parts are the tomalley and the coral. Charlotte! Do you realize that?"

"Realize what?"

"The best parts of the lobster." She laughed. "They're *the* parts, you know."

Charlotte looked at her levelly, then looked away.

"I think we should have a talk about *parts*." She paused. "*If* you are going to keep on making chocolate pudding with John Hamberger, *if* you know what I mean. Are you listening?"

Charlotte heard, but wasn't listening.

"Do you know where babies come from?" Katrinka was asking. "I think we should discuss this—I don't want you learning the facts of life from Gail Bill. Touching uh-uhs or pee-pees, or whatever it is that girl does."

"Mom?" Charlotte asked. "Could we *please* not?"

"They peep, you know?" Katrinka said.

Charlotte pressed on her eyelids, thinking of *pee-pees*, *parts*, of how Ann had something wrong with hers, of the arrow sent by accident through the neck of the dangling gopher. "What does?" Charlotte asked.

"Lobsters," Katrinka told her. "They make little peeps when you dump them into the boiling sleep."

Charlotte stared at her mother, her mouth gaping open. "Where did you get that?"

"Your father, I suppose. He was a wonderful cook. Or I may have read it in Irma."

Charlotte was studying the scuds of soap on the surface of the bathwater—if she said nothing, showed no interest, her mother might move on to something else. The Sunday before, there had been a cartoon on "The Ed Sullivan Show," showing the faces of the Japanese children as their skin melted from the bomb. They were running toward the screen of the TV set. Their flesh vanished first, then their bones, and finally their ashes. As the sky turned to fire, the sound of their screams went on and on and on. It was her own father's ship that had taken that bomb across the ocean to be dropped on them, then was itself blown up because of its failure to zigzag.

Before he had put the cartoon on, Ed Sullivan, with arms folded across his chest, had solemnly advised the parents in the home audience to send their children from the room. Katrinka had refused. She knew him personally, and *he* wasn't such a much in his personal life to tell *her* what to do, particularly by remote control. He always had been bossy as hell, which is why she would never *condescend* to go back on his lousy *shoe*. She had enough of all that, putting up with it from Lionel.

"He doesn't mean just you, Mom," Charlotte had said. "He's talking about everybody."

"Oh, I don't go by *that*," Katrinka retorted.

Charlotte had nearly left the front room on her own at that moment, she was so afraid of what she might see. She would have, but she didn't want her mother to know she was what Katrinka called "a chicken-shitty little coward."

"What's the matter?" she asked Charlotte in the bath. "Don't you like lobster?"

"I don't know," Charlotte said. "I don't think I ever had it."

"What!" Katrinka said. "Those lousy shitasses with all their money have never taken you out to a seafood restaurant?"

"We went to Beadles' Cafeteria once," Charlotte said.

It was after shopping for school clothes at Bullock's Pasadena. Lionel had looked at all the slices of gleaming pie—chocolate cream, banana cream, lemon meringue—but had settled for a cup of coffee. Winnie had had her eye on him, and had spoken out, then, as she often did, about her hope that someone, in the not-so-distant future, would invent the pill that would allow people to get all their nutrition in three doses daily. Winnie felt a pill like that would do so much to cut down on basic nervous tension.

"Charlotte! Lobster is one of the verities. I will not have you growing up deprived!"

"Depraved," called down one of the voices from on high. Katrinka tipped her head up, laughed softly, and whispered back. The dummies were up in the attic.

"What are *verities?*" Charlotte asked her.

"Truths," Katrinka said. "The holy truths. The truths we hold to be self-evident."

Charlotte looked at her steadily. The water was so cold, she was getting goosebumps. There were no towels in the room to get dry with, though, so she couldn't get out.

"As they are, as they ever shall be!" Katrinka looked over, smiling. "Unless the Russians blow us all up into World War III. Liquid cherries is one of them. Jordan almonds. Lobster dipped in mayonnaise. These are the things that taste just as they did when I was a little girl, the same as when Winnie was little, and Big Mother, too. Do you know what I am talking about?"

Charlotte said nothing, so Katrinka went right on. "Do you know what your father once told me? That the worst of the mortal sins is avarice of the emotions? Do you know what that is?" Charlotte, with her teeth chattering, shook her head. "Greed of the heart! As it is! As it ever shall be! Saint Thomas Aquinas told this to your father *personally!*"

Charlotte watched her solemnly for a moment, then dropped her eyes, so her mother's bright look couldn't read her, couldn't read the greed in her own heart.

The Laundry, à la Baba

1. Put dirty laundry into the bathtub. Soak for from three to twenty days.

2. Add soap flakes, stirring occasionally with the handle of a broom.

3. Sit on toilet lid, lifting it to pee occasionally. Talk to yourself or anyone else who will listen about the verities, where babies come from, lobster, Saint Thomas Aquinas, the price of Girl Scout cookies, French literature of 1877.

4. Hide boxes of wet and rotting wash in Sylvia's trailer. Go through Sweeney's pockets where you find a couple of bucks. Think of soaking his clothes but *good*. Think of how Sylvia tells Tony, Sr., "Aw, go soak yer head."

5. Drive to Blackie's for another six-pack and a U-No bar.

6. Forget to remember if the clothes are dirty or clean, are lobsters peeping or sleeping in heavenly sheets so clean you could eat off them! Or rags that have moldered from the

7. Damp. Try to look it up in Irma. Try the index, which Winnie has annotated with her psychotic penmanship, using the Rapidograph Double-Aught or Ought-Not nib.

8. The words swim up, but not because they should, not because of tears, which do not well up and fall but slide instead, like saltwater, down the back of the throat causing

9. Sinus

10. But because you can't find your glasses, which might be lost in the laundry or on the kitchen table under the trash heap of history, or

11. Skip it. Let the water trundle into the tub. Add soap, stirring once with broom handle. Go down the hall to the kitchen, passing beneath the trapdoor up into the attic, where Ogamer is lecturing: Ought, Double Ought, Thou Shalt Not!

12. Sniff.

13. Get yourself another beer.

Charlotte tried to help, but the cards in the box from Winnie had other types of tips on them, such as how to get brown gravy stains out of table linens. She now slept with no sheets on her bed, as all of the linen in the house had been pulled into the vortex of Katrinka's laundry. There were soggy boxes of it all around the backyard, and individual items were strewn around by the dogs who, brought by the stink, ripped the cardboard apart.

Katrinka slammed into the darkened bedroom. How in the *fuck*, she asked, was she supposed to rinse the clothes if there kept being soap in the new water—were they putting soap in the general water supply? Under no circumstances was Charlotte ever again to drink it! And how was she supposed to hang the lousy crap up if the cheap bastard wouldn't give her the money for a clothesline? And even if she *had* a clothesline, like *Aud*rey and all the other *good* wives and mothers all seemed to come equipped with, just as sure as they came with their parts, she didn't have any clothespins—what was Katrinka supposed to use to hold the crappy shit up with, her ventriloquism?

Charlotte pulled the scratchy blanket higher up on her face, thought of the broken woman dying in filth under the stairs. Her eyes were squeezed shut. She didn't know, she murmured. She couldn't even guess.

The black night outside the window was the bottom of the sea where the ship still lay. White fish bumped up out of the darkness, hitting the cold glass. Everything there was white, naked, bloodless. The ship had gone down at a place so deep the sunlight could not penetrate. There was no need for eyes since there was no light to see by. The seaweed, too, was white, white as the moon, as sauerkraut. The tumblers were falling out of that black night, swirling down, as a man's body would after drowning. Some men had life jackets, a few were in rafts. Some had stayed alive for days with nothing, without water, starving, just by floating on the life nets. Charlotte didn't understand why one lived, the next died, why the girl with six months to live acted so delighted, so thrilled by her luck at winning a movie star make-over and the gold Cadillac ride.

The tumblers did it, John had told her, to look like prey, to lead the hawks away from the body of the flock. They dropped as if shot, as if they'd stopped being birds, had turned suddenly into the Wily Coyote—or into the dogs who had come for the sandwich and led Laddie west toward the trash cans on the esplanade, with its view of the sea. On that ocean, Winnie recited, he did sail sail away, in the year Aught One, to an island where the very air was perfumed by! *He couldn't breathe*, she screamed at Lionel, *with his ruined lungs!* She threw the poem she'd written at his feet. *Flowers!* she sobbed, running from the room. Winnie had always hated the smell of them, ever since that day when she was three.

"Queen for a Day" was over when the telephone rang. The kids were on the floor, finished with the sandwiches, watching the cartoons. The roadrunner went off the cliff, then came Bosco, then Betty Boop, then Bosco running again past the same things he always ran by: tree, rock, bush, tree, rock, bush. Then came the roadrunner again with the coyote discovering the law of gravity. The mountains did flow to the sea.

Then came the tumblers, falling down, then the slate blue beachies eating gravel for digestion, then the blue faces of the children running toward the TV screen. The faces melted as they came. The screams went on and on.

The burns and drowning killed the men most quickly. Shark bite was faster than being eaten by the other rapacious fish. Avarice: greed of the heart.

Katrinka has promised that Laddie was killed instantly. He was in the crosswalk but going against the light, and the driver wasn't charged. The dog, one of her mother's dummies liked to say, knows all languages but speaks none. There was not a single voice among them that might have been raised to warn him.

It was the night before the Valentine's party when Charlotte realized she had no cards. Katrinka was completely broke, and the five-and-ten on the Pacific Coast Highway was closed, so Charlotte couldn't steal them. She wouldn't go, she decided. She no longer went on Tuesdays, anyway, because of all the money she still owed the Girl Scouts of America, and she no longer went on Fridays because of the violin.

"Hush now, sug'pie," Katrinka drawled. "Hush now, yo'all hear? Yo baba's gwann fix you right up—dees'uns gwann be da bestest ol' Bal-en-tine dat ever BEED!" Katrinka was holding her cigarette between her teeth, clearing a place in the mess on the kitchen table.

Charlotte looked at her, not smiling at the Aunt Jemima. She hated homemade cards. Katrinka did creative economy, Charlotte knew, to demonstrate how artistic she was and how poor they were. Charlotte was ashamed of her, and ashamed, too, of being ashamed.

Sweeney had fallen asleep in his recliner in front of the TV. Now he came in to the kitchen with wrinkles pressed into his face on the side where his head had been lolling. His head was huge. His golden hair had been greased down, but it was so kinky that some of the curls had sprung loose. A few hairs stood up individually, like important wires.

"You coming to bed, or what?" he asked. Katrinka arched one eyebrow at the picture she was painting and did not look up. "You coulda least sent the kid to bed, you know it? She's got school." He said this without force, without the expectation of a response. For a while he'd been on a kick about her being such a lousy mother, but now he'd given up.

Katrinka lifted her head, taking a deep drag on her cigarette. The cool appraisal she used on the colors and shapes on the paper now shifted to Sweeney. Charlotte, too, looked up at him, but furtively, with her chin tucked in, so she saw the shadow of her own brow. Who did he think he was, anyway, telling her when to go to bed? All he was was some dumb man her mother had picked up in a bar in Hermosa Beach and had married just to give Lionel and Winnie the pip. He didn't have the right to tell them when to go to bed, even if it was his own house.

It was when he was in the wash of strong feelings that the smooth skin of his forehead rippled like that, all along from one side to the other, and then both eyes were yanked shut involuntarily, as if he had been shocked. That was the reason Gail Bill called him spaz, which had once made Charlotte feel a little sorry for him. Still, he wasn't her real father, and he didn't have the right to tell her what to do. He scratched his belly under the ribbed fabric of his sleeveless undershirt, then turned and plodded down the hall.

Katrinka was painting quickly now: roses, rainbows, bowers of flowers, nursery tales, anything else she could think of that was cornball, really really. She ordered Charlotte to get her another beer from the fridge and demanded more names, more crappy ideas—they needed, what? Thirty more of the goddamned things?

"They're pretty, Mom," Charlotte said, surprised that they looked like the paintings on real cards. She brought the beer and the opener, saying, "Maybe you really should go to work for Hallmark."

Katrinka didn't answer. Hallmark was beneath her contempt. What really gave Winnie the pip about Katrinka's being artistic, Charlotte knew, was that Katrinka never used her talent to make money. If she was going to insist upon this ventriloquist business, couldn't Katrinka at least come up with *attractive* dummies, the kind, like Charlie McCarthy, that might turn out to be popular? All Winnie wanted was for Katrinka to live a *normal, happy life.* Winnie's voice always tore apart on such words as these, as if even saying them made her wretched.

"Know where art comes from, sweetie?" Katrinka was asking. Charlotte's head was resting on her arms, which were folded on the sticky surface of the gray marbleized Formica tabletop—it looked like dirty ice. "Beer," she announced. "Beer, cigarettes, and starvation. When my estate is settled and we get my mun-mun and we are very, very rich, I am going to have one refrigerator with nothing but beer in it."

She didn't need one for food, Charlotte knew, because she never ate.

"Know why this isn't art?" Katrinka asked, tilting the painting in Charlotte's direction so she could see it without lifting her head. "Because it's all crappy lies." The painting was of boats in a sunset and looked real enough to Charlotte. "Most people, you'll find, are liars, Charlotte, and prefer things done up this way. But if *Awe-I* were *you* I wouldn't believe a single lousy word of it. One good thing about your father was he wasn't a liar. Another was he wasn't a sentimentalist."

"What else was good about him?" She asked this talking into the skin of her arm, too tired to raise her head.

"Oh, I don't know," Katrinka drawled. She stubbed the cigarette out into the top of a beer can, already overflowing with butts. She got up abruptly, lurched to the refrigerator, yanked it open. "He was extremely good-looking in a ritzy-fitz sort of way. He was much too handsome for his own good, *if* you know what I mean."

Charlotte said nothing. Her mother went right on.

"Because that was the reason so many of them wanted to go to bed with him, and I do mean women awwwnnd men. *If* you must know. Awwwwnnnd it was always because they were so deeply in love with him they couldn't see straight, which showed they were all a bunch of crappy liars. If they loved him so much, why didn't *they* live with him? Why didn't *they* bake him a chocolate cake?" She was rummaging in the fridge, then stood up, her hair standing out from the way she grabbed at it and yanked. She clomped to the table and splurted a new beer open against her palm, then licked the foam from her hand. "He was very intelligent, in that high-IQ-no-common-sense way your grandparents so admire. You know: *Pelican*, literature, architecture. He preferred the peasant type—he was very big on the hovels in Mexico. Anyway, he struck me as being very funny, when he wasn't cracking up over his masculinity, or counting the times he'd just used the pronoun *I*. At any rate, Charlotte, he was *your* father and *you're* entitled to believe anything you want to about him, but there is one story I definitely would not go by."

"Which one?"

"The one with the died-in-the-war sort of crap in it."

"Why not?"

"Because if there was one thing that your father did not do it was die in the war."

"How do you know?"

Katrinka struck a match. She sucked her cheeks in, thinking about this. She brought the match to the tip of the cigarette, saying finally, "He wasn't the type." She looked at the painting in front of her, which was Winken, Blinken, and Nod, and smiled. "The shittiest sort of crap," she pronounced it.

"So, what did happen to him then?" Charlotte was so tired that the words from the nursery rhyme were falling down like stars around her, washing her away, she thought, on a river of crystal light, off to a sea of dreams.

"Now, how in the world am *Awe-I* supposed to know?" Katrinka snapped. "Do you think the Blacks and the Ainsworths and the psychiatrists of the state of California would ever *deign* to tell me?"

Charlotte awoke the next morning, dressed in the same plaid dress she'd had on the night before. Her hair was disheveled, the braids loose and unraveling. Now, sometimes before the pledge of allegiance, Mrs. Brown would call Charlotte to the side of her desk and have her stand there while she combed and rebraided her hair.

Mrs. Brown's calm fingers had great patience at this task and didn't pull or tug. Charlotte almost always loved her teachers.

The shoe box she'd decorated at school with cutouts of hearts and snowflakes and cupids was on the foot of the bed, filled with Katrinka's valentines. These cutouts, Charlotte saw right away, were the worst sort of shitty crap—cupids, snowflake doilies, hearts. None of that was true, as she knew from reading *Compton's*: hearts had four chambers, snow hadn't fallen on Redondo Beach, California, since the last ice age, and what could be stupider than the thought of a baby flying around making people fall in love by sticking them with arrows?

She took out the first valentine, which was of a cute baby bird being fed a cute worm by its cute mother. Inside there was this rhyme:

> *Judy K-nudsen, you have the k-nack.*
> *You are the one who has what I lack.*
> *Judy K-nudsen, I'm on bended k-nee!*
> *Won't you please make me happy by marrying me?*

It was signed: *All my love, Charlotte.*

Charlotte squeezed her eyes shut. Judy Knudsen was a little white-haired girl who was so nearsighted she had to sit right in front of Mrs. Brown's desk—her eyelashes pointed straight down. Charlotte didn't even *know* her, let alone *love* her. The only good thing about her that Charlotte knew of was that she wasn't a Brownie.

Charlotte looked at the rest of the cards, which were all the same—pictures, which were *too* cute, too pretty for children she barely knew, then the poem that made fun of each child's name. Each card was signed *All my love, Charlotte*, which was a joke, Charlotte guessed, about the quality of her own love, that it went out promiscuously to all, and to no one.

Charlotte walked across the cold sand of the backyard to the alley, where the incinerator stood. There were soon going to be leash laws, Sweeney had mentioned, to keep the dogs from running wild in packs. There was going to be a new kind of trash pickup, so you didn't have to burn the papers or sort the bottles and tins.

She shoved the shoe box into the ashes of the old fires and started up the alley to the crest of the hill, gathering her sweater about her. She was going to the pier. She would ask the lady at the candy shack if she needed help packing saltwater taffy. She'd get some new books at the public library on the esplanade; the librarian always helped her.

On the way up the alley, she passed the crater in the middle of the Bills' backyard. It was twelve feet across and a foot deep at the center. It looked like something had fallen there from space, but it was really a hole for the swimming pool Gail was making the kids in the neighborhood dig out for her. The project had stopped the morning Maxine went on "Queen for a Day."

The last time Charlotte ever went to Tulita Elementary School was at the end of February. She walked alone down the alleyway, stopping often to yank the tops of her dirty socks back up out of her shoes. The trees had leaves already and were full of the crisp rasp of larval eating. Walking beneath the canopy of that sound made Charlotte feel sick, as if she were present at the heart of greed.

During the pledge of allegiance, the boy behind Charlotte, whose name was Frank, kept talking when the rest of the class finished, saying in a loud shrill voice everyone would hear: ". . . with liberty and justice for all *of the worms in Charlotte's hair*." Her hand shot up and she felt it, crawling at the top of her braid. Her fingers knocked it away. It was fat and green with blackish spots. It was big; it had heft. It was wrapped around a mulberry leaf, half devoured, as it curled on the floor.

The entire class was laughing, it seemed to her, as she reached down and picked it up, showing it to him in the palm of her hand. "*That*," she told him, "isn't a lousy worm—it's a caterpillar, *which* you would know if you weren't such a goddamned chicken-shitty little idiot." On the skin of her hand she could feel its moving legs and hairs.

For swearing, Charlotte was sent to the office. Katrinka was called to come and get her. Charlotte could see her from the office window, getting out of Sylvia's battered wreck of a car, dressed in one of Sweeney's old shirts, which she tried to shove down into the waist of her wrinkled skirt. Her lipstick was on crookedly. She moved her fingers through her hair trying to make it neat. Charlotte's face was on fire. "Mom!" she cried, as she went out the office door and waved wildly. The children in rows on their way out to recess stared from one to the other. "MOM!" she cried out, because Katrinka still hadn't heard her and was stumbling bewilderedly on the curb; it was making Charlotte weep to see her. "*Mom!*" she cried out loud, *loud*. "Mom! I'm right over here!" She turned around and told the people in the office, "There's my mother. My mother's here." Her voice was very loud.

A few nights later, the door banged open and there stood Katrinka silhouetted by the light from the hall. "There were no worms," she whispered urgently, as she came over to Charlotte's bed. "There were no worms, do you understand?"

"I know," she started to tell her again, that it was a caterpillar.

"I know because his mother called me. She was drunk, but she was telling me the truth, Charlotte—she was pie-eyed, but I believe her. She said they had his body cremated and the ashes scattered on a beautiful garden. All right, Charlotte? A beautiful garden." Katrinka's eyes were glittering.

The lady was standing on the concrete porch when Charlotte answered the door. The lady was wondering if Charlotte was ill or if there was some other reason she was missing so much school.

"Her floors, my dear, were so clean you could *eat* off of them!" a voice cried from the kitchen. That was Nellie Platter, she was *very* ritzy-la-di-da-fitz, half-baked in the upper crust. Like that.

"I'm watching something on TV," Charlotte told the lady, then tipped her chin up.

"You're here by yourself?" she asked, explaining that she was from County Services. Charlotte hung her head down, saying nothing.

She was looking at the lady's feet; she had on the most beautiful shoes Charlotte had ever seen. They were beige and brown pumps with an open toe and a strap around the back of the ankle. There were little pinholes in a pattern on the lighter-colored leather on the top. "Awwwwwnnnd then," Katrinka was saying from the kitchen table where she was ensconced with her entourage, "Awe-I decided to tell them my side of the story."

"They will never believe you, my dear," Nellie said.

"No one ever takes the word of a mental patient," Ogamer agreed.

"Would there be a better time for me to come?" the lady was asking.

Charlotte shrugged—she couldn't really think of one. She was looking at the lady's shoes, then at her own legs and bare feet, which were filthy. They were dark with dirt and spotted with scabs and open sores from the flea bites she'd scratched. The top of each foot, though, was dotted inexplicably with bright white circles of clean skin, where the dirt had been washed away by some event she could not remember—a sudden tiny drizzle of pee or rain?

"Shut up, won't you, and let me finish?" Katrinka asked. "We are discussing my mun-mun!"

"*Silencio!*" Nellie cried. Being delicate, she put all of her harsh words into either French or Spanish. "Ogamer, *cállate!*"

"So what Awe-I told Dr. DePalma and the rest of the goddamned fuck of them was that if Awe-I am NOT the honest-to-Hey-Sue reincarnation of Good Queen Bess and if Joey wasn't William F. Shakespeare come back to sleep with me, then why is it that they have always insisted upon paying so much attention to the two of us? Awwwnnd if I am, why amn't I rich?"

"Amn't?" Nellie sniffed. "Katrinka, really."

"Really *really*," Katrinka agreed.

"Is there someone else then?" the lady was asking. "Someone I could talk to? Could I call your father at his work?"

Charlotte looked up from her dirty feet and squinted at the lady with aching eyes. It was from the sunlight, after the days and weeks of reading, of being inside. "My father is dead," she said.

"Oh, my, I'm sorry!" the lady said, then reached out to touch Charlotte's hand. Her lips, Charlotte noticed, were rearranging themselves, pressing themselves together, as they composed themselves in sorrow.

Sorry—it was what Charlotte hated most about people, that they were so *nice* and they were so *sorry* and that their being sorry didn't do her the slightest bit of good. Charlotte couldn't stand the woman's sorry eyes on her another second, so she began to close the hollow door in her face. Still, Charlotte was sorry, too, for all the harm that she'd done, sorry for the lady, sorry for herself, so she felt she had to offer her something. Just as the door was clicking shut, she whispered, "Churchill 2–3226."

Lionel and Winnie arrived with a new Hoover upright, boxes of cleansers and Bisquik, cans of cream of mushroom soup that made a good, quick gravy. The mess by then was knee-deep in every room. Winnie took one look at it and went straight back home to Vista del Mar. The next day Lionel came back alone, having called a service.

While the cleaners were working, he took Charlotte and Katrinka shopping for new clothes and shoes, then to lunch at the seafood restaurant on the Rainbow Pier. He wouldn't eat in Katrinka's presence, but he did enjoy a cup of coffee with them as they had their meal, and used the opportunity to lecture them on his favorite subjects: probity, sobriety, punctuality, familiarity breeds contempt, and neither a lender nor a borrower be. As he spoke, Katrinka—though stone-cold sober and back on her medication—clicked open her handbag and shoved in all the crackers and rolls from the basket in the center of the table.

Lionel had bought Katrinka a white nurse's uniform. It was made from the kind of material Winnie so loved—Drip-Dry! Wash-and-Wear! Katrinka had it on, along with her new white shoes, size ten, and white hose that slushed in a rubbery way when she walked by. The ripple soles of the shoes eerily made no sound at all. This outfit went with the book Winnie had sent, which was called *Your Career in Practical Nursing*.

When Sweeney got home, the house was so tidy that he went out to get a pizza. Katrinka was asleep on the couch with her huge shoes on, but she woke up when he came back with the food and a six-pack. The windows were sparkling clean. The night was hot with the wind blowing in off the desert. Though it was February, it had the feeling of summer, and the kids were out in the yards, running around in their pajamas. These winds blowing the wrong way were what made people act up, Katrinka had told Charlotte.

But Katrinka, for once, wasn't acting up. She and Sweeney were getting along, discussing the Russians, who, they agreed, were very far ahead. The Russians had spies everywhere; Katrinka had been told about it at the university, where one of her professors had taught them about the conspiracy, diagramming it on the blackboard. It involved Jews, bankers, the telephone company, Washington, D.C. Sweeney nodded in perfect agreement. He knew all this from being in the navy. Why was he *agreeing* with her, Charlotte wondered, when he, technically, wasn't crazy?

He seemed to tick with happiness at his good luck: to go out one day with a mess on the floor you had to wade through, then to come home to this, a nice wife in a nurse's uniform, with nice white shoes. A good clean girl. The crazy colored Glass Wax finally off the windows.

Charlotte was acutely aware of the press of his happiness; happiness of any sort, particularly her own, tended to make her nervous. Sweeney was so happy, she decided to tell him a joke. "Go like thith," she said, demonstrating how he should hold the tip of his tongue between his fingers and thumb—Gail Bill had showed her this. "Now, say: 'My father works in the shipyard,'" she instructed, taking her fingers away.

"My fathah workth in the shityard," Sweeney said, then a hot look swam up into his eyes as he heard what he'd been made to say.

"Very clever, sweetie," Katrinka told her, lighting a cigarette, wagging out the match.

"Who taught you to talk like that?" Sweeney asked her.

"I wasn't the one who said it," Charlotte reminded him.

"Who taught you talking like that's funny?" he asked, his voice rising steadily. "It ain't funny in *my* house. You wanna grow up with a mouth like that?" He motioned with the coils of his hair in Katrinka's direction, pronouncing the world *mouf.*

"Do as I say, honey baby, awwwnnd not as I do." Katrinka sucked her cheeks in, to act serious and to show her deep sophistication.

Go like this, Charlotte could not help herself from thinking, though she liked Sweeney, though she felt sorry for him. Mou*th*, she would tell him, enunciating carefully, turning her head to show him the proper placement of teeth and tongue.

Sweeney's face was bright, hot-looking. "Shaddup," he was saying. "I don't wanna hear any more of it from you."

"Oh, Jesus," Katrinka drawled. "I do believe we have offended his *fine* sensibilities."

"Shaddup!" he yelled. "I never heard a worse mouf on no one!"

"Oh, you shut up," she told him calmly. "You shut *the fuck* up with your goddamned fucking moralizing."

"Go like this," Charlotte then did chime in. "Mou*th*," she said, placing her tongue just so.

Sweeney slapped her. She felt it, heard it, saw her braids flop, one landing, then the other. Then he was turning to strike her mother. The blow was loud; it sent Katrinka out of her chair. She flew back and fell against the wall, sliding down to the floor. She didn't get up. Instead, she reached out to pick up her still-burning cigarette and remarked to Charlotte, calmly, "Go next door and tell Sylvia you have to use the phone. Churchill 2–3226," she added.

"I *know!*" Charlotte cried, already out the door.

The Crustanzos called the police, who got there before Lionel and Winnie. The cops went in, followed by Sylvia, Tony, and Charlotte, all afraid of what they'd see. Katrinka was still sitting on the floor with her back to the wall—her huge feet were sticking out in front of her. That, Charlotte knew, was because of foreshortening, which she'd learned about in one of the Walter Foster art books Winnie had given Katrinka to try to get her to use her drawing talent normally. Walter Foster was beneath Katrinka's contempt.

Sweeney and Katrinka weren't fighting. Instead, each was drinking a beer and talking amicably about the Russians, about which

public figures were undoubtedly pinko-reds. Sweeney was sitting
backwards on his gray vinyl tube chair, with his arms folded along
its top. He was chewing the crust of his pizza, which he put down re-
spectfully when he saw the cops.

"I shouldn'ta hit her," he said, looking up. "But I got sick of it.
The place don't look so bad right now, but it was headed that way.
You shoulda seen it. She ain't no better'n she was. Tomorrow she'll
be back in the aisles down at the Frontier Market, carrying on with
the prize in the box of Wheaties." Katrinka tipped her chin up,
amusedly.

"She's the worst mother I ever seen," he went on. "The kid didn't
own a pair of shoes—I'd give her the money for 'em, but she'd drink
it up. The kid don't go to school, but *she* don't care." He paused,
looking down at Katrinka. "The kid never gets dressed. She wears
her pj's all day long, hanging around reading books about the navy.
You ever heard of it? A little *girl* who don't care about nuffin' but war?

"So I tell myself they got a rough deal, wif them up in Glendale,
which is doozies, by the way. Which is why I ain't already booted
'em out. I even buy the kid a bike, but she would never tell you that,
no, sir. She don't have it. She thinks she mighta *left* it somewhere—
she don't know. She can't *remember.* Or that one pawned it—what
can I tell ya? It's like what they say—you just can't help some people.
I get that one a brand-new bike, cherry red, wif everything on it, but
she don't notice—too busy standing up at the top of the street,
going blind from staring out to sea. And I get this one a forty-eight-
piece set of Melmac, in four tropical colors. Know what she does wif
it? They're plates, so they get dirty, am I right? So you're supposed
to wash 'em. She don't know about that. They get dirty so she shoves
them in the oven, one by one. *Then* she gets tanked up and—outa
the goodness of her heart, I don't know what I did to deserve it but
believe me I could live without it—she *decides* to cook me *dinner,*
right? Know why this place stinks to high heaven? Because she
turned the oven on to broil. Forty-eight pieces in four tropical
colors, all melted together, the smell of which ain't *never* gonna go
away."

Katrinka had sucked her cheeks in, considering this. She sniffed, and licked her lips, and tipped her chin up, and as she did she caught Charlotte's eye.

Charlotte, too, then lifted her chin. She, too, had her cheeks sucked in, and she held her upper lip down over her teeth, to keep from looking too openly triumphant. It was hard not to smile at it, not to laugh out loud, as they watched each other, their faces lengthened with the struggle against the hilarity that rose up at the mere thought of it: that, Katrinka's finest wifey moment.

III

THE AIRSTREAM

Early Summer, 1962

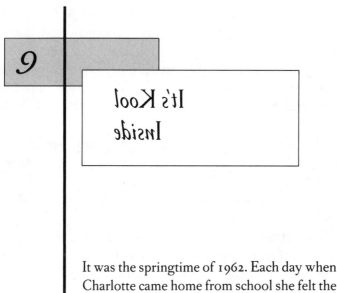

9

It's Kool
Inside

It was the springtime of 1962. Each day when Charlotte came home from school she felt the light grow more palpable. The air, too, seemed to be expanding. Lionel sat in his red leather chair, his fingers groping outward. His fingertips tapped out to take up his pack from the cigarette stand. He smoked while he waited for her; as he smoked, he formulated what it was he wanted to tell her that day. Each afternoon's talk was on the examples set by the lives of the various saints: Horatio Alger, Luther Burbank, Charles Dickens, Herbert Hoover. Or Ike—Lionel did like Ike. Charlotte thought of these talks as "Lionel's Farewell Lectures." They always began in the same way: "Now, Charlotte, I am of the opinion . . ."

"Now, Charlotte," he told her one day, "I am of the opinion that it is possible for a person to live an exemplary life."

"Not in *our* family!" she said out loud. It made no difference that she spoke back to him now, since he couldn't hear her, and he couldn't see that her lips were moving because he now talked to her with his eyes shut.

Winnie said Lionel was keeping his eyes closed to preserve what vision he had left. She told Charlotte that the house on Vista del Mar was an agony for him, the way the light came apart on the beveled edges of the diamond-shaped panes where they met the window's leading. In the afternoon before the sun was down behind the hills to the west, the light was extreme, streaking in brightly colored beams—scarlet, sapphire, or turquoise—through the motes that hung in the air. This afternoon sunlight, in the long moments it spent streaming between the limbs and leaves of oaks, made the smoke of his cigarettes a dimensional thing, thick and well delineated as it swirled upward, like a constant spill of milk.

Winnie told Charlotte that the light was the reason he kept his eyes closed, but Charlotte knew it was really that he could no longer stand the sight of her.

The red leather chair, the one brought home from the bank, stood in front of the portrait of Lionel done in oils by Joshua Winslow. The painting was also from the bank, a formal life-sized, full-figure portrait of Lionel sitting in the same red chair, with the same smoking stand placed next to him. The brass plaque set into the ornate frame read, "L. E. Ainsworth, President." All these years later, Lionel looked very much the same, except that the fat cigar was replaced by the thin cigarette, the chestnut hair was gone, and the eyes were now shut. The portrait caught Lionel so perfectly that a teller had once supposedly approached it while it was leaning against the wall waiting to be hung and had asked it for a raise.

Now, as Charlotte stood in front of him biting her bottom lip, chewing the flesh of one or the other cheek, she looked not at the Lionel before her but at the younger, handsomer one on the wall. He was funnier, then, she saw; his gray-green eyes were full of amusing secrets; all the pie he had probably just been eating, she thought, and other things.

Now, Lionel was off Ike and was onto all the reasons they could no longer take care of her. Winnie was not a well woman. Dr. Greenley was becoming frankly worried. Winnie had not had a vacation in more than forty years. Lionel had hopes of Winnie's getting to go to Hawaii—that was her lifelong dream. She wanted to visit the place where her father had lived while he was dying. It might be possible to convince her to travel, Lionel said, now that there were the polyester blends, which packed so well.

Charlotte was old enough to begin to shoulder the responsibility for her mother. Her mother was going to be Charlotte's burden when Lionel and Winnie were no longer alive, so she might as well begin to get used to the idea. Mr. Dukey would instruct her in the legal aspect of things; Charlotte would find his advice to be invaluable. He would administer the conservatorship, as he'd done for the Ainsworths. Also of great help was Mr. Dukey's legal secretary, whose name was Helen Keller. Charlotte should not hesitate to telephone her.

"Call up *Helen Keller?*" Charlotte asked out loud. She couldn't wait to tell her mother the news: the blind actually *were* leading the blind.

Katrinka could not inherit directly. It would be Charlotte's responsibility to manage things so that Katrinka would be cared for in her old age.

"You mean her *estate?*" she asked him. "My estate" was what Katrinka called her mun-mun, also everything else of value that she imagined was being withheld from her: the insurance from Joey's death, the paychecks still owed to her by the phone company, the bank accounts held in trust by Lionel. There were other things, too, including the body of her husband, his physical person, which had inexplicably vanished from her presence one Wednesday morning as she baked a cake, though his voice was still occasionally to be heard—this was the body that may or may not have been lost at sea, may or may not have been retrieved, may or may not have been cremated and the ashes scattered in a beautiful garden. There were other bodies, too, such as that of Katrinka's infant daughter who was taken from her while still nursing because Lionel and Winnie didn't think Katrinka was capable of caring for a baby properly, and *they should talk!*—they'd then stuck Charlotte in a shoe drawer! Dates were also being withheld from her, also certain facts, pieces of history, whole chunks of memory.

"So I want you to understand that we are thinking of this summer as a trial for each of you. I would like each of you to get used to the idea. Your mother has never understood that the world does not owe her a living. I would like for you to encourage her to try to remain employed." He smacked his lips on the phrase. "The world owes no one a living," he went on. "Your grandmother is not a well woman. Neither of us is going to live forever." She saw him pausing between sentences, listening to their cadences. When he came to the last one, he delivered it well, sonorously but with great good humor, never believing for an instant that it happened to be true.

When Katrinka came to get her, she was driving a brand-new 1962 cherry red Impala convertible with its top down. The car was pulling a shiny aluminum trailer so tall it scraped the lowest leaves of the oak canopy as it came rumbling down El Tovar. She stopped the car with the trailer pulled only halfway around the corner—it would have blocked traffic if there'd ever been any to block.

It was June, a day so hot the air above the roadbed shimmered and bounced, radiating bright shards of light from the silver metal and red paint. Katrinka, too, seemed to shimmy in the heat. Vista del Mar and Lionel and Winnie were all in a dusty olive drab. Katrinka came there as if from a different movie, one being shot in Technicolor.

Charlotte was watching her mother from below the level of the roadbed, hidden by the curve of metal at the opening of the culvert beneath the dirt road. The stream was dry, as it nearly always was. Charlotte stood on its sandy bed, resting one arm on a granite boulder, her ankles itching from the sharp foxtails and the brittle bits of oak leaf that had worked through her socks. She'd come from Patsy's directly down the slope, straight through the brush where there was no path. She didn't really know why she'd done it—she was too tired to think of reasons. She was too tired to bend over, to get the stuff out of her socks. It was only ten in the morning, and she was so tired she could have gone to bed.

The place where she stood seemed to have too much gravity, too much air pressure, as if she were way below the surface of the sea. As she looked up along the steep sides of the house, up the steps, up the tall rows of the diamond-paned windows and the steep shake roof, it all seemed to loom and wobble, as if her looking at it so intently could bring it all down. She was eyes only, these days, eyes and lit-up brain. She saw it all and understood it, too. The looming, she understood in her perfect lucidity, was a sensation known as *vertigo*. She also knew that the wobble was in her and not in the things around her. She knew, too, that the great mental clarity she had these days came from her being so terribly hungry.

Hunger made the air dance and sharpened her sense of smell. There were, for instance, three different and specific dusts she could smell just then—the sage, the oak, and the dust of the granite itself disintegrating. Hunger made animate the natural world: the mica on the granite where her arm rested popped and winked and sizzled against her skin. The brush all around was throbbing, pulsing with the buzz of cicadas.

The only thing wrong with being hungry was the tiredness— that, and the fact that her mouth was too dry to speak. She was too tired, just then, to get out of the streambed, climb up, and say hello to her mother. She was too hot, and she was wearing too many clothes; she had layers and layers of them on, all things she'd been hiding at Patsy's from Lionel and his trash fires.

It seemed to Charlotte that her mother's outfit, too, had been chosen with Lionel and Winnie in mind. Her pants were a pair of khaki trousers that weren't just "mannish"—they looked as if they really were a man's. She had on a big khaki shirt, too, so she looked like she was going on safari. The shirt was open down the front to where the top of her bra showed. She had on ripple-soled sandals, so much like Lionel and Winnie's they had to have been chosen to make fun of them.

Katrinka's hair seemed very red. The skin of her throat and the underside of her chin were pearly and faintly green in the light reflected from a silky scarf she wore knotted around her neck. Where did she shop, Charlotte wondered, to get a thing like that, a scarf made of silk that pulsed in the bounding light like a wave of melted emeralds? Woolworth's, probably, she instantly decided.

Katrinka had started toward the steps when she got out of the car, but Lionel, who was hiding in the cool shadows of the stone garage, went to the bottom step to intercept her. When he got in her way, she went back to the car, reached down to the seat and brought out Ogamer. She jutted her hip out and placed the dummy there, sucking her cheeks in, lifting her chin to him, ironically.

Lionel came toward her silently and took her upper arm in the grip of his long fingers. Together they began to walk the perimeter of his property—this car, this trailer he had bought for them to live in. He kicked gingerly, with one sandaled and stockinged foot, at those things he imagined he ought to kick at: hitch, sewer hatch, tire. He marched her along, then began to talk to the side of her face, rocking her slightly in rhythm to the lecture. Dangling from Katrinka's hip, Ogamer's legs and shoes wagged back and forth in the same rhythm. Katrinka, Charlotte could see, was listening to the hum of something else.

Lionel, still lecturing, took a fat roll of money from the pocket of his trousers and offered it to her. She was gazing up the steps, her lips slightly parted, her face looking ardent, she was so expectant, so he and the money failed to capture her notice. He forced open the fingers of her one free hand and put the wad of bills into it. She stuffed it into the pocket of her shirt, where it made a bulge that was comic and suggestive. His face lengthened at the sight of her contempt for him, and he began then, in earnest, to scold.

She wasn't listening, Charlotte could see, but the words were gaining force, were so loud, so percussive, going *I-me-I-we! Winnie! Winnie! Winnie!* that he could be heard over the roar of the cicadas. Ogamer had begun, slyly, to open and close his mouth to the same beat. Katrinka, however, wasn't doing his voice; Charlotte could see that there was no strain in the muscles of her mother's mouth and neck, where the voices always showed. Katrinka was a great ventriloquist, a genius at it; still, as with the best of them, her lips did move over the impossible sounds—b, f, m, p, and v—which was why the dummies were so important for the illusion. Now her lips were still, shiny with lipstick, her face was shining, too, as it turned toward the stairs.

Because Katrinka wasn't attending to him, Lionel had begun to rock her harder. His fingers, Charlotte could see, were dug into the muscle of her mother's upper arm. As he dragged her closer to his face, his hard lips brushed the hair over one ear. Her face was still turned toward the stairs, and it then occurred to Charlotte that it was Charlotte herself whom Katrinka was so intently waiting for. She thought her heart would break: to have a child and to be so far away from her! to have a father like her mother's was! The only thing worse than having no father at all, she knew, was having one like Lionel.

"Mom!" she cried, as she scrambled up out of the gully. "God! I'm sorry I'm so late! God, I'm sorry! I got here as soon as I could—I came straight down the hill from Montecito!"

"Sweetieheart!" Katrinka cried out. "My baby!" Then, as they held each other, Katrinka asked, "Why are you dressed like that? You look like a mental patient."

"I'll tell you later," Charlotte whispered. "Don't mention it, all right? Okay?" She was thinking, *I could say the same about you half the time, except I'm too polite.*

"She looks like hell warmed over!" Katrinka cried, looking in Lionel's direction. "What is going on around here—have you two been ganging up on her again?"

"Just skip it, okay, Mom? Mom!" Charlotte whispered urgently. "All right? Let's just get out of here!"

"Your mother," Lionel was pronouncing, "is not a well woman."

Winnie came down toward them then, right foot, right foot, watching her feet. She was carrying two big brown sacks from Safeway, which held Charlotte's things. It looked like she was bringing down the trash.

Lionel, frowning, hands on hips, gazed up at the sky. His eyes were gone, Charlotte saw, erased by the glint of sunshine reflected off the surface of his glasses. His lips were pursed into a small dry pucker. It made him look like he was whistling, though no song came out.

Sugarman's was playing the San Diego County Fair at Del-Mar-by-the-Sea. Lionel had given them maps of Los Angeles, Orange, and San Diego counties, which he had gotten from the Triple A, and he had informed Charlotte that she would do the navigating. But Katrinka didn't go by maps. It was easy to get to Sugarman's, she said; all they had to do was follow the water south.

Once on the Harbor Freeway, Charlotte began to take off the layers of clothes. On top she'd been wearing her UVA sweatshirt; she and Patsy had made these themselves with sewn-on letters. Charlotte had told Winnie the initials stood for the University of Virginia, where Patsy's cousin went to school, but they really stood for the club they had invented, the United Virgins of America. Patsy and Charlotte were the only members.

"Slide over here and steer," Katrinka suddenly ordered her.

"I can't drive!" Charlotte cried. "I haven't even taken driver's education!"

"Don't argue with me, Charlotte. I can't see—I have to get this hair out of my eyes." She was trying to undo the knot in the scarf at her neck.

"But, I don't know how to steer!"

"Oh, you do so—you just don't know it. Just aim at that horizon," Katrinka told her. "Drive toward the place you can't yet see, and you'll go straight there." Charlotte held the wheel while her mother undid the scarf, then used it to tie her hair back. The hot wind through the car whipped the ends of it, which were dancing like fire.

"So is that it, sweetie?" Katrinka asked, eyeing her. "You've decided you're above the eating aspect of things?" Charlotte squinted her aching eyes, looking away, wondering how Katrinka always managed to know everything. "There isn't anything that'll land you in Camarillo faster than deciding you don't need to eat. That's what happened to me on Avenue B. Going on the beer and cigarette diet."

"I'm not on a diet," Charlotte said. "I just couldn't stand the food they tried to make me eat. The peanut butter, you know? The liverwurst? And Lionel's mush. Winnie got so mad she took me in to see Dr. Greenley, to get him to tell me about how your body goes backwards and you turn back into a child. She's always trying to get him to tell me the Seventh Day Adventist facts of life."

"Dr. Greenley said your body goes backwards?" Katrinka said.

"That's completely psychotic. You don't grow *down*, Charlotte. You grow up. At least you try to."

"He isn't crazy, but he did shoot himself with the Novocaine once, when he was trying to give me a shot so he could take a wart off my thumb. He's just old, so his hands shake and his head trembles. You know?" Grace, Charlotte was thinking, His grace.

"D.T.s," Katrinka pronounced. "Camarillo's full of the D.T.s, Charlotte, something I hope *you* won't forget."

"I don't know, Mom. Seventh Day Adventists don't drink."

"Charlotte," Katrinka went on, "Camarillo is *full* of people with the D.T.s who never touch a drop. Some of my best friends are Seventh Day Adventists and they all drink like fish. Let me tell you something—it is perfectly easy to go crazy, if that's what you're up to. The hard part is staying that way. You get locked up easily enough, but then there you are, listening to all of Ward G-1 ranting about whatever it was that landed them there. Mun-mun, usually. Getting a little wild with the Charg-O-Matic down at the Jolly Boys Liquors." Katrinka looked over. "I am perfectly serious, Charlotte. What a person usually needs is a nice cup of tea and a hot bath. What you get when you go to Camarillo is shock treatment—you understand me?—when what you needed was a wash and set, and to go out for a lobster dinner."

Charlotte looked over at her.

"So remember that next time you're tempted to get yourself locked up. Charlotte! Are you listening?"

"All right!"

Katrinka fumed, muttered, then announced after quite a long while, as if they were still in the same conversation: "Meanwhile, we are stopping for lunch!"

They pulled off the freeway at Huntington Beach and right into the parking lot of a coffee shop. Katrinka was actually good with the Airstream, Charlotte saw, now that she was out from under the scrutiny of Lionel. She backed the trailer expertly along the fence, turning her head to look over her shoulder, her arm lying along the top of the seat. With Lionel and Winnie watching, on the other hand,

Katrinka had decided to turn the car and trailer around in a space that was too small to accommodate it. When she had backed up, the trailer had shot off at a right angle so far out over the air of the culvert that it had seemed it was going to pull the car into the rich lady's yard across the way.

Katrinka got out, then reached in and grabbed Ogamer and Nellie. "Get the other two, will you sweetie?"

"I guess," Charlotte said to herself, "if I must I must."

"Each of us *is* worth several hundred dollars," Nellie sniffed.

"And someone pro'bly would steal me," Miss Priss added. She was blonde, blue-eyed, a child-star type. It was by Miss Priss that Charlotte usually felt most implicated. The fourth dummy was Buttercup, who was the most innocuous. Like Miss Priss, he was blonde and blue-eyed. He usually stuttered, but sometimes he lisped instead, singing "Thum one's making gingerbread," like Laddie Bill.

"D-don't you l-l-like us?" he asked her.

"Mom?" Charlotte called as she carried the dummies in, following behind her. "Mom? Could we discuss something? Mom? I don't think you understand—it isn't *them*, I mean the *fact* of them, or Space Radio, or whatever you call it. It's that I can't stand it when they talk to me, you know? When they insist that they're *real?*"

But Katrinka wasn't listening. She had stopped on the asphalt and was waiting while a low-slung car waited, too, for her to cross in front of it. It was a rusted white DeSoto with ruined shocks. It was driven by a sun-battered cowboy in a dirty white hat, who touched the wide brim of it and told her, "After you, ma'am."

"Oh, God," Charlotte groaned aloud.

Her mother, cheeks sucked in, was crossing in front of the man, her head held high.

"She thinks she's too good for us!" Miss Priss complained. "She thought she was too good for Avenue B!"

"Too hoity-toity," Nellie agreed.

"We were all too good for Avenue B," Katrinka said, as they came to the back door of the coffee shop. "We're too good for this dump, too, from the looks of it. I can't stand these sorts of orange-and-cocoa color schemes. Is it intended to be appetizing?" she asked, as they went in.

"How am I supposed to know?" Charlotte said.

"I thought you knew everything," Katrinka said as she threw her two dummies down into the booth and swung into it herself.

"She d-does!" Buttercup cried. "She m-made honor roll!"

"Mom! Could you just please not have them talk about me?"

"You heard her, all of you. I want all of you to hush up this instant! Stop picking on your sister! You're making her self-conscious!"

"Mother," she said, through clenched teeth, "I am not their sister." She dumped the dummies and slid in opposite.

"Be that as it may . . . ," Nellie was saying.

"Do you do this in your act?" Charlotte interrupted. "Make fun of your own *family?*"

Katrinka sucked her cheeks in. "Only when I'm hard up." She started patting herself all over looking for a cigarette. She came to the bulge of money and pulled it out with her fingertips, letting it fall in the center of the table.

"Don't you think you should put that away?" Charlotte asked.

"Why bother?" she replied, through the smoke of her cigarette, wagging out the match. "Everyone knows my business soon enough anyway."

The waitress frowned down at the money as she gave them water and the menus. The people at the table across from them eyed it, then one another meaningfully, Charlotte saw. Her face was heating up.

"Want to know the words I live by?" Katrinka asked.

"What?" Charlotte asked her, grudgingly. She was, she knew, greatly in need of words to live by.

"L.S.M.F.T.," Katrinka said, smirking as she inhaled.

"Very funny," Charlotte said, snapping the menu up in front of her face.

"That's right," Ogamer announced. "It was rather funny, I thought."

"It was not," Nellie said. "It was perfectly meaningless. You cannot say something that is perfectly meaningless and imagine people will laugh at it."

"It *means* something," Miss Priss said. "It *means* 'Lucky Strike *means* fine tobacco.'"

"You c-can always say it over again," Buttercup offered. "S-sometimes things are f-funnier the m-more they're re-re-re . . ."

"Katrinka!" Ogamer thundered. "Your mother is not a well woman!"

". . . peated! Yes, in-dee-da-deedy, Mr. Tweet-tweet-tweedy!" Buttercup said, in birdsong.

"The matter with Katrinka is she doesn't always know if people are laughing *with* her," Miss Priss informed Charlotte.

"Are you laughing with me?" Katrinka asked, reaching out to touch Charlotte's hand with four of her own cool fingers.

"I'm not laughing at all," Charlotte pointed out. It was the cowboy; he was passing along the window just then, looking at Katrinka. When she glanced up, he tipped his hat to her.

"Oh, those men in hats!" Nellie exclaimed. "They make me so nervous, Ogamer!"

"Well, you *have* to laugh," Katrinka said. "Otherwise, it'll drive you crazy. Besides, if there is one thing both of your parents were, it was funny, Charlotte. I was always very funny. I was so funny I'd be writing for *The New Yorker* by now if I hadn't turned out to be so mentally ill."

Along the plate glass window where the cowboy was passing, someone had painted animated hamburgers, mud brown, big as car tires, dancing with yard-long French fries. Above their heads the words proclaimed: !ƎDISИI ꓘOOꓘ S'TI, one word per window. It was, Charlotte knew, the law of gravity: get on the Harbor Freeway and you end up in one of two places, either Vista del Mar or Avenue B. The cowboy was sauntering through the first glass door. Now he was opening the second.

"Get the shrimps!" Katrinka ordered.

"I hate seafood."

"You do not hate seafood. Charlotte! I want you to eat something and I want you to stop criticizing, immediately!"

"I'm not criticizing."

"Then what's that beat, beat, beat of the tom-toms we all hear?" Ogamer asked.

"Cowboys?" Miss Priss whispered. "Cowboys and injuns?"

"Now, when Awe-I," Ogamer was saying, Britishly, "went out to In-jaw . . . "

"The word, Katrinka, is *shrimp*," Nellie interrupted.

The waitress was back, then, to take the order. Charlotte, glaring at her mother, said she wasn't hungry. "I'll take the shrimp. Or is it *shrimps?*" Katrinka asked the waitress, smirking as she looked up.

"Ya get five of 'em, so big. Ya get the house salad, thousand or blue, and the fries and the bun on the side, and a little thingie of cocktail sauce." She tapped the menu's colored picture.

Katrinka lifted one eyebrow, looking at Charlotte meaningfully. "How *fun!*" she announced with great purpose. "I'll have *that* and my daughter will have the cheeseburger combo and a chocolate milk shake."

"I don't want a chocolate milk shake."

"Have it," Katrinka ordered. "It's good for your complexion."

When the waitress turned away, Katrinka lit a new cigarette and said, "Charlotte, there is no reason for you to worry about the sort of impression we may or may not be making, do you understand me? This is not Soviet Russia, or wasn't the last time I looked, and it isn't even 3142 Vista del Mar, where you get locked up for looking at people cross-eyed. What this is, in case you haven't noticed, is a lousy shitty little coffee shop in some dump of a beach town filled with people whose opinions of us do not matter one iota."

"I know, Gervaise," Charlotte agreed. "It's Avenue B. Look at the Glass Wax on the windows. And here comes Sweeney now."

Katrinka turned around. "Charlotte! I have never seen that man before in my life! I wish you wouldn't talk like that—it makes you sound like you've gone completely off your rocker."

The cowboy was coming toward them at a tilt, one shoulder carried higher than the other. He stopped to hitch up his jeans. "I meant speaking *metaphorically*," Charlotte said aloud. She was talking to Mr. Greenbaum, her honors English teacher. Katrinka didn't go by

metaphors—this thing being *like* that one—she only went in for *is*,
Charlotte knew: tree, rock, bush.

"Why is it that people's opinions matter so goddamned much?
Don't you realize you never ever see them in your life again?"

Charlotte heaved a great sigh. She was thinking of those people
she'd never see again: Mr. Greenbaum, and Bob Davidson who
danced with her so slowly, holding her so tightly, but still hadn't
even gotten around to kissing her, and Patsy, and even Bingo, the
mooing black poodle shape cut out of the lawn.

Then, suddenly, perversely, she began to miss her grandparents.
She missed the smell of Winnie's Colonial Dames face cream and
the hard little jab of a kiss Winnie launched at her in saying good
night. "*Schlafen Sie wohl*" was how Winnie always said it—*Sleep you
well*. This was the single phrase Winnie still retained from the first
weeks of a course suddenly canceled when the U.S. had entered the
First World War, and all the native speakers of German had been
fired by the university.

And Charlotte missed Lionel, the younger one, the one who had
once read to her, the one who watched the six o'clock news on TV as
part of his perfect day. He sat in the red chair to watch it. His favorite
part was the end when they said, "Good night, Chet," and "Good
night, David." He waited the whole program through, just for that
moment.

"And good night, Li-o-nel," he reminded them. Then he would
haul his long body out of the chair, and, chuckling at his own good
humor, would begin his blue-tinted trudge to the set.

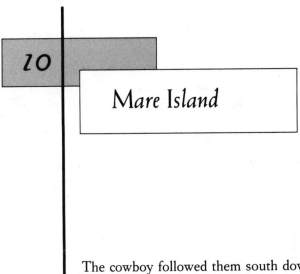

10

Mare Island

The cowboy followed them south down the coast highway to Del Mar, invited by Katrinka to come along in order to help with the sewer line and the electrical hookup. He also did the leveling. He knew all about leveling trailers, he had told them, from his days hauling animals to and from various rodeos. Animals die of bloat, he said, unless they are transported right, to which Ogamer had replied, "I am certain that is quite true, young man. I am quite certain that you would be justified in saying the same of any of us. I am of the opinion that there is a profound truth lurking here about all of human nature," at which Nellie had screamed out into the air of the coffee shop, "*Bloat?* I mean, Ogamer, really! *Bloat* and human nature!"

Katrinka had never heard of leveling. It was mentioned in the manual Lionel had given to Charlotte to read—if the trailer wasn't parked on the level, the refrigerator would begin to scream. Charlotte tried to read the booklet, but it was difficult, full of rules, tips, and dangers, words so fearsome they made her eyes veer off and her heart leap up, words like *propane tank* and *voltage regulator*. Charlotte and her mother were both terrified of electricity, of all other power sources. Then, too, Katrinka flatly refused to be bossed by reference materials of any sort, including the backs of cake mix packages, which tried to tell her what to do without informing her why or how.

Katrinka wasn't concerned about leveling, as she told the cowboy after it was accomplished. She was used to living in places that were off kilter, so to speak. The house in Silverlake that she and her husband had moved into when they were first married was tilted so badly the eggs she cooked for breakfast had a ridge along one edge where they'd been wedged against the side of the pan. *You knew this once?* Charlotte thought incredulously. *You knew how to cook an egg for breakfast?*

The cowboy had done her hookups and, in return, Katrinka was going to make Sugarman give him a job. Sugarman did whatever Katrinka told him because he was in love with her—he also happened to owe her quite a bit of mun-mun, which really gave Roxie Sugarman the pip. Now, Roxie Sugarman was a *real* Wilma-or-Thelma.

The three of them were in the Airstream in the late afternoon: Katrinka and the cowboy were sitting at the fold-down table drinking beer; Charlotte was lying on the sofa trying to read. She'd taken several books from the Glendale Public Library without checking them out. She had a new one on the *Indianapolis*, one called *Abandon Ship!* She didn't check these books out because she knew instinctively that they belonged to her. The light against the plaid curtains made the air seem like water in a hot green sea.

"The trouble with Roxie," Katrinka was saying, "is that *all* she really cares about is lawn furniture. She's much worse on lawn furniture than Maxine was on that goddamned garage." Charlotte read on, trying to ignore her. Katrinka seemed only vaguely aware of the cowboy, as if he were part of a larger, more general audience, one who understood who Maxine Bill was, an audience that was interested, or was at least listening courteously. Tree rock bush, Charlotte thought. The cowboy was learning everything about her mother, from start to finish, although the story didn't proceed with first things first. Instead, the story came explosively, as if the whole thing were packed into every sentence, as uranium had been stuffed into the bomb, with all the subatomic particles ready to come apart and fling themselves out and out and out. Maxine equalled Roxie equalled Wilma and/or Thelma—tree, rock, bush.

About him they knew nothing, aside from his name, which was Wade Winters, and the fact that he referred to his DeSoto as "the Sled." He talked about it as if it were a ship, feminine and somehow alive, which made him sound either babyish or insane. Charlotte thought he didn't actually believe it, though, that if he were given a lie detector test, he could be made to admit the DeSoto was nothing but an old and rusting car. If he were given a lie detector test, she imagined, he could be made to tell if he intended to rape and/or murder them.

"When Roxie Sugarman goes on 'Queen for a Day' what *she* prays for is always to have me fired. Charlotte! Are you listening to me? I want to tell you something about hearts and souls of women! They hate each other! Charlotte, all that Kappa Kappa Gamma type crap to the contrary, women are never happier than when they are the hostess with the mostest in terms of lawn furniture. My psychiatrists all think it's penis envy, Mr. Winters, but it isn't the penises women are interested in, past a certain point. What they care about is having the biggest and best garage.

"Which, Charlotte, was why all of my best friends at Cal happened to be men, and I am discussing Becky, too, and Madge. The only woman who ever truly loved me was Becky, and she was a lesbian. I have nothing against lesbians, Charlotte, except that I really would prefer for you not to marry one—I can't stand all that immaculate conception sort of crap that they love to go by. Believe me, there is nothing all that *immaculate* about it, isn't that so, Mr. Winters?"

"Her floors, my dear!" Nellie cried out. Katrinka whispered back to her.

"Excuse me?" the cowboy asked. He frowned, rubbed his cheek, tipped his hat back farther on his head. He had, Charlotte saw, all the elaborate and distracted courtesy of the chronic alcoholic. Other drunks were always one of her mother's favorite sorts of types.

"You don't agree?" Katrinka asked him. She was getting up, stomping to the little refrigerator to get each of them another beer.

"I'm not sure I understood the question."

"The point is this—that when my husband died, Mr. Winters, I was living in Silverlake and my friends were all still up at Cal. Arch was there, and Becky and Madge and the rest of *Pelican*, everyone except for Watson, who'd graduated and gone east and was married to a Connecticut type who used to shop at Town and Country, but moved to the Village to try to be more interesting than she was, which was not remotely. Am I now being perfectly clear? So there was no one around when I started cracking up, aside from the Ainsworths and the Blacks—who were even worse than Lionel and Winnie in their own not-so-subtle way.

"Awwwnnd when I called Becky or Madge, they thought I wanted to go to bed with them. When I called P. I. or Watson, their wives hung up on me. It was Watson, Charlotte, who took me to Jones Beach. He took me out to the beach on Christmas Eve to discuss having an affair. He said he would have had an affair with me at Cal had it not been for his abiding love for your father, and I told him they *might* have talked it over with *me!* His wife couldn't stand me. They were living in the Village because she was trying to be a painter—she was perfectly lousy at it. Their apartment was all one room, like this dump, to illustrate how poor they were when she was really rich as hell. Awwwnnd so people would be forced to look at her crappy paintings. The bed was in the center of the room to make a point of some risqué type—they had a black and white kidney-shaped coffee table and a fuzzy black bedspread, made of dog fur, I'm sure. They drank martinis with onions instead of olives. Talk about Wilma-or-Thelmas! My point is this, Charlotte: it wasn't s.e.x. I was looking for after your father died—it was friendship. But it's impossible to be friends with a man after he is married. Roxie will never allow it! Sugarman is the chief psychiatric resident around here but *she* is charge nurse! You should see it all, Mr. Winters!"

"Sorry?"

"Her goddamned lousy lawn furniture. The nurses are the absolute worst, believe me—they're the ones who make you play Scrabble when you'd much rather lie on your bed, smoking and talking out loud."

"I thought you liked to play Scrabble," Charlotte said. She was still trying to read. She was still thinking, *tree rock bush.*

"It isn't that I *like* it," Katrinka said. "It's just that if I *must* I *must*." She said this grimly, then was up again, opening and closing the cupboard doors, all of which popped out satisfyingly, then clicked firmly shut. The name of this model was the Tartan Squire. Everything in it worked, fit, matched. It was all done in red and green plaid, a decor Katrinka had groaned over, pronouncing it "*pure* Sears and Roebuck, *pure* Monkey Wards." She yanked open a cupboard where the dummies lay on their backs, as if in state, on shelves designed with a lip for cans. "Now which one of you little bastards took my cigarettes?" she asked, then explained to the cowboy, "I hate them all equally."

"You put them in the drawer next to the stove," Charlotte reminded her.

Katrinka stomped over, took a pack from the drawer, ripped it open, and bent over to light it on the blue gas flame of the stove. "The problem," she announced, inhaling, "is always what to do with the non-normal. Now, my parents, being Republican, believe mental patients ought to go kill themselves out of civic pride, as part of the war effort, and to save the taxpayers mun-mun. But then my parents are pretty non-normal themselves—I really mean it, Zero Sub Minus. They just get away with more because they're richer than I am, and for some reason I have never been able to figure out they are less conspicuous.

"But what do you think, Mr. Winters? I mean you're an intelligent man, and well educated in the School of Hard Knocks sort of crap your type likes to brag about. Do *you* think we ought to close the mental hospitals?"

"Pardon?" he asked, craning his neck out to place his face over the top of his beer so as not to spill, not to offend. His eyes were the faded blue, Charlotte saw, that came from staring hard and without intent. The furrows etched into his brow were permanent, pinched in by studying the broken line down the center of an endless, glaring highway. His face and neck were deeply tanned, a pebbled reddish brown.

"My role, I'll have you know, in their lousy little morality play was Star Mental Patient. I was the most interesting one they had ever had—DePalma's always made a point of telling me that. Talk about being written up by Walt Disney! His first name was *Donald* and his maiden name was *Duck*." She slammed to the refrigerator. "As in *quack!* It was those chits," she said, "for the fucky little *tasks* they invented that made me tender *my* resignation. What they liked to do was refer to it as art *therapy*, though it had nothing to do with anybody's ever getting any better. If he was so great a doctor, why didn't anybody ever get any better?"

"But you were good at the art classes," Charlotte said.

"So what?" she asked, narrowing her eyes. "Charlotte, I have been on Ed Sullivan—I don't work for chits. Anyway, the art they all did was so mental patienty, *if* you know what I mean. And so is Thelma Watson's, by the way, though she does it like that on purpose to try to be interesting. Her painting is about as interesting as this floor." Katrinka motioned with the cigarette toward the green-and-red-and-black-spattered linoleum. "She should stop wasting her time with all *that* and go back to playing bingo with Roxie and Maxine, really really."

"You were on Ed Sullivan?" the cowboy asked. He looked at her with his weak blue gaze, squinting over the bright metal of his beer can.

Katrinka sniffed, jabbing the cigarette out. "I wouldn't be too overly impressed by Ed Sullivan, if I were you, Mr. Waters. Ed Sullivan isn't so high up in the muckedy-muck that *he* can lord it over the rest of us in terms of his personal life. That we should be all *that* overly impressed by him. I mean, Ed Sullivan had a few problems of his own. It's just that as with the Blacks and Lionel and Winnie—the problems have never been diagnosed on the front page of the newspaper."

"Such as what?" Charlotte asked.

"Oh, never you mind, Missy Miss. You'll find out about all that soon enough, won't she, Mr. Waters?"

"Winters," he told her.

"Or whatever it is you're going by these days. Just let me tell you this about that," Katrinka said. "A really big *shoe* is not what Ed Sullivan's problem happens to be!"

She talked to the cowboy until the beer was gone, then she threw him out. She gave Charlotte a fifty-dollar bill and sent her after corn dogs on the midway. Outside, in the clear sea air, away from the smoke of the cigarettes, Charlotte was amazed to see that the sky was gathering into an ever more luminous blue and that, beneath this pulsing twilight, the carnival was being invented out of the dark and mounded shapes of tarps on the backs of trucks. The shadowy half-dressed men moved slowly, their skin suddenly glistening as they were hit by the truck lights. The carnival was going up almost silently, with only a few sharply barked orders, groaning heaves, clipped words, grunts. As with all cities and villages, the carnival was constructed of little more than will, Charlotte saw. This was one place built only to be pulled down again. It was a little town assembled temporarily with lanes fanning out from the huddled shape of the racetrack and its low rows of stables. It was made out of nothing but the strings of naked lights swinging out from the poles as they were yanked up, and the sounds of greased machinery, and the heavy smell of fuel, the masculine fumes that caused her to breathe in deeply even as they made her sick.

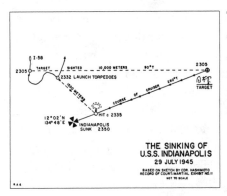

THE SINKING OF
U.S.S. INDIANAPOLIS
29 JULY 1945

The ship was built twice: once before the war, then again at the end of it, when radar was added to the superstructure. Still, it had no air-conditioning and was ill-equipped for war in the Pacific. It was hit by a kamikaze at Okinawa and might have been sunk then, except that the captain, Charles Butler McVay, was able to save it against all odds. Nine had died, in addition to the kamikaze pilot. Charlotte's father hadn't yet been aboard.

The attack by kamikaze was the reason the men were stationed at

Mare Island while the ship was being repaired; its being available was the only reason such an old, slow ship was chosen to carry the uranium to Tinian. That was the summer that Katrinka, Madge, and Becky were sharing the place in Benicia, while they counted out old rifles at the arsenal. That, Katrinka liked to say, was their contribution to the war effort—as coeds, they'd learned to count to ten. They could also count backwards from one hundred, having practiced with all the bottles of beer, beer, beer in the cellars of Eshleman Hall.

No one on board the *Indianapolis* knew what the cargo was, even Captain McVay. The ship had delivered the uranium and was steaming home, zigzagging by day but not under the cover of darkness. It was top-heavy after the retrofitting; when Admiral Spruance saw it at Mare Island, he had remarked that it would sink like a shot if it ever took a direct hit. On the night of 29 July 1945, shortly before midnight, it was hit by two Japanese torpedoes, and it sank within twelve minutes. There were 1,153 men on board.

This event was important, Charlotte knew. There were a number of different accounts of it, but the years had gone on, and now no one paid much attention to the drama of the story—how the location was so precisely marked in the sub commander's log, how Lieutenant Commander Hashimoto himself was brought to Washington to testify, how he told how he had broken radio silence to report the kill to Tokyo. He read a poem from his log into the records of the court-martial. He reported what his men had had that night in celebration: eel, sweet bean curd, beer, sake. He'd been in the war since Pearl Harbor but had only just received this command.

Three hundred men died of burns immediately or went down with the ship. Eight hundred men, it was estimated in each of the various accounts, were alive, however, when they went into the water. The cruiser, because of secrecy, had no escort, so there was no one to pick up survivors. There were different versions of the story regarding the SOS: no distress signal ever went out, or it did go out but was garbled in transmission, or it was picked up and read at Pearl Harbor but never relayed to Leyte, where the cruiser was expected.

When the men went into the water, they were hundreds of miles from the nearest land. Only two boats were launched; each was capable of holding thirty, but the choppy seas dispersed the men so widely and so rapidly that neither boat was even filled. Each had capsized during launch: the caches of food and water were lost, and neither boat was left with oars or medical supplies. Some of the men in the water were in life jackets, but the equipment was old, and many of the jackets had lost their buoyancy. Most of the men simply dangled from the life nets.

The ship had no sound gear that might have detected the submarine; it had been built for colder wars, ones fought on northern seas. It was out of kindness that McVay had ordered all watertight doors and hatches left open for air circulation. Most of the crew had gone naked to their bunks or were wearing only shorts. McVay himself was naked, he testified. For the act of keeping the hatches open on that hot night, he was charged with laxity in failing to secure the ship. Because it wasn't buttoned up, seawater rushed from compartment to compartment, which was why it was so quickly swamped.

The standing order for the fleet was for all ships to zigzag when there was the possibility of enemy sighting, but that particular night was so dark, because of a thick cover of clouds, that the men on watch had trouble seeing one another's faces. Survivors testified to this and Hashimoto corroborated. The moon, according to his log, rose at 2200 hours, by which time McVay had already gone to bed.

Hashimoto was at the periscope on such a dark night only because he was too anxious to sleep, afraid the war would end without his having made a kill. He had been at it for so long, his eyes seemed to be conjuring the shape of the dark ship on the faint horizon; then the clouds drew apart for an instant and he saw the shape grow darker and more defined: the cruiser lay five and a half miles away, silhouetted by a single moonbeam.

He was so awed by his luck, as he told the court, by the event's foreordination, that he was moved to write the words of Mitsune in his log to remind himself to be humble before fate. All *I-56* had to do was wait, and the cruiser itself would steam into position. Then he remained lucky: though he had it directly in his sights, he had overestimated the *Indianapolis'* speed, and fully four of his six torpedoes missed. Still, the final two were clean hits, one forward, the last shot amidships. He saw the line of lights erupting on the waterline, then saw the flashes spread. It was just before midnight that the shape of the cruiser was altered abruptly in his scope. It rolled toward him, before slipping quickly beneath the surface, less than an hour after his initial sighting. Hashimoto had done nothing but watch and wait as the skies grew brighter. The cloud cover was breaking up and the moon was full.

In his jubilation, he signaled Tokyo. When he went to his bunk at dawn, after drinking sake and quoting poetry with his men, he dreamed of a hero's welcome. But, as he steamed home, he was not told of Hiroshima, Nagasaki, of how these words had suddenly loomed up, positioned themselves mightily in every language. When he stepped ashore twenty days later, he was shocked to realize his country was so stunningly defeated that it had completely forgotten him.

When their ship was sunk and the eight hundred men went into the water, it was as warm as a bathtub's on the surface, though their legs and feet dangled down into the colder current. They would not be overdue in the Philippines for another two days—no one aside from Charlotte missed them, and she hadn't even been born yet. Charlotte hadn't been born—still, as a full moon or as a comet or as another celestial event she did witness it. She was a shooting star, the tail turned backwards, the hot and furious length of her going first through the heavens, pulling the fist-sized shape of her hurt and iciness down with it into light. The men, she observed, floated there without food or water. The fuel oil had blackened all their faces; only by their voices could they tell themselves apart. There were hundreds of cabbages bobbing with them, which were also covered with sludge. The cabbages looked almost as much like men as the real ones did.

The fuel oil was still burning in patches on the surface of the water. The men continued to die of burns, of other injuries. They drowned as the sodden life jackets gave out. They died of exposure. Still they held hands as they were buffeted by the winds and waves, and they sang; the men sang and at first the cabbages did not sing back.

The current carried them outward from the site of the sinking in an ever-widening whorl. McVay, who happened to be in one of the boats, was carried to the very edge of the massive slick, and so could see a few of his men but he couldn't get to them. When he was picked up and stood on the deck of the rescue vessel, he was shocked to look out over the miles of devastation; the sea was like a great black plain with all its floating bodies. The cabbage heads still bobbed. It looked to him the way he'd imagined Gettysburg.

It was on the second day that the sharks came, and then the other rapacious fish. It was when they realized that the SOS had not gone out that they began to die of despair. It was on that second day that they began to kill themselves. It was on the third day that they began to kill each other.

It was easy to go crazy, as Katrinka always said; the harder thing was to stay that way. There were enemies on the lines among them: these were the Japanese. The killings were orderly. The Japs were tried and found guilty by a jury of their peers, stripped of rank and their life jackets, held underwater by their hair.

Their final delusion was of their own city all lit up like Christmas, their *Indianapolis*, resting just beneath their feet, having sunk in shallow water. She had air for them; she had fresh water gushing from the taps. There was food set out in the galley. When they all fell silent, they could hear the sound of it: the throbbing of her mechanical heart. The engines were still at full ahead when she had gone under. She had not abandoned them but lay just below the surface, brilliantly lit. She was paradise. One by one they slipped out of their life jackets and went back down to it.

No search was ever mounted. The oil slick was spotted accidentally by the American plane, flying alone and far off course. It took a day and a half from the time of that sighting for the first help to arrive. By then only two hundred twenty men were still alive. In the accounts, the survivors referred to themselves as "personnel."

At the court-martial, McVay was charged with having failed to issue a timely order to abandon ship. The engines were at full ahead because the lines were down, and he was unable to get word to the engine room, except by runner. He had issued the order to go into the water eight minutes after the first torpedo, when he had heard the sound of the hull breaking up. The ship had shuddered each time it had thrust forward through a swell, he told the tribunal. The engines were shoving the ship forward, scooping tons of seawater into the ruined hull. This was another reason it sank so quickly.

McVay was also charged and found guilty of having failed to zigzag "in anticipation of moonbeams." He was convicted, although Hashimoto was brought to Washington to testify that, since fate had arranged the event, the ship's zigzagging would have made no difference. Hashimoto used the notes in his log to show what he meant. He had actually sunk the cruiser accidentally; he had overestimated its speed and had hit it with only two torpedoes but was in such a good position for the strike that he could not miss. Had all torpedoes failed to hit, he still had the *kaitens*, the torpedoes that were more accurate because of their human pilot. The *kaiten* was infallible—a torpedo ridden by a man as heroic as the kamikaze. And even had the ship been zigzagging, the submarine was so much faster it would have overtaken it on any probable course.

There was public outcry over the huge and needless loss of life. There was another public sentiment: that Captain McVay, having lived when nine hundred of his men did not, had suffered enough. He was found guilty, stripped of rank, then restored to full rank, but only after the ordeal of the trial.

What Charlotte could not stand about the case of the *Indianapolis* was this: that as the days went by and the oil slick spread and the men lost their minds and they and the cabbages still bobbed there equally, and they tried on the first day to help one another, and they lost heart on the second day and began then to kill themselves, and on the third day began to kill one another, the U.S. Navy had known all along exactly where they were.

Hashimoto's message giving the true and accurate position of the cruiser and the class of ship it had been was picked up immediately, relayed to Pearl Harbor and almost instantly decoded. There

it was analyzed, then discounted without checking. For days the
men bobbed there, still alive at 12°02′N, 134°48′E. A day or two
later the message was relayed to Leyte, where, though the *Indianapolis* was now due, it was again discounted. It was as simple as this: the
U.S. Navy was not in the business of taking the word of a lousy Jap.

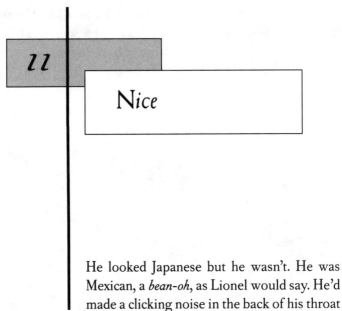

22

Nice

He looked Japanese but he wasn't. He was Mexican, a *bean-oh*, as Lionel would say. He'd made a clicking noise in the back of his throat at her that was causing her insides to wither, like a leaf curling in a fire. His hair was jet black, greased back. His teeth were white and perfectly straight. He was a ridesman, putting together his kiddie ride. "Wanna go on it?" he asked her, pitching his voice low across her path, tossing the words like pennies.

"No, thanks," she told him. It was for two-year-olds; it had frogs, ducks, doggies. She held her beach towel to her chest to cover up the letters on her sweatshirt: *UVA*. The letters were bright red and slanted. Everyone always assumed, from the look of them together, that they stood for something dirty.

She was coming back from the beach where she'd been lying out, getting tan, observing the behavior of other, more normal teenagers, ones who weren't mistaken for two-year-olds. One girl surfer had yelled at the boy who'd cut her off on a wave, "Hey, Burlingham! You asshole!" Charlotte was so entranced by the throaty sound of the girl's shout over the crashing water that now she wanted to meet an *asshole*, just to be able to call him that.

This ridesman wasn't it. He was handsome to the point of beauty, which was not Charlotte's sort of type. He was too old for her, way older, all the way up in his twenties. His flirting seemed deadly serious, as if something might actually come of it. His eyes were copper-colored, brown with gold flecks, slanted, squinting in the strong light. He was too good-looking. Even his long brown fingers looked dangerous.

"You decide you wanna ride, then you come see me," he was telling her, the words low, accreted with meaning.

She fixed her face to look pained, to look like a stuck-up high school girl from Verdugo Woodlands. "Sure bet," she said, then tsked. As she walked by him, she could feel his eyes on her; she could hear only the swack, swack, swack of her rubber zoris as they hit the flesh of her heels.

Sugarman was DePalma, did Charlotte understand that? He was chief psychiatric resident, deciding who got shock treatments, so it was best not to get too palsy-walsy. Katrinka and Charlotte had eaten a dinner of junk from the concession stands and were now walking back to the Airstream, while Katrinka continued the lowdown. Charlotte's skin felt tight with sun. She was thinking of the ridesman's eyes, of the way they had rested on her. The cowboy and the DeSoto seemed to have vanished, to have rusted away, which also raised Charlotte's spirits.

Even the smells were hopeful: popcorn, salt air, the day's heat evaporating, the tarry smell of the still hot blacktop. They were passing by the glass box of a vendor; he shoved a paper cone into the box and a cloud of cotton candy materialized from the flying threads of fluff. The filaments were white at first, turning pink as they cohered. She stared so hard the man thought she wanted it. "Gratis," he said, as he held one out to her.

"Take it!" her mother ordered. "Charlotte was brought up not to take candy from strangers," Katrinka was telling him, "but you remember old Pete, don't you, sweetie?"

"Not really," Charlotte admitted. He was an old man who looked older because he was toothless and grizzled. His clothes smelled of heat and burned sugar. She pulled a big piece of the cotton candy off the cone and stuffed it into her mouth; it melted immediately. She was staring away into space, wondering how her mother imagined that she'd been brought up any one way at all.

Calliope music was plinking down from the speakers above them. Beyond the games in rows in the Fun Zone, the roller coaster was up and running empty, the cars rattling along in a businesslike way, then falling in a loud swoop. The track ratcheted them back up the steep ascent, then the cars pitched out and off the back way, like an organized suicide. "Sure bet," she said aloud.

Katrinka was now on the concessionaires, how they generally considered themselves very high up in the muckedy-muck of this particular fleabag Dogpatch, big as A. P. Giannini, who had started out with a pushcart too, historically speaking, except that his was full of mun-mun. These concessionaires owned their own little wienie stands, their crappy Tilt-a-Whirls, but the truth was this, if Charlotte *cared* to realize it: Sugarman *was* Sacramento, and all he had to do was throw anyone he wanted off the lot and they'd be out of business. There was no one to work for anymore aside from Sugarman & Associates Amusements, and the associates were all Roxie Sugarman and her lawn chairs. It was Walt Disney who had ruined the carnival business—Disneyland didn't have freaks; it had Mouseketeers. Talk about mental patients! Had anyone taken a good look at Annette recently, all grown up and still wearing those goddamned ears?

All Disneyland was good for was a person like Lionel, who was so sick he *believed* in it; it was *Main Street* but written by that crappy Horatio Alger. It was *nice*, and all that: no freaks, no Negro pick-pockets. It was the threat of Negro pickpockets, Charlotte knew, of the long, dark Negro fingers, that kept Lionel and Winnie from going most places, including Dodger Stadium. Disneyland, Katrinka was going on, was the worst possible kind of lousiness, built on a dairy farm out of actual cow manure. Walt Disney was the type of mental patient only interested in the truly infantile—smearing pooh-poohs on baby bottoms for s.e.x.—like that. All this, she wanted Charlotte to realize, was historically accurate, since things that were historically accurate were Charlotte's top favorite sorts of issues these days.

Charlotte's hands were at her face, her fingers pressing to keep the sight out. Her mother kept on talking, while Charlotte went off somewhere to think about things other than old men and babies' bottoms. A few moments later, when she felt it was safe to pay attention again, she spoke up to agree: "It is," she said. "Disneyland is pure Normal Rockwell." She was sucking the grit of the last of the cotton candy from her teeth. The paper cone was gone from her hands. Missing it, she understood that she had littered. This tiny Katrinka-like act had been accomplished entirely without consciousness—Lionel and Winnie would never commit such a gaudy, public crime. Charlotte had done it while ghost walking beside her mother—she walked along as if she were in a trance. At times like this, when her attention came unhinged, she was capable, she felt, of doing nearly anything.

While she'd been gone, she'd been imagining. She was thinking of Lionel, of how Katrinka used to say his face as a boy had been painted by Normal Rockwell, with the big brown freckles placed there one by one. Charlotte understood this two ways: that Lionel had actually posed for the true-to-life Norman Rockwell, as he later had for Josh Winslow, and had had his portrait done in oils. But it also meant this: that Norman Rockwell had conjured up Lionel's boyhood face. Charlotte experienced this from inside the skin of him, feeling the thrill of the wet touch of the pointed brush applying the paint of the cheeks, the freckles.

"Hey! Katrinka! Brink me dat chilt!"

"Oh, shit," Katrinka said. "It's that crackpot Kreminski. Ignore him, Charlotte. He thinks we're related to him."

"Related!" Charlotte had never met anyone she was related to aside from her grandparents and Great-Aunt Hoppy and Little Winnie. She had only been to Orange to see them with Katrinka, since Winnie was still mad because Little Winnie had been named after her, then turned out to be an imbecile. Still, as Katrinka liked to remind her mother, it had been intended as a compliment, besides which, Little Winnie was a very *high-IQ* type moron, since she was an idiot savant. Little Winnie could play Chopin, or anything else she heard, from memory. The only trouble with that, as Katrinka pointed out, was that she had only ever heard that one lousy nocturne.

"Because our names start with the same letter, or we both refer to ourselves as Awe-I, or something equally deranged on the subject of *identity*," Katrinka was adding.

"Vait!" he cried, "I haf sometink!"

"Oh, Jesus God!" she yelled. "All right! If I must I must!" She grabbed Charlotte by the upper arm and marched her up the steps of a tiny trailer. It was snail-shaped, balanced on bricks at its hitch, and it rocked with their weight.

"Charlotte, this is Herr Kreminski—Kreminski, this is Charlotte. She's my daughter; he's the ringleader of the circus, a really big *shoe!*" she said, and smirked.

As her eyes adjusted to the darkness, Charlotte got the joke: Herr Kreminski was a dwarf.

" 'Lo," she told him. He was pressing something moist into the palm of her hand.

"I am makink you tea," he said, "to go vif your sweet."

"Tanks," Katrinka told him, "but ve ist never touchink the shitty crap." Under the influence of the dwarf, her stance, too, had become vaguely European: leaning back against the wall with the sole of one foot flat, she held her hand fully cupped over her mouth to smoke and breathed out rapturously, eyes veiled à la Dietrich, à la Garbo. "Vile," she added, "*ve* ist on the subject of *identity!*"

Charlotte held the article of food, which was already warm from his hand—she was trying to give it back. "Thanks for the muffin or whatever it is it goes by, but my mom and I just ate dinner. Then she made me eat this whole huge thing of cotton candy, you know, not to he rude, so I just can't have this because I'm too stuffed. Plus I'm on a diet. Thanks, though."

"Rude, schmude," Katrinka said. "Forget it, Charlotte—what is it you're so worried about? He isn't listening. You aren't listening, are you, Kreminski?"

He didn't answer. He was watching Charlotte intently, with dark, bright eyes and lips that were slightly parted. The bottom of his face was pushed in, which at first made him look young, cute, puppyish, like a Pekingese, but then she saw that the skin all over his face was finely wrinkled, as in extreme old age. She took a small bite of the muffin, which tasted like honeyed clay.

"You do voices?" he asked her, on tiptoes, whispering up to her.

"No!" she shouted, so loudly that he jumped back.

"But she is in the school play. Now finish that so we can get out of here."

"I am not!" Charlotte told her. "How can I be in the school play if I don't even know which school I'm going to be going to yet?"

"It doesn't matter one iota," Katrinka told her. "They all do the same lousy crap: *South Pacific* for the musical and *Death of the God-damned Salesman* if they're stuck on the pseudo-intellectual. I never could stand Arthur Miller."

"Why?" Charlotte asked her. "Did you ever meet him *personally?* What's wrong with him? Is he some kind of an *asshole?*" She felt suddenly uncontrollable, as if the voice coming out of her were someone else's—a real teenager's.

But Katrinka was going right on: "Your father and I actually preferred Arthur Murray, who taught us dancing in a hurry. We preferred the funny ha-ha, Charlotte. Musical comedy might have been okay for us song-and-dance type Lunts, you know, like that, except we both drank too much to ever remember our lines, and neither of us could carry a tune in a lousy bucket. He did play the piano. He was much better than Little Winnie—at least he knew Cole Porter. Musical talent is obviously something you have not inherited. My God, the sound of that violin screeching on Avenue B was sending me right back to the mental hospital, which is the real reason why I pawned it."

"You never told me that."

"I didn't want to hurt your feelings."

"Thanks," Charlotte said, her cheeks hollowed out by this news.

"Well, really, what do you want me to do, lie to you?"

"No, but I still have feelings!"

"Ist zat zo!" she told her, sniffing, "as our small frient here vud zay."

"I haf an act," Kreminski was whispering, conspiratorially—for this was the opening he'd been waiting for—"vere it's *all* small, you know? Pygmy horses, I got? dachshunds? Ve hat a girl but she was no goot—too bik. Do you like horses?"

Charlotte sighed her huge sigh. "Well," she sighed again. "I guess not really. I mean anyway not *that* much, you know? Not like some people. Like when I was in the fourth grade most of the girls thought they *were* horses, you know, sort of, and my best friend was *really* good at it, with the neighing and tossing her mane around?" Kreminski, she saw, did not know what she was talking about; still, she went on talking. "I used to ride my imaginary horse over to her house so we could ride to school together, imaginarily, I mean, but then I had stuff to do so I never really remembered to ride it home. Sugar was what I named it. So in the morning, I was home but Sugar was still at school, if you believed in it, I mean. I never really believed in it, but I couldn't really ride it to school all over again, you know? I think it's just that I never liked imaginary things as much as some people—for instance, I never had an imaginary friend."

"Are you quite finished?" Katrinka asked. "Or are you going to give him your whole personal history?"

"You should talk!" she told her mother, who was marshaling her toward the door. "Thanks for the watchamacallit. Anyway, I can't do the job because I'm still growing. Everybody in my family is really tall. My father was six foot three."

"Von tink ve notice," Kreminski was telling them, "in this place, this California? Dat you are drifing and drifing down a different road, and you are alvays comink to dat same Safeway."

"I know what you mean," Katrinka told him as she marched Charlotte down the steps.

"My vif ist dere now." Kreminski was following them. "You

come another time and she ist tellink you your fortune. You're very lofely, not too bik. And you have your fadder's eyes."

"What do you mean by that?" Charlotte yelped, deeply startled. It was like the time she had first heard the expression *Ah, your fadder's moustache!* Her father, as far as she knew, was clean-shaven—she had no way of understanding what the saying was intended to mean.

"He means," Ogamer's voice boomed down, "that his brain has been pickled by alcohol!"

"Ogamer!" Nellie shrilled. "I cannot stand it one second longer. If you insist upon applying the nervous pressure I am going right straight back to Camarillo!"

Still, because Kreminski was holding one of her hands in both of his and because his eyes were still on her and looking at her so expectantly, she could not leave. His fingers and the pads of his small palms were plump and dry, utterly smooth and without muscle. Like Lionel's feet, they seemed as if they'd hardly been used. "Come back," he whispered, "so Celestina can tell your fortune."

"All right," she whispered back. "Bye-bye."

Katrinka was already out and down the steps. "You will do *no such thing!*" she told Charlotte. She was scuffing the sole of her ripple-soled sandal back and forth in the gravel. "Gum," she told her, looking down.

"But did he actually ever meet him?" Charlotte asked.

"What are you talking about?" Katrinka asked sharply.

"You know, what he said? About my father?"

"Of course not." She was still scuffing.

"Well, I was only wondering because I never really met anybody who actually met him, except you. And Lionel and Winnie, of course. Did Aunt Hoppy and Little Winnie come to the wedding?"

Katrinka stopped scuffing and stood with hands on her wide hips. "I know it," she said. "I know I never should have married him, but would you please not start in on how your life is ruined? I'm sorry that your father died and that your life is ruined. I formally apologize."

"I wasn't aware that my life was ruined," Charlotte said. "I mean, absolutely."

"Well, you should see your face go through the floor every time the word is mentioned. If you think it is so gawd-awful wonderful to have a father, take mine, why don't you? Or go back to Sweeney— he at least had bikes!"

"All right," Charlotte said. "You've made your point." No one could compete with Katrinka on the subject of wretchedness; it was one of the rules of their lives.

"It's all my fault."

"It is not your fault."

"Don't argue with me—it is! It's my fault, for instance, that the Blacks never paid any attention to you. They were mad at me, but they took it out on you. My advice to you on the subject is to grow up, get rich, join the Chevy Chase Country Club, give a luncheon, and *not* invite Aunt Nan. The trouble with you is you blame yourself."

"Aunt Nan?"

"Old bean," Katrinka said. "Your father's sister."

"Mom?" Charlotte was saying, her voice going high up, getting breathier. "Mom? Know what? You don't have to take it *personally?* Know that? You just take everything so *personally.*" Charlotte told her this all the time, so she didn't have to think about the words as she said them. What she was thinking was *Aunt Nan, old bean!* and how she would look her up in the phone book. Still, with her luck with relatives, this aunt would probably turn out to be another idiot savant of one type or another.

"What other way is there to take things?" Katrinka asked. "Besides, think about it logically, the way you're so big on. What would your father be doing slumming in a dump like this, knowing a midget like Kreminski? Your father graduated from Cal Phi Beta Kappa."

Aunt Nan, Charlotte was pronouncing, *you don't know me, but I wonder if you'd like to meet me for lunch at the country club?* She was talking out loud, too, telling Katrinka, automatically, "He isn't a midget. He's a pituitary dwarf."

"What's the dif?"

"Actually, there is a difference," Charlotte said, then suddenly interested in the conversation. "A midget is perfect in proportion, with six or seven heads to the body, whereas a dwarf seems to have a big head because . . ."

"No," Katrinka interrupted. "You misunderstood. I meant, what *the fuck's* the difference? I mean in the whole hellish light of the world?"

This, Charlotte thought, *is what I will go to my grave hating about you, Mother. You are only interested, ever, in the thing you've just said, or are saying, or are about to say.* Aloud, she told her coldly, "Actually, I learned about that in my anatomy and physiology class, and some of us, who *are* in the honors science program, do happen to care about the ways things are different rather than just the same, *Mother.* Which you wouldn't know about. Things start out the same, but they do not necessarily end up that way. The rule for it, in nature, is *Ontogeny recapitulates phylogeny,* really really! And my father was not a Kappa because college sororities do not happen to take men."

Katrinka threw her head back then and laughed out loud—something she hardly ever did. They were in front of the Airstream by then, each facing west toward the sun, which was going down hyperdramatically behind the contorted black shapes of the Torrey pines along the rim of the cliff. Katrinka's throat was stained magenta. "All right, Charlotte," she said. "you win. You are the one who is absolutely right about midgets. Now are you satisfied?"

"Or is it shrimps?" Nellie inquired politely.

"I never knew these things, Charlotte," Katrinka went on, "and they are *very* interesting, although the honors science type crap, delivered as a speech, does make you sound a little cracked, so I'd watch it if I were you, unless you want to turn out to be a schoolteacher. I don't know anything about anything—why should I? I've had seven series of shock treatments. But I do remember this: a kiss is still a kiss, *awwwnnd* you are to go nowhere near that trailer."

"He was nice," Charlotte said. "He only wanted to give me a summer job."

"They are always *nice,*" Katrinka said, and the word came slurring out of her, smeared by a drunkenness that couldn't be, since she had not been drinking.

Charlotte's eyes dropped to the tops of her tennis shoes, which she wore without socks when Winnie wasn't around to worry about fungi. Tennis shoes were supposed to be a little dirty, so they wouldn't look new, but these were getting grungy. She observed them with a welling sadness, wondering how Katrinka imagined the two of them would ever be able to accomplish such a thing as the laundry.

"Charlotte! Answer me! Do you understand what I am saying?"

"Yes."

"Well, then, as long as we understand one another, that you are the expert on certain things, science and history among them, and that I *am* the mother around here and that you are strictly forbidden from going over there, let's not be downhearted." She raised Charlotte's chin with the three dots of cold that were the tips of her fingers. "Want to know what he once told me?"

"Who?"

"The dwarf, of course. What else were we talking about? He said he never drinks a *think* but water." She smiled as Charlotte brought her face up.

"What's so funny about that?"

"Welllll," she drawled, "as he was saying this he was fillink his teacup and my own with vodka, sayink, 'Wadka, my darlinka, ist da Russian vort for vater, but dis ist da vater in vich da fish don svim!'"

"Ho-ho-ho," Charlotte commented.

"Well, really."

"I know!" Miss Priss said. "I have the best idea: let's let Charlotte be the boss of history, of science, and what is and is not hilarious."

"I will be the boss of that," Ogamer said.

"What I have always thought," Nellie said, "would be *hilariously* funny would be to have George Gobel come out in front of the curtain on his show, all dressed up in bubbles to advertise his commercial sponsor Dial soap? I wrote out the idea on a three-by-five card and sent it to the television studios. He could sing 'Life Is Just a Bowl of Cherries.'"

"T'aint funny, McGee," noted another voice. This was the new one, low down, gravelly. This was the one who had no body.

"God, Mother," Charlotte said, "don't you ever just get sick of yourself? Do you have to make something *funny* out of everything?"

Katrinka jutted her chin out. "I'll tell you one thing, Charlotte, and I am perfectly serious when I say it: you must find this funny. If you don't, then Lionel and Winnie win and you end up in the mental hospital."

"Well, you don't have to worry about that kind of stuff with me, okay? All right, Mom? I'm not cracking up over anything. So don't worry about it, okay?" What Katrinka had never understood about her daughter was that Charlotte intended to practice sanity as her own private form of revenge.

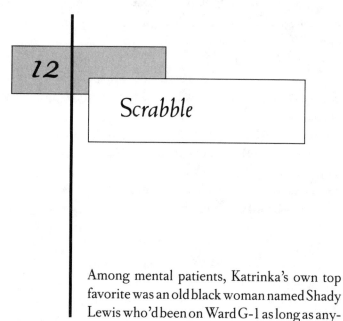

12

Scrabble

Among mental patients, Katrinka's own top favorite was an old black woman named Shady Lewis who'd been on Ward G-1 as long as anyone could remember. Diagnosed as catatonic, Shady Lewis never spoke to a soul, never smoked, never watched television, never even drank instant coffee. What she did all day, every day, was sit in the corner with one eye open, the other squeezed shut like Popeye, and wait for Sacramento.

Sacramento came through a few times a year, Katrinka said, in order to make itself feel better. Sacramento came just as people went to the freak show at Sugarman's. Sacramento viewed mental patients as if they were dead, or on the other side of a one-way mirror, which they sometimes were, or as if the state of being mentally ill had also rendered them blind. Some were blind, of course. Some of them were blind and deaf and dumb and they did act up, just like Helen Keller, not Mr. Dukey's secretary, but the other *real* one, who had acted like a mental patient until someone got through to her. At Camarillo, though, people did not get through: Helen Kellers were given shock or tranquilized. Some were mentally ill *and* mentally re-

tarded like Little Winnie. But it was Shady Lewis who was Katrinka's top favorite, because it was she who lifted her skirts over her
head and held them there the whole time that Sacramento was looking things over. She never did it at any other time. She was catatonic,
but she knew enough about how high up Sacramento thought itself
to be that she'd made sure she'd taken off her underpants.

As Katrinka told this story, she was setting out the Scrabble
pieces, placing them face down on the table. The wooden squares
were spotted with flecks of tobacco. She kept rolling tobacco and
Goody Butts in the Scrabble box for cigarette emergencies. Goody
Butts were those cigarettes that had been smoked only once and
were still too long to throw away. "All right, then, sweetie-pa-toot,
what *is* it you need to know?"

"I know the rules," Charlotte said. "You get some letters, mess
around with them. Spell things."

"I mean about Whosits."

"*Kreminski?*"

"I'm talking about your father 'tis of you, of whom you perpet-
ually sing. I am perfectly willing to discuss it, if you get up and get
me a beer and another pack of cigarettes and *if* it is such an issue
with you."

"What do you mean, an *issue?*"

"That's what they always call it in group therapy, which they
make you do in Camarillo. Sacramento says to Shady Lewis, 'Shady,
why don't you tell us what you are *truly* feeling,' when she already
has! When what it is she is *truly* feeling is none of their fucky business! So what is it you *feel* impelled to *have* to know?" She was moving the letters about on the slanted holder in front of her, peering at
some of them ironically as if they were old friends.

"Well," said Charlotte, getting up to go to the fridge, "where'd
you meet him, for instance?" She took a beer out, then began opening and closing drawers to find the place where her mother had last
hidden the cigarettes.

"Cal," Katrinka said, looking over the top of her glasses, which
rested way down on her nose.

"In classes?" Charlotte asked as she sat down.

"No, he was older and in architecture. He should have already graduated except that he'd lost some years when his parents slapped him in the sanitarium. That's what they call the ritzy-fitz type mental hospitals, and Glendale Sanitarium is no exception." This was the Seventh Day Adventist hospital where Charlotte had been born. "I've been locked up in there," Katrinka said. "They give you little nutcakes that are pretending to be hamburger. Awwwnnd, though *you* are in the nut house, you are *not* supposed to take it personally." She smirked. "Twenty," she said, snapping down the letters to play the word BONEY.

"How old were you?" Charlotte asked, leaning forward across the table.

Katrinka raised her arms above her head and stretched luxuriously. "Do you really want to hear the *whole* story?"

"Okay," Charlotte said. She played BOX. "That's twenty-six," she told her, adding, "I'm ahead."

"Thank you, sweetie, but I'm not so addlepated that I cannot still count." She bent over the paper, occupied with the writing of the figures in the two columns; the thickness of her glasses made her green eyes first bulge, then seem to slide away as she turned her head. She sat back and lit a cigarette, taking a tiny piece of tobacco from the tip of her tongue with her ring finger. "Tell me, Charlotte," she said, "have you ever heard of *primogeniture?*"

Oh, God! Charlotte thought. *Not this!* Primogeniture was the reason Winnie had not been left the ranch in Montana; it had gone instead to her stepbrother Franklin, Big Dad's real son. "I thought this wasn't going to be about *them.* It was supposed to be about *my* father. For once."

"It is," Katrinka said, "but you have to let me finish, awwwnnd you haven't even let me get started. If we discuss this issue, Charlotte, you are going to have to drop all that war-hero crap, do you understand me? It has obviously all been hallucinated by Winnie in one of her pips about the navy, and I don't want you to go by it. I mention *primogeniture* because I want you to get a good idea of those types who ended up in California, and I'm not discussing the issue of Hollywood movie stars."

Charlotte picked her letters, growling audibly, curling her upper lip.

"What I am talking about is the ones who did *not* inherit the ranch or the family banking business in South and/or North English, Iowa, if you see what I mean. I mean the ones who had severe emotional problems from a *very* early age, who were thrown out of Grinnell for public drunkenness and/or for contracting syphilis and/or gonorrhea from one's own cousin Elmo." Charlotte was not listening; still, Katrinka went on. "The important thing to remember is that bankers are congenital liars. They tell you they are going to give your money back, but they never do. Who do you think owned most of California after the Depression? A. P. Giannini, who toddled off with all of everybody's mun-mun in his pushcart, to the happy tune of his organ-grinder's monkey. Which was the precise moment that man stopped being a wop and his wife Sylvia started being asked to bingo at the country club! Talk about big she, little he!" *Tree rock bush*, Charlotte thought. *Bush rock tree.* Katrinka, still muttering, smacked down the letters for the word ZANY and went right on: "*Which*, I have noticed, has shown up in you, Charlotte, I mean congenitally."

"What? Mental illness?"

"I mean, Missy Miss, that bankerly flintiness, sweetieheart, which I would watch out for if I did not want to turn out like our dear Awwwunt Nan."

"Which is how?"

"Bi-homosexual."

Charlotte heaved a great sigh. "Do you think it would be okay to just change the subject?" she asked her. "What's the score, for instance? Or, do you want something from the fridge? I'm getting myself a Coke. *Which* Patsy's mom pronounces Co'Cola, did I ever tell you that? Or do you think she still says it that way to sound dumb for boys though she's a total grown-up?"

"What's the matter with you?"

"Nothing." She sighed again, noisily: Arrrgh. "It's just that it's impossible for you to ever talk about anything without going off on some sickening tangent."

"I was not aware that my tangents were *sickening*," Katrinka said, seeming pleased. "Forty-eight," she said as she wrote it down, then started picking new letters from the clotted ones. "All *right!*" she announced, lifting the letters up, peering at them, replacing them with a smacking sound on the wooden rack. She didn't finish what she was saying, so the exclamation hung there. Katrinka's words were three-dimensional, Charlotte felt. Her mother didn't so much think them as manufacture them, put them out into space as objects to be italicized, dangled, jostled, joked with, walked around. Words for Charlotte were more interior, a darker, more secret matter. Charlotte was more like Shady Lewis, either unwilling or unable to say anything about what she was *truly* feeling. Normally Charlotte had no wish to know what anybody was truly feeling.

"But," Katrinka went on, "if you are going to be *that* way about it, we will not discuss it. I was trying to make a point, *which* is this: that his family and my family were too much alike, that we were surrounded by primogeniture, which was why we were doomed to fall deeply in love although no terrible good could come of it." She sucked her cheeks in humorously. "Present company exempted."

"You were too much alike?"

"Similar," she sniffed.

"How?"

"Oh, I don't know, Charlotte. We were similar, though he was much better-looking." Katrinka was drawling this, to show she meant it in some special way. "But you first have to understand about Lionel, how he was kept in dresses until a very late age, and his hair was all done up in ringlets."

"I know the photograph you're talking about," Charlotte said. "Remember I told you it was a christening dress?"

"Which is what they would have you believe!" Suddenly Katrinka was notably angry. "Face it, Charlotte, Lionel is bi-homosexual! DePalma even told me so. He said that was half my problem!"

"What's the other half?"

"Winnie. She's bi-homosexual, too."

Charlotte looked at her levelly, squinting over her bottom lids.

This was, she decided, no better than Lionel on the couch, or having to listen to Winnie go on about their *relations*. She stretched theatrically. "Gee, Mom, I'm really pooped. I think I'll go to bed."

"Don't you get passive-aggressive with me, Missy!" Katrinka told her. "Why don't you just say so if you're angry at me?"

"Well," Charlotte drawled. "As a matter of *fact*, I really can't stand the way you tell a story. It's tree rock bush. It's stupid, dumb. Plus every story you ever tell is always full of these bi-homosexual assholes! Have you ever noticed that? That everybody is exactly the same?"

"Actually, that is just my point," Katrinka told her. "That you must understand the historical background if you want to understand what happened. If you're so big on history. Anyway, I need you to help me with this, Charlotte."

"'What happened to what?'"

"Everything. Your father. My mun-mun."

Charlotte sighed. Why should this time be any different from the way it always was? She sighed, started in, "Mom? I told you—don't you remember? Remember I told you all about the ship and the bomb and . . ."

"There was no ship."

"No, *really!* Want me to show you? I have a book that has pictures in it. A map, Mom. This was *real*."

"I'm not talking about all that," Katrinka said. "I am talking about what happened to your father, and honest to Christ, Charlotte, I am really worried about you and your faulty understanding of things. Did you realize, if you're so big on the U.S. Navy, that Harold Ainsworth was in Washington, D.C., during the war and was very high up in the Pentagon on the subject of ship movements? He bragged about it to Lionel all the time, to be boysie, you know, to make Lionel feel even lousier than he normally did. Call Harold if you want to talk about ship movements, Charlotte, but don't bring it up to me!"

"He's dead."

"I meant it metaphorically," Katrinka said, heavily ironical. She was smoking furiously now and muttering into the smoke, "Those three brothers all turned out to be sick—Ina did it, with her god-damned crappy pies. They loved to take things away from people after being brought up like that. Harold and Lawrence had other people's farmlands for them to repossess; Lionel had only the two of us for his acts of masochistic sadism." She pronounced the latter as in "the Marquis de," so it sounded like a joke way of saying "sad." "I'm sure he did it, the phony shipshapes, like that."

"What are you talking about?"

"Your Great-Uncle Harold and the conspiracy he invented. The one with the *Indiana* in it."

"Mom!" Charlotte said. "The *Indianapolis* was real. But it was just an *ordinary* conspiracy, like they *always* have in wars. They have normal codes, you know, and secrets that don't have anything to do with us, you know? With psychiatrists driving by in sets of threes? It was just the cargo, that it was the uranium for the bombs, that it was so secret. Remember that I explained this? They didn't tell you he was dead at first because they were keeping it from everyone? No one knew except the navy. They only told the families after the war was formally over."

"That," Katrinka said, "is completely insane."

"What I mean is it didn't pertain to our family *personally*."

"Then what does this have to do with my estate?" Katrinka asked.

"Plenty, probably. You should have had widow's benefits. A medal of some kind? He would have had a medal. Lionel probably did keep it all. Or Eleanor Ann."

Katrinka's green eyes stared out, her pupils large. "Where did you get all this?"

"I'll show you!" Charlotte said, going to get the books. This, she then realized, was why she'd taken them when she'd read them so many times before: she would need them as evidence. "Books!" she said triumphantly, piling them up on the Scrabble board. "I got them from the Glendale Public Library."

Katrinka looked down at them over the rims of her glasses, flipping a few pages of the top one. Charlotte pointed out Hashimoto's map, and the spine with the spindly white-inked letters and numbers, indicating that the book was nonfiction. "Get me another beer," Katrinka said, and she looked at the books for a moment. She seemed to Charlotte to be considering. "Charlotte," she said finally, "I do not want you to go by any of this. None of it has anything to do with your father."

"All right," Charlotte said, her own cheeks sucked in as she gathered up the books. "Now can we just drop it?"

"You were the one who brought it up."

"No, you were." Charlotte was getting her pajamas and her toothbrush out. "You really were."

"Quitters never prosper," Katrinka sniffed.

Her mother's skin, in the light of the green shade, which matched the curtains, looked otherworldly. Charlotte stared as if she herself were Sacramento, on the outside of the glass peering in. She stared at her mother to try to understand how she could stay so impervious to reason, although Charlotte already knew the answer. She had figured it out long before: Katrinka had to remain immune to the truth about Joey, because if she admitted he had gone off and joined the navy, it would mean he'd run off to get away from her and the house in Silverlake that was sliding so seriously downhill. Charlotte knew this; she simply never remembered it.

"The expression," she reminded her mother, "is 'Cheaters never prosper.'"

"Ha!" Katrinka said. "Bankers are all rich as hell."

When Charlotte came out of the little toilet, Katrinka asked, "Want to hear how I met your father?"

"Not especially."

"All right, then, Missy Miss, be like that if you so choose, this being a free country and all that crap, but no one has ever been able to stop me from talking out loud, except when I've been forcibly pumped full of Thorazine. Get me a beer from the icebox while you're up and get yourself one, too, because this is a long story." Charlotte got out a beer for her mother; she never drank beer herself because she didn't like the sweet and sweaty taste of it, which she knew from the taste of her own lips after they brushed her mother's shining cheek.

|||||||||||||||||||||||||||||||||||

"Once upon a time, and a nicens time it was, we did meet, really really. They were coming downstairs and we were going up, men and girls. Arch was there; he was carrying the human skull we had for a mascot at *Pelican*—no, I must be making that up. Becky and I were going upstairs to dress for dinner. *That*," she inhaled, "was what it was like in those days and what we were like: we all dressed up for dinner, even at a crappy place like I-House. Arch was the one who introduced us."

"You all lived in the same dream?" Charlotte asked—she meant *dorm*.

Katrinka nodded. "On different floors. The name did suit your father. It stood for International House, but he thought it was all about him. When he went south during the summer and wrote back to me, he always went through the letter circling every place he'd used the pronoun I." Charlotte handed her the beer and the opener and sat down. "That was to convince me what a mess he was. He was working for his father. He was always very sick when he was working for his father."

"Doing what?"

Katrinka painted the air with the end of her cigarette: puffs and clouds emerged. "Doing, you know, that washing-machine-agitator type building Los Angeles was getting so wrought up over. Modern. *The machine designed for living in*, you remember?" With the cigarette smoke Katrinka was drawing shapes in the air; her lips pursed, she was hunting for the words that had once expressed these ideas. "Bauhaus," she settled on. "Le Corbusier. Like that."

"His father was an architect, too?"

Katrinka nodded. "Which was undoubtedly why Joey was so good at it and why he hated it so damned much. Which is to say it was not your father's top choice. Your father would have rather had a beer-and-lobster joint down on the pier in Redondo. He would have rather played the piano in the Rainbow Room."

"Or been a sailor?"

"Oh, for Christsake, Charlotte! Are you really back harping on that? Actually, if you must know, he was a sailor. He and Nan had their own little sailboat, I told you that. He and I had met before. He was from Glendale, too, but he went to Hoover. He was ahead of me in school, so I didn't know him. We were on the same science trip, though, out to the Mojave, where Winnie and Josh used to rendez-vous to paint, or whatever it was they wanted us to believe they did. We were out there to get snakes' skins, bones, spiders, those sorts of types of things. I remembered him vaguely. He was the one who was supposed to bring silver but forgot it. He cracked up over that, slightly, as I remember. Or his parents both showed up in the middle of the night to check up on him—it might have been *that* he cracked up over, the two of them looming over his sleeping bag."

"My God!" Charlotte said. "What a coincidence. The same field trip!"

"Right," Katrinka smirked. "A marriage made in heaven, or if not that, at least in the Mojave Desert. Except we never spoke until Berkeley. We all sat together at the French table, speaking Ig-pay Atin-lay. Then he and I walked up to the Claremont Hotel for a drink. One thing led to another. We decided to take the A-train to San Francisco to go dancing. We went to the Top of the Mark and told one another our life stories about Glendale High versus Hoover versus the Oak Knoll versus the Chevy Chase country clubs versus psychoanalysis, which interested your father profoundly and me not one iota. He was very big on Freud—Freud and martinis. We each had twenty-six or -seven martinis and we got so drunk we missed the last train and had to take a cab back across the bridge.

"Arch was in love with me, too. He was the one who made your father and me work on *Pelican*. It was very funny then. It had to be funny because the war was on."

"Whatever happened to him?"

"Arch? Oh, he got a job teaching philosophy at Cal and wrote a book mathematically disproving the existence of God." Though this seemed to Charlotte to be the kind of thing her mother would normally approve of, Katrinka was smirking over it.

"Why is that funny?"

"Well, really, Charlotte! How unfunny can you get, writing a book counting all the crappy shitty things that have ever happened to anyone to mathematically disprove the existence of God? Atomic *bombs?* Imaginary ships being blown out of the water with great loss of life? Like that?" She arched one eyebrow contemptuously at Charlotte's pile of books. "Which shows you Arch had completely lost his sense of humor. Also, it was so babyish of him, don't you think, to act as appalled as all that?"

"What did he look like?"

"Oh, I don't know. Kind of short and geniusy, you know. Not my type. He got boozed up once and asked me to marry him. Thank God, I didn't. Thank God, I didn't end up drinking twenty-six or -seven martinis at those goddamned Berkeley cocktail parties where all anyone ever talked about was his latest book disproving the existence of *Gawd!*"

Charlotte had meant her father. The last time she'd asked Katrinka what he looked like, Katrinka had told her that the skin on his back was so beautiful the Nazis would have used it to make a lamp shade.

"Honest to Christ, Charlotte—you think I'm bad, but you should go to one of those Berkeley cocktail parties, if you think all *that* is so absolutely wonderful. You should go and listen to them go on about themselves—Awe-I wouldn't have got a word in edgewise! Someone should stand there and circle *them* whenever they use the word *I*, really really! I could not have stood it, being pregnant all the time, serving little meatballs sopped in that orange crap, breast milk dripping from the bodice of my basic black, which is all one wore to that type of crappy soirée, that and a clever little *hat*. Arch and his wife have at least five children, all of whom are named Sasha. How would *you* like it if someone had named you Sasha? Talk about ruining someone's life."

"I meant my own father."

"Welllll, he was much better-looking than P. I. Arch, and he was better adjusted than Alan Watson, if that is what you're driving at. And he was taller than Lionel, which gave Mr. Tweedy the pip, really really, because he is so goddamned good at looking down on people. He had hair like yours, but darker—his was nearly black. He did have eyes like yours, but his were a deeper blue—which is not to say the dwarf is to be believed on any subject whatsoever, Charlotte, any subject aside from the scientific fact that fish do not live in vodka—*do* you understand me? His skin was lovely, really really, freckled all over, golden and brown, like the stones on the bottom of a creek. In the summer when he sailed he was actually dappled."

Because Charlotte was in horror of her mother making the same joke about Nazis, skin, and lamp shades, she abruptly stopped listening. Her attention came unhinged and, though she could hear the words Katrinka was pronouncing, she stared away, thinking nothing, letting them go through her without effect, like an unread ticker tape. One of the first times this had ever happened was the time she'd been sitting on the table in Dr. Greenley's office. Another time was once when Katrinka was telling the story of a man who'd shot himself in the upstairs bathroom of his house in Glendale—Katrinka had met the daughter at Camarillo. Charlotte had listened to that point, but then Katrinka had gone on and on and the effect of words being spoken had suddenly ceased. Instead, the event had begun simply to unfold before Charlotte's eyes: the grown son reaching down to pick up the bits of bone and broken teeth from the tile floor, the shape of the man's outstretched fingers, the tiles, which were perfectly white and cold, grouted in black; they were hexagonal and smaller than a quarter. The punchline of this story was uttered by the girl's mother, talking to her bridge club. When she told the story of her husband's suicide, she always ended by saying, "And my floors, my dears, had been so clean you could *eat* off them!" This sounded so much like Nellie that Charlotte never knew how much was true and how much was Katrinka's fabrication.

"He had a space between his two front teeth," Katrinka was going on, having skipped the Nazis. "He looked like Johnny Mercer, except taller. Sometimes it seemed to me that your father *was* Johnny Mercer—but that was only when *I* was cracking up over something or other. There was a lot of that sort of thing in those days, everyone being a little cuckoo competitively. It was very chic, like the clever little hats. But I always knew your father was not Johnny Mercer because he wasn't that rich."

"But he was kind of rich."

"Rich enough for twenty-seven martinis each at the Top of the

Mark. Rich enough for a cab ride. Hell, we were all rich in those days, sweetie; our parents had been through the goddamned Depression, which was depressing enough to last us. Lionel and Winnie used to send me one hundred dollars a month just to get my hair and my laundry done, and to tip the maid. If I needed another basic black or a cleverer little hat, they sent me an extra check. That was when I was still on their good side. Now my allowance is down to a crappy five dollars a week." Katrinka looked at Charlotte with her chin tipped up. "Are you still on their good side?"

Charlotte dropped her eyes, shook her head.

"That's good," Katrinka said.

"But he was funny?" Charlotte asked.

Katrinka nodded. "It was expected of us. Someone had to be. The war was on and everyone was going around taking all *that* very seriously."

"But not you."

"As I have already explained, Miss Girl Scouts of America, I did my own fucky little bit, counting those crappy rifles. I also drank a lot of beer with boys from the navy base, and I did shut up every once in a while and listen to their lousy homesick stories."

"The boys from Mare Island?"

"Charlotte!" Katrinka said. "Are you really back on that?"

"Where my father was."

"Actually, no, he was not. He was in Los Angeles, designing concrete bunkers for the twenty-first century, cracking up completely over his masculinity and writing me letters enumerating how many times he'd just used the letter Awe-I! Which Awe-I have just explained. The one who was most seriously interested in me *that* summer happened to be Madge. Speaking of enlisted men, Madge turned out to be a Wac." Katrinka, squinting at her letters, smiled her grim smile.

"What's so funny about that?"

"Sweetie! Honey! Everyone knows that Wac is the way you spell Homo-*Homo*-Sexual in Ig-pay Atin-lay."

It always came back to this, Charlotte realized, this *issue*. Katrinka reminded her of something Mr. Greenbaum had once told the class when they were discussing *Oedipus Rex*. "All roads lead to Rome," Charlotte said out loud, adding, "Tree rock bush."

"Where'd you get that?" her mother asked.

"Honors English."

Katrinka sniffed, as if smelling the words for truth. She peered out at Charlotte from behind the rim of her glasses and tipped her chin up. "That," she said, "isn't English—it's geography."

13

Nescafé de Camarillo

- *A giant economy-sized jar of instant coffee*
- *Tap water, run as hot as you can make it*
- *Mug, paintbrush jar, or other large vessel*
- *Something to stir it with*

While talking aloud to yourself or to anyone else who might be there to listen, bang jar against the rim of the mug to dump in a heap of coffee. Run under the gushing faucet. Stir with anything handy. Some suggestions: Knife handle, eraser end of Scrabble pencil, twin handles of the turn-around can opener. Serve immediately.

"Awwwnnd then," she was saying, "she started in serving the mental patients squirrel meat."

"Who did?" Charlotte asked, opening her eyes.

"Tina White," Katrinka answered. "The one with the board-and-care place in Ventura. Talk about Okies and Arkies! There ought to be a law against it."

"Being an Okie or an Arkie?" Charlotte moved past her mother at the sink and on into the bathroom.

"That awwwnnd serving board-and-care patients squirrel meat! That awwwnnd being allowed to name your children Pearl White and Lily White or Sasha-Sasha-Sasha! Why doesn't Sacramento do something about *that* if they're so high up in the goddamned crap heap that they think this is Soviet Russia!"

The clothes for the dummies lay around on the floor and on the Scrabble board; the war books had been left out on the table. The fabric of the dummies' clothes still smelled dusty. The dust came from the old house in Orange. Everything about Aunt Hoppy and Little Winnie's house was dusty, it seemed to Charlotte, stinking of exhaust and the exfoliation of stucco from the motel and apartment houses that surrounded it on all three sides. The two old women lived in a Queen Anne Victorian on an acre of land. The brick walkway was lined with gumdrop trees and bushes of blue hydrangeas, the blooms as big as a lady's head. Aunt Hoppy cut the woody stalks of the huge flowers with a kitchen knife, the blade dull against the large flat plain of her wrinkled thumb. The flowers were dry and brittle, standing without water in a big glass vase on Little Winnie's grand piano. The sign on the front porch read "Hemstitching" but in letters too small to be read from a car moving at modern speeds. No one ever came asking Aunt Hoppy for hand sewing, as far as Charlotte knew. The only reason anyone ever came up that walk was to inquire if she would like to sell her land.

Katrinka was stirring another big mug, and, when Charlotte passed, she handed it to her. Charlotte looked down at it. There were darkened bubbles floating on the surface of the brown water. They burst and the lighter powder floated out. "Maybe we should drive to the Safeway and buy some breakfast stuff," Charlotte said, taking the mug, then setting it down on the sink.

"Such as what?"

"Like doughnuts. You know, whatever." Charlotte meant whatever it was that more normal people ate for breakfast. Once, Katrinka had taken her out to the movies on a Saturday afternoon but hadn't brought her back to Vista del Mar. Instead they'd driven to Malibu and rented a seaside cottage where they had stayed until Katrinka's money had run out. That had taken a couple of days. The cottage was built on stilts out over the water. All through the night the waves had rushed up under it, smashing onto the rocks. They had slept in the same double bed. It was the first time they'd been together overnight since Avenue B, and Charlotte's longing for her mother was terrible. She was also revolted by having to sleep so close to Katrinka's beer-sweaty skin. She had listened to the rasp and wheeze and had turned away so she wouldn't have to look at the dark of her mother's nostrils and open mouth.

They'd spent the evening in the bar across the parking lot. Charlotte had eaten peanuts and candies out of the nickel machines and voted over and over again for Miss Rhinegold. She had studied each ballot carefully; the printing of the faces' bright red lipstick changed so that the one who was prettiest on one sheet might look weird, skewed, crazy on the next.

Katrinka had sat next to her at the bar, singing theatrically with Doris Day on the jukebox, motioning out the window with one grand hand to the moonlight jittering on the water. She sang, "*Que sera sera. Whatever will be, will be. The future's not ours to see. Que sera sera.*" At the time, Charlotte had thought it meant something poetic about her father and her mother and herself, all zigzagging home from one place or another in order to be together.

Winnie had asked specifically about the breakfasts. Charlotte told her about the Campbell's soup Katrinka had made on the hot plate, even using the can opener herself and serving the soup in coffee cups. She hadn't imagined she was telling on Katrinka. She had actually been trying to brag about Katrinka's ingenuity, that she had managed to make something hot that a child would like, that might have had nutrition in it. But Winnie, hearing it, had run off to the service porch holding onto the flesh on either side of her face, yelping, "Bean with bacon soup for *breakfast!*" She screamed as if she were about to have a heart attack.

"Hand me that can and I'll make you a chopped olive sandwich," Katrinka told her.

"No thanks." Charlotte had skewered a slice of white bread on the tines of a fork and was holding it over the gas burner. The air of the trailer filled with scorch. "Thanks, though," she added.

"You used to love chopped olive sandwiches," Katrinka told her. She was struggling with the turn-around can opener, holding it at the can's rim, but positioned upside down. Charlotte took it and turned it the right way, then ran it around the tin. "Where'd you get that trick?" Katrinka asked, with her cheeks sucked in. "Honors home ec?"

Charlotte shrugged. This was praise, but it came with an insult in it, the way the cob of corn had been shoved up the loaf of French bread. It was hard, *hard* to get things right: to do things just well enough to get by, just well enough that her mother wouldn't feel criticized by her success.

Katrinka glopped mayonnaise from the Best Foods jar into a large Pyrex measuring cup, then she dumped the chopped olives on top, stirring with the twin handles of the can opener. "Did I really ever love chopped olive sandwiches?" Charlotte asked, incredulously. "I don't remember that." The smell of the mayonnaise was making her sick.

"Of course you did," Katrinka said. "Or maybe that was me. You were the one who loved Cambridge tea." Cambridge tea was what Katrinka called the real tea with sugar and so much milk it was nearly white. She had made it for Charlotte to go with her play tea set. This must have been at Avenue B. She'd always heard the word "Cambrick"; its sound was so indelible that the word "Cambridge" still sounded mispronounced.

"Vile ve ist on the subject of identity," Katrinka told her, breathing out smoke through her nose, then going off in her apricot-colored satin dressing gown to sit at the table with her coffee. The issue of identity had always baffled Katrinka, Charlotte knew. Once she'd told Charlotte, in all seriousness, that she had never really understood why Lionel and Winnie hadn't remained *Awe-I* all the time, and why Katrinka couldn't have just stayed *you.*

"Vile ve ist on the subject of history," Katrinka was going on. "*She* read my mail and she took the five-dollar bills Winnie had tucked inside. Being an Okie or Arkie, she'd never heard of such a thing as 'enclosed please find,' which your grandmother always wrote at the bottom in her increasingly psychotic handwriting."

"What *are* we talking about?"

"The types who came to California during the Depression.

There were two basic types, aside from the bi-mama-sexuals like your grandparents. *Which* we will not go into. There were the Okies and Arkies and the Negroes."

Charlotte had finished scorching the bread, and after picking some bits of tobacco out of the butter cube, she now buttered the toast on the less-blackened side. "That's more than two types," she mentioned.

"Okies and Arkies *comma*," Katrinka informed her. "That is just one type. Remember Rufus Fountain?"

Charlotte nodded, studying her bread. Rufus Fountain was a Negro Katrinka had once planned to marry. She called the Ainsworths at three-thirty in the morning to tell them so; they then placed a person-to-person call to Dr. DePalma, which was how they had found out the kinds of things you could not do when you were living as an outpatient in a family-care facility. Marrying Negroes was one of them.

"Did you ever know that Winnie was really surprised to find out that there even *were* Negroes in Camarillo?" Charlotte said. "She didn't think their IQs were ever high enough for them to even have mental problems. Plus she thought they were too relaxed for nervous tension, you know, from the way they spend all their time laughing and singing, just whiling away the time eating low off the hog in the shade of trees, all the doo-dah-day."

"She said all that?" Katrinka asked.

Charlotte shrugged. "I added the part about all the doo-dah-day." Katrinka tipped her chin up and sucked her cheeks in. *She likes me*, Charlotte thought, with some astonishment.

"She sounds like she's gone completely off her rocker," Katrinka was saying. "If she does ever crack up absolutely, let's just keep her home in a straightjacket, shall we, sweetie? She couldn't stand Camarillo. The music in Camarillo is pure Africa, bongos, congos, played with bones in the nose, like that. Rufus was high-class type blackamoor. He played the alto saxophone. He spent the war up north, too, working in the shityard."

Charlotte's heart leapt. "Mare Island?"

"Frankly, Charlotte, it was Richmond. Tina got him out of Camarillo after the second or third time he'd cracked up. She was keeping him as house nigger."

"Don't say 'nigger,' all right? You might hurt somebody's feelings," Charlotte interrupted.

"Whose feelings is it exactly that you are always talking about, Charlotte? Yours? There is no one listening, particularly Rufus who, being *Negro* and from the south and all, knew full well that it was squirrel meat and that he was a nigger. What else do you imagine mental patients are? She fried it up with a mess o'sumpin' and tried to get us to believe it was chicken, just the *darker* breed. But I wasn't *that* deranged, and neither was he. It may have been slightly psychotic to imagine I could have married him and had a mess o'little pickaninnies in order to save race relations, but I do happen to know . . ."

"Okay, just don't say 'pickaninnies,' all right?"

"Why shouldn't I?"

"It's prejudice."

"The word, Charlotte, is *prejudiced*, and you can't accuse me of that because I hate everybody equally. I am talking about the history of California, and I do not mean according to MGM."

"MGM?"

"I mean Joan Blondell exclaiming all over the place about how goddamned wonderful to be *alive* during the Depression, being bossed around by that psychopath Busby Berkeley. Talk about gestapo! I mean the real facts of this case and not those written up for the fans in *Photoplay*."

"What case?"

"Mine, against the state of California. I have proof, Charlotte, which is this: there were two types who were not considered good enough to die for their country and Rufus happened to be both. Talk about preju*dice!* Preju-*dis* and preju-*dat!*"

"You mean Okie and Arkie *and* Negro?"

"Sweetie! Honey! You can be as Okie and Arkie as you want in this country! The Okier and Arkier the better, really really! Look at

Maxine Bill. I'm sure she is at least Queen of the World by now. What I mean is that Rufus was both a Negro awwwnnd a mental patient."

"So?"

"So, so was your father. I am referring to Black, Joseph Jordan, Jr. The one who did not work in the lousy shipyard."

Charlotte sighed, yawned, squinted. "Sure bet," she told her, wondering how it was possible to be so completely exhausted when she had just gotten out of bed. "Mom, know what? Wanna know something? That just because a person's last name might be *Black* or something doesn't mean he's a Negro, do you realize that? If he was really a Negro, he wouldn't have had freckles and my arm probably wouldn't really look like this." She demonstrated by holding out her sunburn.

"He was classified Four-F," Katrinka pronounced with utter finality. Her hands were held above her head, the cigarette chuffing out puffs like a smokestack. "Both your father and Rufus were hospitalized at the beginning of the war," she went on. "Rufus for something he did or didn't say—I frankly cannot remember because I didn't happen to be around. That was in Richmond where your father and I did go one time to a Negro jazz club but did not meet Rufus. Rufus was too busy putting together Willy Bill's car parts, going "*Y'sir! N'sir!*" and like that. Shuffling, looking down, saying things like: '*Feets get moving!*' They locked him up anyway, Kingfish or not.

"Your father was classified Four-F by the draft because he'd cracked up right at the start of the war. His father was a war hero from the first war; it may have been the pressure of all that. He was out at least a year from Cal. It was when he came back that I met him. So you can't really blame me for *all* of his mental instability, my dear sweetie, though I know you would love to. The iodine bottle he liked to carry around! Like that!"

"I'm not blaming you," Charlotte said, but she was no longer listening. *The brain*, she was thinking, *is run on electricity and blood.* She brought her fingertips to her eyelids. It was a physiological reaction, she would later decide, a dropping off in her brain's physical ability to pay attention. She experienced it as a plummeting off into a form of unconsciousness, like narcolepsy: she was awake but existed in a state of benign paralysis, unable to speak, to move, to really hear. This happened to her whenever a conversation with her mother became too horrible to bear. The conversation went on and on, but Charlotte wasn't there to hear it.

Her mother was still talking. Charlotte took her hands away. She held the green plaid curtain back and watched the lines on the blacktop weave in the waves of heat. *A dog*, she thought, *understands all languages but speaks none*. She thought of other things. She imagined the force of the water in the state park showers in the concrete building on the edge of the cliff. It was possible there to take a good shower and to get really clean. In the Airstream, the water pressure was so weak that the shower just dribbled out, like pee. The park provided a big stone washbasin at one end. There it would be possible for Charlotte to wash out her underpants, to scrub them with soap. Her mother had sometimes gone to Camarillo, she knew, over nothing more than the issue of her own dirty underpants, mounting up and up.

"Talk about acting mental patienty! Charlotte, you should see your face, right this very instant. You go around looking like you are right on the verge of cracking up completely! I will not stand for it, really really! I promise you, Charlotte, that if you decide to fall apart over all this, I won't be able to take it. If you don't stop looking like that, I am going right straight back to Camarillo."

"Looking like what?" Charlotte asked, mildly, turning away from the window. She hadn't heard a word of it.

She was turning away from the window, and was going to get her towel, her zoris, her O-Dor-O-No. This was Winnie's brand of deodorant, which Lionel had started buying for Charlotte too. It was bright red, the color of the punch served with cookies after services at Patsy's church. The liquid was dabbed on with a plastic wick that stuck down into the bottle. It was an old-fashioned brand, something that a person would have taken to Cal during the nineteen forties. The chemicals in it were so strong they made Charlotte's eyes sting and the flesh of her underarms raw. It was the sort of thing a suicidal person might drink.

Katrinka was still talking and suddenly, then, the narcolepsy began again. Charlotte turned back to the window. She was staring away, into the blaze of light, away into nothingness. Her face was immobilized but she understood that its muscles were frozen like one of those mummified at Pompeii: horrified, agonized, aghast. She could not stop staring. It was as if a ticker tape fed through her, providing her with images only now, without words. She saw the hand reaching down toward the cold tile of the bathroom floor. She saw the fingers picking up the bits of bone and teeth and pale brain, and she then understood, completely, thoroughly, that the hand reaching out there, out and down, did belong to her.

Her mother was furious, Charlotte saw when she turned around. She was stomping, threatening Camarillo for both of them if Charlotte did not knock it off *instantly!* She was picking up the dummies, shoving them into their clothes. Charlotte automatically began to help her.

Katrinka sniffed, watching her. Charlotte looked up, smiled, lifted her shoulders. "The point is this," Katrinka said, having decided that her daughter had recovered from her mental breakdown. "The war gave all of them a complex about their masculinity, can't you see that? All of them, Watson, Arch, Rufus, your father, Willy Bill, my father, too. That's why they go and do the things they do afterwards, spending the rest of their lives building shopping centers out of materials that made you want to kill yourself, which is what Joseph, Sr., did, or getting Wilma-or-Thelma pregnant and naming the children Sasha, Sasha, and Sasha! Do you understand me? Or mathematically disproving the existence of God? What they are doing is trying to prove they are *consequential* after a thing like that. It makes no difference whether or not they fight a war or whether or not they get killed in it. War is always this sort of an issue with them: how boysie am I, really really? How much boysier is Harold or Thelma? Whose torpedo fits through the eye of Ina's darning needle? But I did not happen to invent any of this, so don't blame me!"

Charlotte said nothing, but turned, as if dreaming, back toward the light. She had long since gone away. She had gone and come back again, transcendent, and she now sat calmly, listening without listening. She could remember the bits of bone and blood only vaguely.

She was sitting cross-legged on the rumpled bed in her nightie, putting on Miss Priss' knickers. Miss Priss did a cancan in Katrinka's act sometimes, while singing something to Sacramento about *Widdle she, Big big he. Big I and you, and me and thee!* In Katrinka's act Shady Lewis had been immortalized.

"No one's blaming you," she told her mother, just as she always did, and as usual she was thinking of something else. She was remembering playing dolls with Little Winnie. Great-Aunt Hoppy was actually Winnie Ainsworth's half first cousin, or something like that, and so she wasn't an aunt at all, though she was old enough to be. Little Winnie was only ten years younger than Charlotte's grandmother, so she too was now an old woman. Still, Aunt Hoppy kept Little Winnie dressed in short white dresses, the way girls were dressed in the days of Aunt Hoppy's youth. She still did Little Winnie's hair up every night on wet rags, so her long hair hung down her back in ringlets.

Charlotte, dressing the dolls with Little Winnie, tried to be patient, tried to teach her back from front, tried to help her learn buttoning, but the clothes Aunt Hoppy made had many, many tiny pearl buttons that were hard to do up. These clothes made Little Winnie furious. When she got mad she would swing her handbag—a grown woman's leather purse, kept so crammed with rocks and coins that it felt like a sledgehammer when she walloped Charlotte. The second time Little Winnie hit her in the head, Charlotte had grabbed this ancient baby at the nape of her neck by a whole handful of the sticky steel-gray ringlets and had yanked her head back. "The next time you do that," she had whispered down at the small eyes in the dim and crafty face, "I am going to tell."

Kreminski's little circus was in a striped tent near the midway. Inside, high in the rigging, a small flock of beach pigeons were roosting, having come in for the discarded food. Charlotte and Katrinka stood in the tent's back opening and watched the little clowns doing their run-through. When one fired his blank gun at a tiny dog dressed as a lion, the blue-gray swoop of birds startled, took flight.

Katrinka's act was done in an open-sided circus wagon in the sideshow with the freaks. She shared her wagon with one of the freaks, a giant named Sam-Sam. During the act, a hand-painted screen was moved into position behind her. Katrinka had done it, a group portrait of herself and the dummies with the name of the act written in a banner above them. The first line read: "Katrinka L. W. Ainsworth, M.P.," the second, "& Associates." The "M.P.," Charlotte knew, stood for "mental patient."

"What gives me the pip about Sam-Sam is the way she allows Sugarman to play up the bit about the ambiguity, *if* you know what I mean," Katrinka announced as they walked to the wagon.

Charlotte put her head down. "I don't know and I have no wish to know . . . *if* you know what I mean," Charlotte told herself. Then she saw the sign. The giant was billed as a "Womanly Man." Charlotte squinted, thinking of other things: the loud slap of a gun in the empty tent and the slow fat flapping of the captive pigeons against the canvas, of the way the Chihuahua lion had been taught to play dead, with its little paws folded on its chest. She thought of her red pigeon, which was named first Juliet, then Romeo. She wondered what had ever happened to John Hamberger, the first boy she had ever loved. The people she loved always left her life: tree rock bush.

The name Sam-Sam, Katrinka was going on, was as bad as Sasha-Sasha-Sasha! The whole goddamned carnival was just as bad as Cal had ever been, the way everyone went around justifying whatever his and/or her latest productions were on whatever the shitass subject: la-di-da *lawn* furniture, French literature of the hellhole launderette! Or counting the rifles in Benicia to demonstrate there had never been a Gawwwwd. The main difference was the sideshow didn't give cocktail parties where people swilled down innumerable martinis, but that was not to say they weren't just as bad, weren't all quietly thinking, "Now, Awe-I . . ." as much as anyone at Cal.

"Present company not exempted," Charlotte said out loud.

Sam was a very tall bearded lady but, aside from the hair, she wasn't very masculine; she had hips and breasts and a little waist. Even the wispy beard was shiny, as if she used cream rinse on it. What she was was shy, Charlotte saw; her shyness, like her height, was exaggerated. She was much taller than Lionel, probably close to seven feet. As Katrinka and Charlotte entered, she had gone to the darkest corner of the wagon where she now huddled.

"Sambo, sweetie," Katrinka said, "I know you hate like hell for people to look at you, but we have to get some light on this goddamned subject." She flipped the switch but nothing happened. "Oh, my God, *now* what have I done? It's Reddy Kilowatt, isn't it, Charlotte?" Reddy Kilowatt was the cartoon who had sent letters to Katrinka on Avenue B, trying to joke and cajole and boss her into paying the power company.

"It isn't you, Katrinka," Sam-Sam whispered down from her great height. "The electricity is broken." She had a beautiful voice: soft, musical, childlike. Charlotte remembered the first time she'd seen the album cover to a record her mother had played all the time on Avenue B, called "Ella Sings Johnny Mercer." Charlotte had been trying to pick up the mess one day, to put things away, when she had seen the picture on the album. She was astounded that the voice of a beautiful thin blonde woman came out of that big dark face. Sam-Sam's voice, Charlotte thought, was like that, like something which seemed borrowed from another person.

"Oh, don't be so goddamned infantile, Sammy," Katrinka told her lightly. "Electricity doesn't get broken, does it, Charlotte? Charlotte knows everything like that because Charlotte is in honors science," she added.

"Mom!"

"True's true." Katrinka had put the dummies down and was shoving debris from the top of the dressing table onto the floor. "Anyway, what had we planned to do about it, cower there in the corner all day, praying for rain?"

"I was going to go ask Mr. Sugarman to send the electrician," Sam-Sam breathed from up near the ceiling.

"That sounds perfectly geniusy to me, Sam-Sam," Katrinka told her, lighting a cigarette. "So what's stopping you?"

"I was waiting for a while, so the sun could get a little bit higher."

"She's afraid of her own shadow," Katrinka told Charlotte. Charlotte was already shrugging, just about to agree, "Well, aren't we all, I mean one way or another?" when her mother added, "I mean, really *really*."

"It's long," Sam-Sam whispered. "As big as a building's. If I walk facing the sun, I don't see it, but then when I have to turn around to come back, there it is right in front of me, and I have to watch it as I walk down into it."

"Awwwnnd all that," Katrinka added sardonically.

"Well," Charlotte said, then sighed in a huge way. "We all *are* afraid of something."

"I most certainly am not!" Katrinka retorted. "Aside from being afraid of running out of beer and cigarettes and ever again being tried by a jury of my peers. Did I ever tell you this, Charlotte? About when I was working for the phone company on Ninth and Hope?"

"Katrinka says it's a phobia," Sam-Sam whispered down.

"Then maybe you should go see a psychiatrist," Charlotte whispered back.

"Why *go!*" Katrinka cried out, opening drawers, getting things out. "Just wait right here! They come by here in sets of threes! There's one due right about now!" She turned to Charlotte and glared. "What are you forever telling people to go to the psychiatrist for when they never did either of your parents one bit of good?"

Charlotte, startled, stared right back. She could feel her own mouth setting in a hard O like Lionel's. "Now, would *someone* please cut out this goddamned crap and go do something about the lights?"

"Why are you so mean?" Charlotte asked, but she already knew: it was because she and Sam-Sam had been talking to one another and not to her. Katrinka was like anyone sometimes, simply jealous.

"Oh, why shouldn't I be? Women are always perfectly wretched to one another. Now, when Awe-I was working in Disbursement Accounting at Ninth and Hope, I wouldn't ride the elevator . . ."

"See?" Charlotte interrupted defiantly. "My mother is afraid of elevators and almost all electrical appliances."

"I most certainly am not!"

"And we are both afraid of electricity."

"She is making this up out of whole cloth," Katrinka told Sam-Sam.

"I am not! My mother is afraid of the Hoover upright, toasters, every brand of washing machine. You are! You are! *You* are the one who loves olive-glop sandwiches made with so much mayonnaise it spills down your arm. That much mayonnaise makes a normal person throw up! *I'm* the one who hates mayonnaise, remember that? I'm the one who's afraid of barf rides and the Ornt Tree and Geeh-ah!-Geeh-ah! cars."

Katrinka sucked her cheeks in. "Charlotte," she said. "This is a tirade."

"So what! You aren't Lionel and Winnie! You aren't the boss of what human beings say!"

Katrinka lit a cigarette. She seemed to consider this.

"What's an Ornt Tree?" Sam-Sam whispered down into the lull.

"Something my mother made up," Katrinka said. "The tree outside the window that loses its leaves in winter and scrapes along the pane."

"It looks like the finger bones of a skeleton," Charlotte chimed in, to be friends with her. It was terrible not to be friends with Katrinka. She couldn't stand it for more than an instant.

"My mother had us each believing that it came to get ornery little girls on windy nights, but we *try* not to be babyish about it, don't we, Charlotte?"

"Ornery? Ornt Tree? Get it?" Charlotte asked Sam-Sam. Her heart was still pounding.

"Clever, wasn't she?" Katrinka asked, raising one eyebrow at her reflection in the mirror. "She scared us *half* out of our mind. Which is one reason I hate women. There is nothing like those Disbursement Accounting types who decide who should and should not take the elevator awwnnd when. But the elevator really was not the issue. The issue was the little black grate they pulled across the opening because there was no door."

"No door!" Charlotte cried, aware that she probably would have agreed she did hear voices, right then, just to get back to Katrinka. "At the phone company! But that's against the law!"

"Law," Katrinka snorted. "There are laws against lots of things, which doesn't stop people from doing them. There was a door on every floor, sweetieheart, to keep you from killing yourself by pitching yourself into the shaft on your coffee break, which is what working in that place made you feel like, but there wasn't one on the car itself. You had to watch the floors whiz by, which I must admit did not seem to remotely bother anyone else. Of course, I was cracking up completely. That was what I was *really* being tried for by the Safety Committee. It fired me for nonconformity because I went up and down the stairs. That was before I was even talking out loud. Know why women hate each other, Samula? Because they hate their mothers. DePalma told me so. He told me I have grounds. Your father," Katrinka said to Charlotte, "felt our whole generation had mother problems. Father problems, too."

"Which would about cover it," Charlotte said. It came out sounding sarcastic.

"I love my parents," Sam-Sam whispered.

"Well, lucky you," Katrinka told her grimly. She was staring into the mirror of the vanity, holding great handfuls of hair in either hand, as if she had been decapitated in a war and was both victor and vanquished. "Gawd, I wish I had a beer. Do you know why I drink? Because I get up looking like hell warmed over, and it's only after I've had three and a half beers that I am stark raving beautiful. I can't see a goddamned thing. Throw the shutters open, won't you, anyway? I have an act to do! I can't find my fucky bobby pins!"

"Oh, I must say that getup is terribleeee natty!" Miss Priss shrilled out in a British accent.

Sam-Sam blinked. She was covering her muscle-man outfit with a huge trench coat that could have been Paul Bunyan's had he been a detective in an old movie. "What's a Geeh-ah!-Geeh-ah! car?" she asked Charlotte, as she was putting on her hat.

"I thought that up," Charlotte told her. "They were the old-fashioned cars, the ones with the horns that go like that: *Geeh*-ah! *Geeh*-ah! I had a gray dress that was covered with a yellow and black pattern of them. They scared me. I used to think there was a time at night when it would finally be every person's bedtime and that then the cars down on Verdugo Road would stop. Then, when everyone was sleeping, time would go backwards and all the old-fashioned cars would come out, and it would be dead people driving."

"Oh," Sam-Sam breathed.

"That," Katrinka snapped, "is quite enough of that."

"Why?" Charlotte asked her, incredulously. "Does it bother you?" She had never heard of any subject that bothered her mother, aside from the sinking of the *Indianapolis*.

Katrinka's mouth was full of bobby pins—she spat them into her hand. "Of course not! I am not afraid of electrical appliances, and I am not afraid of Geeh-ah!-Geeh-ahs! They simply do not interest me one iota!"

"Wh-wh-wh-wh-wh-what's an iota?" Buttercup asked.

"You hush up! You may speak when you are spoken to! I have a show to go and goddamned do and the two of you are acting as if this is group therapy in the Camarillo State Hospital for the Mentally Shitty, where we are all sitting around acting sick as hell, telling on our craphead parents!"

"Which you would never do," Charlotte mentioned.

"Tell DePalma?" Katrinka asked haughtily. "Of course not. Haven't you ever heard of family loyalty? Sam-Sam! I need those lights." Sam-Sam was already out the door.

"I am of the opinion . . . ," Ogamer started, when Katrinka slammed her fists down, saying, "And you shut the fuck up! You are all making me nervous as hell. Charlotte, go over to that crappy Palmengarten and buy me a beer, this instant!"

"They won't sell it to me," Charlotte said. "I'm underage."

"I don't go by that."

"Well, they do."

In the half-light of the circus wagon, Katrinka started doing her makeup as Charlotte watched. She was wearing a green sheath dress, sleeveless in the style of Jackie Kennedy, and a matching pill-box hat. She had on elbow-length gloves that were still so new the fingertips were not yet blackened at the seams; she yanked them off, finger by finger.

The makeup went like this: she poured a sparkling gush of baby oil into the cradle of one palm, applying it with the fingertips of the other hand to lips, eyelids, brows. She stared impassively at the face in front of her, then took a deep drag on her oily cigarette, saying, "And *you* shut the fuck up, too!" She put the cigarette back on the edge of the table, then rubbed her hands together. She wiped her face all over, as if she were a raccoon washing; she ran one oily hand up one arm, then the other up the other arm, paying special attention to her elbows. Katrinka was always very proud of the pliant skin of her elbows.

"What it *was* at the phone company was," she paused to smoke, "that the place was so full to the rafters with the most gawd-awful A-number one–number ten G.I.-Maxine-Audrey-Roxie-Wilma and/or Thelma bitches that I had to go into the ladies' room to sit on the toilet to get away from them and even *then* their voices didn't quit. They left their blotted lipsticky mouths on tissues all over the place to sing to me. Of course, I was completely off my rocker by then. Lionel and Winnie had taken you out of our room and put you in the shoe drawer in the front bedroom."

"They put me in the shoe drawer? And you *let* them?"

Katrinka was twisting the end of the lipstick tube. "Well, it *was* filled with pillows, and it wasn't *shoved back in!*" She drew a wide slash of crimson across either gleaming cheekbone, then rubbed it into rouge with the tips of her shining fingers. She drew her lipstick on, top then bottom, then rubbed her lips together. She blotted them with a clump yanked from the roll of toilet paper she kept on the vanity, and tossed it to the floor. She peered into the smoky mirror, then sighed her heart-attack-in-the-food-store sigh: *Aut! aut! aut!*

"The mouths on the tissues used to sing to me in syncopation, like the Andrews Sisters, but much, much sicker." She tipped her chin up. She seemed almost to be listening to those voices again.

Her shiny brows moved together almost imperceptibly. She looked up and found Charlotte staring. "It was, you see, all about him."

Charlotte's stomach felt as if it were suddenly shorn away. Her empty hands ached, and she held them out toward Katrinka, palms up beseechingly. Her eyes were filling with tears. "My father!" she cried. "You knew he was dead then?"

"Oh, I knew that all along."

"Because you had a feeling?" Charlotte asked her, her voice breaking, the last word cracked in two.

Katrinka, regal, arch, looked back at her. She pressed her lips together amusedly. "Uh-uh, sweetie, because I could hear him."

14

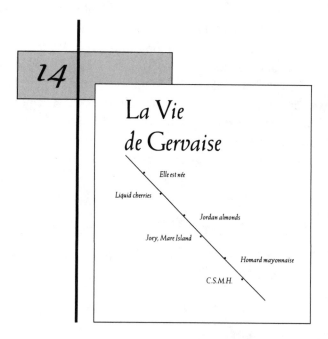

La Vie
de Gervaise

Elle est née

Liquid cherries

Jordan almonds

Joey, Mare Island

Homard mayonnaise

C.S.M.H.

Charlotte and her mother were in the Palmengarten having lunch. The German beer garden had been put up under the dark green mesh of the enormous tent over the horticultural displays; the tent was open on the sides. High above them the sun was gleaming, but dimly through the filmy green.

They were only a week into the fair, and Charlotte was already raging with boredom. There was nothing to do except listen to her mother talk and go to the beach to lie out. She lay alone there on a wide white beach strewn with the bodies of surfers and half-dressed marines who came in their fatigues but took their shirts off to sit upon. Lying around like that, Charlotte noticed, made people look dead.

Two of the marines had come up to Charlotte the day before and sat down on either side. Each had sat with knees up, staring out at the waves crashing, watching her only when the other one was talking. They had wanted to know if she and a friend might like to go to the movies in the village sometime.

It was the look of their white skin, she knew, that was so repellent, though her own skin had been that white just the week before. One had pimples in the hair follicles on his chest. Their short haircuts made their ears stick out. She had told them she wasn't allowed.

Charlotte was never getting married. No one was ever going to marry her because she had Katrinka as a mother. Her mother was bizarre. It was in everything—the words she said, the way she said them, the ways she moved her face around. Charlotte noticed it most in public. Now, in the beer garden, Katrinka was holding her arms stiffly above her head, as if she were hanging by her wrists. Charlotte couldn't get married because she would never be able to leave her mother to these people in the Palmengarten who were turning to stare at her. Like Little Winnie and Aunt Hoppy, the two of them were going to live forever, the one talking out loud, the other silent, furious, weighing the words for clues as to who they were and how they'd come to be that way.

"Gawd, how I hate nature," Katrinka said, and her face went off into ironic contortions. "Na-chur! Winnie was always very big on it, the horned-toad-and-fishing aspect of things. Lionel preferred the dank stink of library paste."

Charlotte sighed and looked around. Next to their table an artificial stream burbled along over a creekbed where the black plastic was held in place by rocks. The flowers and bushes alongside it had not been planted, but sat in their pots stuffed down into dirt and covered at the base with dried moss. The azaleas right next to the creek were already looking crisp. Wide beds of petunias and snapdragons had wilted in the shady heat.

"Nature," Katrinka repeated. "This is more like Camarillo for plants." She smirked and muttered. She was muttering more to herself these days, which was the way she did the dummies secretly. "Why, hideee!" she cried suddenly. "Why, do tell! Don't look now, sweetie, but it's Wade-in-the-Waters, his very full-sized self!"

The cowboy was coming up to them at a definite tilt. His face was worn but smiling. With him was the Mexican ridesman. They were both wearing pale green shirts with names sewn into the oval patch above the pocket. Beneath the words "Sugarman Amusements" each shirt read "José."

"I wanted to thank you for setting me up like that," the cowboy was telling Katrinka, though it looked as if he wanted to apologize. "Do you know José Delgado? I'm working with him over in the Fun Zone."

"If you're all *that* grateful, why don't the two of you buy me a beer?" Katrinka said, and the two men sat down.

"I go by Joe," the Mexican told them, looking at Charlotte. Her stomach dropped. Their shirts were faded from being washed so many times, but were not ironed. Charlotte understood that to mean the ridesman wasn't married, or he was married to a person like Katrinka who wasn't very wifey.

She was looking at him. He looked back. His look lay on her skin like the press of coins that had been left out in the sun. His lowered eyelids were so shiny they looked like they'd just been licked.

"Oh, you two *know* each other?" Katrinka said.

"No," Charlotte said.

"Well, *I* do know Joe, Charlotte. Joe and I go back a *long* way, don't we, Joe, and he's a perfect louse so I don't want you to have anything to do with him." Katrinka smirked. "Aren't you a perfect louse?" she asked him, then turned back to Charlotte. "He's always been the first to admit it."

"Mother!"

"Don't you love the way she says that? With six or seven syllables? And every one of them accusatory?" Again she turned to Charlotte, saying, "And as for you, Lady Fancy, I wouldn't get too snazzy, if I were you, unless you want to end up half-baked in the upper crust like all your fawtha's family." She reached her long white arm over Charlotte's shoulders, telling the others, "Lady Fancy is what I call her when she's being particularly irritating." She was trying to pull Charlotte's face over to her own proffered cheek, but Charlotte shrugged her off, crossing her own arms across her chest.

"Don't!" Charlotte whispered harshly.

"Don't what?"

"Don't talk about me and don't call me things."

Katrinka arched her brow and sucked her cheeks in. She took a cigarette from her pack and waved it until the cowboy struck a match. She inhaled dramatically, then exhaled, saying, "All right! Ignore her, all of you. The trouble with my daughter is that she was orphaned at birth and has never gotten over it. She has never received the proper kind of attention, which has led to this painful and quite inarticulate self-consciousness, which is her *deal*, as she says."

"Her deal?" the cowboy asked.

"Her issue in group therapy. You are not to discuss her, do you understand me? Ignore her, and whatever you do, don't call her *things!* I thought you were going to buy me a beer?" The cowboy's arm was reaching high into the air to get the waitress's attention. His wrist was flat across and bony. He was pathetic. All of them were pathetic, including Charlotte herself. She heard the scrape of the back of her chair legs, felt herself standing up. "See!" Katrinka said. "Now, you've all gone and called her *things!*"

"*Schlafen Sie wohl,*" Charlotte whispered as she leaned toward her across the table, "which is German for *fuck you!*"

"Oh, for Christsake, Charlotte! Can't you for once be teased?" But Charlotte was already out from under the tent and into the sun. She hated the headachy brightness of a day like this when paint and metal were made to gleam so violently. As soon as she was able, she was moving to a rainier climate. She went into one of the exhibition halls to get out of the sun; there she bought a piece of chocolate cake from a plump lady exhibitor and ate it, deciding that she was going on a diet as soon as she had finished it. The lady brought out a piece of needlepoint she was doing—two kittens playing with a ball of yarn—and she sat patiently working on it as Charlotte ate. Charlotte had to close her eyes, so perfectly appalled was she by the sight of the plump lady contentedly doing a needlepoint design so cute it was beyond belief or despair. She did this work, Charlotte imagined, to make herself believe she was living, that she was consequential, that she had significance. The sun, the boredom, the rage she felt at her goddamned craphead mother, who had called her *inarticulate*, the cake were all making her sick. She was going to get really sick, she knew, and Katrinka would be no help. Once when Charlotte had been sick on Avenue B and had been lying in bed fast asleep, her mother had tried to feed her peas.

Walking up another aisle in the food hall, Charlotte stole a jar of pickles. She did it brazenly, right in front of a family of two nicens parents and their three nicens children. "Wanna know something?" Charlotte asked them, as she held the pickles in front of her. "Know how Marie Antoinette was supposed to have said that junk about letting them eat cake? Well, that isn't what she said." The mother and father were holding their children to them. "What she really said was, if they are all out of *pain*, then let them eat *brioche*, which is a whole lot different from *gâteau*," Charlotte told them, but they were already gone. She kept talking anyway: "About as different as chicken is from squirrel meat," she called after them.

She went into the next hall, groaning loudly, horribly, over the sad lives of everyone, over that of Mrs. Arthur Dickson, of Poway, California, who had collected more than thirteen hundred different pairs of salt-and-pepper shakers, which were here displayed. "Oh, my God!" Charlotte said, talking out loud. "Talk about something stealing the meaning of life!" It was the Blandito who was responsible for this, Katrinka sometimes said. He was one of the voices she heard that was not assigned to a body.

The next display was done on poster board. The title was the kind of writing that always made Charlotte want to kill herself—upper and lower case all mixed together. That was bad enough, without thinking of what the words said. She stared and stared at the dullness of them: "112 diFFErEnT tyPES OF bArBEd wirE." She put her two cold hands over her face and made the sound of sobbing into them, although she was really laughing. She was laughing at the words she was telling herself: "Consequence. Significance." She was, she observed quite clearly, cracking up in the exhibition hall of the San Diego County Fair in Del Mar, California.

Walking as quickly as she could to get out of there, she passed a huge jar holding a portrait of John F. Kennedy, done in pickled vegetables. It was all she could do not to push it to the floor to smash it. She walked on, imagining the crash and the great wash and splash of glassy brine and the olive and peppers and little onions that had made up the president's eyes and mouth and teeth wildly hopping around as if in total ecstasy at their escape.

Katrinka fell apart just like this, Charlotte knew, overwhelmed by sights and sounds while zigzagging down the aisle at Safeway, the music plinking down, the giant Chiquita bananas and cans of Del Monte peaches in cardboard cutouts all perched and dancing above her on the wires. She would forget then that it was she and not the things all around her that were made animate by meaning. The boundaries broke down at times like this. She would abandon her shopping cart in the produce aisle and lie down next to the sacks of onions and potatoes. The clerks would come to help her up, to throw her out: there would be no lying down in Safeway! She would then lie down in the parking lot next to the taxi stand. It was then that the police or the ambulance would finally be called.

Schizophrenia, Winnie always said, was the form of mental illness that had been clinically proven to be caused by the chemical properties of grief. That was one good reason, she told Charlotte, she should not make it a habit to go around feeling sorry for herself. In addition, Charlotte was going to need all the gumption she could get. "Gumption!" Charlotte said out loud, snorting at the nineteenth-century sound of it. Plenty of the Japanese children had had gumption, she imagined, and still had had an atomic bomb dropped on their heads.

She was walking through the horse barn, thinking of the fact that she was so dispassionate about horses, that she was so basically lousy at being a girl. She breathed the clean sweet smell of hay and horse manure, wondering if there were some special *significance* in the fact that Winnie painted her crappy art in the toilet off the service porch. Charlotte thought she would ask her mother, but then remembered she wasn't speaking to her. Katrinka always knew all about that kind of thing, the pseudo-psychological *deal* of whosits doing this or that. She also knew how to conjugate verbs such as those in phrases like "go mind your own fucky little business," which she said to a Safeway checker trying to help her out of the potatoes. She knew a million words for blotto, stinko, bombed, and all the various plurals of "gins-and-tonics."

But it was Charlotte, not Katrinka, who knew about the chemical properties of grief: it was heavy, as low down as ether, it bubbled in the bridge of her nose. It hollowed a person's hands out, made them so empty and desperate that they would grab onto anything or anyone in order to be held. It could sheer away the organs of feeling: the stomach, the bowels. It left the heart dead and the brain alive, to hear words, to think of them, to whisper them in Winnie's voice: "Grief! What do you know about it! *My* father died when I was three and *I* was the one who was *heart*broken!"

This was grief, Charlotte knew. She stood in the horse barn in the smell of manure and wept for the loss of all she'd ever loved. She had never cared about horses. She had played horses with Cheryl only to be like her. She clutched the pickles and saw herself living in the broken-down house in Orange with Katrinka, surrounded by the sparkling motels and apartment buildings. They were both old, both dressed in long, white, mental-patient nightgowns left over from the days of Aunt Hoppy and Little Winnie. Reddy Kilowatt had turned the lights off so the house was lit with candles.

The plumbing was long broken, the toilets stuffed up with dried and ancient shit, clogged with toilet paper. They lived on peanut-butter-and-cheese crackers from the Servomation machines: Charlotte sneaked over to the motels at night with their twenty-seven centses, using the dimes and quarters. Sometimes she took her nightgown off and slipped naked into the pool's blue water, thinking of the life she might have had if she had not had to stay home to take care of her fucking mother. She looked down at the shape of her body, but couldn't remember what it was supposed to be good for. She watched her long gray braids float out and out. When the social worker came by to bring their welfare checks, she asked Charlotte why she'd done this, if it wasn't really just a question of family loyalty. Charlotte sucked her cheeks in and sneered at the social worker, cracking a beer, lighting a cigarette. She wasn't talking. It was a rule in their family, something her father was famous for always saying: *Never apologize. Never explain.*

The 4-H kids were outside the beef barn sudsing their animals at the pens by the concrete tubs. They were about the same age as Charlotte, but the clothes they wore were entirely different. Both boys and girls wore brand-new extremely blue blue jeans that were so long they bunched up at the heels of their boots. They wore white T-shirts or white Sunday school shirts and each had a tooled leather belt. One big red-and-white steer was ready, and the boy who owned him was moving him down the chute constructed by the swinging gates.

Suddenly, as one gate was swung halfway around, Charlotte, too, was enclosed and in the same grid as the animal. "Sorry," the boy said, raising his eyebrows. "I'll get him turned around." He jabbed the steer in the haunch with the prongs of a currycomb and yanked the lead, but the steer had started to back up. The side of his flank was against her chest, pressing her to the gate. Steam from the bath was rising from his red hide.

"Goddamn you, Spenser!" the boy said, yanking on the lead. Charlotte lowered her face but still looked up at him. She liked boys who seemed to know what they were doing.

He couldn't get the steer to move out of the pen toward the barn, so he yelled for someone to bring him the cattle prod. "My father's over in the pig barn with my sister," he told Charlotte. "He'll be here in a second with the Hot Shot." He said it as if anyone would know what that was.

He was good-looking, tall; his eyes were humorous and were bright turquoise in the redness of his face. He had freckles, and his nose and lips were smeared with zinc oxide. "God, I'm sorry," he said, still yanking, although the steer was clearly determined not to move.

"Oh, it's okay," she told him. "I mean I wasn't really in a hurry." She held the pickles in one hand and gestured toward the exhibition hall with the other. "I was just over there, you know, where I saw some of the stupidest junk I ever saw in my life, I mean, not to hurt your feelings if you like junk like that."

"Like what?" he asked across the back of the animal.

"Oh, I don't know," she was saying, "like one hundred twelve different types of barbed wire. But maybe you would like it because you live on a farm. Or a portrait of the president made out of pickled vegetables. But then maybe you're a Democrat." He was looking at her very somberly when the steer took one more step backward and crushed the toes of her foot. She said, "*Oh.*" It sounded like air going out of a tire.

"What's the matter?"

"He's on my foot," she tried to say, then realized she hadn't spoken. She licked her lips and tried again. Her face was suddenly wet with the steam from the animal's haunch and with tears. Since her eyes were not shut, and she made no noise, it was hard for her to understand that she was crying. This was a different sort of remove from the narcolepsy: she was now in the movie, and was watching herself.

The boy was underneath the steer jabbing his hoof with the point of the currycomb, but the steer had settled in and wasn't moving. "Someone, tell my dad to hurry! Spenser's standing on this girl's foot and she's got on sandals!" He stood up. "He's right there—he'll be right here," he was telling Charlotte, still jabbing the steer and yanking the lead. "I hate this animal," he told her. "Born obstinate." He socked Spenser with his fist on the pink of his snout.

"Oh, that's all right," Charlotte wanted to say, to be polite. "It's all my fault anyway—I should have been wearing some sort of different outfit, boots, the way you guys do. I should have been a different sort of type." She would have said this, but the pain was making her dreamy.

Quite abstractedly, she was thinking of the pain, taking it apart in order to analyze it. There was the ignominy of weeping uncontrollably before this cute boy and the crowd of kids who were gathering, kids who all knew one another, who dressed alike, who spoke the same language.

Then there was the pressure of the foot of a thousand-pound steer standing fully on top of her. The four biggest toes on her right foot were under the crushing weight of it. There was also an unbearable pinching of the skin at the sharp edge of his hoof. She thought of the pain, the parts of it, the way it felt hot, then cold, then dull as if it had gone away, only to come reeling back again. It was the Blandito, Katrinka said, who steals the meaning of life. He was the inventor of pain so bad it is unbearable. It is unbearable, but still there is no release from it.

"I can't stand it," she whispered to him, and he reached across the steam and patted her hand where it rested. She sighed through her sobbing and put her face down on her arm as if taking a nap at her school desk.

The father was there then, tawny-haired like his son, and they began trying to get the people to move out of the way so the steer could see a place to move. Charlotte heard all the voices clearly. Everyone was offering yet another helpful suggestion.

The steer's face was white, and his eyelashes were white and long, and as thick as brush bristles. He turned and looked at Charlotte impassively. But still the pain would not cease. It went out and out. It spread from her to him who would soon be dead, since he had been raised for slaughter. She saw it synapse, leaping in the flinch of the prod's current that rippled his steaming flesh. She felt the shock in her hand. They were united by it, both inured to it. The fucker wouldn't move until he'd been shocked four times. She was like that too: good at pain, having grown used to it.

The pressure lifted. She was suddenly light then and was being lifted, carried as if in triumph through a crowd that was pleased with her. She was a hero but the pain didn't stop. It went on and on, out and out and out. She could still feel the imprint of the bones of the animal's tail against her chest: each, each, each. The pain made it hard to breathe. She watched the sunburned neck of the boy's father as he carried her to the first aid bunker. The boy followed behind with the pickles. His head was down. It looked as if he were following a trail. Drops of blood were flung off from her toes with each of the man's bounding steps.

"Oh, my God!" Katrinka was crying as she came into the first aid room.

"I don't think the toes are crushed," the nurse was saying, and Katrinka was already whipping that word into the vortex of her lifelong soliloquy, Charlotte saw, and had immediately spun it out again.

"My baby's toes! Crushed???? Crushed???? *Crushed* by the *weight* of a *steeeer!*" It was Baba, Charlotte saw, the joke of a dutiful mother who'd come to take Katrinka's place. She was wearing her ventriloquist's dress, more or less clean, only slightly rumpled. It was a sheath in the shade called raspberry. Lionel bought her these dresses at Bullock's. Katrinka wore them until they turned into mental patient outfits, then they were thrown away.

She reached around Charlotte with her naked arm and tried to hug her to her. "Don't get worked up over it, all right?" Charlotte said. "All I have to do is go get a tetanus shot."

"Tetanus!" Baba screamed. "Jesus H. *God!* That's what Teddy Roosevelt's son died of! His shoes were too tight! He got a blister! It became *infected!*"

The boy and his father were watching them. Katrinka's hair was wild. She was wearing a single long sherbet-colored glove.

"Lockjaw!" she was screaming. "Charlotte, listen to me! I want you to open and shut your mouth."

Charlotte's teeth were tightly clenched, and she spoke under her breath, without moving her lips. "Mother, will you stop it, please? Don't you get it? This isn't your act. This isn't even your *deal.*"

The cowboy had come earlier, bringing a corn dog smeared with gaudy mustard, but Charlotte had taken a pain killer the doctor had given her and had been sleeping in such a leaden way that she was removed from appetite. She saw the thing as an object, smelled its grease, and told him she was sorry but she wouldn't be able to eat it. She asked him to throw it away because she was nauseated. "Not in there," she told him, when he started to put it into a big brown shopping bag from Safeway. "She still wants those. Those are her Goody Butts." The words were strung out, gauzy, a series of pink-tinged clouds.

So when he showed up later and stood in silhouette in the door against the lights of the parking lot, the one shoulder hunched up, chin tucked in as if warding off a punch, she remembered it as a dream she'd had once and was embarking on again. "Sorry," she said, "but I just can't eat it. The pill makes me feel filled up, you know? Like my head and stomach are stuffed with cotton?"

He used his elbows to hitch his trousers up. He scooted his pants halfway up his chest; they started to slide down again. "It's her," he said. "She needs you."

Charlotte was already out of bed, still in her pajamas, wrapping herself in Katrinka's satiny dressing gown. Her mother's smell was all around her: the smoky sweetness of the sweat and breath and perfume. She hobbled down the steps after him, walking on her heel. All four toes were broken, but none was crushed. She would lose the nails. The foot was bandaged. Charlotte would live; it was her mother, as always, who was in actual extremity.

"I don't want you to think nothing," he was telling her as they walked along. The moon was out and it lit up the fog that lay low to the ground. "We went out for a couple of beers. She got a little looped and started acting sort of crazy. I didn't do nothing to her, you understand?"

She didn't answer him. She had never been able to tolerate anything anyone ever said about her mother. She hated the person for commenting, even hated Dr. Greenley's saying Katrinka's fate was in the hands of God. As if Dr. Greenley himself were exempt from fate by virtue of his being a Seventh Day Adventist, such a *good* and *kindly* doctor! As if God had ever given a shit about anything that had already happened to Katrinka. She went through life like a baby, Charlotte knew, almost totally defenseless, screaming to call attention to herself.

The foot throbbed. The cowboy was drunk himself and stumbling in his high-heeled boots through the drifts of sand that had come up onto the blacktop of the parking lot. Now they were on the road along the top of the cliff running next to the state park. The waves on the beach below pounded down, sucked in, slushed, grew awed and silent, then the sound began again. Behind them in the darkness, a car's tires slipped on the wet pavement. Everything in their lives was so precariously balanced that the slightest, most normal accident would pitch them off into catastrophe, Charlotte knew.

The car they had heard behind now came along the road, stabbing its headlights out in front of them. The lights fell on the white DeSoto where it was parked in the shadow of the pines. This was a lovers' lane. Katrinka sat in the driver's seat. Her lips were moving. "I didn't do nothing to her," the cowboy said again. "She got her clothes off herself and . . ."

"Just shut up," Charlotte told him.

She came to the side of the car and reached in to touch her mother. "Mama?" she asked. The skin of her mother's arm was frigid.

Katrinka looked up, knew her, but only vaguely, as Shady Lewis recognized Sacramento. Her eyes looked hurt, shrewd. Her cheeks were sucked in so extremely that the flesh of her face was pulled down. "He took my cigarettes," she whispered.

"Mama, it's okay, really. We have more at the Airstream. We have Goody Butts, remember? Mama? Come on out. I think this man wants to drive somewhere."

"He took my money awwwwwnnnnd he took my cigarettes."

"She hid my car keys. I think she threw them into the sand out there. She started saying things. *I* didn't take nothing from *her*."

Charlotte opened the door and tried to take her elbow, but Katrinka shrugged her off. "Well, anyway, put the robe on, all right? All right, Mom? Mama, we have to go now. I think this man wants to drive his car someplace."

"Maaaaannnnn?" she asked. "Maaaaaaaaaaaaaaaannnnnnnnnn?" Her head rolled around. "This is not a maaaaaaaannnnnnnnnn! This is a crappy piece of filthy shit awwwwwnnnnnd this is not a *car*. This is a lousy shitpile." She reached into the foot well and brought out a handful of trash, which she tried to throw past Charlotte toward the cowboy. "His floors were so clean you could eat off of them," she cried, pelting him with a hardened piece of hamburger bun.

"The squalor we have found her in." This was not the cute, jokey Winnie, the voice Nellie sometimes did, but the actual malignant thing. It might have been Winnie herself sitting there, except that it was really Katrinka naked.

Katrinka was shoving hard on the heavy door of the car, trying to get it open. Charlotte pulled on the handle; the door then swung away, which made Katrinka lurch toward the opening. Charlotte caught her before she tumbled, righted her with her hands in her mother's clammy armpits. Katrinka swatted her away, saying, "Don't you condescend to me with your crappy social worker act. You're not so high up in this pisspot stinking shithole that you can condescend to me."

"I didn't say I was," Charlotte told her. "I was just trying to keep you from falling on your face." *Your drunken face*, she added, for her own mean pleasure.

Even in the moonlight Katrinka's face was haggard. Her upper body slumped over her thighs, casting her belly into shadow. Her breasts sloped down and away from the white of her chest. Charlotte was always horrified to look at her mother's body, to see it, be made to think of the ways they were so intimately united by that flesh. Katrinka's legs were apart. She made no effort to cover herself. "Just take this, all right?" Charlotte said, holding out the robe. It was so new it still had creases from its pressing at the garment factory, but was already spattered down the front with various liquids.

Katrinka shoved her away, then reached back into the well of the car to retrieve her handbag. It was black, beaded in jet, and it swung on a gold chain. She put it in her lap. Then she reached around and got her shoes, struggling into them by arduously raising one big foot and then the other. She planted them in the sand, all the while muttering amusedly to herself. She looked up again and saw Charlotte. "Miss *Missy* Miss. Miss Missy Missy Miss of the UVA." She launched the handbag out on its chain in a slow arc up and out in the direction of Charlotte's face. "We know all about it, don't we, Charlotte, the mayonnaise and the icky ick, and the way it comes dripping down the leg?"

But Charlotte was gone now, translating it all into coded numbers, putting it onto ticker tape; she noted all the details clearly but as a camera only. She saw how her mother reached beneath her seat and pulled out the car keys, how she sent them off the cliff in a high tinkling arc, how she shoved at Charlotte's body as she stood up, saying, "You are perfectly disgusting to me. Did you imagine that I would find you attractive, drunk and unclothed like that, just because *she* likes it?" This was in Winnie's voice. Charlotte did not know who any of the people were: *I* or *she* or *you*.

Then Katrinka started off, staggering on her high heels but with her head held high. She held her evening bag with its chain in the crook of her elbow so it swung as she lurched. The moon was out from the fog, and the wind-bent Torrey pines cast eerie horror-movie shadows. Katrinka's back and long buttocks were starkly white in the moonlight.

She was stumbling back the way they'd come, right along the cliff. The black was where the world ended. Charlotte watched it: a white shape now there, now there, now not. "Mother!" she screamed then, ripped awake. She hobbled after Katrinka, overtaking her, placing the luminous robe around her shoulders.

But Katrinka had already turned from the dark of the cliff and was lifting her face toward the haloed lights of the parking lot. The face Charlotte looked into wasn't that of a suicide: it was cold, bemused, haughty. "I know all about it," she said, as Winnie. "What the two of you do with your icky icks."

Her mother's wasn't the face of a suicide, Charlotte saw as she stared into its cruel impassivity. Katrinka would never kill herself. She didn't need to. She was still dead from way back then, from the time when her parents had killed her.

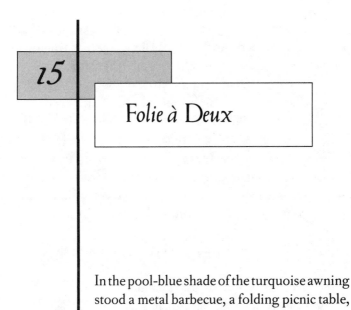

15

Folie à Deux

In the pool-blue shade of the turquoise awning stood a metal barbecue, a folding picnic table, redwood benches, lawn chairs. On the steps of the mobile home there was a nubby rubber mat that said, "The Sugarman's." Charlotte noted that the apostrophe was in the wrong place, pocketing that information for later, to hate them with.

"Who's there?" a woman's voice asked from behind the screened door. Charlotte told her that she was Katrinka's daughter, that she needed to see Mr. Sugarman.

"Well, he's eating lunch right now—come back in a little while."

"What is it, Roxie?" a voice inside asked.

"Nothing. Some girl."

"Come back when?" Charlotte asked, thinking, *Lunch? At ten-thirty in the morning?* "This is kind of urgent," she told her.

"What do you mean, *kind of* urgent?" asked Roxie Sugarman. "It either is or it isn't, am I right?" But she was opening the screen to let Charlotte in. She had on harlequin glasses studded with rhinestones and was wearing bright orange capris and a white sleeveless shirt with a turned-up collar. The shirt was spotted with huge orange polka dots. "He's got stomach troubles," she told Charlotte. "He's got to eat regular or his stomach gives him grief." She seemed to be addressing Charlotte as she said this, or perhaps a third party standing to the side of Charlotte and slightly behind her.

Charlotte limped into the room. Her whole foot ached in a throbbing way with every step, every thump of her heart. She hobbled to the place where the aluminum strip on the floor showed that the living room ended and the dining room began. "Alex, this is Katrinka's kid. You ready for this? You want to hear it when you're eating?"

Alex Sugarman was hugely fat and sat at a table covered with platters of food. He seemed to be made weary just by looking out at all he had to eat, and he hadn't yet begun. He sadly reached with his fork to spear a sausage; touched, it gushed yellow juice. "So what's up wid your ma?" he asked without looking at Charlotte.

"She's sick."

"Sick!" Roxie cried from the kitchenette, where she was heaving a huge pot of corn on the cob into a colander in the sink. "How sick?" The corn thumped out like logs coming over a waterfall.

"She means sick *how?*" he explained.

"Run down," Charlotte told them.

"Oh!" Roxie exclaimed, her mouth small with humor. "*Run down* is what we're calling it?" This was addressed to the third party. Charlotte turned with narrowed eyes to glare at her. The lenses of the harlequin glasses were white with steam from the bowl of corn she was carrying.

"She has the stomach flu," Charlotte told her.

Sugarman took a corn on the cob and began laboriously to butter it. A dinger dinged, and Roxie went to the oven and took out a loaf of garlic bread. "My husband's Jewish," she told whoever it was she imagined was interviewing her. "I'm Italian. He married me for my cooking. He can't stand Jewish food. Matzo balls? Can't stand them. Chicken livers? Wouldn't touch them with a ten-foot pole." She said it all in a rote way, as if she had said the same thing to a thousand different people over the course of their marriage.

The fragrant steam of the spaghetti rose up into Sugarman's face. He took his napkin from where it was tucked into his neck and used it to wipe his forehead. He looked up and Charlotte saw that he had beautiful features: deeply brown eyes, curly lashes, a long straight nose that came out from his brow without an indentation, like the profile on an ancient coin. His lips were fat, red, wet. "She been drinking?" he asked. Charlotte jumped as if she'd been jabbed with the Hot Shot.

"You been eating?" she retorted, but silently. "She has the stomach flu," she repeated sullenly, looking out at him from under her eyebrows.

"Stomach flu!" Roxie cried, distractedly. She was carrying in another platter. "Now, Alex, what have I forgotten before I sit down? Tell me so I don't have to get up again."

"Nothing, Roxie. Sit down."

"The cheese," she said. "You go ahead, Alex. You start," and she was gone again.

"So, I heard she had a little trouble wid her act last night," Sugarman said, not starting. "That she got a little wild wid the language."

"Fuck you," Charlotte said under her breath. She shrugged. "She's trying out something new. Something with the Blandito in it. The one that steals the meaning of life."

"Is that right?" Roxie Sugarman asked the interviewer over the rhinestone rims of her glasses as she passed by, winking at the invisible audience. "Alex, what do you want to drink? I have sodas. I have ice tea."

Charlotte looked over the mounds of food. She closed her eyes and recited mentally: igneous, sedimentary, metamorphic. That was to avoid the words *consequence, significance, the meaning of life*, which might have made her laugh out loud. "Why doesn't she have as much right to be sick as the next person?" she whispered, with her eyes still closed. "She needs a day off to rest up. She needs to wash and set her hair."

"She told me about that one, the Blandito," Sugarman said. "I told her, 'Katrinka, correct me if I'm wrong, but I don't think it's such a good idea.' I told her, 'Go easy on that intellectual stuff—this is entertainment.' Now I know your ma's a smart lady, the only one around here with a college education, but still and all, people don't like to be talked down to. Which is what she does when she gets going. Anyways, I told her, 'Katrinka, you doing voices without the bodies ain't original. You just look like any other nut, talking to yourself.'"

"You know what the matter is?" Roxie asked. "She's got a lot of talent but you can't count on her. She's on three days, off the next. She may be the best, but what good does it do you, Alex, when she's always taking a couple of days off to wash and set her hair? God! Think of what would happen if she decided she needed a manicure!"

"She'll be better tomorrow," Charlotte said.

"I don't really want to tell you your business, Alex, but how many times is it that we've had to call her parents to come after her, to get her someplace where someone can take care of her? She doesn't *seem* dangerous, but you never know what that kind will do. Remember in the papers? That one in San Gabriel? That one who tied up the family on the weekend and slit their throats for no reason and even killed the family dog?"

"Roxie, that's enough."

"The people maybe I could see, though he'd never even met them once, but *to kill a dog like that?* To slit the throat of a *dog?* You have to be completely crazy for that kind of thing."

"Roxie, I got a bad stomach. I'm trying to eat." He had paused with his wrists resting against the edge of the table. His head was bowed as if in prayer.

"He was a certified public accountant. Start!" she told him, then turned to Charlotte to confide: "Who would expect a thing like that from a certified public accountant?" She was still standing, waiting to show Charlotte out. To the interviewer she added, "It was a fox terrier. You know, the kind the Thin Man had?" She twisted her dish towel in her hands. Sugarman hadn't started.

"A person still has the right to get sick," Charlotte whispered, watching Sugarman's soft eyes. "This isn't Soviet Russia," she reminded him. She felt they both were hypnotized. She was going to win. She was going to win though she couldn't ever really win. She'd win this one, and what she'd get would be Katrinka.

Slowly scooping peas onto his plate, he sighed with the effort of it. "You didn't need to come around here," he said, and, as she opened her mouth to argue, he went on, "Because I never do fire your ma, you know that? I just don't want those ladies from the Legion of Christian Decency coming around here, sitting down with my wife to wait for me so they can complain about how women and children are hearing that kind of language. I run a nice place, and your ma has to respect that. I don't need the Legion of Christian Decency ladies on my neck. Remind her. Tell her, 'Legion of Christian Decency,' and she'll know what I mean. We had this talk before. Tell her too to remember our deal."

"Deal?"

"I give her a bonus for promising she won't smoke in the circus wagon. Remind her she ain't allowed. If she's gotta smoke, she can step outside."

"All right," Charlotte breathed. His face was glowing, beautiful; she felt sickish with love for him, a love that was physical, a love surpassing gratitude.

"Tell her to come see me when she's feeling better. I need to talk about the act."

"Okay," Charlotte said, and words began. "Thanks," she told him. "*Thanks*, really, *so* much. She's going to be a lot better, really, because really no one except me understands how it is with her and now I'm old enough, you know, to help out? To pick things up? And to help with the business kind of stuff?"

He looked up at her through the steam of the peas. "Your ma and me?" he asked. "We got an understanding: I'm the way I am, which is fair. She's like she is, which is . . . ?" He shrugged. "We don't try to change each other." He stared at Charlotte deeply. His eyes were beautiful—they were also perfectly tragic. "But you're a smart kid, so what am I telling you you don't already know."

The boy was sitting on the steps of the trailer, holding the jar of pickles. "I knocked," he said, "but no one answered. I think somebody's in there, though. I heard voices." He stood up on the bottom step.

Charlotte shut her eyes. She looked like hell warmed over, she knew, from staying awake all night, holding her mother's head on her lap, holding her own hands over her mother's hands, which were covering Katrinka's ears. Charlotte opened her eyes but he hadn't yet disappeared. "How're the toes?" he was asking.

"Okay."

"God, I'm sorry about it."

"About what?" she asked him suspiciously. How many people, she wondered, had heard about Katrinka? She hated people who were *sorreee*.

"Spenser."

"It's okay. Anyway, it was my fault for not having boots on. Anyway, your dad paid the doctor bill."

"I have to pay him back when the son-of-a-bitch is slaughtered." He said this matter-of-factly.

Charlotte squinted up at him. He had an old-fashioned look from the way the waves were pressed into his golden hair. His nose was broad and straight, his mouth small. She felt woozy. Through the wooziness swirled the wonder that a boy this good-looking could be involved in anything cruel. "You don't do it yourself or anything?" she asked him.

"The packers do it. Then my family buys one side back. We have a locker."

"Side?"

"Of beef. I get two calves every year and raise them at school. You really never heard of any of this?"

She shook her head. "You keep animals at your school?"

"Your school doesn't offer animal husbandry?"

Charlotte stared up at him, forgetting to answer. His eyebrows, like her own, ran straight across without a lift to them. It looked better on him. The conversation was becoming taut, sexy, though she understood neither how nor why. "Animal husbandry," she said, sighing deeply. This had to do, she knew, with breeding.

Then she glanced down and saw the ragged filthy bandage. She looked like Avenue B, like a mental patient who couldn't take proper care of herself, she realized, or one of the hobos who tape their shoes together. "I have to go in now," she told him suddenly. "I have to go in and help my mother." Her face was getting hot with the thought of what an asshole she was to have imagined anyone this good could ever be interested in her.

"Well, my dad says the least I could do is take you out for a pizza."

She smiled at him bitterly. "Forget it," she said.

"My dad says . . ."

"Really," she told him, trying to wave him out of her way. She was thinking, *Pity, pity!* in Nellie's voice. "It was all *such* a pity," Nellie liked to say. "Anyway, I'm not allowed to date."

"Well, I didn't mean a date," he said. "Anyway, not a *date* date. I meant a movie, you know, if you don't like pizza."

Charlotte stared up at him, wondering what was a *date* date? What was a date date date? He seemed to loom over her. He was tall and she was exhausted and he was standing above her on the trailer's first step, as if it were his trailer and she'd come to see him. The Airstream had begun to rock. That would be Katrinka awake, ripping it apart to find cigarettes. She might come out if she heard them. She was wearing only the spotted dressing gown, if even that.

"All right," Charlotte told him. "Okay, but I have to go in now." He was good-looking and sweet. He was smiling down at her. All of this made her miserable, made her believe she was going to cry.

Katrinka was inside at the table, digging in the shopping bag for the longest Goody Butts. She had wiped her ashy fingers down the front of the apricot robe. "I am smoking this," she announced, showing it to Charlotte, "then I am going right straight back to Camarillo."

Charlotte said nothing. She went into the bathroom and looked for herself in the mirror that was hinged at the top, so it hung down from the ceiling. Katrinka had looked for cigarettes in the medicine cabinet, dumping everything out into the sink. The mirror was still swinging, so Charlotte's face went up and back, up and back. Her braids were loose, her eyes dark in the hollows under them. She looked like a whore or a refugee. "Pity, pity," she told herself, feeling the grief swelling in her glands like a sickness. The pump of sadness was palpable at all pressure points: throat, collarbone, hands.

"Charlotte!" her mother was pronouncing. "Charlotte, I want

you to place a person-to-person collect call to C.S.M.H. Call information in Camarillo to get the number. Are you writing this down? I want you to tell them that that mole on my stomach is changing and that I need to have it checked."

"Mom?" Charlotte asked, coming out of the toilet. "Mom? Why don't you just not?"

"Because! Because I'm broke and he stole my cigarettes and that Jew bastard fired me."

"He didn't fire you," Charlotte said. "He never fires you."

"Of course he did—I was acting up."

"Matter of fact, he didn't. Matter of fact, Mom, nobody really cares if you act up or not—do you realize that? He just wants you not to burn the place down. That and watch your language."

"Where did you get this?"

"He told me. He said to tell you, 'L.C.D.—Legion of Christian Decency and L.S.M.F.T., but only outside the wagon.'"

"He did not!"

"He did. Anyway, I can see what you mean about the Wilma-or-Thelma lawn furniture, but Mr. Sugarman is really nice."

Katrinka, with her mouth wide open, made a horrible animal *arrrghh!* "You *talked* to him! You talked to Sugarman! Jew bastard pimp craphead! Fat man! You *bitch!* What did you two do, *talk* about me?" she screamed. "Who do you think you are, my parents? My social worker? You can't talk about me to him, Charlotte! This isn't your *deal*, your life, your business!" She stood up and stomped to the bed, where she sat with her fingers dug into her cheeks. "Damn you! What did you do, go tell him how many beers I'd had?" Charlotte sat down at the table, closed her eyes, thought of the boy, whose name was Duncan, and how the cleft of his upper lip was made prominent by the way he held his mouth. She thought of taking her first finger, reaching forward, touching the declivity with her fingertip.

"In case you're interested," she said, opening her eyes, "I told him you weren't feeling well. I told him you have the stomach flu." Her mother was sitting with handfuls of hair gripped in her fingers. Or is it *handsful?* Charlotte wondered.

"You what!" Katrinka screamed. "Jesus Christ God, Charlotte! Everyone knows that 'stomach flu' is just another way of saying *tee minny martoonies!* Haven't you ever heard of family loyalty?"

"Fuck you," Charlotte said.

"Get me ready," Katrinka ordered.

"Get yourself ready."

"I can't! I'm having a nervous breakdown!" She stomped to the Scrabble board where her Goody Butts were lined up on the grid according to length. "I am smoking these, then I am going back to Camarillo." She sniffed, tipped her chin up, then sat down with great dignity.

"Oh, why don't you just really not?"

"Because," Katrinka screamed, "I can't bear it! I can't stand living like this! With my only daughter hating me!"

"I don't hate you."

"But you don't love me either." Charlotte chewed her lip as she looked at her. Katrinka was abstracted now, watching the match move close to the end of the shortened cigarette. Cross-eyed, she watched it miss, pass, move back to the center. She puffed and puffed; the blackened end of the butt finally caught. "Do you?" she demanded, through the smoke she was coughing out.

"When I go out to wash my hair," Charlotte told her, "I'll stop by and get you some at the machines."

"With what? That cowboy stole all my money."

"Lionel gave me some, too."

"I thought you said you weren't on his good side." *Were en't* was now two syllables, Charlotte observed.

Charlotte shrugged. Katrinka's eyes were bright green, their expression shrewd. Still, there was a little hope in them, that she had by some miracle been blessed with a daughter so clever she might be able to buy her a pack of cigarettes. Even that little dollop of God's grace might be enough to forestall a trip to the insane asylum.

Charlotte looked around at the wreck of the trailer. Both the life-sized clothes and the miniatures were strewn about. There were beer cans and food cans and smoked-up Goody Butts on the table and on the floor. The sink was stopped up, and black water filled it to the level of the counter. In this sweetish water floated cigarette filters and the bloated orange crusts of Wonder Bread.

Things always started off all right, Charlotte thought. Katrinka was like a bride at a foreign wedding, going away in a neat trailer, her dress pinned with dollars. But this sort of immigrant hopefulness had nothing to do with their family. Nothing would come of getting to know that boy. There was no good boy on earth who would marry her after seeing the mess that was her life. She wished she hadn't said she'd go to meet him.

Still, Charlotte now had more energy than back when she was trying to be a Brownie, and she decided she was going to clean the trailer while it was still possible to swing open the doors. "As soon as I get the sink cleaned out," she told her mother, "I'll shampoo your hair if you want me to. I'll set it for you, too."

"Why? Because I'm stinko? Is it really necessary for you to hate me so! It is not *all* my fault, you know, though most of it is, I imagine."

Charlotte ignored her. She was scooping the soggy crusts into the sacks of Goody Butts. The smell of the water was like rotting fruit. Water sucked out through her fingers down the drain, which was not stopped up; the basket was simply clogged with chunks of garbage.

"Know what he told me once?" Katrinka asked.

Charlotte didn't answer.

"All right, Charlotte, *ignore* me! *Don't* speak to me ever again! Be just like Lionel and Winnie! But honest-to-fucking Jesus, doesn't it embarrass you to act so goddamned teenaged?"

Charlotte didn't answer. She did wonder how it was possible both to be like Lionel and Winnie and to be teenaged, but she was not about to go into her mother's logic.

"With the pouting and the sulking," Katrinka went on anyway, "how stereotypical, really really, Missy Miss. It won't be necessary for you to wash my hair. I'm stinko and I'll stay that way."

Actually, Katrinka was clean, lying on the newly made bed in Charlotte's clean nightie, with her black high heels on. She had taken a shower in the Airstream, with Charlotte's help, but the water pressure wasn't strong enough for a good shampoo. Charlotte was worried about her hair because Katrinka always said dirty hair was one of the things that would slap her right into the mental hospital.

Katrinka was smoking her new pack of cigarettes and staring at the ceiling. "I eat and I eat," she said in Sugarman's New York accent, "but my appetite don't come." Then she said in her own voice, "Awwwnnd just exactly why must I wash and set my hair? So I'll be clean for Camarillo."

"You aren't going to Camarillo."

"Of course I am. I'm going as soon as Lionel shows up."

"He isn't coming."

Katrinka smirked at that and whispered, "Missy Miss Fancy Pants. Missy Miss Teenaged Minister of Shock Treatment of the UVA."

Charlotte remembered the electrical shock, how the steer's flesh had leapt with it beneath his damp hide, how her own nerves had picked it up and had jumped in sympathy. The current races—black goes white. An appliance, she knew, was fitted to one's mouth so one did not bite off one's tongue.

The brain is run on electricity and blood. What was wrong with Katrinka was in the chemistry, how the genes came down through generations, Winnie said, bringing along the little particles of grief. Someday soon, when there was nutrition by pill, when there was the perfect weather in the domed cities of Walt Disney, this grief-carrying gene would be isolated by scientists. Then these babies— those like Katrinka, those like Charlotte who didn't have it but who carried it—would not even have to be born.

Charlotte's hair was wet from her own shampoo, and it hung unbraided straight down her back. She imagined the jolt, the electricity leaping from nerve to nerve, black going to white as all nerves synapsed at once. She thought of Duncan's mouth, of the way he held his front teeth together on edge with his lips closed and moved them slightly; it was as if he were chewing the tiniest bit of paper. Black goes white, she thought, when the jolt hits. Stars fly out, then up and up as they break apart and the sky lights up. She'd go see him, she decided. She needed the distraction.

"Vait!" he cried out. "Dis is my vif! She's tellink your fortune!"

"No, thanks," Charlotte told the dwarf. She was on her way to the beef barn to meet Duncan. Her heart was a fist so tightly clenched it could hardly beat.

"Free," the gypsy said. She was taller than Charlotte. She was wearing drapey scarves and bangles. Her eyes were smeared with dark makeup.

"And ve haf that picture, don ve, Celestina? Of her mudder and fadder ven they vas married?"

"Sure bet," Charlotte said, but she realized she had fallen in step with them and was going along, so strong was the tug of the hopefulness she couldn't even give credence to.

The dwarf walked with a roll, duck-footed, on the deck of a tossing ship. His wife glided along without taking any steps at all, as if sliding over ice on the soles of her shoes. Charlotte looked down to see the shuffling shoes. They were covered by the hem of her gypsy skirt and by the scarves flowing down all around her.

She was a very ugly woman, Charlotte saw, with a great hooked nose and snaggle teeth, but she had an arrogance to her bearing that had tricked Charlotte at first into thinking she was beautiful. She was just the opposite of Charlotte herself, who was probably okay-looking but usually felt her looks were dismal.

"You vant to know you fortune?" she asked Charlotte, out of the side of her mouth.

"Not really," Charlotte said. "I don't really go by that sort of junk. No offense."

"You don belief," the gypsy said. Her dark eyes in their smear of black were cold, unamused.

Now they were at the little trailer. The dwarf was up the steps first, with the key in hand, opening the door, turning on the lights.

"I'm turnink on the vater. I'm gettink you a sweet. Then I'm gettink out that picture."

"Picture?" Charlotte asked.

"The weddink."

"Sure bet," Charlotte said again. She had already seen pictures of her parents' wedding: Her father with his arm around her mother's shoulders holding her tightly to him, him looking down, her looking up. Their expressions were ardent. They were standing under the oaks at the top of the stairs on Vista del Mar.

"It's in vid the other clippinks," the gypsy said, already sitting on the little sofa and pulling Charlotte down to her.

"Don't bother with tea for me," Charlotte called to him. "I have to go right away."

"For nothink," the gypsy said, without letting go of her. "Free," she pronounced quietly, as if the price were the issue. The pressure of the woman's fingers spread Charlotte's hand open on the fabric of her skirt over her knee. The gypsy's fingers felt smooth, shiny in an unnatural way. The skin looked as if it had been bathed in chemicals. "I'm seeink a dark man," she was saying. "Vat do they call them here, Felix? *Brunatnie?*"*

"Niggers," Kreminski replied, coming forward with a large, stiff old photograph. Charlotte stared at him. The word was uttered without feeling of any sort, as if it were any old word, not even intended to be humorous, the way Katrinka used it.

"Not dat one," the gypsy said. "The one dat's lighter."

He wasn't listening. He was shoving the photo at Charlotte, pointing to the members of a little European family circus. They could not be Americans, Charlotte knew, because they all faced the camera full on but not a single one was smiling. "Dat bik one is my brudder," Kreminski was saying. "He did not survif. Nor dis von, nor dis von. Dis ist your fadder." He was pointing to a muscle man standing behind a dark woman with puppets on her lap. "There's Katrinka," he said, pointing at the woman with the puppets with his stubby finger.

*Brunatnie: Polish colloquialism meaning: "Beaner."

"She hat *courage*," the gypsy said, pronouncing it in French, placing her slick hand on Charlotte's chest above her heart. Charlotte's eyes filled immediately at the sound of the word, and her mouth gaped open, it, too, filling with water. She moved back, away from the heat of the woman's hand which she felt through the fabric.

"Yes, they did have *courage*," Charlotte told them, but neither seemed to be listening. The woman Kreminski pointed out resembled Katrinka in no way that Charlotte could see. Charlotte stared though and was suddenly engulfed by the smell of the gypsy's clothing: onions, sawdust, something else that may have been mold. "She still does have courage," she informed them. "She's had a terrible life."

Kreminski went waddling away to the sink and then came back with the tea tray. "Those vere evil days," he was saying. "Budapest, 1942."

"My parents were in college then," Charlotte was telling him, "in Berkeley, California."

"You tolt their fortunes, you remember, Celestina? So even on their weddink day they both knew he would not survif. It vas the next veek the Chermans marched. She marriet him knowink he vas a Chew." The Kreminskis were looking at one another deeply.

"They had *courage*," the gypsy repeated to her husband. They were, Charlotte saw, talking about themselves.

"My parents," Charlotte said loudly, and to no one unless it was Roxie Sugarman's interviewer, "were married in 1945 in my grandparents' living room in Glendale 8, California. My mother wore a white linen suit—she spilled cake on it. The cake was devil's food, which was my father's favorite. The recipe came from *The Joy of Cooking*. My mother says the batter was salted with her mother's tears."

The dwarf and his wife were still looking at one another raptly. "That's a joke," Charlotte told them, but they didn't look up. They were, Charlotte saw, as crazy as the people who call the Joe Pyne Show to tell him about how they went for a ride on a UFO just to suffer his abuse. These people believed they had gone for a ride on a UFO, believed in past lives and future lives and that they had ESP with which to tell fortunes. But people like the Kreminskis and those who called up Joe Pyne didn't end up in Camarillo, while Katrinka did. Katrinka, Charlotte felt, didn't even really *believe* in Space Radio. "I have to go," she said abruptly, standing up. Her knees hit the tea tray in front of them and the jostling sent a bright slosh of amber out from each of the cups.

"I didn't finish," the gypsy said. She had not let go of Charlotte's hand. The slick brown skin seemed to have been burned or tanned as leather is tanned.

Charlotte ripped her hand away and clutched her fists to her chest. "I *have* to go," she told them. Her voice was slightly hysterical.

"Then you gotta pay," the gypsy said.

"You said it was free!"

"Free if I do the fortune. If I don do it, you vaste my time."

"You told me! You said *brunatnie!* All right? *Brunatnie*—I got it! Anyway, I don't have any money."

"You gotta pay me," the woman said, holding her palm out so Charlotte had to look into it. The hand was flat, stiff, the skin melted, then frozen in scarring so the joints no longer allowed the fingers to curl up. She used her hands with the fingers held together like a lobster's pincers. Charlotte knew then the woman had been tortured by Nazis, burned on her palms and maybe on the bottoms of her feet. It was a peanut-butter scar like Gail Bill's.

"Here, then, take this," Charlotte dropped her ring into the ruined palm. The gypsy grabbed it with the other hand. She used her hand just as an elephant grasps with his trunk. The ring was an opal, given to Charlotte by Lionel on her sixteenth birthday. It had belonged to Ina and was inscribed, "With Love to Wifey." The gypsy dropped it down her blouse. "Take it," Charlotte said, to assuage her own guilt at the damage something had done to this woman. "It's worth a lot of money."

"You still gotta pay in money." The awful palm was out again.

"Are you crazy?" Charlotte yelled at her.

"No," she said, "I'm a thief. You gotta pay me money."

"I don't have any," Charlotte said, trying not to think about the fifty-dollar bill she had stuffed into her pocket. That was the last one she and her mother had. "This is robbery," Charlotte said, appealing to the dwarf. He was spooning sugar into the tea; he was lucky, happy in his marriage to this chiseler, and wasn't paying attention. They had what Katrinka called *folie à deux*, Charlotte saw, the madness of two, which was, Katrinka said, what plagued most modern marriages, Lionel and Winnie's in particular. "How much?" she asked, looking down at the slick brown palm that was still held out to her.

Charlotte was conjuring up her other money, the five-dollar bill she also had, thinking of its picture, the numerals, the soft way it felt after so much use. The fifty had been folded only once and was still crisp. She called the five-dollar bill forth in case this crappy gypsy really *could* read minds.

"Four," the gypsy said, after looking her up and down.

Charlotte breathed out. "All right, four, for one lousy stinking word in some language I don't speak and nobody else does either, not even, probably, dogs. But I'm telling Sugarman on you!" She could hear him already, saying: "So what can you tell me I don't already know? The woman's a thief. Did you ever meet a gypsy who wasn't?"

Charlotte got the five out, offered it. The hand snatched it, shoved it down the blouse after Lionel's mother's opal ring. "You owe me change of a dollar," Charlotte told her, tipping her chin up. The dwarf, miraculously, was offering Charlotte a cup of bright tea, but she was pushing by him to get out the door. She turned and told him, "Your wife still owes me change of a dollar," then she was gone down the steps.

Charlotte's thigh felt warm with the heat of the new money, the ink of which was so strong she could smell it rising in the popcorned air. Her heart, too, was rising up in triumph. Gypped, cheated, she had still once again escaped from thieves with her money and her life. She could never quite believe her luck.

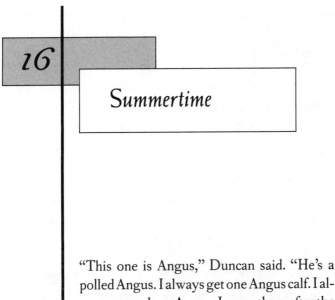

16

Summertime

"This one is Angus," Duncan said. "He's a polled Angus. I always get one Angus calf. I always name them Angus. I name them after the breed and because the name goes with Farrell." The two were standing in the beef barn next to a pen made from stacked-up bales of straw. This steer was jet black, shorter, stockier than Spenser, who was in the next pen over.

"Polled?" Charlotte asked.

"Bred so they don't grow horns. So they can't hurt each other on the feedlot. Spenser's been polled, too, but mechanically. His horn buds were burned out when he was castrated."

Charlotte looked over at him, at the white blaze of his T-shirt showing beneath his Pendleton. Duncan was so matter-of-fact in saying this that it was obvious he wasn't just trying to bother her. "So do you always name the Hereford Spenser?" she asked him.

"No," he said. "I name them different things. I named Spenser after Spenser steak, which may be why he's so obstinate, except I think really he was just born that way."

She sighed hugely. She wished she was like Katrinka, who always seemed to have innumerable interesting things to say at any time.

"Think that's bad," he went on. "My sister Dory raises pigs and she names them things like Pork Chop and Bacon. Spenser at least sounds like a name."

"Pork Chop!"

"Drives my father nuts," Duncan said. "Also that she's a vegetarian. He can't stand that. He tells her to think of the starving people in China, and she says, 'Well, pack my pork chop up and send it to them because *I* sure as hell am not eating it.'" Duncan was smiling down at her.

"My grandmother had pigs," Charlotte said, looking away. "On their ranch in Montana. She raised them to earn money for college."

"Same here," Duncan said. "I'm going to college to be a large-animal vet."

"I'm going to be a simultaneous translator."

"What's that?"

"You work for the U.N., or something? You travel to different countries? I have an uncle—an uncle or something like that?—he works for the State Department. His children were all born in different countries where we get oil: Venezuela, Persia, Indonesia."

"Texas?"

She looked up at him. She was holding her breath. Oh, the luck, her luck, to meet a boy as cute as this, a boy who was cute and smart!

"Does she still keep them?" he asked.

"What?"

"The pigs?"

"No, well, my grandmother's sort of old now, kind of, I mean, and I don't really think they let you have pigs in Glendale, California." Why, she wondered, was it always necessary to say Glendale, *California*, as if it could possibly be anywhere else? "She can call quail, though," she added.

"That's neat," he said. "I don't like pigs," he told her.

"Really? Why?"

"Well, they act like *pigs*, I'm not kidding. They oink and wallow in their muck and they're tricky. They're prone to disease, and they're temperamental. Dory lost a whole year's money when hers got erysipelas. And sometimes they're bred plain nuts. She had one sow who ate her whole litter."

"God!" Charlotte said.

"And they always roll over on them."

"Really?" Charlotte said.

"It seems that way to me. Cows never act like that. They have one calf. Two at the most."

They had left the beef barn and were walking toward the Fun Zone, past the dairy barn, past the display where the girls gave away samples of homemade ice cream, past the stall where there was Bosco, a live cow with a porthole fitted in her side so you could see the workings of the four-chambered stomach of a ruminant. Charlotte felt as though she had gone there, stood in line and peered in, although she knew full well she had avoided it. By day, she avoided it; still, she'd gone back at night in her dreams. She had gone and seen that the cow was a ship, that the four-chambered stomach was a whale's, that men were inside and could be seen working the engine, half-naked in the condensing steam.

Duncan took out a box of Marlboros, tapped a cigarette out, held the box out to her. She took a cigarette and inhaled as he lit it with the long flame of his lighter. Her lungs were huge with heat but she didn't choke.

This is what I've been waiting for my whole life, she thought—smoking a cigarette with a cute guy. She liked everything about smoking, the taste and smell of it, and the look it gave her. It made her look like she knew what she was doing. Smoking was so much better than eating food, which had to be cut up, put on the fork, raised to the mouth, then chewed. She could never eat in front of this boy.

"Do you know all these people?" he asked her, when they came to the freak show.

"Some," she said, both proud and ashamed. "I know her," she said, pointing at Sam-Sam's sign. "And I think I met them once, one time when I was little." She nodded toward the picture of the Good Twins, who were joined at the base of the spine. Katrinka had done the billboard on the side of their wagon. It showed two girls with blonde hair and big blue eyes with a banner above their heads. It read, "What God Hath Joined Together Let No Man Put Asunder!" Their costume had two bodices but only one flouncy skirt.

"Weird," Duncan breathed.

"I suppose," she told him with little prickles of irritation starting up. But not that much weirder, really really, than burning out horn buds and putting portholes in the sides of cows, which is what agricultural types like to do. "Want to meet them?" she asked him.

"Okay. Couldn't they have been separated? We had Siamese-twin calves once when I was little, but only one was viable."

"Viable?" she asked.

"Able to live. The other was vestigial. It came out of the side of the live calf's neck. The vet removed it."

"Oh," Charlotte whispered. She closed her eyes to imagine the calf going out into life wearing the ghost of its twin about its neck much as the gypsy had draped her scarves. "My mom said they could have been separated," Charlotte told him as they were going up the steps of the wagon, "they just didn't want to. You know how people get to be?" she asked him. "Sort of in love with the way they are?" She said this, then walked around it, awed, startled, by the way it sounded true.

She knocked on the wooden door and they heard two voices, in unison, asking them to come in. They opened the door and stepped into the blaze of a spotlight. "Oh, my God!" Charlotte cried, trying to back out. "It's show time," she told him, "and we've walked in on them!" He was right behind her so she couldn't go down the steps. The light from the spots was blinding them.

"Sorry!" she cried. "We're sorry we disturbed you. Sorry! We'll come back another time!"

"Oh, do come in, dears," they said together.

"You aren't disturbing us," one said.

"We aren't busy, are we, dear?"

"Oh, my, no! We're never busy!"

As her eyes adjusted to the bright lights, Charlotte could see beyond the two women to the darkened passageway between the wagons where the people were passing by on their way into the circus tent. The twins did nothing in their show, Charlotte saw, except smile and wave. It was as if they were in a parade passing by the people, instead of the other way around. Did people stop to really *listen* to Katrinka, Charlotte wondered, or were they more like Sacramento, passing on as soon as they had registered her and the dummies as a phenomenon? From out of the darkness, a woman's voice piped up, "Jason, I think it is positively criminal for money to be made like this on human misery!"

"We're really sorry to come in like this," Charlotte told them. "I'm Charlotte? My mother is the ventriloquist?" *Is this so?* Charlotte thought, as she always did whenever she said a thing like this aloud.

"Oh, yes!" one said. "Such a lovely girl! Don't we always say?"

"Yes, lovely! So sweet-natured, and so competent!"

"Yes, competent!"

Charlotte shut her eyes. She opened them and things were still just as they'd been. "This is Duncan," she whispered. "He has steers."

"Steers," one cried.

"Oh, my goodness gracious!"

"How interesting!" the other cried. "I don't believe we've met anyone with steers before, have we, dear?"

"No, I don't think so. Not that I recollect."

"Nice to meet you," Duncan said. He didn't move to shake their hand. *Hands*, Charlotte said, correcting herself.

They were seated on a love seat facing slightly away from one another, so they had to arch up and around, straining with their necks in order to look into the other's face. This facing away from one another, the listening to the voice behind, must have been like being blind, Charlotte thought; like the blind, their faces were perfectly open in expression. Their delight at having Charlotte and Duncan visit them was painful, extreme.

"Nice to see you," Charlotte told them, "but now we have to go." She shut her eyes, to keep out the look of their terrible disappointment.

"Oh, don't go!" they cried together. "You just got here!"

"We don't get out much to meet people, you see," one said.

"Because of the way we are."

"And it's been a long while since we've had such an interesting conversation."

Duncan nudged Charlotte slightly, which made her feel she was going to bubble over with feeling, the need to laugh and to cry twisted together with equal force.

"Do you have steers, too?" one asked her.

"No," she said. "But I had a pigeon once. Its name was Romeo and Juliet." Duncan behind her made a little noise in his nose. "I mean first it was named Juliet, then Romeo." She breathed in and out. "And I have a friend who has a dog that moos instead of barks." She said this, then raised her fist to her mouth and bit hard on her first knuckle to keep the laughter from escaping. Duncan, behind her, was utterly silent. If one started, both knew, there would be no end to it.

"How lovely!" one cried. "How lovely to have a pigeon!"

"How lovely to have a dog!" Each listened over her shoulder to the musical voice of the other. One spoke, then waited for the confirming echo.

"My mother gave me a dog once," Charlotte said. "My grandfather named it Pip after the one in Dickens." This story was sad, terrible, but still she felt the need to laugh pushing up behind the telling of it. "Also, *Pip* because it gave my grandmother the pip. Its fleas, you see, preferred her blood to that of dogs. *She* had a dog once, too. Its name was Nicodemus Boffin."

"What happened to it?" Duncan asked behind her, his voice muffled from the effort of shutting down the laughter.

"Which? Nicky or Pip?" She turned around and saw him mouth the words: *Let's get out of here!* "Either," he said out loud.

"Welllll," she took a huge breath and swallowed the air to shove the laughing down. "Nicky, I don't know. That was before I was born. Nicky was the last good dog, the only dog my grandmother ever loved. Pip, she had gassed." Though the loss of Pip was one of the great tragedies of her life, the word made her giddy. Laughter was a sea: she was going off a cliff and into it. If she were swimming in it with him, even the saddest of stories would be funny.

"How interesting!" the twins said together. "You have such interesting lives." Charlotte could hear Duncan making little choking noises. The twins were craning their necks back toward the doorway to hear more news. The crowd in the passageway was thinning out, the circus beginning.

The twins were very old. They wore their hair in puffy blonde curls. They wore bright red lipstick that bled out from their mouths into the wrinkles running like rivulets from their lips. When they moved to wave at the passing shapes in the corridor, the smell of dust came from the crinkling material of their skirt. This was the same as the smell at Aunt Hoppy's house: old lives, lives in disuse. It smelled to Charlotte like mummies, like the ball gowns in the museum at Exposition Park. The colors had bled from these clothes, and they were so dingy, so ugly, she fervently believed they should not be on display, but rather should be thrown away or burned. "Aren't they beautiful?" some of the girls in her class had asked one another on a field trip. "I wish I had that dress."

"Are you insane?" Charlotte had shouted out. "Are you completely out of your mind?" Was she the only one with vision left, she wondered, the sight to see that the clothes were terrible, wretched, the colors as grayed as the stucco on Avenue B? "Those clothes," she had shouted, "are all that is left of dead people!" The mannequins wearing the dresses didn't even have hands or heads.

"I had a goldfish once," she was telling the twins lightly. "I won it in the dime toss at the school bazaar. But it flipped out of the bowl somehow, and we found it dried to the tiles of the sink."

The twins' mouths had moved into two little kisslike shapes, still listening, staring behind them, their eyes rolling back a little. Their faces were poised: ready to smile if the fish, rehydrated, had turned out to be just fine, but willing, too, to collapse in commiseration if that was not the case. Charlotte broke the bad news: "We had to chip it off the tile with a knife." Duncan gave her a little push. She turned and saw that his eyes were watering hopelessly.

"Bye," he was saying, choking. "Bye. We have to go."

"So soon?" the twins asked. "We were having such a lovely visit!"

"It was lovely, wasn't it?" Charlotte asked, looking up at him, her cheeks bitten in, her eyes filling. "But we have to rush off. Bye-bye," she told them.

"Oh, don't be late!"

"We'll see you next time!"

"Thanks for stopping by!"

"Give our best to your lovely mother!"

"Bye-bye!" the twins cried. "Bye-bye! Bye-bye!"

Charlotte and Duncan got out of the trailer and down the steps and to the steps of the next trailer before they sat down, helplessly laughing. "Dried to the sink," he said. "That was the worst. I could stand it until that."

"This," she said, laughing, "was worse than once in my honors English when the substitute had a fly sitting on his toupee the whole period, buzzing up, then landing again." She showed him with the flutter of her fingers. "He couldn't feel it. One girl laughed so hard she wet her pants. Not me," she told him, wiping away the tears. "It wasn't me," she emphasized.

"To the sink," he covered his wet face with his hands. "Dried. It was worse," he said, then stopped talking to laugh. "That was worse than having to sit in some girl's living room talking to her father while she takes three weeks to get ready."

Charlotte stopped laughing abruptly. She took the cigarette he was offering her and watched him light it through narrowed eyes. How many times, she wondered, had poor Duncan been put through this terrible ordeal? "Have you ever seen anything so weird in your life?" he asked her, rubbing his eyes, still laughing.

"Oh, I don't know," she drawled as she tipped her chin up. "Maybe," she breathed.

His car was a '56 Chevy painted forest green, upholstered with tuck 'n' roll and equipped with Vibrasonic. He drove her up the highway to the Safeway the next day, while the speakers in back boomed,

"Duke, duke, duke, duke of Earl, Earl, Earl, Duke of Earl, Earl, Earl, Duke of Earl," and then the high voices came in, in falsetto: "When I, I walk through this world . . ." The speakers spread the voices all around the car.

They went up and down the frigid aisles of Safeway assembling the things Charlotte thought her mother might like: a carton of Salems, which Duncan could legally buy since he was already eighteen and had graduated from San Diegito High, a box of Jordan almonds, cans of chopped black olives, a jar of green ones with pimiento, liquid cherries at two for a quarter, a loaf of French bread, corn on the cob, Campbell's bean with bacon soup, a big jar of mayonnaise, pickled herring, baby food.

"Want to get a pizza?" Duncan asked. They were hanging out in the frozen food section while Charlotte tried to remember if her mother liked succotash. With a name like that, it seemed to be something weird enough for her to like.

"Okay, if you do." She picked a box up and was reading the directions. It had to go into a preheated oven. She sighed deeply. How would they ever accomplish a thing like that when she couldn't ask Duncan to come into the Airstream? She didn't want him to see her mother the way she was, lying on her back on the bed, one arm with a lighted cigarette held straight up from her chest, the glowing tip descending to the dried-out lips, the glow brightening, and then going straight back up. Katrinka was now no longer talking to anyone aside from herself. She sighed again. "My grandfather calls pizza 'pieces.' I used to never know what he was talking about. I'd go, 'Pieces of *what*, Lionel? Pieces of candy? Pieces of gum?'" She was still studying the directions. It was the bossy tone they took, the first-do-this-and-then-do-that that Katrinka could not abide, Charlotte decided, since the directions were not that hard.

"You must really like your grandparents," Duncan commented.

Charlotte was so startled, felt so accused, that she physically jumped. "Why do you say that?" she asked him. She closed her eyes against the thought of Lionel; the smell of his lunch seemed suddenly to be all around her, like an olfactory hallucination.

"Because you talk about them all the time."

"I do?" Was this a criticism? Didn't other, more normal girls, girls with living rooms and fathers waiting with Duncan in them, talk about their grandparents? Or was it that they had grandparents who were different from Lionel and Winnie, who were more normal themselves, who weren't from South English, Iowa, and who talked to other people sometimes and had therefore learned how to pronounce the word "pizza," in California?

Charlotte and Duncan were in the checkout line. She had the fifty-dollar bill. She knew other, more normal girls shopped for their mothers with more normal types of money, fives or tens or twenties. Still, the fifty might make him think she was rich. Her head was bent down so she was looking at her feet in their zoris. Her four toenails were black but they hadn't yet come off, so her foot didn't yet look totally disgusting. Suddenly his fingers went up under her hair at the back of her neck. She shivered so violently he felt it. His breath next to her ear was warm. "What's the matter?" he asked. "Are my fingers too cold?"

She was shivering; her teeth were chattering slightly. She shook her head. He took her cold hand in his cold hand as the checker bagged the groceries. He picked the bags up and carried them out to the car for her, as if they were in love, as if they were already married.

It was on the hot front seat of the Chevy in the heat of summer in the early afternoon that he tipped her face back and shaped her lips into his. It was in the parking lot at Safeway that he first kissed her, the sort of place in which her mother would lie down in order to be put back into the mental hospital.

Their skin was still cold from the air of the store. He tipped her face up and his mouth came down to hers. There was nothing wrong with him. He knew what he was doing. He had kissed people before, then she amended: *Girls.*

They had to take her mother the groceries. Charlotte dropped them by while Duncan waited in the Chevy. She raced in, unpacked them, and put them away. She changed into her bathing suit. They were going to Moonlight Beach in Encinitas, a ways up the coast where

Duncan lived. Charlotte looked at her mother swinging one white knee back and forth. Charlotte might do whatever it was she thought she was doing—kissing, being kissed by a person who could talk to her, a person who was funny, who had a mind behind his mouth to kiss her with, but she couldn't get away from this—*this.*

Katrinka's eyes appraised her as Charlotte told her where she was going. She muttered something to herself. Within it was the word *righteousness.*

"I got you cigarettes," Charlotte told her. "A whole carton, but you really need to eat something, don't you think?"

"For his name's sake," Katrinka was telling somebody, gutturally.

That evening when Duncan brought her home, Katrinka seemed to be a little better. "Mom," she told her, "you really have to eat something, okay? Do you want a liquid cherry? Can you believe how much they cost anymore? Liquid cherries may have tasted just the same in Big Mother's day, but they probably cost her about one penny. Want an olive sandwich? I'll make it for you. Want some applesauce? What is it? Are you worried about your teeth?" Katrinka, when delusional, sometimes worried that all her teeth had been loosened by the shock treatment and were about to fall out. Charlotte got out the applesauce and dumped some into a bowl. She sat on the edge of the bed, feeding her mother that and vanilla tapioca baby food. She was eating the Gerber's plums herself. She fed her, looking down into her mother's face, but she saw his instead. She was, one day, going to get married. It would be like being born another time, into another family. She would get another name. She hated her middle name, the way "Katherine Ainsworth" had been plunked down for bad luck.

"Summertime," she sang, as her mother had once sung to her, "an' the livin' is easy. Fish are jumpin', and the cotton is high. Oh, yo' daddy's rich, an' yo' mammy's good-lookin', So hush, little baby, don' you cry." She smoothed the hair away from her mother's forehead. Katrinka glared at her. Her lips were parched. "Can you drink?" Charlotte asked her, seeing that she was paying attention.

"Of course!" Katrinka said, in her own strident voice. "If you don't drink, you can't work on *Pelican*." Katrinka smirked, then went on. "It's my mother who is rich, Charlotte, by the way. It was Lionel who was the one who was too damned good-looking."

Charlotte looked away, eating the fruit from the jar. She was thinking of the way Duncan's T-shirt slid over the smooth skin of his back and of the way the sweet and tart taste of the plums slid down her throat so easily, as if it were jellied nothing.

17

Alight with the
Same Desire

Why do I chide the summer insect
For flying blind into the blazing flame?
Why should I be an exception?
When I am already alight with the same desire?

From the log of Lieutenant
Commander Takashiti Hashimoto*

Charlotte was trying to explain to Duncan how it was on holidays, growing up in a family like hers, how the holidays made everybody act up, like themselves but worse, as if they were themselves augmented to the *n*th power.

Katrinka cracked up nearly every Christmas over what a lousy mother she was. It was only at Christmas that she imagined herself to blame for everything, and would accuse herself of drinking up Charlotte's college money, of spending nearly every Christmas in the mental hospital away from her only daughter. She seemed to feel justified in going nuts at Christmas, almost as if it were expected of her. Christmas was a very popular time for having a nervous breakdown, she always said, so popular that there was traffic backed up all the way to Camarillo with cars crammed with loved ones being

*From the entry dated 29 July 1945, read in testimony on 26 February 1946, in Washington, D.C., at the court-martial of U.S. Navy Captain James Butler McVay.

dropped off at the loony bin. The reason people cracked up over the holidays, Katrinka said, was they still wanted what Normal Rockwell promised them, their own good Grandma and Grandpa, the ones with cheeks like apples.

The holiday Winnie cracked up over was Thanksgiving. She thought it had been invented by the men in fedoras or the one in the attic or by Lionel just to spite her. Although the Ainsworths never had guests, Lionel always bought the biggest turkey the butchers could get for him. He brought it in and presented it to Winnie with the look on his face that said he was Ina's own best boy. He was already smacking his lips over the leftovers—why, with a turkey that big, they'd probably last him most of the rest of his life!

Winnie touched the turkey, then cried out: Another frozen one! After what they'd been through the year before? Didn't Lionel remember a frozen turkey had to be carefully and scientifically thawed?

The turkey wouldn't fit in the refrigerator, so Winnie sat up with it all night, monitoring the spoilage, hectoring it along toward the state of being defrosted. At three in the morning, the rattling and banging in the kitchen began, like an earthquake that went on and on. It was Winnie; she had just discovered the turkey was too big to fit in her roasting pan.

Lionel was then out in the car at eight, looking for a store open on Thanksgiving Day, though there was never any hope of finding one. He came home hours later with his face smudgy, as if he'd been drawn in pencil, then partially erased. He was empty-handed, as expected. He seemed like he'd been drinking except he didn't drink. He didn't drink because drink was poison to his system.

And by then, anyway, Winnie Rutherford Ainsworth, Daughter of the Golden West, whose family had come in covered wagons to settle The Dalles on the Columbia Gorge and then the town of Orange, had intimidated some materials into impersonating a roasting pan. She had pounded holes in several cookie sheets with nails, bent them, then roped them together with picture wire, covering the whole with aluminum foil. The turkey nestled in the cradle she had constructed; still it was so large the oven door was kept from closing. The nail holes leaked grease, and flames shot up three feet from the propped-open door of the oven. She doused the fire with baking soda, then washed the turkey off in the sink. She began to hack off limbs. After hours of cooking, the meat thermometer still said the bird was freezing. No wonder! The thermometer was made in Japan! She yanked it from the turkey thigh and threw it out the window into the tops of the windy trees. All the windows were standing open because the house was filled with smoke. Winnie made the gravy. Finally it was time to sit down. They were dressed in their winter coats.

Blood gushed out when the knife went in. Charlotte mentioned that she'd learned in home ec that that *might* mean the turkey *might* need another couple of minutes in the oven. "Don't you home ec me!" Winnie screamed at her. "How dare you be so impudent! Lionel, did you hear what she said to me? I'm going to run away and join the navy!" She slammed the peas down with such force that they all hopped up and down in the bowl together. Then she went out the door and right foot, right foot, down the steps. She spent every Thanksgiving on the Harbor Freeway, foot to the floor, searching for her own good bright-cheeked Grandma and Grandpa—the ones who had a turkey cooked through and through—weeping, going ninety.

Lionel and Charlotte had peas and gravy sopped up with buttered French bread. Winnie's gravy was delicious.

"But you had trimmings," Duncan told her, looking over for confirmation. They were driving up the coast highway.

Charlotte narrowed her eyes. She had known him for over a week and still hadn't figured out what was wrong with him. Maybe it was this: he just didn't get it.

"There aren't any trimmings on Vista del Mar," she told him. "I don't think they go by that."

"Cranberry sauce?" he asked her. "Your family's American and you never had cranberry sauce?"

"It might be poison to my grandfather's system."

"You never had pumpkin pie?"

"Pumpkin pie is, for sure."

"You're making this up," he told her, looking over again. His eyebrows going straight across gave him a sober, wistful look. Do I look like that? she wondered, looking back at him.

She shrugged again and sighed. "Well, sort of," she said. "Half." Then she added, "Actually, I wish I was making it up."

He now believed she made things up because she'd told him the fish dried to the sink wasn't her own story but one she'd snagged from Patsy's little brother. She had told Duncan she stole it so he'd know from the first she was a liar and a thief. She lied easily. She half-believed her own lies. The lies, she often felt, were as good as the truth, or better.

The truth in the fish story was this: Charlotte had been born blessed, lucky—Dr. Greenley had even told her so—but who could ever believe that once they'd witnessed the facts of her life? She had always been the type to pitch one bright dime and win the goldfish. The trouble with having such glittering luck was the fact of her mother looming darkly there, that it was Charlotte taking all the luck that should have been more equitably divided. Charlotte won the goldfish easily, and there was Katrinka, still stuck back in Camarillo, still having her teeth knocked loose by electroshock therapy. Luck that lucky was hard to enjoy. Over and over again, Charlotte won the lousy fish, then left it to die on the tiles of the sink. She came back to it when it was stiff, when the glitter had all dried away.

"Your mom was never there?" Duncan asked.

"They brought her home one time," she told him. "That was the worst. She made Winnie furious somehow. It couldn't have been by what she said because she had come out of the hospital directly and was all drugged up on Thorazine. People on Thorazine," Charlotte told Duncan, "sit around like this all day." Gripping her arms at the elbows, she hugged herself and let her chin rest against her chest. "They look like Ed Sullivan or Jack Benny." Charlotte told him that, although she knew it was exactly the sort of thing people normally had no wish to ever know.

"That time," she went on, "Winnie screamed at her for no reason whatsoever, then used the ladle to slosh the gravy from the gravy boat all over the walls and drapes. The turkey was frozen, as usual.

Lionel started calling up Beadles Cafeteria to see if it was open. He called the dining room at the Hotel Glendale, but we didn't end up going anywhere because Winnie had gone off in the car."

Duncan wasn't smiling, as people usually did when Winnie went weeping down the freeway at one hundred miles an hour, blinded by tears, driving backwards in time, trying to catch up to the covered wagons and find her own apple-cheeked Granny and Grandpa. Instead, Duncan looked sad.

It occurred to Charlotte that it was because she wasn't funny. As her mother always said, it was she, Katrinka, who was funny. It was Charlotte who was smart, sweet, pretty, and *nice*.

Duncan didn't get it. Having Lionel and Winnie as grandparents was part of her luck. Charlotte was glittering with hope, with risk: the hope that she might go forward in time, that she would never be one to have to fling herself backwards, sobbing, weeping, trying to find those particular shits, those ancestors whose cheeks were neither full nor rosy.

They were on their way to a party on the beach at night. Each stretch of sand up through Leucadia and Encinitas had a name: Fourth Street, Moonlight, Snack Shack, Trestle, Diamondhead. Each was a surfing beach.

The kids were sitting around a bonfire drinking beer and Everclear. Everclear was an alcohol so pure it tasted of nothing. It was so strong, someone said, that you didn't even have to drink it to get drunk on it. Duncan handed Charlotte a cup; it looked exactly like water. This, she thought, is the water in which the fish don't swim. It evaporated on her tongue, the liquid simply vanishing.

One boy was drunk already. "Hey, Farrell," he said, coming up to them. "Gimme a cigarette." He grabbed at the box-shaped place in the pocket of Duncan's Pendleton.

"Get off me, Finn," Duncan told him, whacking the reaching hands away.

Duncan introduced her to kids, but there were so many of them and she was so nervous she could only remember the one name: Tom Finn, a name that might have come from literature. His parents, she guessed, must have liked him, must have hoped to have had a funny baby, to have given him a name like that.

She watched him. He was eighteen, maybe nineteen, but he was already totally wrecked. His face was cute, with bangs to his eyes, but he was so drunk he was staggering. She saw that it wasn't girls, either, that he cared about. He wanted the attention of boys. He went a few feet away and wanted someone to come pee with him. No one would, so he came back to the group to try to pee the fire out. "Pull your zipper up, Finn," someone told him. "Nobody wants to see your dick," this boy added. Charlotte turned to look at the boy, amazed at the fact of the word coming out of his mouth. She saw the vehemence carved into the planes of his face by the shadows of the dancing fire.

Duncan drank from the cup. "He's so fucked," he said. "His father killed himself but that's just his latest excuse. He always was a complete and total prick. He was a prick before it."

Charlotte, sitting on a rolled-up sleeping bag, felt physically shocked. She stared at Tom Finn with her mouth open. It was as if she'd been introduced to someone who was her brother, each born long ago, both then given up for adoption. Someone gave him a cigarette and he shoved it up one nostril. He was trying now to stand up, to balance on the log that had been dragged back in a long and swooping curve from the wet sand to the fire. "I wrote a poem," he said. "Wanna hear it, Farrell?"

"God, what an asshole," Duncan said. One girl tsked. Charlotte was already drunk on the Everclear, her collarbone becoming number, inch by inch. She looked at this boy, her brother, trying to balance on the log with the cigarette shoved up his nose, and the pinpricks of sorrow started to tingle all along the bridge of her nose. "I do," she whispered, looking up at him, but Tom Finn wasn't listening.

"Farrell?" he asked. "Wanna hear it? It's a love poem. I wrote it for you."

"Let's get out of here," Duncan said, pulling her up. "The guy's totally crazy. Know where he got it? His father. Know what a prick that guy was? He drove the car off the end of Dana Point. He did it on Christmas Eve."

"Jesus," Charlotte whispered. No wonder Duncan hadn't thought it was funny about people going crazy on the holidays. She turned around and saw in perfect clarity of moonlight what was left by an act like that: Tom Finn was a ruined child. "Farrell!" he was crying out, "I wrote it for you! Doncha! Wanna! Even! Hear it?" He staggered, stumbled up, slipped off the log but still was determined to declaim his poem. "Farrell?" he called. "*You say that the world is shit? Well, I say that you shitted it.*" The cigarette was still stuck up his nose.

They went to the water's edge and dropped their outer clothes. Charlotte didn't look directly at Duncan but watched him from the side. His body, she imagined, was the same as her father's must have been, tall and broad-shouldered. His hair was like his, too, in the waviness, the way it looked old-fashioned.

The water was warm and smelled of a fishiness that was not unpleasant. Duncan said it was the red tide, that the water was full of the bodies of trillions of infinitesimal plankton, that when the red tide was in full flower it would begin to kill the fish by depriving them of oxygen. The plankton was phosphorescent. Moonlight danced in the surf, making the water glow in a deeper white than anything Charlotte had ever seen before, a white that had layers to it. Wherever their hands moved or their feet kicked, the bluish yellowish white sprang away, bubbled up. The shapes of their bodies were illuminated, as they faced one another treading water; they turned dark against the glow. The effect was so beautiful, it made her laugh. He laughed back, his teeth lovely in the light the sea was giving up to them.

He kissed her. He kissed her lips, then moved his hands against the fabric of the top of her bathing suit. They were going to sleep together, she knew: she'd been waiting all her life for this. He moved his hands over her breasts, then stood with his feet touching bottom and held her to him so he could kiss her seriously. Then he let go of her, brought his hands to his face and groaned. There was nothing wrong with either her or him—still, there was something wrong.

"What's the matter?" she asked. She couldn't breathe, could barely speak. She should have stopped him. Another, more normal girl would have stopped him.

His hands came away, and she saw that his face was agonized. "What you need . . . ?" he was trying to ask, to tell her, but she just shook her head stupidly: what she needed wasn't so much, just this one cute boy who wanted to go to bed with her.

He kept on trying to talk. He had rehearsed this, she saw. He was thinking of it even as they were coming up the coast highway and she was doing imitations of someone on Thorazine. What was wrong with him was a simple thing: she was falling in love with him, while he only *cared* about her.

He cared about her. That alone was a shock. He cared about her, which was the reason he was going through some kind of emotional agony, right here, right before her eyes. He wanted to sleep with her, she deeply felt. Still, something was wrong. Was she supposed to have whacked his hands away, as he had when the boy had reached out to him? Charlotte knew she was supposed to be better at this, at pushing people's hands away: she just became entranced, though, whenever someone wanted her. She was always so grateful, she never could remember to be aloof.

"Don't you see?" Duncan was asking, but she shook her head. She was still smiling at him: he had wanted her. It was all right with her, she needed him to know. "That it isn't what you need?" he went on saying. He was stumbling over the syllables. He seemed agonized, ashamed of himself, or of them, or maybe just of her. "What you need?" he asked, and she wondered if he was drunk to have suddenly become so inarticulate. "Don't you see?" he kept asking.

She shook her head: she just didn't get it. What she needed was so simple. She watched his mouth move as if she was lipreading, and she deciphered these words: ". . . that we don't go anywhere?"

We don't go anywhere. The beach towns came down the coast like a necklace strung along the black of the water. The waves broke white and white. The words went in a line, ducklike. *We*, she told herself. *We don't go anywhere.* He had put a question mark at the end of it. She studied this mark. Wavelike, it broke, tumbling the statement, making it into a question.

Again, she tried to parse the sentence: *We*, she imagined, had to be the two of them. *We*, she told herself again.

He cared about her. That startling fact shone out from his face and hands the way a single window miles away will suddenly glint with enormous light as the sun catches it, going down. He had called them "we." The word, most definitely, stood for the two of them together.

But then the sentence grew more difficult. Was this one of those phrases that danced with itself in obverse, one of the religious ones that she never understood, one with an apology built into it for the thing they should not do but were going to do: go to bed together? Duncan was Catholic. Had he said it to sound good in case God was listening? Catholics *did* go around trying to act like they were good, Charlotte had observed.

In going to Patsy's church, Charlotte had been startled by how abject they all were. Rich Episcopalians would say the abject thing over and over again three times, as they softly struck their breastbones: *Lord, I am unworthy to gather up the crumbs under Thy table, but speak the word only and my soul shall be healed.* Were they really sorry, she wondered, and for what sorts of crumbs? Was Duncan trying to say that kind of thing?

Did he really imagine it was a sin, she wondered. She didn't understand the sin in it: it was so normal compared to other things, but then sin seemed small, quaint, personal. She only thought about the enormities, cosmic guilt and innocence. Who, say, was to blame for the deaths of the children of Nagasaki, Hiroshima, and those in the Warsaw ghetto? She could not imagine the God of the modern world taking time out to worry about two kids on a darkened beach, kissing with their mouths open, kids who touched each other this way or that way, kids who wanted to be together at night rather than all alone, kids who wanted for once to act alive instead of dead.

All of it was too hard. It was the same old question, Charlotte saw, of guilt and innocence. Or did Duncan say things backwards, as Katrinka often did, saying Sugarman *was* DePalma, when he most assuredly was not, that this *was* Sacramento, when it was obviously and to everyone, including Katrinka, really Del-Mar-by-the-Sea.

Or maybe it was plainer. Maybe it meant the most simple thing: that together, she and Duncan, the two of them, were not going to go anywhere, including to bed. If it meant that, then it was the kind of thing that was inevitable. Her life was a wreck. She was as bad off as Tom Finn; it just didn't show as obviously because she got good grades. She was ruined; she had been since the moment of her birth. Charlotte, deep down, had always known this. Still, she found it a continual surprise.

She had known specifically since she was twelve that her father was one of the men of the ship who had killed themselves. She had read it in her chart in Dr. Greenley's office, by reading the first page upside down and backwards. She had read it that way since he was holding the pages of the chart up in front of his face to shield his old eyes from the sight of her, a twelve-year-old girl sitting before him in her underclothes. Winnie was making him tell Charlotte the facts of life.

She had read it upside down and backwards, and his hands had been shaking with Parkinson's. Still! Still! The words were unmistakable: *Charlotte Ainsworth Black, 4/20/46, mother diagnosed "paranoid schizophrenic," 20 (?) yrs. at onset, father suicide, 1945.* Dr. Greenley was going on about a girl's mother's menarcheal age as one of the determinants of the onset of menses. Charlotte, who already knew the facts of life, was thinking: Blah, blah, blah!

She knew all about it, all about life, luck, how it was genetically determined by the blah, blah, blah, or the chromosomes, how this sort of blah, blah was exactly the sort of luck a girl like Charlotte would end up with: she would have the father who did not survive; she would have the suicide, the one who took his own life. And she wouldn't be Japanese. With the Japanese, at least there was honor to be found in it.

What she never understood, though, about the things written

down on her chart was the placement of the marks of punctuation and the way the doubt was thereby misassigned. "What!" the whole thing asked. A baby could be born to this kind of parentage and still be expected to live?

Even Dr. Greenley didn't believe it, Charlotte saw, and he had the facts: the words, the dates, the correct spellings. Dr. Greenley, devoutly Seventh Day Adventist, had the objectivity: he was the man of science and had the evidence and *still* he didn't believe it. That showed in the way he put the question mark after Katrinka's age, and again in the way he put quotation marks around "paranoid schizophrenic." Dr. Greenley must have asked himself, when had she stopped being the bright, sweet, smart, and hopeful Ainsworth girl and turned into what the experts were calling this thing that was so hard to spell? The words showed all Dr. Greenley's puzzlement: twenty years, maybe? Maybe maybe this or that, maybe this at onset? Or maybe not. But why then had that same man on the same day written of her father so definitively? The words were terse, tightly scrolled, black with confidence: *suicide*, Dr. Greenley had written, *1945*.

"Your mom must be a lot better," Duncan was telling her.

"A fuck of a lot a normal person like *you* would know about it," she thought, but did not say out loud. "A whole hellish fuck of a whole goddamned lot, to be known by *such* a normal person! Normal! Catholic! Bi-homo-momo, too, just like that wimpy shitty little creep of a fag of yours that they tacked up, the one who always looked much too skinny to *me* to have ever really been *alive* in the first place, let alone to have been G.A.W.D! Your type, Duncan, the type of homo-momo I most certainly am *not* going to go anywhere with, would not know the first thing about this kind of word: BETTER." She believed she was keeping this to herself, though little hisses did seem to be escaping from between her clenched teeth. She sounded to herself as if she were huffing; then she realized that it was because she was just about to cry.

By *better*, Duncan meant this—that while they were gone at the party up the coast, Katrinka had taken off in the car. The Impala was gone, and the door to the trailer was standing open. From the doorway a pool of bright light was spilling. This was the thick and buttery yellow that Normal Rockwell would have used to backlight Gramma and Gramps standing on the steps at Christmas. It was the tone of light that had been expressly devised by Hallmark to paint the color of welcome.

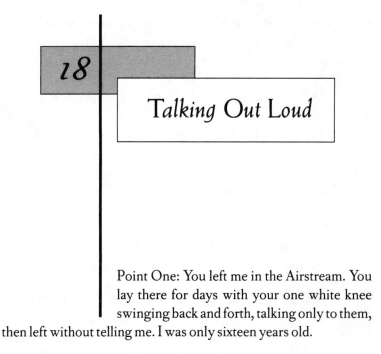

18

Talking Out Loud

Point One: You left me in the Airstream. You lay there for days with your one white knee swinging back and forth, talking only to them, then left without telling me. I was only sixteen years old.

Point Two: This was not the first time.

Point Three: The note you left was not a note and it did not apologize. It was only the wooden Scrabble pieces that you placed on the wooden rack to read, in code, you bitch: BK blank SN blank LV blank MAG, leaving it to me to get it: *Back Soon Love Mag*, to know that you, you goddamned fucking bitch, were now going by Mag the Hag, leaving it to me, as always, to translate, to try to make sense out of the psychotically insane things you did, leaving me with the Ainsworths, *when you knew how they were*, leaving me in the Airstream.

Point Four: I was so busy being your daughter all my life, Mother, trying on your damned psychotic point of view about things—Disneyland, the musical comedy history of bi-homo-momo mental patients, according to A. P. Giannini or MGM— that *I never even knew I was mad at you.* Hag is right! Know what else I really hated? The gunk that was always caked under your fingernails! That and the patch of skin from your bottom lip that came off and off! You were so dried out you'd have stuck to the sink! You were dying your whole shitty damned life, mother, both of you, first him being spectacular, heroic, then you in dried-up bits. And you left me in the Airstream!

Point Five: You never learned to blow your nose. Also, you never once in your life put the top back on the mayonnaise jar. It congealed, turned hard and yellow, then became transparent. Do you realize that any article of food left in proximity to you, Mother, turned almost instantly to garbage?

Well, Katrinka sniffed out of nowhere, it must be lovely to have gotten all *that* off your chest.

MOTHER! Do not interrupt me! You drove away and left me! You were much too sick to drive! You were so insane you ran the car off the cliffs at Cardiff, and I'm glad, *glad!* Because now I don't have to spend every moment of the rest of my life poking through the rubble of the houses you've burned down by smoking drunk in bed! And anyways . . .

The word, Charlotte, is *anyway,* awwwnnd I did not die like that. And you know it!

BE QUIET! I'M NOT FINISHED! DON'T INTERRUPT ME! *Anyways,* do you know who you really thought you were? Dorothy Parker! Know what she's famous for these days? *Nothing!* She was just one more mean dead drunken bitch who ridiculed her husband in public!

I wasn't the one who picked on him, sweetieheart. He was so busy picking on himself there was no need for me to ever criticize.

You made jokes about lamp shades!

Oh, so what? So does he. I wish to hell you'd hurry up and become a lawyer, so you can take your case to the Supreme Court.

You drank up my college! You drank up my law school! You left me in the Airstream!

Drama, Katrinka said. Oh, the drama at high noon. I wasn't the one who died, Charlotte, and you know it!

Right. He did. I killed him first. I killed you later.

No, awwwctually, you didn't. You couldn't kill us, sweetie, any more than you could keep us alive. Now, not to change the subject, but Awe-I would do things differently, less stark raving tragedy. More show tunes. *Awwwwwk-cent-chuate the positive*, she started in. *Eeeeee-lim-innate the negative. Latch! On!—to the affirmative. Don't mess with Mister Inbetween.*

Your singing voice, Mother, was so terrible it hurt my ears.

She started over, in a lower, more mournful key: *One of dese mornin's, yo gonna rise up singin', yo gonna spread yo wings, an' take to the sky.* Breath pause, she stopped singing to say. *But till that mornin' there ain't nothin' gonna harm you, with daddy and mammy standin' by.*

Charlotte, looking out past the green plaid curtain into the darkest night, was weeping steadily, uncontrollably. *Breath pause!* she said, choking; then she added, You were much too sick to drive.

So the angels helped me. The angels sing, my sweetie, in syncopated harmony like the Andrews Sisters, something *you* would not know about! *Turn here*, they sing. *Change lanes. Katrinka, we believe you've left your clicker on, my dear.* The angels, you see, are often very kind.

You don't go by that! You never believed in anything until you started hearing voices. You went off the cliffs at Cardiff. You were dying your whole damned life.

Sweetie, that just wasn't me.

I always hated you. I hated your lousy Goody-Butt-trash-heap-beer-can life! How was I ever supposed to turn out to be a girl with a mother like you? Girls are supposed to be neat!

Katrinka sniffed.

What did you think, that if you sniffed enough Winnie would come along and help you blow your nose?

I do believe, Katrinka, that we have finally given Charlotte the pip, Nellie commented.

W-wanna know wh-what I've been w-w-wondering? Buttercup asked. Wh-what, exactly, *is* the p-pip?

Shut up! Charlotte told them.

It's another word for *auditory hallucinations*, Katrinka explained.

BE QUIET! Charlotte screamed.

¡Cállate! Nellie agreed. *Tais-toi!* The sound whistled between her teeth.

I almost burned you all! Charlotte said. I did throw your gunky Scrabble board away. I dumped it into the trash cans by the park showers. I threw your bags of Goody Butts in there, too! Talk about Annette, Mother! Going around with dolls at your age! Know the only reason I didn't burn them? Because it was such a mental patienty thing to do!

How about a song right now, to relieve the nervous tension? Miss Priss asked. We could sing "Fresh Paint!"

Mother!

Fresh paint! Ogamer started in. *On these wooden heads of ours! Knock-knock-knock!*

Fresh paint! Nellie added. *Painting out the frowns!*

Instead of tra-la-la-gedy and sadness! sang Ogamer. *We need to show we're ho-ho-ho with gladness!*

Can't you *ever*, Mother, not for one single instant *ever* just knock it off?

Miss Priss added, *Knock-knock-knock!*

Frankly, no, Charlotte, Katrinka sniffed, I awwwctually cannot. Charlotte! she then went on. I'd call it "Hemstitching." I'd put in some innocuous form of mild social commentary, something that nobody *really* cares about, the treatment, say, of Negroes and/or mental patients in board-awwwnd-care as conducted by the Awwwndrews Sisters, Roxie, Maxine, awwwnnd Awwwwdrey. I'd put in the first banking families, the Rutherfords, Ainsworths, like that, for ritz. And of course A. P. Giannini for verisimilitude. The backdrop is spatter painted rather psychotically by set designer Wilma awwwnnd/or Thelma Watson awwwnnd/or Arch. The neon along the top of the backdrop flashes hot pink to yellow—in obverse. Get it, sweetie? How the high-and-high-uppety-up have all fallen through the looking glass and ended up in this crappy hell.

Stage center! she went on, there stands a Queen Anne Victorian in much need of paint. Stage right: Abstract expressionist hydrangeas. Chopin's Nocturne, opus 9, no. 2, drifts through the window. The curtains lift out, settle back, in the still air. The music is played perfectly but without emotion in the phrasing. Stage left, Charlotte, all the wee widdle waundry is hung out, snapping in the bweeze. The glitter in the stucco is lit up by the headlights of passing cars: One! Two! Three! The curtain has risen on "Hemstitching," the latest meisterwerk by K. L. W. Ainsworth, music by Dementia Praecox. Costumes, she added, by Coco Chanel.

Do you know what it must have been like for them, one, two, three, to try to help you, Mom, when all you could do was stay busy thinking up the next clever thing you were just on the verge of saying?

She sniffed. As I have said, when I need their help I will . . .

Which you never in your whole life did. Do you know what the best thing about your dying was? That it did finally shut you up.

Oh, it did not. Honestly, Charlotte, death never shut anyone up. Do you honestly mean to tell me you can't hear your father?

Charlotte, in spite of herself, strained to hear. She heard a voice whisper from far off: *Flea circus, notions counter.*

Charlotte! her mother said. We have been meaning to speak to you about your talent for self-dramatization!

You should talk! You called yourself "Drama" sometimes, when you were at your most worse! When you weren't going by Mag the Hag or Baba or Toothless Crone Out of Hell! Out of Shakespeare!

Well, I should have had my adenoids out.

Drama! Charlotte yelled. As if you were some tragic principle instead of a mother who should have been trying to learn how to screw the top of the jar back on! They should have put you in vocational rehabilitation! How would you have liked growing up with a mother who constantly referred to herself in the third person, or the first person plural?

Well, at least we don't think we are Mary, Queen of Bloody Scots, like some Missy Misses I've met.

Oh, the hell you don't, deep down.

Awwwctually, the one I really always thought I was was Queen Elizabeth. I'd tell DePalma-Moody-Maudlin awwwnnd the rest of the schizoid FBI they had following me, Hie thee, all of you, to the goddamned fucky nunnery! Psychiatry hasn't been invented yet! I was, at my best, she sniffed, a handsome woman, while you, Charlotte, were always very sweet and pretty. You were very sweet, smart, pretty, *nice*, awwwnnd neat!

Your floors, my dear! Nellie started in.

I am sick, Mother, of your endless insults.

Awwwwnnnd your ankles were much thinner than mine, which you got from your diminutive Grandmère Eleanor Awwwn with her shoes sized one! You were always very sweet, very sweet, smart, nice, pretty, awwwnnd very, very neat, while I was merely funny.

You left me in the Airstream.

You lived.

Well, isn't that just the whole crappy goddamned point, Mother? That I lived and you died. That the whole weight of sunshine falls on me? That woe is unto Y.O.U.?

My dear, Katrinka sniffed. My true and utter dear. How can I tell you enough that I am sorry for the deaths of the six millions, for all that is truly and utterly evil in the world, and *all* that? *Which does not happen to be my goddamned fault?* Dear, my own dear sweetie, what I mean to say in the kindest way possible, is can't you cut this crap out, really really? I was the student of musical comedy. It was your father who was interested in the home, home again, homeward aspect of things, the Gertrude Steinishness, awwwnnd all that was Freudy-Freudy. I, actually, preferred Porter, Gershwin, Mercer.

Now! Ogamer boomed out, I am of the opinion that it was Charles Dickens who suffered hardship in the most extreme. He was not one, Katrinka, to imagine that the world owed him a living. There were none of these communist programs for social welfare in those days, no sir! Such as those instituted by FDR. Now, Charles Dickens was my kind of man. He went to work in the blacking factory at the age of twelve. He pulled himself up by his bootstraps.

Charlotte took a deep drag on her cigarette and breathed out. "Shut up, you asshole," she told him, out loud.

Charlotte! her mother said. This is what I'm thinking. Act three, Aunt Hoppy dies, how about that? Then who is there to take care of Widdle Winnie? We could stick her up in Ventura with Tina in her big house paid for by board-and-care? But do you think Little Winnie's smart enough to get it? To tell the difference between chicken and squirrel meat? You know? No IQ but high common sense?

Mom, it's not Aunt Hoppy's death we happen to be thinking about, *right at this very moment!*

Well, honestly, sweetie, I always have had a fairly hard time telling the difference between the quick and the dead. In your father's case, for instance. Your grandparents all assured me he was fit, fine, sound in body if not mind and had merely been shipped off to the sanitarium, which was their ritzy-fitz way of saying "nut house," really really. They actually all told me, Charlotte, all four of them, together and/or separately, that he'd gone on a business trip, that he was staying at the Palmer House in Chicago. They believed, Charlotte, that I was so insane that I might have gone insaner still. Still! Still! I was not so insane that I didn't know the difference between *Palmer* House and *nut* house, to think this place in Chicago would register a person who could not pronounce his own name, membership in the AIA notwithstanding.

Charlotte drew back the plaid green curtain and looked out onto the glowing asphalt. The light was too bright. She pressed her fingertips to her eyelids to stop the sight of it. "So?" she asked, barely breathing.

Though these words had all actually been spoken days before, when Charlotte stood at the window entranced, it was only now that her mother was gone that her ears could bear to hear them.

So! If you're very sure you aren't going to crack up over it, your grandparents didn't know that someone at the office had already called me at home. He was Czech, or something, married to a Japanese. They brought flowers and a bowl of fruit to me at Vista del Mar. Your father was really crazy about them, about the look of them.

Mom? she pleaded.

Well, fuck, she said, he had to go by the look of things! He was an architect! Form, you know! Substance!

Charlotte wept for a while, then wrapped herself in the smell of her mother's robe and said, "Go on." She spoke now, but the past was all she had to listen to, her mother now being gone.

I have always noticed, her mother had then said, that death makes me hungry. I had a cake in the oven when Sam Planc called. It was sloped to one side because of the slant of the house. He called and I ate it while it was still hot, piece by piece. I was staring out the window toward the hills in back of Hollywood. I ate the cake, then started to make another one for Joey, since, by then, I had started to hear him.

Charlotte looked out the window of the Airstream, saw the view from the kitchen at Silverlake. She had taken her hands away. She was stunned again by the white look of grief, and by the knowledge that she was going to be able to stand it.

It was devil's food, her mother said, out of Irma. Awwwnnd, Charlotte, I don't really mean to bring up the bad tidings of tragedy and weep, but frankly, your father did happen to be depressed as all hell. Which I wish you would not take personally.

Charlotte, frozen like Pompeii, had not been able before to speak or move.

I was starving, Katrinka went on. I'd started out to make the cake because I thought it might cheer him up. There was the cake smell hanging out into the air of the hot morning. There was the laundry the landlady put out every day, to make a point about how blessed—weren't we all?—it was to be girlsie. There was the shape of the recipe, black on the white of the page.

You didn't cry? Charlotte asked. Even then? Even then did the tears go down the back way, slipping down your throat like sinus?

Katrinka sniffed but did not answer.

Why? Charlotte breathed. Why did he?

Oh, I don't know, Charlotte. Honest to fuck. The war, I suppose, awwwnnd the last war, if we'd ever had any interest in that. And there was the issue of being boysie. There was Joe, Sr., who had the loaded gun at home on Melrose. Your father grew up with all that war-hero crap, which is why I wish you would drop it, *right now!* That and the architecture of the city and county of Los Angeles, which was, frankly, the sort of thing your father would have killed himself over had he not killed himself over everything else.

"Like what?" Charlotte asked, turning from the window to go to the bed where she began to dress Miss Priss, as she'd done days before. Now, however, her mother was gone and could no longer answer.

Her mother had always told her it was easy to go crazy and only hard to stay that way. Being crazy was always pitched as a preferable way of operating—the better, more reasonable, more interesting thing to do than washing the Melmac or hanging out the laundry.

Now, Charlotte lay on the couch of the trailer, wagging one knee, smoking, thinking up ways to kill herself. After a day or two, she decided she would rather kill her parents, although one or both were more than likely already dead.

She did it gorily, over and over again, with and without heroism, with and without a musical soundtrack. She did it as directed by Busby Berkeley, who always made his swimmers grimace, made them smile much too hard. They always stayed underwater much, much too long, way past human possibility.

During her own days underwater in the Airstream, Charlotte learned nothing very interesting—that sweat smells like Campbell's beef with vegetable soup, undoubtedly because of the heat and salt and water-soluble proteins. She ate salad with her hands. She understood what was wrong with every member of her family: that, because of the cause-and-effect nature of mental illness, no one ever had a chance. She started in forgiving them all back through history like dominos: one by one.

Forgiveness was easy; she'd been practicing it since before her birth. It came from her as easily as silk is extruded from the guts of a spider. It came in endless amounts, unreeling with the ease of the roll after roll of kite string that had taken the kites on Avenue B out and out until they had vanished, sunk by the weight of the string itself.

She smoked and she forgave them, going "Our father which aren't in heaven," while her mother's voice voiced over, "Jesus H. Shit! Charlotte! Must we? Must we really really? I mean really really *really!* This is really oh-so-Camarillo! Don't you really think? If I'd known you were going to crack up over the subject, I never would have brought it up!"

On the second day after her mother left, Duncan came back. He wanted to know if Charlotte wanted to go to Tijuana with him and a bunch of other kids. This wasn't to be a date or anything. He just thought they ought to go on being "peripheral friends."

She watched his mouth moving. She no longer spoke the English language. What, she wondered, did it mean to be "peripheral friends"? Was it boysie? Girlsie? Boysie awwwnnd/or girlsie? Bi-baba-mama-mo-mo-sexual? Her brainpan rocked. Her eyes ached. She wanted to tell him he got her name wrong, that she was now going by "Sparkle Plenty," but her mouth didn't seem to operate.

What was wrong with her family, she decided during her days in the hot green sea, was that it was all the same. They all had a proclivity toward marrying themselves, which she had almost been tricked into doing with Duncan. The evidence of that was the eyebrows.

They were all crazy, and they made a point of marrying other people who were also crazy, so no one would find out. They married themselves, then named the children they had after themselves. Every one of Charlotte's great-grandmother's granddaughters was named Katherine after her. When Charlotte was little, she had never quite understood why they hadn't been named Big Mother, since that was who they were going to turn out to be.

And Lionel's family was just the same: Harold was Harold Lawrence, Jr.; Lawrence was Lawrence Harold. Lionel's middle name was Elmo after his cousin, Elmo Lionel.

Whether she slept or did not sleep, she never figured out. On the third day she ran out of cigarettes. She went out to get some and decided to wash her hair. Her family was all dead. She was going to the beach to lie out.

She was interested in picking up a marine or someone else equally poorly educated, someone who would know enough not to talk out loud. She was sick of people who were funny—funny *odd*, and also funny *ha ha!* She was sick of the type of person who said he wanted to be peripheral friends. The beach was littered with corpses. Not one marine came near her.

She went back to the beef barn, but the steers were gone. There was no longer a crowd at the side of the living cow equipped with a porthole so she could easily see into the steamy darkness. There was noise, commotion, but no small men requiring rescue. The girls in the dairy pavilion who gave away free samples of ice cream all were missing. The sky was white with wind and mist. Gulls flapped backwards; time was going retrograde. That, Charlotte knew, is how it always is when your mother dies. There is, she reminded herself, a silence then that is vast and that travels out and out.

She was interested in getting married. Her family was all dead. She was, therefore, an extremely wealthy young woman. She was smart and pretty and would have been a very good catch aside from the fact that she was mentally disturbed. She was the type to eat salad with her hands, to do smeary things with mayonnaise. Mayonnaise, Charlotte understood, was an inherited trait, passed on genetically in much the same way as hearing voices was. She was the type who would grow up to sit for hours in coffeehouses called things like "The Esoteric," smoking, drinking too much. She was the type who could stop any conversation dead in its tracks with this sort of statement: *My mother was a paranoid schizophrenic, twenty years at onset. My father killed himself at twenty-six.* She would say this, then smile a private little smile, then check her watch.

The Mexican was packing up his kiddie ride. When she saw that, she understood: the fair was over, the world had really ended. Before that, in telling herself it had, she had only been being amusing. The world had ended and she had not survived it. Her mother had abandoned her on the edge of an ocean, in a parking lot, a place that had neither past nor future. The air was white. At this place, the coastline fell away. Time was being dismantled, to be reassembled elsewhere.

It was the same as when she was two or three and Katrinka had died the first time. Katrinka had left Charlotte next to the canned goods in the store and wheeled the cart out of sight, going: *Aut! aut! aut!* in her supermarket heart-attack groan as she had turned onto the next aisle, which held the paper products. Charlotte always felt her mother's deaths profoundly, all through her body. Her knees were made weak by it. Her mouth watered and opened wide, and she felt the need to clutch herself the way Winnie did when overwhelmed by the sudden need to pee. Charlotte became a leaf curling in on itself, a caterpillar spinning itself into a cocoon, so mighty was her terror whenever this happened.

"Never got your ride," the ridesman was saying. It was the same, Charlotte saw—then and now. Then, the sky was white as it was now. Now, there was the smell of salt in the air; then, there had been refrigeration. She didn't answer him. She was too disturbed to talk out loud. She was happy to observe that he, too, was dismissing stupid words from utterance, dumb words such as *you* and *I*.

She watched his lips move, wondering when he was going to ask her to marry him. He would, of course. She wanted him to and she always got everything she wanted, aside from a mother, a father, Duncan.

"Going over there?" he was asking. "Over to Lake Piru?" He really meant *up* to Lake Piru, as it was north on the map; that was where the carnival was headed. She didn't correct him. She didn't correct him and she instantly forgave him, realizing that everything north on the map probably seemed like *over there* to a Mexican. Anyway, what people said made no difference, she knew. The language was being dismantled. Soon nobody would say anything to anyone for any reason.

She watched his mouth work. His teeth in front were white, pretty, but on one side the fourth one from the left was missing. That didn't matter to Charlotte. This was just the sort of flaw she always used in order to fall in love with somebody; it was just the kind of detail she could use later to identify his body as that of her husband after he'd been burned beyond recognition in this or that type of conflagration.

She had her hands shoved down hard into the pockets of her sweatshirt. The tug of the collar was yoke-shaped around her shoulders. He was moving his hands in a rag, cleaning machine parts in gasoline. He thunked things into a coffee can: nuts, bolts.

My father, she told the ridesman, though not out loud, was an architect. I was going to be one, too, but I turned out to be the only girl in mechanical drawing and I couldn't stand it. The boys did stuff to bother me. They held up their drawings of the three-dimensionality of screw threads and they'd ask me, *Hey, Charlotte!* so I'd look up. Then they'd go, *Hey! Wanna screw?* as they showed me the drawing.

And, well, yes, actually I really did. But the trouble was to find someone who would ask me without asking me, someone who didn't have to say the word out into the air with the shape of itself in it. My mother was the same about words and sex, while she lived. She didn't like anything about s.e.x. in any way, shape, or form, which people didn't ever realize. She used to scream at my grandparents, *You mother fuckers! Youmotherfuckingpimpandwhore!* but she wasn't swearing. She was only saying the things that were literally true.

"Going into twelfth grade?" the ridesman asked her. "What school is that?"

Sweeney always said she had the worst mouf he ever heard. Charlotte went on, saying what she was not saying. Still. She never said a word that would make parts of the body figure forth. If you know what I mean. She never said *butt*, for instance. She would never say a word like *glands*. She did say *pee-pee, pooh-pooh, touching icky icks*, things like that. My mother, while she lived, did not usually say *up yours* or *up yours with a ten-foot pole*.

"Got one uncle in Bernal Heights," the ridesman was saying. "And another in Echo Park, which is pretty close to Glendale. Their kids are all Americans."

I could of been an architect.

Could *have!* Katrinka interrupted.

If I would of been able to get past mechanical drawing. The boys made me blush so hard tears came up in my eyes, condensed out of perspiration. They did it by ventriloquism, by not moving their mouths and by placing their voices down real low so the teacher at the front of the room couldn't hear them.

Charlotte! It is would *have*, could *have*, and *really* low! Really low down, really really! Awwwnnd, while we are on the subject of which of us speaks the most South Englishy English, Awe-I have never in *my* life ever said the word, *arthur-I-tis!*

I never said you did! I said you said tor-*til*-la when the word is tor-*tee*-ya.

"Twenty or thirty cousins," the ridesman was saying, "over in Pacoima. Most of them are American."

Well! Nellie cried. In that case let them come to the wedding!

Tits, they'd say, Charlotte went on. *Charlotte! Boobs. Wienies!* They'd say these things and each item would then swim up out of the white of my drafting paper. My skin stung with the heat of it, the blushing. *Dong*, somebody would then mention, just when I thought they'd quit. Still! Still! My drawings were the neatest! Still, I got an A in it. I always get an A in everything, which is why I was accelerated.

The shittiest sort of crap, we both could say, Charlotte continued. *Bastard* but not *prick*. *Pee* but not *piss*. This is the reason: *piss* has the shape of a man standing in its sound. He's holding himself over the toilet bowl, pondering the state of his glands, get it? *Pee*, you know, dribbles down more, more down, you know? Less out?

Charlotte! Katrinka asked. Are you quite finished?

No, Charlotte said. I'm not. I'm actually only coming to what the point of all this is. *If* you don't mind! The point of which *is* this:

The worst thing I ever heard anybody say was Maxine Bill. She'd go screaming out the kitchen window. She'd go, *You get in here before I whip your filthy butts and give you something to really cry about!* I used to have to hide in the bathroom on Avenue B, with my thumbs in my ears and my fingers shoving hard against my eyelids to stop the sight of it. My vision went blood red, then was dashed with bright stars, racing out and away, breaking up. I had to hide to keep the sound out, to keep the sight away from me. She beat them twice— first, with the words she screamed at them; then, really really, in the yard or wherever it was she caught up to them. She used Willie Bill's belt.

Well, Katrinka said, she was too stupid to live.

Still! Still! She didn't die of guilt and shame and grief, like we all did. She wasn't in our family. She wasn't insane, was she? She used Willie's belt, the belt he used on her. She used his language, too, the exact same words. See? Mom? *You get in here before I whip your filthy butts and give you something to really cry about* was only the second worst thing I ever heard a person say. The first worst was this:

When Laddie was killed, Maxine said, *Shit! We've six of them. We can always get another one. And the same damned way!* Willie Bill said it first, those exact words, remember, Mom? He was standing with his face purely open and empty, on the dirt next to their mailbox? He meant they'd *had* six of them, but neither you nor I corrected him. His hands were down, clutched, holding onto nothing.

Then she started saying it, quoting him, with the tense still wrong, and when she said it, she'd leer in that way of hers to make sure you were going along with her to that sickening place she meant to take you. See, Mom? How the language had come apart in their mouths? How Maxine was trying to discuss s.e.x. when the issue was really grief!

"She left me." Charlotte didn't mean this. She'd made it up on the spot to explain to the ridesman why she had suddenly started crying when he'd been talking about where you could get the best tacos in and around the city of Glendale. The ridesman, unlike Lionel, did not pronounce the word *tay*-cos. She said it was over her mother, but Charlotte didn't mean it. What Charlotte was really thinking was of Maxine and Laddie, of the loss of her own children, the children she'd never have because no one was ever going to marry her, how much greater a grief was that, to lose a child, than to lose your parents, or how much greater a grief it *ought* to have been.

Her arms were at her sides. His were then around her. He smelled of gasoline. His shirt was the gray-green of a Girl Scout uniform washed a hundred times. The places where her tears fell darkened it.

He brought her into the camper on the back of his pickup. First he took her clothes off, then his own. His chest was shiny, his back smooth down to where the two sides of his buttocks started. At that place there was a patch of soft hair. His skin was smooth but less silky than Duncan's had felt, the way she'd touched it with her fingertips slipping along as she'd moved the fabric of his clean T-shirt. Now there was his weight on her, now, the taste of his mouth in her mouth and the feel of his teeth and tongue. His weight pressed her down against the ridges of the truck, and he was moving into her. It was not as bad as the sound of its words had made it seem—the pain was less bad than having a tooth filled at the dentist.

Walking back, Charlotte saw the lights in the trailer and understood that she now had the smoker's knack for conjuring. She now knew what all smokers know: that, in order to get the bus to come, all you have to do is light a cigarette.

She now understood all there was to know about the lives and deaths of those around her. Forgiveness issued forth from her as easily as silk, smoke, kite string. She felt him still. She said his name. She tightened and the stars swam up out of the black and red, then pitched away to nothingness. Everyone she'd ever loved was now safe, wrapped with her in the silky cocoon of her blessedness.

She could smoke and make the bus come. She could bring her mother home. All Charlotte had had to do was to give up waiting, leave the trailer, go out herself and find him. His name was Joe. There had been sand down in his sleeping bag.

Katrinka stood on the steps of the Airstream in one of Winnie's Butte Knit suits, which was black in color and baggy. "Charlotte!" she was crying out. "Where in the *hell* have you been!" It was late. The parking lot was made hollow with fog so her voice went out and out into it.

Charlotte looked around, looked down at the place where she stood. Now, as then, his name was Joe. Now time was exactly as it had ever been. There, in the supermarket, there had been linoleum; here, now, sand was drifting up over the lines painted to mark the trailer spaces. She shut her eyes for a moment, then as now, and her mother died. She opened them, and there Katrinka was again. A flatbed truck started up, revved its engine. The whiter exhaust bloomed up into the less-white fog: *putt, putt, putt.*

"It's your grandfather!" Katrinka said. "Charlotte! Are you listening? Do you understand me? I will buy you a hot fudge sundae if you make me a solemn promise that you will not crack up over this completely! Will you promise me?"

"What?"

"That you will not use Lionel's death as an excuse to crack up completely! Because he's dead, Charlotte! Lionel is good and goddamned dead!"

IV

GLENDALE 8, CALIFORNIA

Late Summer, 1962

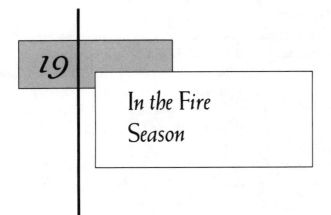

In the Fire
Season

The climate of Southern California, Charlotte had read somewhere, was half wind and half water. The place was actually a desert that just happened to lie alongside the ocean. All of it, all the way south to the tip of Baja, was a geological anomaly, unrelated by either weather or topography to the rest of the American continent.

Having never been to any other place, however, she had no way of knowing what it would feel like to be in real weather. Here, people all congratulated themselves and one another over all the sunniness, as if they were corporately responsible. "Nice weather," they'd say, looking up, squinting. "Yup, another nice day."

Because so many topics—politics, religion, M.O.N.E.Y., S.E.X., and anything else that was even vaguely personal—had been excluded as suitable topics of conversation, Lionel, in public, at the butcher's or the barbershop, talked of only two things: the weather and the Dodgers. "Nice weather, Mr. Ainsworth," Rico would say. Lionel then would smack his lips over it and tell him, "You bet your life!" Charlotte would flip the slick pages of the magazine she was looking at, wondering why he didn't get a headache from saying the exact same thing.

Upon hearing this, the fellow in the chair next to Lionel put in, " 'S'why we come here from Des Moines."

"Des Moines?" Lionel asked, with his green eyes wide. "Why, I was born and raised in South English! I'm a Grinnell man! An Iowan, through and through!" The naked look his face had with his glasses off and the sheet tucked up around his neck made Lionel's head look as if it were being served on a platter. There, in the ledge above either ear, a shiny gutter had been worn by the press of his eyeglasses' earpieces.

The man in the next chair grunted but didn't answer. Lionel went on, "We came here in 1923. My wife was expecting—she had family here. Her grandfather settled the town of Orange. We've been here all these years. Still, I miss it. I miss those hot summers, sleeping in the sheets we'd wet in a tin tub. And the corn, the sweet taste of it. How we'd walk out, my brothers and I, with all those stars pressing down upon us, up and over the little hillocks and out into the fields, where we could hear it, the actual rustle of the corn as it was growing."

"Been here ten years," the new man said. "Don't miss it."

Charlotte chewed hard on the flat slab of Double Bubble that Rico had given her. It was thick and big enough to be broken in two along the crease at the center. It took a long time to get it going. Lionel let her chew it, but she had to spit it out before Winnie saw her. Winnie saw chewing gum as a vice as grave as the piercing of one's ears.

Charlotte chewed the whole thing. She chewed and listened, waiting for the weather joke. Lionel had to tell it to the new man quickly before the silence that was threatening thundered down again. "Know what they say about the seasons here?" Lionel asked him. The man stuck his lower lip out: he didn't know and he didn't necessarily need to know. "That there are only two? The dry one, when it never rains?" The man looked up with mean blue eyes; no laugh would be squeezed from him. "And the wet one," Lionel said, "when it never rains, but might?"

The man from Des Moines thought about this for a moment, then gave a grunt as he got it. That was good enough for Lionel. He began to rock a little beneath his sheet. "Yes, indeedy! Mr. Tweedy," Lionel said, winking up at Rico.

"Name's not Tweedy," the new man said.

Charlotte chewed, hard, hard, and thought about the joke. She got it, anyway, unlike the cartoons in her mother's *New Yorkers*, which usually remained opaque. This joke was funny, or was at least supposed to be, because it was both true and not true at exactly the same time. In that it was like the question of Captain McVay's guilt and innocence.

It was like a story she'd just read in *Life* magazine about a girl having her arm ripped off by a bear while camping in Yellowstone Park. As she was being carried off, she screamed back to her friends, "My God! He's killing me! I'm dead!" It was true, the bear had killed her. Still, as she was saying this, she obviously wasn't dead quite yet. It was as if she had happened upon the event of her own death so suddently that she was more than vividly alive: she was alert and able to offer commentary as she presided over the fact of her own dying.

All was true and all exaggeration. It never rained, and then, when it did, the rains that came down were hyperbolic, rains out of fairy tales, out of the Bible. Cliffs crumbled, walls of creeks and gullies melted. Torrents of the salt-smelling rain were scooped up directly out of the ocean and were dumped right on the land as out of a firehose. That was when the movie stars would show up in the newspaper, photographed in their bathrobes. They would look like other people then, tousled, surprised. There behind them in the picture was the empty sky where their cliffside house had stood only hours before.

Once, two new houses in the canyon next to Lionel and Winnie's fell down together. They'd been built out over the slope on stilts. A crowd had gathered to watch it. Because of her affinity for disaster, Charlotte was there. The first came down all in one piece, while the other dismantled, carefully, as if in slow motion. The stilts came out all along one side, then along the other. The house tilted one way, righted, tilted the other, like a camel sitting gently down.

It never rained in summer, and summer came several times a year. There was one summer that came along right at Christmas or in early January, blowing in off the Mojave. The hot winds then blew all the smog out to sea and the smell of the air changed. Dogs barked at the dry scents and at the sounds of the circular clotheslines going around the wrong way.

Statistics showed that more robberies were committed during the Santa Ana winds, that more people killed themselves then, and more people killed each other. It did not have that effect on Charlotte. The pure blue of the sky looked almost purple without its usual high white milk of moisture from the sea. She smelled the sage and believed it might be possible to awaken one day, to find herself living in a clean, new place, to have a new name.

"Smoke," Katrinka mentioned. They were headed north through Los Angeles on the Harbor Freeway, pulling the Airstream. The sky was burnt umber, fragrant with woodsmoke from the two brush-fires that were burning out of control and had been for days. One was in the Angeles National Forest and another was in Big Tujunga Canyon.

"I noticed." Charlotte had set out not to talk to her mother, but didn't have the energy.

"I was talking about the issue of your grandfather," Katrinka said. "About what was done with his remains. I was trying to put it tactfully."

Charlotte stared at her. "Tactfully?" she asked.

"You know. Not to have to mention the word *cremation*, Charlotte. I have noticed how you tend to come apart over this sort of type of business, and I have had just about enough of that with Winnie, who is lying in the Glendale Sanitarium trying to compete with Lionel over who is the dyingest." Charlotte had guessed it was a car crash that had killed her grandfather, but Lionel had actually keeled over of perfectly natural causes while eating one of his endless breakfasts. Winnie broke her hip trying to pick him up and carry him someplace, right foot, right foot, Charlotte imagined, down the steps. She'd lifted him, but he had then fallen back down on top of her. She was saved by Jehovah's Witnesses who had heard her when they had come to the door selling *The Watchtower*. The Witnesses had interpreted it as a sign, but Winnie had interpreted their arrival as pure and utter impertinence. They had tried to convert her and to get her to pay for tracts while they waited for the ambulance.

"Your grandmother is hallucinating cancer of the bowel," Katrinka said. "Greenley has her on vegeburgers." Charlotte sucked her cheeks in so she wouldn't smile at this; she was never going to be amused by anything her mother ever said again. "She thinks she can hear every word said in the whole wing of the hospital through the ventilation ducts. She's just livid. She probably will burst a blood vessel, sweetie. It was Lionel, you know, who reminded her to take her calcium and her blood pressure pill."

"Does she really have cancer?"

"I don't know. He always used the vegeburgers on me to try to get me to be less intoxicated. I really have the distinct impression that Seventh Day Adventists think Loma Linda is the answer to everything. Remind me to pay him back when our ship comes in."

"For what?"

"The cremation, Charlotte. What have we been talking about? He had it done at Forest Lawn, and it was expensive as hell, which ought to pay Lionel back a little bit for what a shitass he was in real life."

Shitass, Charlotte thought. She added that to the word list she was keeping.

"He shipped the ashes up to The Dalles parcel post, Charlotte. Isn't that the most amazing thing?" Katrinka looked over but Charlotte was staring straight ahead, hoping her mother wouldn't become too enthusiastic about all this until she had finished driving. "I didn't want to bother Winnie about mun-mun until we get through all this."

"All what?"

"The fire season."

Charlotte didn't answer.

"That *was* what I came about, Charlotte, as I have explained. It's two hours up to Glendale, two hours back. They had the mun-mun, honey. I had the time. But when I got to Vista del Mar they just weren't there."

"You've already told me this."

"You don't seem to believe me."

"No. It isn't that, really really. It's just that I don't want to hear all these same stories over and over again any more times."

"People in the canyons are out on their roofs with garden hoses," Katrinka said.

"Where'd you get that?"

"Radio."

"Well, these two fires aren't very near to us, Mom, so don't get too upset about all that."

"How do you know I'm upset?"

Charlotte didn't answer.

"How do you know whether or not I'm upset and what it is I may or may not be upset about?"

Charlotte looked away. Far off over the mountains she could faintly see the shapes of the bombers working the fire. No flames were anywhere in evidence. These two fires were general, had not been contained, held no line. She'd seen one brushfire close up as it had come over the crest of their hill. The flames then had seemed tiny, little licks of faint light. The burning itself had entirely lacked color; it was a shimmer of intense heat that made the brush wobble, melt, before it exploded in an audible rush. In that one single emergency, the authorities had come to get her; she and her grandparents had all been evacuated to the multipurpose room of John C. Frémont Elementary.

"Your father was cremated, too," Katrinka said.

"So you've told me. Could we get onto something else?"

"I have not told you!"

"You sure as hell have! Don't you even listen to yourself?"

Katrinka sniffed.

"This, Mother, is a *hankie*," she said out loud. "Awwwnnd *this* is the way we screw back on the top to a mayonnaise jar."

"Welllll, Charlotte, I honestly don't remember telling you that he was cremated. I wasn't the one responsible. It was Eleanor Ann, Queen Loverly of Aquitaine, who called me once to inform me that they had had his awwwwwwwshes scawwwttered in a beautiful garden. You ought to be happy you missed her, sweetie. She was very tra-la-la! Very sherry splash! splash! in the teacup!"

"Missed her?" Charlotte asked.

"Oh, she's dead, too, of course."

"Of course."

"Charlotte! Why are you acting so hysterogenic, if I may ask? Why are you curled up like that?"

But Charlotte couldn't hear her. She was bending over at the waist so she lay along her own legs. She had her thumbs hard on the flaps of her ears and her fingers were pressed against her eyelids. She was saying, "Shut up! Shut up!" into the skin of the insides of her knees, which were pressed tightly together. She could not stop remembering the sound she'd heard once on Avenue B, when a boy named Norman had put a live lizard in a shoebox into a bonfire. They'd stood with toes curled, hearing first the sizzle, then the delicious *pop!*

Winnie was as angry as Charlotte had ever seen her. Mr. Dukey had been in that morning to read Lionel's will, and the wording of it had started Winnie off. Lionel made her cross! He made her tired! Calling her his "beloved wife," leaving her all his earthly possessions and his "undying love"!

"Well, what else is there?" Charlotte asked.

"Really really," Katrinka agreed. "His last silver dollars?"

"The property was mine already!" Winnie ranted, staring at the heating duct. "It was my shrewd business sense that rescued him from the blacking factory! It was my inheritance that was invested. He was a ruined man. He was ruined by that demon who called herself Ina. She dressed him on the wood stove until a very late age and splashed him with toilet water!"

"Nice to see you're feeling better," Katrinka said, arching one eyebrow at Charlotte.

"I feel perfectly wretched!" Winnie exclaimed. "I detest this place! There is no one here aside from old people complaining about their miseries."

Katrinka reached her slim fingers out to touch Winnie's brow beneath her gray bang where the sweat had turned her perm to a steely frizz. "I'll go get Dr. Greenley, Mother. I'll make him give you a pill."

"I don't want a pill and don't call me that!"

"Of course you do. We could all do with a pill or two, couldn't we, Charlotte, right about now?"

"Why are you wearing your hair styled like that?" Winnie asked, turning toward Charlotte. "It makes you look like a pony."

Charlotte shrugged. She didn't answer.

"Don't you start in on her, Mother, unless you want to make her cry. Charlotte has had a hard day at the office."

"What is that supposed to mean?" Winnie stared at Katrinka, who was pressing her finger to her own lips, as if reminding her mother that the two of them shared a secret. "Oh, these nurses make me so tired! They make me cross! All they seem to want to do is watch me while I try to eat."

Katrinka lit a cigarette. "They're probably just trying their best to be social workerish, Mother. I always thought people like that were trying to do me in, being so *friendly!* and *helpful!*" She dropped her match on Winnie's untouched food tray. "We'll come back in the morning. We'll bring you the paper and your radio. Would you like to play a game of Scrabble?"

"I threw the Scrabble away," Charlotte told her.

"I'm sure you can buy another one in the gift shop," Winnie mentioned.

"Would you like me to? Would you like to play a game of Scrabble, Mother?" Katrinka asked. She touched the shine on Winnie's worried forehead.

"Oh, I suppose," Winnie admitted.

"Is there anything else we can bring you? Do you want a hamburger from Bob's Big Boy, with two pieces of real meat in it? Would you like me to bring you a bottle of scotch?"

"I do not drink," Winnie announced.

"Well, maybe you ought to start," Katrinka informed her.

They went out into the smoky parking lot where the hospital maintained an aviary filled with tropical birds and plantings. As they passed along the fence of it on their way to the car, a mynah bird cawed, swiveled its head, and cried out toward them, "Bad boy! Bad boy!" Charlotte's eyes ached. The bright colors of the bird's beak and face hurt her eyes so much, she had to look away.

"I'm starving," Katrinka said. "Death always makes me starving." Charlotte was startled to realize just then that her mother was wearing new glasses, bifocals with a transparent plastic frame on the bottom and charcoal plastic along the tops of the lenses.

"Mom!" she said. "Those are Lionel's."

Katrinka shrugged. "From each according to his means," she said, "to each according to her needs. Or something shitty like that. Did you know your father was a communist?"

"He was not. He was a Democrat."

"Why are you so contradictory?"

Why are you so insane? she retorted, but without saying it out loud. Charlotte was struck anew with the fragility of all of them. She had always known it about Katrinka, but the fact that Lionel and Winnie were also mortal was completely surprising. As she had touched her grandmother's hand in parting, the skin had suddenly been loose over the large knuckles. How had she become so old without Charlotte's even really noticing?

"Honest to crap, Charlotte, if Awe-I can take it, then so can you."

"Take what?"

"Having one's father be demised."

Charlotte narrowed her eyes at her, suspiciously—another trick word, tragic yet frosted with comedy.

"Don't you see that it isn't anybody's fault?" Katrinka asked.

"Who said it was?"

"He was blue as hell," Katrinka told her, as they came to the car and stood opposite one another under the hot amber sky. It was impossible to tell what time it was—morning, mid-afternoon, early evening. *My life*, Charlotte announced to herself, *is the middle of the ocean at midnight.*

"He'd stopped talking. He wasn't sleeping either so he was up all night painting the woodwork in the kitchen three shades of Dutch blue: Dutch, Dutchier, Dutchiest, you know, like that. The walls were Old World cream. Sam Planc and Kiko-Kiko, or whatever her Japanesy-type name was, were very Old World, very Old World and tragic. Your father was crazy about them. The flowers were lilies, Charlotte, gilded, dipped in that same crap they splash on the what-do-you-call-it of Bibles. What do you call it, Charlotte? You know what I mean? The ... ?" Katrinka moved her fingertips around three sides of the block of the invisible book, which she held in the other hand.

Charlotte shrugged. "The opposite of spine?" she asked, adding the *blank* of it to her word list. *My mother—while she lived*—Charlotte was thinking, *would conjure a word out of thin air, would conjure a word, then paint it.*

"Doing that to a flower is very un-Japanesy," Katrinka said. "It must be something Czech." Each was getting into the car.

"But why?" Charlotte asked. Her voice was a whisper.

"Oh, Awe-I don't know," Katrinka drawled. She was fumbling with the keys, peering at them nearsightedly to see which was which. The glasses had slipped far down on her nose. "Oh, the same lousy things, I suppose. I don't go by that all-Ina's-fault type crap, by the way, but Eleanor Ann did happen to be perfectly awful."

"Like what?"

"She belonged to Eastern Star, for one thing."

Charlotte turned to look at Katrinka, who was poised with one white arm resting along the rim of the door's window and the other shielding her eyes. The cigarette smoke twirled and drifted up. She took a deep drag, then held the cigarette in her mouth as she leaned forward and turned the key in the ignition. "People don't kill themselves just over a thing like that," Charlotte told her mother.

"That, Missy Miss, is what *you* think," Katrinka said, as she shifted into drive. With the cigarette jutting up and clamped in her teeth that way, she looked like FDR.

20

A Word Turned Inside Out

Katrinka sat in the red leather banker's chair, in the gloom of the living room. The orange ash glowed above the brass of the smoking stand, rising to her lips, and then descending. Behind her, on the wall, the Lionel in the portrait dangled his own ash. Their two long faces, their straight noses, the long upper lips that were deeply cleft, had never looked so much alike. It was because he had been her age now, more or less, when the portrait had been painted, and because she was still wearing his glasses, Charlotte decided.

"They got the fires out," Katrinka told her. Charlotte was still in the shadows by the telephone table, hiding her body by crossing her arms in front of herself in her nightie, in case he really was still alive and was just off in the bathroom, where he seemed to be, or there in his darkened study. "Or they were at least *brought under their control.*"

"That's nice," Charlotte told her. Katrinka was wearing only a full slip, without a bra. The strap of the slip dangled down off her shoulder. Her other clothes, most of which really belonged to Winnie, lay in a heap at her feet, with the two nylon stockings piled up on top. The nylons caught the rays of the purplish light that came from the street lamp; this made them look like water was caught in the interstices.

"Oh, I don't know," Katrinka said, raising the beer to her lips, drinking, going on. "I thought you would have loved the idea of being burned out, of having this place burned to the ground around our ears. I mean the *drama* of it. That *we* would then be able to add it to the list of all of our other calamities." She was sounding drunk, ironic, mean.

All the doors of the house stood open; open, too, were all the diamond-paned windows that lined both the living room and the dining room behind it. Many of them had been painted shut long ago, but Katrinka had somehow pounded them open. Now the darkening rooms were filled with the rasp of crickets. How had this racket happened without waking her up? Charlotte wondered. The house had never smelled like this to her, so alive with the crushed-sage smell of the out-of-doors.

"Then we could have felt *good* and sorry for ourselves, couldn't we?" Katrinka asked. She was reaching down to put her beer can in the line with the others that marched along the pattern in the Persian carpet. She stubbed the cigarette out elaborately, elegantly, then struggled up from the recesses of the chair and lurched toward the dining room, banging her hip hard on the corner of the table. "I made muffins this morning, before I went to visit Winnie. I was being girlsie while you slept." She was calling blithely from the kitchen. "Are you hungry?" she asked. "You damned well ought to be."

"Why?" Charlotte asked. She had slept, she was then realizing, not for the few hours it had first seemed like, but for at least one entire day and night besides.

"What day is this?" she shouted, suddenly furious, sputtering.

"Oh, Awe-I don't know. The day before tomorrow."

"And you let me sleep in the middle of a forest fire?" Charlotte screamed at her. "When the roof might have started smoking and the whole place might have been engulfed before they even brought in a hook and ladder?

"Mom!" Charlotte came to the kitchen door. "Do you realize I was asleep! That I was helpless! That you didn't wake me up to tell me you were going? That you just went to the hospital. That you have done this kind of thing a million times before?"

Katrinka considered this, then said, "I know I'm a terrible mother, Charlotte, and I *truly* hope that in your next life you'll get a better one. Would you like a muffin?"

"Oh, you shut up!"

Katrinka approached. The satin of the big slip glowed in the dapple of light from the street lamp. She held in her outstretched hands a muffin, one that she had made. She offered it to Charlotte ironically. "Take. Eat. Because that's all there is around this dump. I think we ought to get dressed and go to Bob's."

Her fingers smelled like cigarettes and tangerines. The skin of her wide chest and shoulders was luminous; so, too, was the skin of her pale arms. She tricked Charlotte like this constantly, trying to make her laugh, trying to get on her good side. Still, Charlotte took the muffin from her, asking, "What is it?"—by which she meant "What was it supposed to have been?" She took a small bite. It was old food, dry; it tasted like a major ingredient had been left out.

"Mush," Katrinka told her. "I used what was left on the stove."

Charlotte spat it into her palm and threw the rest of it, the bite and the other part, too, out the window into the treetops. "You *what!* Lionel made that! Mother! It was left over from when he died!"

Katrinka turned and swaggered to the kitchen, coming back with a large book open to a place that was marked with a red ribbon. She pointed to the place with a certain sincere reverence, as if it were a dictionary or something else they both really did believe in. The recipe was called "Cooked Cereal Muffins"; she tipped the page up into the spatters of light so Charlotte could read it. "See?" she told her. "It came right out of Irma."

"I don't care what Irma says!" Charlotte screamed at her. "You cannot do something so insane as to use things that have been cooked and left uneaten by someone because he has dropped dead in the middle of eating them!"

Katrinka sniffed and tipped her chin up.

Charlotte was suddenly washed by a strong and poignant memory of once, long, long before, when she'd been very small and she was sitting at this same table, listening to her mother and her grandmother discussing the preparation of this or that food. "Irma says," each told the other, and there was no cruelty or belittling in either one's tone, no charges were being leveled.

It was as if each were referring to an old, dear, very well-respected relative, someone of whom each was immeasurably fond. Charlotte hadn't known then who Irma was, but she had always hoped and imagined that she might one day be discovered in some nice branch of the family that wasn't too far away. The blessed influence of this woman was so great that it enabled Charlotte's mother and her grandmother to stand together at the sink with the window open, looking out into the treetops, handing one another a platter back and forth, or the silver cake carver, or a soap-bubbled glass. Each had hands equally wet and shiny. This, Charlotte understood when she later came to know who Irma was, was why this magical relative had named her book *The Joy of Cooking*.

Now, though, Katrinka stood before her breathing in a noisy way, and the stink of her beery breath was ghastly. She had been off there in the kitchen all day, Charlotte saw, smearing things with mayonnaise. It appeared to Charlotte suddenly how easy it would really be to push this bitch of a hag of a crazy drunk out of the open window and be left with only the shape of trees in the starry night. She wasn't any kind of mother: she had left Charlotte too many times. She would have let her child burn up, let her starve to death while sleeping under a smoldering roof.

Charlotte's physical hunger then became so palpable, so painful, that she was assailed by it. It rocked her, burned up through her throat, and she was dizzy with its sickening, bitter taste. The heat of it illuminated the shapes of all her organs: it was hatred, she recognized coldly, of all of them, of *her* and of *him* and of *them*, all who had left her to save herself. The hatred was so intense, so profound that she felt altered by it, as if her stomach had been physically shorn away and was to be ever after that phantomlike—there, but also missing.

"Watch out for bankbooks!" Katrinka cried. "And more last silver dollars!" She was in the kitchen, Charlotte in the front bedroom, a few days later. They'd been in to see Winnie in the morning, and now they were ransacking the house.

"Mom! Come here! There's a drawer in here that is filled to the brim with jewelry!"

"Oh, that," Katrinka said, as she appeared in the doorway of Winnie's bedroom. "That's the crap from her spinster schoolmarm days in Power, Montana. She used to let me play with it for dress up."

"Rats!" Charlotte said. "I thought we were finally rich."

"Know what I'd like to do if we do find some mun-mun?" Katrinka asked. "Let's go to the Biltmore. The Lunts are in town, doing Dürrenmatt's *The Visit.*"

"Are you sure none of it is real?" Charlotte asked. She ran the strands of diamonds and rubies and topazes and emeralds through her fingers. She clipped on earrings, pinned on brooches.

"Woolworth's," Katrinka said. "Otherwise, why would she keep it in a shoe drawer?"

"She never got to wear it," Charlotte said, suddenly feeling a little weepy. "He never took her anywhere."

"He gave her some of it, too," Katrinka went on. "She always burst into tears over his gifts, because all she ever really wanted was a new toilet or something for one of her slumlord rentals. Now, what in hell do you suppose this is all about?" She showed Charlotte a three-by-five card on which Winnie had printed:

EMERGENCY! Place T. in unopened bag into pan of cold water. Change water often! It will take 6 to 8 hours until pliable.

The letters were blurred by water drops, so Katrinka asked, "What's the 'T' stand for, do you suppose—tears?"

"Turkey," Charlotte told her. "The big one Lionel always got, remember? The frozen one he got huge, for leftovers?"

Suddenly, Charlotte's head was bent over and large tears were splashing down from her eyes onto the floor in front of her. She was crying silently, looking down at her missing toenails, so Katrinka, who was leaning on the doorjamb, drinking a can of Pabst Blue Ribbon, didn't notice at first. When she did, she reached out the cold tips of the fingers of one hand and patted Charlotte's arm. "There, there," she told Charlotte. "There, there, there, there. I know you loved him dearly, and *all that*."

"It isn't him," she wanted to say, but she wasn't able to talk. "Breath pause!" Charlotte was thinking, trying to suck air in past the weeping.

Katrinka went on, "I could see how someone *might* have loved him, I suppose. He was much better when I was younger, really really, during his Great Depression, when he'd get all beered up. He was much sweeter then, believe me, Charlotte, than what you had to put up with."

Charlotte, still ornamented by the fake jewelry, was sobbing now. She was thinking how they all had tricked her into weeping, how she was always weeping over all the wrong things.

What Charlotte was weeping about now was her dog Pip, the one Winnie had put to sleep, and also the horned toad Winnie had given her as a replacement pet. Winnie had brought it back from the desert, and Lionel had bought Charlotte an aquarium with sand in it to keep it in. Charlotte, still crying, put out one empty hand, to show her mother what she was crying over, and then, seeing her hand palm upward, remembered suddenly the small heft of the horned lizard, the softness of its belly, the perplexing smoothness of its pointy back that felt silky in spite of its scales.

Katrinka sighed, shrugged, murmured something as Charlotte wept. She rolled her eyes and grimaced with her whole face to ask, *Now what have I done?* She patted Charlotte's arm again, awkwardly, then raised both arms up over her head so that she seemed to be offering the beer can and the cigarette to the ceiling. Then she sighed her heart-attack sigh, to tell anyone who was interested that it was simply too much for her: *Aut! aut! aut!* Katrinka said. *Aut! aut! aut! aut!*

"Her floors, my dear, were so clean you could *eat* off of them!" That was Charlotte's ritzy-fitz grandmother Eleanor Ann in the kitchen, talking things over with Charlotte's fancy Aunt Nan, the one who said "Old Bean." Katrinka was doing them, as she emptied the contents of drawer after drawer into a giant pile in the middle of the floor. The contents, Katrinka announced, were utterly psychotic; she was working hard these days to keep Winnie out of the mental institution.

The drawers *were* crazy, Charlotte saw. They all seemed to contain the same mix of crappy junk: torn-out recipes; notes half-written-out in Rapidograph, then abandoned in midword; discount coupons for new products that were no longer new; sample swatches of drip-dry fabrics for the modern house Winnie planned to build one day—the place where she would live better electrically—order forms for the orthopedic sandals; and thousands and thousands of rubber bands, all rotten and crumbling.

The rubber bands were from the newspapers, which Lionel saved up and tied with twine into bundles. The bundles were stacked from the floor to the ceiling along two walls of his study, in front of the windows in that room, and in the closet there, as well. There were also bundles in every available space in the basement. Katrinka had begun to haul these bundles out, one by one, dragging them by the twine to the old and crumbling incinerator. Charlotte had already told her mother that the burning of trash in L.A. County was no longer legal, but Katrinka did not go by that. She had cleaned out Lionel's study because she was now sleeping there, in the same dirty slip, on top of the daybed that was covered in red corduroy.

Katrinka wore the slip by day, too. She wore it under the same Butte Knit suit that she put on whenever she went to the hospital. The suit still looked okay, Charlotte saw, because it was black and Katrinka seemed to be making an effort to pick off, with her fingernails, the food that hardened on it.

Though Katrinka still had other clothes, even new clothes, down on the street in the Airstream, and Winnie had other suits, Katrinka wore only this one. That was, Charlotte knew, because of its color, because Katrinka seemed to be pretending that she had landed the role of the bereaved daughter or wife in a movie about some ironic sort of mourning. In reality, she didn't seem sad at all.

Katrinka played Scrabble with Winnie at the hospital. Charlotte would not play, would never again expose her spelling and vocabulary to their ridicule. She had played the word "ignominy" in the last game she ever played with them. This was an impossible word for a sixteen year old; still, she understood it inside out. The trouble was she'd got it from reading and had learned it mispronounced. She had since learned to spell it, but the sound of it was indelible and could never really be corrected. Just as she now knew Cambridge wasn't Cam*brick*, that the hymn did not go "ground round version," that the cleanser was not called Bone Am Eye, she still thought the words this way, as she had said them, too, snapping the right letters down triumphantly as she told them: *ig-no-MIN-i-ty!* and Katrinka and Winnie both broke into jeers. Katrinka was right, Charlotte decided right then: women in a pack together *were* nothing but a bunch of Wilma-or-Thelma bitches.

While they played Charlotte went to the cafeteria and bought a tart milk shake made with something called "yogurt," and watched for Dr. Greenley's trembling mane of white hair. She saw him, greeted him, but never asked him to show her the words again, so she could clarify what she'd read there or see exactly where the question and quotation marks had fallen.

She both did and did not want proof these days. She wasn't very certain of anything, including how sick anybody was supposed to be. Winnie had a broken hip and had been brought in suffering from dehydration; she was supposed to be recovering, but she obviously felt herself to be dying. Katrinka was totally insane, as usual, but nonetheless was experiencing moments of taut, luminous lucidity when all she said brought the past forward so dramatically that Charlotte was certain she herself was reexperiencing it. Charlotte, too, now seemed to have suddenly become equipped with ESP. She could stare at the wall so hard she saw the outline of the gilded lilies where they had once stood on top of Lionel's console radio. The bowl of fruit she saw placed right there, in the center of the dining room table.

Katrinka was busy hallucinating this scenario: she was the humorously dutiful daughter of a sick woman who was somewhat grouchily dependent upon her. The amazing thing to Charlotte was that Winnie seemed to share the delusion. *Folie à deux*, Charlotte told herself, looking at the two of them, seeing their two heads bent forward over their Scrabble letters. Katrinka smoked in spite of the sign that said "No Smoking." Winnie didn't tell her not to.

Now Winnie, too, was suddenly loquacious, reminiscent. She liked to tell about when she was at Saint Helen's Academy, which was her happiest time. Things then, she said, were simpler. Girls then did not pluck their eyebrows out! The war wasn't on! Even music then was different. It was performed by instruments that people knew how to play. A boy sang and friends joined in singing around a piano. They all knew the same old sweet songs.

It had never been America's war. Still, the boys from the university and Winnie's own hometown had gone off to fight in it. One boy, whose name she did not remember, had been sent off to France. He sent her French dirt in an envelope, so she could see it, know the different feel of European soil falling through her fingers. It had had an older feeling, Winnie said, like that of face powder. But she never told him that because she never wrote back to him.

This boy had stepped on a land mine in a French field a week after the armistice was declared. He was to have shipped home the next day. His commanding officer wrote Winnie a long letter about all this. He sent along the boy's knapsack; inside there was a gold pocketwatch with her picture in it. The boy had cut the picture out of the Saint Helen's yearbook. Winnie had stared at it where it was glued, in back of the watch facing the works. She was utterly horrified.

"Why?" Charlotte asked. "That he loved you and you never knew it! That you never wrote back to him! And that now it was too late!"

Winnie glared at Charlotte as if she were a simpleton. "Of course not!" she snapped. "That the vile person had taken my picture with him, that he had *thoughts* about me, don't you see?" She had thrown the knapsack into the root cellar at the ranch. It was probably still there, as Franklin had probably never gone down there to clean it out. Franklin always had been a very slovenly person.

On the way home from the hospital, they stopped at Big Boy for hamburgers to take home, then at the Jolly Boys Liquors, where Katrinka had opened an account in Lionel's name. The Impala and the Airstream were parked up the road. She was now driving the Nash Rambler.

The heat of early August was oppressive, enervating. It was only noon or one, but already both of them were completely exhausted. The work of the day, seeing Winnie, was done but did not seem done. Charlotte did not call Patsy, did not go to the Y to swim, did not walk up to Montrose to steal or to eat or to get money out of her bank account. They were supposedly fixing up the house for whenever Winnie might come home. Katrinka had been trying get someone to put in a funicular. Katrinka didn't know about Charlotte's bank account, how it was hidden in plain sight at the Bank of America on Honolulu, waiting for her college education.

Katrinka drank beer and worked at what she called "getting through" the house. She imagined that they were cleaning, but the mess they were making grew more enormous and more complicated every day. The debris in the backyard was so widespread that Charlotte imagined they were going to be arrested for it. She imagined that in the city of Glendale there would have to be a law against trash heaped outside in such a demented and obvious way.

When Katrinka wasn't cleaning, often enough she lay on the red corduroy in her slip and whispered. Often enough, it was Ogamer lecturing her on poverty, on the world not owing her a living, on pulling herself up by her bootstraps. "Bootstraps," she would repeat, then go off into her whispers, the words like water being dragged back through the pebbled course of her phlegmy laugh.

Charlotte, too, changed out of her street clothes when they got home. She wore a pink satin nightie, one she had found folded in tissue in its Bullock's box in the bottom drawer in the center hall. Katrinka said she thought it was another of Lionel's gifts, given for the sole purpose of ruining Winnie's Christmas or birthday, but Charlotte did not see how that could be. The nightie, she decided, had been sent by someone mysterious, someone who was in love with Charlotte herself. It fit Charlotte perfectly.

She walked through the heat of the wrecked house, stepping

carefully over the creaking floorboards, watching, as always, for land mines. She carried herself as if she were something old and valuable, a Ming vase, an object that had survived so long because of just such careful and deliberate transportation. Charlotte carried herself this way now because she had decided she was pregnant.

She was not so stupid that she didn't realize that her life now was utterly ruined. She would not go to college, would never live up to all her fine potential. Still! Still! In this simple thing, this act that had been so easy, she had become unempty. She remembered him only vaguely, really only the line of his teeth. Yet she remembered him in the way she'd been shaped to him, how she'd once been and was now no longer empty, how she now held the shape of a man and was suddenly now filled and filled.

Her life was utterly ruined. Still! She would have the baby and maybe one day marry someone. They would run a printing shop. They would live in a room made out of his parents' garage. They would try so, so hard. His hair would be black, like the baby's. The baby, she hoped, would be a boy and would look nothing at all like the Ainsworths nor the Blacks. The baby would have a brand-new start.

She went to the refrigerator, opened it, and looked inside. The bulb was burned out, but on the top shelf she could see a note written out by Winnie, entitled "Not To Be Forgotten!" Below was a chart of the different medications she and Lionel were each to take, and at what times. The bottles of pills were all there, lined up along one wall of the refrigerator.

She took a carton of milk from the shelf and turned to the window to get a glass from the sink. As she rinsed it out, she saw Winnie's Colonial Dames cold cream on the ledge of the window and the note taped below it: "Wash face twice daily. Rinse well and pat dry. Rub cream in gently, with the fingertips only, then wipe off excess with tissue." The words had been copied verbatim from the label of the jar. Winnie was self-conscious about her penmanship, but this was her best: capitals and lower-case letters, printed on a slant, each perfectly formed. Added later, though, in a shakier hand and done on a tilt, as if from standing, were these words: "Or skip it!"

Charlotte was thinking about the directive and about its addendum, wondering whether it was an admonishment, written out by Winnie to scold herself when she was cross, or whether the last part was a joke, added by Katrinka imitating Winnie's rigid printing. The two of them did write in a similar way, and her own handwriting, Charlotte noticed, was going from cursive toward printing as she got older. Now there were only a couple of letters in each of her words that were in any way connected.

As she was thinking, she poured the milk into the glass and took a big swig of it. She gasped and choked and spat it into the sink. She poured the glass out, then turned the half-gallon over the drain. As the sides of the carton heaved huge glugs, the air all around her began to fill with the stench of sour milk.

"I made the cake to cheer him up," Katrinka was saying. "He'd stopped talking, by then, but he was still cooking and he still had an appetite. He was very good at a leg of lamb. He served it with mint jelly. They were both so interested in having the two of us be the sick ones that they were paying for the psychiatrists."

"Who was?"

"Eleanor Ann and Joe, Sr." Katrinka was eating a hamburger from Bob's. She wiped her fingertips down the front of Winnie's suit and went on, "Lionel and Winnie never had all *that* much interest in my seeing a psychiatrist. They thought I'd tell on them, although I never did. They thought my problems could all be solved by my getting a decent job.

"Anyway, it was a waste of cold hard mun-mun, sweetieheart, since neither Joey nor I ever told them a goddamned thing. He was seeing Maudlin and I was seeing Moody, or it may have been the other way around. He wasn't talking so he *couldn't* tell them anything, and I *wouldn't* talk to them on principle. I always felt they were trying to get the dope on the Ainsworths so they could have them locked up. The Ainsworths probably did deserve to be locked up, but then where would I have been, I mean really *really?* Those types are always interested in the parts of everything that have most to do with s.e.x., have you noticed that? The bi-homosexual saga of

Power, Montana, versus The Dalles, Oregon, versus Glendale 8, California, versus South English, Iowa.

"But, Awe-I had nothing to say and I, on principle, refused to dream. I never dream anyway, but I made certain I didn't dream then. I made some dreams up though, so they'd have something for their report to Sacramento. I put lots of cigars, hot dogs, you know how those sorts of types all *love* that sort of shitty crap: blimps going *put! put! put!* meaning *blank! blank! blank!* Pistols popping out, going: Boing-cuckoo!

"I left out the bottle of iodine your father carried around in his pocket at Cal in order to be psychodramatic. I left out Mr. Tweedy, and Charles Dickens, Ogamer being 'Grandmother' turned inside out. I left out Winnie's horned toads. I left out Joey's stopping talking. It seemed to me that it was a lot like Lionel's Great Depression, though Joey still went to work. Joey worked and painted the kitchen, and he did the leg of lamb. One of the last things he ever said to me was perfectly matter-of-fact: 'I am going to work here until I die,' he said one day, as he got out of the car. I simply had no idea, Charlotte, that he was thinking about things with such immediacy.

"I drove him in the Willys. I had packed him a lunch, that day, but I don't think he ever ate it. Remind me to show you how to make a sandwich with . . ."

"Mom?" Charlotte interrupted. "Could you try to just stick to the main story?"

"The office," she sniffed. "*Which* was on Wilshire and *which* was ugly as hell! One thing that did distinguish your father's father's firm's architecture was its complete and utter gawd-awful ugliness, Charlotte! Still, it was just the kind of thing that all the high ups in the uppety crap all *loved* to *love* to *love!* Are you listening to me?"

"You aren't sticking to the story."

"These, Charlotte, are the words *you must* go by: when you are making your husband's sandwich, I want you to spread the mayonnaise all the way to the edge of the bread! It is also a very good idea to pack the damp crap in a separate little package so the bread won't get soggy! When our ship comes in, I'll show you how to slice the tomatoes very thinly and to wrap them in their own square of waxed paper. This is what your father taught me! In those days in our dream shack! *When* the rent was cheap because it was falling off the foundation!

"Arch came down and it was hot as hell in the house with the oven on, so we picked the Dutch blue kitchen table up and carried it outside. The front yard sloped away so when the butter melted it ran to the downhill side of the plate. Your father made a leg of lamb, charged at the butcher's. Eleanor Ann and Joe, Sr., paid that bill, too, of course. I don't know why, since your father was AIA, we never had any money. I think it was because we owed our souls to the company store.

"Arch thought this was all too romantic. He thought we were very F. Scott and Zelda in our crappy dump sliding off the hill into the streets of Hollywood. He got drunk and wanted to sleep with both of us."

"Did you?"

"Did we what?"

"Go to bed with him?"

"Oh, for Christsake, Charlotte! That is none of your damned business, really really! Did you ever know your father made a tuna casserole that had a topping comprised of broken-up potato chips? That sounds perfectly lousy, I know. It sounded lousy to me, too, but it was actually quite good. Awwwnnd did you know your Grandfather Joe had a blend of pipe tobacco named after him—the J. J. Black blend? Very high up!" Katrinka said, sucking her cheeks in. "Very la-di-da-fitz!"

Charlotte watched her from beneath her brow, waiting for her to go back to it.

"The Blacks were paying for everything, butcher, baker, Jolly Boys. They were also paying the druggist. Your father was taking medicine by the handfuls. He thought it was keeping him going, but I think it was making him sicker."

"Thorazine?"

"That was before Thorazine. I'm not sure what he was taking. He was really quite sick, but we won't go into all that."

"All what?"

"Charlotte! I don't want you cracking up over all this! It didn't happen to you, do you understand me? And you are *not* to take it personally! He had father problems, we all did. Maudlin was trying to get your father to be more boysie, I think. Awwwnnd I was supposed to be girlsier. I think that's what it was all about, with the lopsided cakes and the little packets of sliced tomato leaking all over his one clean shirt. I could only ever manage to iron the cuffs and collar, so he had to work in his suitcoat all day. I do regret that. I regretted that I was so sick and that nothing either of us could do could help the other one.

"I think that after Arch came down, Joey decided he was bi-homo-homo or whatever. I did tell him, well, aren't we all, more or less? Aren't we all, one way or another? So why get all worked up over it? We both knew by then we'd never get away from our parents. Joey imagined that if he died you and I would have at least a million dollars in insurance money."

"So he killed himself," Charlotte said, not a question, but a statement.

"Oh, I don't know." She glared at Charlotte as if some of this really were Charlotte's fault. "I'm not certain it ever was proven."

"Did he do it so it looked like an accident, like he stumbled over his gun or something?"

"Where the hell did you get such a lurid thought?"

Charlotte shrugged.

"The truth," Katrinka said, "is this." She stopped and lit a cigarette, wagging out the match, dropping it in her food. "They wouldn't ever tell me. They called to tell me the Palmer House crap, first the Blacks, then the Ainsworths. Did I ever tell you Eleanor Ann made me write these lousy poems for her for her Eastern Star luncheons? They were perfectly shitty, the lousiest shittiest sort of lousy shitty crap, *worse* than Hallmark. Then she'd call me, stewed to the gills, to ask if I would be oh! so! terribly *offended* if she took credit for them!"

Katrinka laughed, then, and had to stop talking to cough her thick cough. After coughing a while, she stopped and then whispered for a moment or two, keeping up her side in a private argument from long ago. "They told me that he'd had a hard day at the office," she went on, "so he was going on a business trip. *Business trip* was what they always called it when they put him back into the sanitarium. This was a very We-say-*eye*-ther sort of place, sweetie. No Negroes ever went through the doors into *that* particular Slumgullion for the Pathologically Enthusiastic and Others Depressed as Hell!

"When I was talking to Winnie, it occurred to me that none of them had really got it right, that Sam Planc had called me and had said, with his great Old World formality, that my husband Josef had so very regretfully committed suicide. I resisted believing him, Charlotte. I imagined that the name Josef, as pronounced in Czech, went more readily with another person. I also could only go so far as to imagine Joey *attempting* suicide, but not him actually succeeding. I also worried about the construction—who was doing the regretting, if you know what I mean."

"I told Winnie all this. I told her as tactfully as possible because I didn't want her going to pieces over it."

"Then what?"

"She told me to pack my shoes in tissue, to then put them in brown paper, and then to place them in my suitcase in the sleeves along the side that had elastic, the sleeves which existed for that express purpose. She told me to place tissue in the creases of each of my blouses as I folded them. Then she told me to drive very, very carefully up and over the hill past Griffith Park to Verdugo Road."

"She didn't tell you she was sorry! That you were right and she knew it!"

"No," Katrinka said, sizzling her cigarette out in the saucer. "As a matter of fact, she said I was wrong. She said I was to drive very carefully because I was hearing things. *The phone has not rung, do you understand me!* I remember her telling me. *The phone has not rung!* Of course the phone had rung! It hadn't stopped ringing. I was standing at the telephone table talking to her on it. See, Charlotte? Your grandmother has always been completely out of her mind."

"Mom!" Charlotte shouted. "Don't you see? Winnie was driving you crazy! Telling you you were hallucinating when you knew you weren't! When you knew what was true!"

"True?" Katrinka smirked.

"About my father!"

"Your father?"

"That is what we were talking about!"

Katrinka tipped her chin up and looked away. "Winnie didn't make me start hallucinating, sweetie. I was already hearing things." She looked back. "Him."

"Did he ever, you know? Did he ever say anything about me?"

Katrinka sucked her cheeks in. Inhaled, exhaled, thinking this over. Her lips were pressed together bemusedly. "He sends you all his love, sweetieheart," she said when she did again speak. "He sends you *all* his love and kisses."

Katrinka's estate was composed of this: three one-pound coffee cans filled with silver dollars, quarters, nickels, and dimes but no pennies; fifteen one-pound coffee cans filled with pennies only; the Kappa silver teaspoons (pawned); a Singer sewing machine (pawned); Big Mother's pearl-handled opera glasses (used by Charlotte and Katrinka at the Lunts' performance of *The Visit* at the Biltmore Theater in downtown Los Angeles, then pawned); Winnie's real father's three-quarter-sized "Washburn" guitar, taken to Hawaii by sailing vessel, then returned with his body and the rest of his effects on the same ship after his death in 1903 (pawned); and the old *Joy of Cooking*, by Irma Rombauer. The cookbook was wildly annotated in Winnie's Rapidograph pen, with such comments as these: "*Too dry!*" and "*Broiled! Not boiled! This is a typographical error!*"

Charlotte's estate was composed of this: the brand new 1962 edition of *The Joy of Cooking*, which was clean and modernized, bought by Winnie to go in her clean new all-electric kitchen in the new house she one day intended to build. The "Dedication," by Marion Rombauer Becker, read in part:

> In revising and reorganizing "The Joy of Cooking" we have missed the help of my mother, Irma S. Rombauer. How grateful I am for her buoyant example . . . [and] for her conviction that, well-grounded, you can make the most of life, no matter what it brings!

And its epigraph, from Goethe's *Faust*:

> That which thy fathers have bequeathed to thee, earn it anew
> if thou wouldst possess it!

And the recipe for "Roast Turkey" on page 479, which was scribbled entirely out.

Charlotte could see him clearly: He's only a few years older than she is. He's walking down a wooded path that runs along a creek beneath oaks and eucalyptus. This creek is still running, though it is nearly summer. He has just left a small building, one surrounded by larger ones. The courtyard behind him holds a bronze sculpture of a bird in flight. The tilt of its wings is lyrical and solemn, caught in a powerful downbeat, but because of the distension of his pouched bill and the openings at the side for the water to be squeezed out, this pelican has a comic look, as if it were making wisecracks.

The young man is very good-looking, very well dressed. He's wearing a tan tweed jacket and darker trousers that are pleated at the waist, and a white dress shirt, open at the throat. His shirts are done for him each week at the French laundry a block off campus.

He carries no books, and, although he is an architecture student, he carries no rolled-up blueprints. Still, the fabric of his jacket is suffused with the scent of wood shavings, from the pencils he sharpens by hand with a penknife, and the side of his drawing hand is smudged with graphite.

As he passes from the bluish shadows out into the sun, light blazes up off the white of his shirt and illuminates his face. It had been in shadow because he is looking down. He is looking at the ground, and he would look dejected if it were not for the fact that he's smiling. He smiles with his teeth showing, lips drawn back tightly; there is a space between the two front teeth.

He smiles because of his plans, his projects, which he keeps in the hand he has shoved deep into his front pocket. His pants look wide there, from the width of his clenched fist. The one hand holding the small squared-off bottle of iodine is darkened with the bruise of lead. This bottle is his future, his fortune, his luck. He holds onto it.

He holds onto it.

21

A Room with a View

"I want to talk to you!" Katrinka says, clomping in.

Charlotte looks up, but with great difficulty. She is reading the L.A. *Times* with rapt attention. Her mother is standing before her in her dirty slip, weaving slightly, waving her cigarette around. The only other clothing she wears is her black high heels. Charlotte cannot force her eyes to stay on Katrinka, so they drift down to what she was reading. The paper is spread out on the dining room table, among the beer cans, the white paper bags from Big Boy, old hard French fries, the full ashtrays, and the neat piles of nickels, pennies, dimes, and quarters, all of which, in different combinations, add up to twenty-seven cents—just the amount needed to buy a pack of cigarettes or a can of beer or a gallon of gas in August of 1962.

"What?" she asks, but she is already reading again. The newspaper is full of the death of Marilyn Monroe, whose body was found the morning before in her Hollywood bungalow. She and Katrinka first heard about it yesterday, when they were at the hospital having cake with Winnie to celebrate her birthday. Katrinka made the cake, which was chocolate but was not sweet and which seemed to have been made with grease.

Charlotte and her mother now go to the hospital at an appointed time each Sunday, to sit with Winnie while she enjoys old "Amos 'n' Andy" programs on the shortwave. This ritual is, Charlotte thinks, the event in their lives that most closely resembles church.

"You aren't listening!"

"I am, Mom, really. Really—what were you saying? Mom, what does it mean when they say 'bungalow'? Wouldn't you think somebody like that would have a mansion, at least, or at least a good, nice, really big, pretty house?"

"Charlotte, don't talk to me about bungalows! I want to discuss this! I want to discuss a serious issue. I want you to promise me that none of this is going to send you to Camarillo."

"Okay, sure. All right. I really do promise. But, Mom, get this. I'm not kidding. Really, you should listen to this—you can take it personally. Her parents were pretty lousy, *really* P.U., but her psychiatrist was seeing her every single day to try to keep her alive. Do you think he was in love with her? Probably, right? Lookit. Let me see if they put his name in. God! Mom! Did you ever think it might be Moody or Maudlin?"

"Charlotte!" Katrinka is trying to say, but she breaks off, erupting into a fit of coughing. The sound of the cough is so awful that Charlotte's eyes go out of focus as she reads, and she is forced to look up.

Katrinka is standing at the head of the table with one hand on the back of Winnie's chair to steady herself. Her other hand is curled helplessly in front of her gagging mouth. Her irises are vivid green behind a bright shine of water that has filled each eye, the whites of which are suddenly so red they look diseased. The first two fingers of this limp hand are stained a deep yellow ochre on the inside, which is, Katrinka says, the mark of a true mental patient. "Want me to get you a glass of water, or something?" Charlotte asks her.

Katrinka keeps coughing, all the while shaking her head from side to side, so her hair hanging down in a limp bang goes back and forth, wobbling. Her whole body is convulsed by the coughing.

"Want me to pound you on the back, at least?" Charlotte asks, but Katrinka squeezes her eyes shut and continues to shake her head. Her mouth, shaped open by the coughing, still struggles to get words out, Charlotte sees. *The best thing about my mother,* she thinks, *is that she just doesn't quit.* The worst thing is this: the whitish look of her fat and contorted tongue, made perfectly evident by this hacking.

Then, abruptly, the coughing stops. "I want you to promise me, Missy! I want you to promise me that!" and the coughing starts in again. Charlotte bends her face back to the paper, trying to concentrate on the stories about Marilyn Monroe. She tries to read this article, but then begins to wonder when she should telephone for an ambulance. Winnie was delirious with dehydration by the time the ambulance had come for her and Lionel. She had thought the Jehovah's Witnesses were the snoops from Power. She had called the ambulance their wedding hearse as it had taken them both away.

"Mom! Mom! Could you do me a favor and not stand there doing that?" By which she means: *dying.* "Could you please at least go lie down on the couch?"

"I most certainly will not," Katrinka snaps, coming back to life. "And I will thank you very much not to try to change the subject."

"From what to what?" Charlotte shouts after her, because Katrinka is already clomping away back into the darkness of the hall.

"Mom, Mother! *really!* You have to read this," she continues as Katrinka comes back in. "Really. They've ruled out foul play. It was pills, they think. Do you think that's what it was with my father?" She looks up and finds her mother assessing her, searching the features of her face. "What?" she asks, startled by Katrinka's acuity.

"You aren't listening to me."

"I am so."

"Then promise me."

"Mom, I *did,*" Charlotte tells her, "I *have.*" *You,* she thinks, *are the one who is never listening!*

"I have never understood why you were so eager to get involved in everybody else's tragedies," Katrinka says, "when we have always had *more* than enough melodrama of our own." She hands her a packet of newspaper clippings, yellowed, tearing on the folds. "I found this stuffed on the shelf up behind the toilet on the service porch, behind all her brushes and turp. Do you realize what a fire hazard she has there with all that linseed oil?"

The clippings were from the L.A. *Times*, the day after the Japanese had surrendered, the headline reading: "JAPAN SURRENDERS! PEACE DECLARED!"

"Sleep in heavenly peep, and all that," Katrinka says, impatiently, trying to get Charlotte to open the newspaper so she can show her what it is she wants her to see. Charlotte, though, is reading the first article, when her eyes shift to the one in the left-hand column: "*Indianapolis* Sunk by Jap Sub on Eve of Peace, Hundreds Lost." At the bottom of the column there is a note that a partial list of the dead and missing can be found inside. She turns to page four.

"You passed it."

"What?"

"This," Katrinka says, opening it up, so the old newspaper lies crumbling upon the inky crispness of the new one. She points and Charlotte sees it:

ARCHITECT LEAPS TO DEATH

Joseph Jordan Black, Jr., 26, apparently took his life yesterday morning by leaping from the roof of the office building where he was employed. There were no witnesses. He left his place of employ at approximately 10:30, saying he was going to get a cup of coffee. When he did not return, a search was instituted. His body was found in the parking lot behind the building, which stands at 2189 Wilshire Boulevard and houses the architectural offices of Mr. Black's father, Joseph Jordan Black, Sr. A colleague, a Mr. S. Planc, reported that Mr. Black had recently appeared to become increasingly despondent, but the family declined to comment and no note was found. Mr. Black was a graduate of the School of Architecture at the University of California, Berkeley. He was married to the former Katherine Ainsworth, and resided in the Silverlake district. In addition to his wife and father, he leaves a sister, Nan, and his mother, Eleanor, both of Glendale. A coroner's inquest has been scheduled. No memorial services are scheduled, a spokesman for the family has said.

"Some coffee break," Katrinka says. Charlotte says nothing. She is reading it again.

"Why did they put 'Katherine'?" she asks as she looks up.

"That's my name."

Charlotte is reading it again. "He didn't leave a note?" she asks. Katrinka shrugs.

Charlotte reads it again, then looks up. "It doesn't say why."

"Journalism doesn't do *why*, sweetie. It does who, what, where, how, when. You really should sign up for the school paper with Mrs. White." Charlotte has explained to her mother that she isn't going back to Glendale High, but this has not yet sunk in.

"He didn't say good-bye," Charlotte says. Katrinka, though, has sucked her cheeks in and is looking off into the moving treetops. "Why?" Charlotte asks her. Her own dry lips, top and bottom, catch and stick.

"Oh, I don't know, Charlotte. His family was very big on 'Never apologize, never explain.' Like that. And like it or not, we are a part of the crappy shit of our own families. I mean that in the kindest possible way."

"Not me!" Charlotte screams, standing up.

"Jesus God!" Katrinka is saying, as Charlotte shoves by her. "I should have known! For once, my lousy shitty parents were goddamned right about something! I should, really really, have thrown the lousy shitty crap on top of the bonfire and torched the whole mess! You promised me, Charlotte! You promised that you would not have a nervous breakdown over this! Haven't I done enough time in the penal colony for both of us?"

Charlotte is gone, though, gone barefoot in her satin nightie over the warped and creaking floorboards where the splinters are, beneath the phone table in the central hall, gone back into her room where she is face down on her bed on top of all her clothes. These things are folded or are still bunched up, still to be tried on for style and fit, to be taken, or left behind in the rubbish of the growing piles outside. As she chooses something she will take, she packs it into one of the boxes Katrinka has brought home from the Jolly Boys. Charlotte will take her clothes off to this fancy girls' school in cardboard boxes marked Jack Daniels and Wild Irish Mist.

There was no funeral, she tells herself. There were only the gilded lilies standing on the console radio, from Mr. Planc and his Japanese wife. They came to call, bringing fruit in a woven basket, fruit which Lionel and Winnie would not touch. That was all that had happened. They alone showed up because they weren't from California and they still remembered how things once were done.

Leaving no note, Charlotte thinks, isn't the same thing as saying, "No note was found." Her father and Marilyn Monroe were both *apparent* suicides. She struggles to turn the words around, to force them inside out and backwards, to fit them to the luck of failure. To have tried to kill yourself and to have failed at it! What could shine out more brightly than the luck of that? To have tried to die and have failed?

Charlotte thinks these words: *They hated him so much, they wouldn't bury him.* The words *There was no funeral* seem suddenly inscribed, as if carved by the fingerbone of the Ornt Tree into the living muscle of her heart.

There was no funeral, Charlotte thinks again. And she wails into the pillow her face is buried in.

"I will," her mother says behind her, "simply not put up with this."

Charlotte looks back over her shoulder and sees that her mother is gripping her own upper arms, as if to keep the parts of herself from flying away into outer space.

"Get out of my room," she tells her. "Leave me alone! What business is it of yours? He was *my* father and you never shed a tear over him!"

"How do you know?" Katrinka asks her coldly.

But Charlotte is beyond arguing with the old crazy bitch. Charlotte is up on her feet now, weeping at the window indignantly, looking out at the heaps of trash that grow every day. *The ignominy*, she thinks, *of people's old wet things*.

"I would kill myself, too, if I thought I had to spend the rest of my life with you," she tells her mother. She does not turn around to measure the effect these words have. She is looking steadily out and out, out past the grape arbor, out past the victory garden that still! still! struggles up.

She is imagining the shape her own life will take, her looking for him. She sees the precipitous arc out and upward toward hope, toward love, toward forgiveness, then the tumbling back down. It will be as it was with Duncan. She will never stop crying. She will always look out and see that body falling past her window.

Then she sees herself firing the bow and arrow down into the gopher hole in the field and sees her face with the surprise in it and the limp body dangling on the end of the shaft. It is always startling to remember how closely love and hatred lie at the heart of things.

There was no funeral, she reminds herself. She reminds herself of that and that the newspaper didn't mention her. Nowhere was it written that he was going to be a father, that the baby was going to be a girl, a daughter who would love him faithfully without ever meeting him, that she would stand here forever at this back window staring out at the ruin of her family. Her wails grow loud and Charlotte is doubled over.

Behind her Katrinka is saying, "I really will not stand for this. Charlotte, if you don't stop that *this instant* I am going to call the police!"

Charlotte stops crying abruptly and turns around. She stares at her mother incredulously. "Mom?" she asks. "The police? *You* are going to call the police?"

"I simply will not have it in my house!"

Charlotte stares at her. Katrinka perfectly serious. "What are you going to do, tell them to come to *your* house and arrest me? What would the charges be?"

Katrinka ignores the question. "If you don't stop that right now, I am going to call your grandmother."

Charlotte's mouth has dropped open. Her nose is still running, but she is too astonished to wipe it.

"Your grandmother," Katrinka tells her, "is not a well woman!"

"Know what, Mom?" Charlotte asks her coldly. "You really are *insane!*"

Ten, fifteen, twenty times a day, Charlotte goes into the bathroom, pulls down her underpants, and waits. While she waits she thinks about the nature of luck, how Marilyn Monroe had so much luck she couldn't stand it, even with the best psychiatrist trying to help her, even with all the money in the world, even with the men who loved her, who were smart and good-looking and maybe even funny, even with someone to do her laundry!

Still, it was hard to say about luck from the outside. Her parents, Charlotte knows, had the look of being lucky but they actually were not. They were the type who had what was called *advantages.* But even with all that, all they had been able to come up with between them was one disadvantaged child.

Charlotte thinks about luck until a little pee finally trickles down. She wipes with the big wad of toilet paper that she has been clutching. She wipes, then tips the wet place toward the light from the window. She is looking for the filament of red or the faint pinkish blush that will mean there really is a God.

She *tries* to believe in God, tries to imagine that all hardship might just be a test, to make faith difficult. She had read this once—that the fact that you don't believe in God could be leapt over, you could begin by jumping, by leaping away into faith. Maybe her father believed this as he went off into the air above the parking lot and went down, going *God Is! God Is!*

Or, then again, maybe he did not. Her mother has told her he was raised as an Episcopalian but was an ardent and thoroughgoing atheist. If he was an atheist, Charlotte thinks, she will be one, too.

Charlotte waits for more pee. She's thinking of Ogamer, of why Nellie wasn't named Ogamer if it's the word grandmother turned inside out, then of Ogamer's voice booming in his Cockney accent, singing, "Wif a widdle bit o' bloomin' luck!"

She remembers the blue egg:

It was when she and her mother were living on Avenue B. It was Easter, almost at the end of the time they lived there, and some ladies were having an Easter egg hunt on the lawn in front of the steps of the library. Charlotte could see by their outfits that these ladies were the sorts of types who were nice, and she walked way, way out of her way to go around them. *Niceness, ladies, Easter*: these were exactly the sorts of words which did not interest Charlotte even remotely.

Charlotte was already on the steps when one of the ladies stopped her. It was because she was so obviously an orphan, with her bare feet and the rips at the sides of her dress where the sashes had been but had somehow fallen away. The fabric was sticky there where it touched the undersides of her arms. That was from the masking tape her mother had used to try to tack the sashes back on.

The lady was so happy at the thought of having an orphan on their hunt that she was not going to let her get away. She *made* Charlotte take the basket, then guided her down the steps. The ladies were all watching her, imagining that Charlotte was the sort of person who never had any luck. To show them, Charlotte walked right over to the first-prize egg and picked it up.

This egg was dyed sky blue; on its side, in a technique called "wax-resist," was written "$10" in the crayon that shows up only when the egg is dyed. Charlotte knew all about it. She knew all about luck, all about their goddamned egg, which she couldn't help but find since it was hidden in plain sight. She knew all about how lucky it made these ladies feel to have an orphan to cluck over for two or three minutes, and not for the rest of their lives.

She held the egg in the cup of her hand. The smooth cool shape of it filled her palm. She considered eating the egg, since she was very hungry. It was *her* egg, her luck; still, she couldn't eat it, and she couldn't turn it in for money.

If she took the money home, Katrinka would have to have it, and Charlotte would hate her for making her hand it over. She made Charlotte give up all the money she ever got from Lionel and Winnie, or from Sweeney who gave her dimes for pigeon feed and a quarter for her dues as a member of the pigeon club. Katrinka would get the ten dollars and call Blackie's Liquor to have Blackie deliver. She'd get herself a six-pack and cigarettes and a jar of pickled herring so she wouldn't smell too completely boozed. She would get Charlotte a candy bar and a Seven-Up. "You know?" Katrinka would wink at Blackie, as she took the soft drink out of the bag, "YOU like IT! awwwwwnnnnd IT likes YOU!" All of the words she said would be made hefty with terrible meaning.

The ladies were watching her. They were all too nice. *Well!* she could already hear them saying, *we were only trying to help!* What they didn't understand was that some people just could *not* be helped, that the others were going to have to save themselves, that some still liked to say, "When I need their help, I will ask for it!"

She tipped her chin up. Someone tried to speak to her, but she lifted her shoulders and shook her head, as if she did not speak English. She put the basket back down on their table, then she started up the library steps.

She put the bright blue egg down on top of the paws of one of the library's stone lions, hidden in plain sight. It was the brightest thing out on that cold gray day. Still, Charlotte imagined, it was going to take a resourceful child to turn her back on the hunt to come up there and find it.

Charlotte's luck had been written down for her on the day she was born: *Mother diagnosed "paranoid schizophrenic," 20(?) yrs. at onset, father, suicide 1945.* She had read the words upside down and backwards; still, they were hard to mistake.

She tries to remember them, tries to wrap herself around them as her hand had gripped the egg. But the enormity of being born with that sort of luck is the same as that of children looking up, with their eyes already on fire, to notice that the world has ended.

Still, she knows the words, has memorized them, can recite them. She tries to hold onto them, but can't. She can't think of them for longer than a moment or two. Then she sits on the toilet, waiting, humming show tunes. She thinks of the tumblers falling out of the sky and how they always did flap up again before they hit the ground.

She thinks of the weight of birds, of how the fact of homing is built into the hollows in their bones and is a separate thing from migration, which is thought to be a function of the inner ear, as balance is in humans. She thinks of the way birds eat gravel for digestion, and of how their intestinal organs are lightened by that evolutionary fact, of how the weight of gravel is temporary and does not therefore interfere with flight.

She remembers in the bones of her hands the weight of the egg, of the witch hazel, of the horned toad, and of Juliet-and-Romeo when she had held the pigeon out and up to the sky and the bird had lifted off, sunk the slightest bit as its weight hit air, then flapped on up, as birds are born to do. She has weighed the facts.

She is remembering the words on the chart that stood in front of the ones Dr. Greenley was saying out loud, the blah blah blah of the twenty-eight-day cycle of the blah blah blah, and so forth, which, blushing, excruciatingly embarrassed, sitting flat-chested in undershirt and underpants, Charlotte had not imagined really applied to her, and she had therefore barely listened to. There was Winnie shrilling, *Tell her! Tell her just what might happen!* and Dr. Greenley with his white head trembling *trying* to tell her, but he was embarrassed, too. He was intent on saying the other things: that she'd been born with a good brain and with God's grace.

But it was Charlotte's luck that she did happen to have been listening. She was listening attentively to all of it, even as she refused to listen. She listened, she heard, and she remembered it as birds remember to go where they've never been by the bones in their inner ear. The difference between Katrinka and herself, she decides, is the difference between homing and migration.

She had listened and she had heard, and Dr. Greenley's information was detailed, accurate, precise. In spite of his religion, or maybe even because of it, he was an utterly scientific man. Scientific knowledge had always appealed to Charlotte: it was so logical, so contrary to the way Katrinka conducted her thinking. Charlotte's father, on the other hand, was cute in his beliefs. He believed children were something a person picked up at the notions counter, or so Katrinka has said. Children then might be too easily discarded, just as he had apparently discarded himself.

Charlotte wants to be logical, rational, more like Dr. Greenley.

To be more like Dr. Greenley, Charlotte tries to pray. *Oh, Lord, we are unworthy to gather up the crumbs under your table*, she thinks, then adds: *And all that crap.* Her thoughts fly up with the flock, then tumble down and away. She no longer thinks in words but with her stomach. It is by thinking with her stomach that Charlotte first understands that she is saved: twenty-eight days after her last period, she has menstrual cramps.

Charlotte is saved. She has this one blue egg: another chance. Her heart, like Juliet-and-Romeo, flaps out, starts up. It was her luck to have been born with a high enough IQ to remember you don't get pregnant without slightly wanting to. You don't get pregnant by sleeping with someone the day your period's ended.

This is *her* luck, she thinks, just as they are *her* parents and she wants to scream it out, just as she called to her mother that day when Katrinka came stumbling up the sidewalk in front of Tulita Elementary. *Mom!* she'd cried, and she'd looked around at the people in the office, furious, weeping, daring each one of them in turn to even look as if he was going to say a word against her. Katrinka was so bad then that even she seemed to know it. She told Charlotte later that she wouldn't have blamed her at all Charlotte had refused, that day, to claim her.

They are terrible parents, Charlotte understands; still, they are her own. They are her luck and she is proud of it, of them, even of how bad they were. *They were worse than anyone's*, she thinks, and she is proud of it. Her luck was being born with the ability to hear even when she isn't listening. When the blood starts and her life is saved, Charlotte isn't the slightest bit surprised. It is her own luck. She has made it. She will not thank God for it.

Across the road from Lionel and Winnie's was the back edge of the large estate owned by the woman whose house was far away, facing down onto Montecito. The big yard took up the whole block. It was traversed by the creek and studded by the oaks that were left to stand where they'd been, in order to look natural. The ground though was covered over entirely with planted ivy that now grew knee-deep. The ivy made it impossible to walk out into the yard and the old woman never came there.

Down by the creek near the culvert, three ceramic deer had been positioned; they had stood there as long as Charlotte could remember, and were now pitted, weathered. She didn't know why someone in Verdugo Woodlands would feel the need for ceramic deer since there were still the real ones. The statues, she knew, were like her mother's dummies, and both were also akin to the wrought iron Negro grooms that stood by the picket fences up and down Montecito, waiting with rings in their hands to tie up people's imaginary horses.

Cute things are used to stand in for the past, Charlotte thinks. Ceramic deer and Negro grooms and her mother's dummies all stood in front of real memories: the job of cute things was to make the past less wretched than it had really been, to make it sweeter, funnier, more glamourously wealthy. Cute things are pathetic for that very reason. She had always hated cuteness not for the lure of it but for the fact of its weakness in the face of such mighty and terrible wretchedness as the past had really held. She thinks: *Notions counter, my ass.*

"What was he like?" she asks. She and her mother are sitting on the davenport, looking at the moldy photo albums they've dragged up from the cellar.

"Oh, I don't know—witty."

"What was so witty about him?"

"He used to say all he wanted in life was a room with a view."

"What's so witty about that?"

"He'd say it like this: 'Womb with a vu.'"

"Pretty witty," Charlotte says. "About as witty as the four-chambered stomach of a ruminant."

"He used to have a dream about a house with a hundred rooms. Every door he opened would open into more and more rooms."

"He did!" Charlotte shouts. "Mom! Guess what! I have that *exact* same dream! That I open door after door and there are rooms and rooms and rooms! And they all open out and out!"

Katrinka has her lips pressed tightly together and does not smile at this, though Charlotte can see she is tempted. It amuses Katrinka to see that her daughter still dreams, that she still imagines there are *possibilities!* "Then *you* be the architect, sweetie," she tells her. "In your father's case, this happened to be a nightmare. It was the same house he was always working on, one that was never finished, one his father was making him do for some big shot high uppety-up from Sacramento and/or Camarillo. Your father went to bed at night and couldn't sleep. When he did sleep, he remembered he had forgotten to put in exits."

"Was that why? Was that why he killed himself?"

Katrinka turns away, then looks back at her and lifts her eyebrows to ask again what the question was.

"Because he didn't want to be an architect and his father was making him?"

"Oh, I don't know, really really," Katrinka says, and sighs her *aut! aut! aut!* "It was all fairly complicated. If we'd had any money, he'd have quit, I suppose. If we'd had any money at all, we would have gone to live in Paris."

"And been what, artists?"

"Oh, I suppose. That awwwnnd the sorts of types who sit in cafés and drink heavily." Katrinka smirks and tips her chin up. "Do you know what Gertrude Stein said when she came back to California? About there being no there here?" Katrinka is searching Charlotte's face as she does frequently these days, studying her: eye, eye, mouth, frame of hair. She seems to be studying her in order to remember her. "She didn't say it dismissively. Charlotte! Do you know what I'm saying? What she meant was there *had* been a there there, but it *was* gone, that she had grown up and gone away and that, when she came back to the very same place, the *there* had disappeared? I mean the here that had been there? Do you understand this? We had tried to get away from Glendale. We were happier up north. We might have been happier in Paris, but we really didn't see how we could raise children living in a garret, and all that. Silverlake, actually, was quite bad enough."

"You mean you wanted to have children?" Charlotte asks. "You both did? I always thought it was a complete accident!"

Katrinka tips her chin up. She's remembering, but the look is just the same as when she's listening to something else. This is because the past is always with her, right before her eyes, just as for Charlotte it is irretrievably lost. She looks at Charlotte, then draws her upper lip down over her teeth to keep from smiling. She raises one eyebrow ironically. She touches the tip of her tongue to the circular patch of dead skin that sits in the center of her upper lip now too, and she finally does smile as she looks away.

She gazes out into the treetops, transfixed by the sound of the slushing leaves. The light in the room is dusty green. She stays that way for a long time.

When she looks back, her eyes are huge, black with wonder. She lifts her shoulders to answer Charlotte's question—she has not forgotten it. She smiles ruefully at the two of them, her daughter's parents, who'd had such funny hopes: of falling in love, getting married, having children, like other people.

Design by David Bullen
Typeset in Mergenthaler Fournier
with Weiss display
by Wilsted & Taylor
Printed by Arcata Graphics/Fairfield
on acid-free paper